R.C. MARTIN

Heartless

Heartless

R.C. Martin

Cover and Interior Design by Cassy Roop at Pink Ink Designs ©2017
www.pinkinkdesigns.com

Para Jenny, *quien ayudó a darle vida al héroe de esta historia. El té hizo suspirar antes de conocerlo y a quien amaste hasta el final. Me encantó compartir contigo este viaje riesgoso. Gracias por ser parte de mi trayecto de escritura.*

Heartless

Prologue

"WHAT IF HE DOESN'T?"

I look up from my *Wisconsin Brat*, catching her gaze from across the table. Absentmindedly tracing my finger along the edge of the red, plastic basket, I ask, "What if he doesn't *what?*"

Her pretty brown eyes grow sad, and my heart aches at the pity I see in her expression.

"Blaine—darling, what if he doesn't actually leave her? What if he doesn't come back?"

I shift my gaze down into my lap and stare at my hand. With my thumb, I spin the ring around my middle finger over and over, all the while reminding myself that her *what ifs* are just words. I convince myself that what he and I have, it's bigger than our circumstances. I shield my heart against the lies that lie in *what if*—in the silence—in the *waiting*.

"Blaine…" she murmurs, leaning against the table to shorten the distance between us.

I curl my fingers into a fist and lift my eyes to meet hers once more. I ignore the way her worry tugs at her brow and the regret I know she harbors in her thoughts. I ignore it all. I have to. For Michael, for *us*, I have to.

"He will," I state resolutely. "He'll come back to me."

"But—"

"He *will!*" I insist, pounding my fist against my thigh. "He has to. He *has* to."

One

Michael

We enter the house through the side access door at the rear of the mansion, just as we do every morning. When we reach the end of the hallway, I lift my chin in a silent expression of appreciation to Clay—my security detail and running mate. Still as breathless as I am, he dips his head in a nod, offering me a wave before heading to his quarters. I glance up the stairs and then make my ascent to my own bedroom, well aware that we'll both be taking our leave with the sunrise.

Even though it's barely five-thirty in the morning, and I'm sure I made not a sound when I got up for my usual run an hour ago, I return to the master suite to find Veronica is already awake. I don't see her when I sit on the cushioned bench at the foot of the bed to unlace my sneakers, but the sheets are empty, and the lamps on each nightstand flanking the mattress are illuminated.

"Morning, sweetie," she murmurs softly, walking into the room.

I look up and watch my wife exit our closet, her short, black robe left open. I let my eyes take in the matching black negligee she wore to bed last night, the silky material hugging her hourglass figure. Her long, black hair hangs down her chest, hiding her full, heavy breasts, but that doesn't stop me from remembering that they are there.

Lifting my gaze to meet hers, I pull off one sneaker and then the other as I reply, "Good morning."

"How was your run?" she asks, as she so often does.

"Good," I assure her. "It's brisk out, but I appreciated it after the first mile."

"Good." Once she's closed the distance between us, she leans down to pick up my shoes. On her way up, she stops and puckers her lips. I accept the invitation thoughtlessly.

"You're up early. What do you have going on today?"

"Do I have to have a reason to be up?" she asks, turning back toward the closet. "Can't a wife just wish to see her husband off to work?"

A smirk tugs at the corner of my mouth as I follow after her, yanking my sweat soaked t-shirt from off of my back. Joining her in the closet, I toss the soiled garment in the hamper as I reply, "You say that like I haven't been paying attention to you for the last decade. I know you better than that, Vee. Idle hands are not something you're familiar with."

She chuckles—the sound throaty and mischievous—and discards my shoes before she starts picking through my suits. "Your new interns start today, don't they?"

I sigh, having forgotten that to be true. I spent the duration of my run thinking about the session that I called for today. Legislatures have been on my ass about this bill, but I won't sign it until it's right. "Yeah," I mumble, tugging off the rest of my clothing. I think about what that means for my day, and I rake my fingers through my hair as I head for the shower.

"...you know how I like to stop by."

"What was that?" I ask Veronica, only catching the tail end of her sentence as I start my water. I turn away from the glass stall and come face to face with her.

She smiles, holding up two ties, and I point to the solid blue one before she repeats, "Cookies. It's tradition. You know that."

"Right," I nod, stepping into the shower.

"Anyway, I've got a busy day," she goes on to tell me, speaking loudly so that I can hear her as I wash. "I thought I'd get the cookies baked this morning before I went to Mercy Hill. You know I'm in charge of the clothing drive this Saturday. Your dad wanted to meet and get the run-down on the morning I have planned."

"Right," I repeat, trying to remember if I knew about this clothing drive.

The truth is, the First Lady of Colorado is all over the place all of the time. When she's not running one committee or another at my father's church, she's volunteering at the Boys and Girls Club, or organizing a charity gala, or baking *cookies* for my new group of interns. Keeping track of her feels nearly impossible sometimes, especially on top of my own schedule. I swear, some days it's a miracle we even see one another.

"I have to be there around seven, but if you could stop by around nine, that'd be perfect."

"Wait, nine? This Saturday?" I ask, my hands freezing in my hair, drenched and thick with shampoo.

"Yeah."

"Babe, I can't this weekend. I've got a golf game. I tee off with Lawrence at seven."

"Oh," she murmurs contemplatively. "I could have sworn I told Heidi—"

"I'm sure you did," I assure her, rinsing my hair clean. "I know she had to move some things around on my schedule to fit in this meeting with Lawrence. I'm sorry, Vee, but—"

"No, no, it's okay. It's *Lawrence*. I know the only time you can get that man to have a serious conversation with you is on the golf course. Besides, you've been so busy lately. You deserve a morning game. I'll just let your dad know when I see him today."

Stepping out of the shower, I grab my towel and wrap it around my waist. Veronica is sitting on the short stool at her vanity mirror across the room. Her phone is in her hand as she types something—no doubt adjusting her plans for the weekend. Looking up from the device, she smiles at me and points out, "You forgot to shave."

"Damn," I mutter, reaching up to rub my chin.

"I'll go start your breakfast," she says, making her way toward me. "Oatmeal? Eggs? Toast?"

"Eggs and toast."

"Okay." Placing a hand on my chest, she pushes up on her tiptoes and presses her lips against the top of my cheek—above my stubble. "I laid your suit out on the bed. I like the way that one is cut on you. Big day today. You should look *extra* sharp." She winks and then she's gone, and I go about squeezing in a shave.

By the time I'm dressed and headed into the kitchen, Veronica is making her way out, two plates full of food in hand, and the newspaper underneath her arm. I follow her into the dining room, and we both catch up on the local news while we eat—a routine we've grown quite accustomed to over the last couple of years when we share our breakfast. She knows this is about the only time I have to read the paper before my day gets hectic.

When we're finished, I follow her back to our bedroom, where she helps me into my jacket and straightens my tie.

"Well, I hope I get to see you when I stop by this afternoon. If not, tonight?"

"I'll be late," I warn.

"All right. Oh—I'm having dinner with your mom and sister. We're finalizing the details for the party Saturday evening. You *cannot* miss it. If Heidi—"

"I won't miss it," I promise, leaning down to press a quick kiss to her lips.

"Good. Your mom is so excited."

"No doubt." Glancing down at my watch, I see that I'm a couple of minutes behind. Sure that Clay is already waiting in the car, I announce, "I have to go."

"I know," she says, sliding a step away from me. "I'll talk to you later."

"Love you," I say automatically, taking my leave.

"Love you too, sweetie."

"How'd it go in there?" asks Heidi, catching up with me as I barge through the double doors leading into the lobby.

I ignore the murmuring at my back, confident in the decisions that were made during the session. I'm also hopeful that the next presentation of the bill won't lead to a veto, like I had originally feared. My shoes are not the easiest to fill, and I find myself so often toeing the line between approval and disgruntled frustration. I take no pleasure in being perceived as *the bad guy*. Rather, I simply work in the best interest of the businesses and special interest organizations constantly lobbying the legislature for better or more favorable laws to be passed—for the *people* who make up the beautiful state of Colorado. It has always been my goal to serve my state fairly, respectfully, and determinately, even if that means putting up a fight.

Today, the battle was fought—and hopefully won.

Glancing down at Heidi, I hide my smirk and button up my suit jacket as I inform her, "Better than I had hoped."

"Congratulations, Governor Cavanaugh."

"Don't congratulate me yet," I warn with a slight shake of my head. "Wait until the bill comes back from the House in a couple day's time."

"Always so humble, our good governor," she teases.

This time, I don't hide my smile, but couple it with a friendly wink.

Heidi has been an integral part of my staff for the last two years. I first met her when I held the title of District Attorney. She was just getting her feet wet then—an administrative intern I couldn't help but notice. She was sharp, professional, and ambitious; not to mention, she had no interest in *flirting* her way up the food chain. She worked late, arrived early, and earned the respect of her peers and superiors alike. When I announced my candidacy for governor, she was anxious to take part in my campaign.

Now, at thirty years old, I find her far too beautiful, amusing, and intelligent to be chained to her desk for the likes of me—but so long as she continues to show up, I won't turn her away. Some days, she's the only reason I can seem to keep my head on straight.

Keeping pace with me, she informs, "I'm afraid you missed your wife by about thirty minutes."

"Mmm," I hum, nodding my acknowledgment. "I suppose she saw who she intended?"

"As always," Heidi says with a grin. "She was a hit. I swear, she makes the biggest cookies in Colorado. Hopefully your interns don't fall into a sugar coma before the day is done."

"Only the strong survive, Heidi." Tipping my chin at the stack of files she has in her arms, I ask, "What have you got for me?"

"I've got another budget proposal that came across your desk an hour ago. If you want to glance at it now, you can—but the press corps is also scheduled to arrive in fifteen minutes. Your lunch is still untouched on your desk. You know you do better talking to the press after you've eaten. It's getting pretty late, so I thought maybe—"

Cutting her off as we turn down the hallway that leads to my office, I instruct, "Grab an intern from the finance team. Have him or her meet me in my office. I'll eat, they can tell me what's in the file."

"Throwing one into the lion's den on their first day, huh?" she asks through another grin.

Chuckling, I remind her, "Only the strong survive, Heidi—only the strong survive."

"CAVANAUGH," I MUTTER into the phone, not bothering to look at the caller ID.

"Mmm. I know that tone," she says, pulling me out of the paperwork in front of me.

I sigh, running a hand down my face—scratching at the stubble that has already started to grow in on my jaw.

"I just got home from your parents' house. I'm still dressed. If you need something, I could have Noah swing me by your office for a minute."

"No," I tell her, shaking my head, even though she can't see me do it. "Don't bother. I'm fine."

"Mike?"

"What is it, Vee?" I ask, raking my fingers through my hair.

"Don't stay at the office too late, okay? Whatever it is, it'll keep until tomorrow. It always does."

"I'll be home before midnight," I promise, shifting my focus back onto the files in front of me. "Don't wait up. I know you've had a busy day."

"Skip your run tomorrow?" she asks hopefully.

I hesitate, trying to remember the last time we had sex. It's been a few days. A week. Maybe more. We've had a lot going on. Not to mention, with shit like this hitting my desk, I'm not always so sure that sex is the release I need. It's a lot easier to take my frustration out on the pavement of the street than on my wife in the sack. She's a gentle lover. Always has been. Twenty-one years, I've known her body; and in twenty-one years, not much has changed.

"Mike? You still there?"

"For me or for you, babe?" I ask honestly.

She pauses for a breath before she replies, "It's been almost two weeks."

"For you, then," I answer for her.

"For *us*."

I nod, wondering if I could manage to squeeze in some time in the weight room at some point tomorrow.

"Mike…"

"Tomorrow morning, I'm yours," I assure her. "Vee, I've got to get back—"

"Right. Of course. I'm sorry; don't let me keep you. Remember what I said."

"Before midnight," I repeat.

"I love you."

"You, too. Night, babe."

"GOVERNOR?"

My head jerks up at the sound of Heidi's voice, and I see her face peeking through my cracked office door. I glance at the clock, note the time, and then furrow my brow at her. "It's almost ten. What are you still doing here?"

"What are *you* still doing here?"

I toss aside my pen, drawing in a deep breath and letting out a heavy sigh as I lean back in my desk chair. "I swear, some days I take one step forward only to take five steps backwards. This budget?" I shake my head, at a loss for words.

"You have a team who can help you with that, you know? 'Course, they've all gone home for the evening, but you have analysts on your payroll for a reason, Governor."

I stare at her for a moment, noting that she's right, but still wishing I was given something better this afternoon. After my interview with the press, the rest of my day was full of meetings. I didn't get a chance to really dissect the numbers until after people started heading home for the day. At times, my impatience for a solution can get the better of me.

"Cavanaugh," she laughs, stepping into my office. "I say this with all due respect—but you need to get your ass out of here. Clear your head. Seriously—that'll be here waiting for you tomorrow."

"Now you sound like my wife," I tease. She grabs my suit jacket from where it's folded across the back of one of the chairs on the opposite side of my desk.

"Then I must be right," she says through a smile.

It isn't until she thrusts my jacket out toward me that I realize—"That's not what you were wearing earlier." My eyes do a quick scan of her attire from head to toe, noting how the little black dress she has on is something I've never seen her wear to the office. "Are you going somewhere?"

She shrugs, still holding my jacket for me, and I quirk an eyebrow at her.

"If I tell you, will you leave the office?" she asks with an eye roll.

"Eventually," I retort, snatching my jacket out of her hand.

"It was a date. A bad one."

"You're telling me you went home, went out on a date—a *bad* date—and then came back to the office?"

"What?" she asks with another shrug. "It was only a couple of blocks away. I felt like a stroll. The guy gave me the creeps. The bar was great, though. I'd never been before. You should check it out sometime. Now, actually. Now would be a great idea. Nightcap. I'll even tell Clay where it is on my way out."

I cough out a sigh. Shaking my head, I toss my jacket across the edge of my desk as I tell her, "Maybe another time."

"What time did you tell her?"

My eyes catch hers, and she raises her brow at me while folding her arms across her chest.

"Don't look at me like that, Mr. Governor. What time did you tell Veronica that you'd be home?"

"Before midnight," I admit with a scowl.

"All right. So, let's think about this logically. If you're to keep your promise, you have an hour and a half before you need to be on the road. You've been in the office since before seven. You had a late lunch, but I didn't feed you dinner, so I'm guessing you didn't eat—which means your mind is basically mush."

"I had a protein bar," I argue, hiding a smirk.

"Mmmhmm," she chuckles. "Like I said, I didn't feed you dinner, so you've done nothing but consume numbers you can't crack because it's been a long day. Not to mention, you're not a financial analyst. You're smart—brilliant, even—but you're a politician at heart. So get up. Go have a drink. Relax for a minute, and start again tomorrow."

"Heidi, I appreciate—"

"All due respect, sir? I know about the bottle of bourbon you keep in the bottom left drawer of your desk. A gift from the Mayor on your first day in office. Don't tell me you can't appreciate a nightcap."

Leaning back in my chair once more, I fold my arms across my chest, mimicking her stance as I counter, "If you know about the bottle of bourbon, you know it's not been opened."

"Of course not. You're too honorable to drink while you're at work. Which is why I'm suggesting you try out the swanky bar I've just come from." Backing her way toward the door, she goes on to say, "I'd join you, if only to be sure that you took my advice, but something tells me that tomorrow's going to be a long day. My boss is kind of a stubbornly determined hard-ass on a mission, so I should head home and get some sleep."

"Tell your boss to lighten up on you. You work too hard," I mutter, lifting my chin at her—only half teasing. The fact that she walked here from this bar she keeps talking about is proof that she works too hard. Furrowing my brow once more, I call out, "Grab an Uber. It's late. Too late for you to be walking around downtown Denver by yourself. We'll make an intern go pick up your car tomorrow."

"Yes, sir." She salutes me before making her exit. As she steps over the threshold, she shuts out my overhead light, leaving only the light in the next room for me to see. "Prohibition Lounge, Governor. I'll see you in the morning."

I free a heavy sigh, peering through the darkness at the pages before me that I can no longer see. Heidi is right. I could use some food. More than that, I could use a minute to take a breath. It's been a long day. If I don't step away for a minute, tomorrow will be even longer. Grabbing my jacket, I fold it over my arm and make my way into the next room. Clay is sitting on the couch in the reception area, messing with his phone. When he sees me, he stands to his feet, sliding his device into his pocket.

"Ever been to the Prohibition Lounge?"

"No, sir."

"Neither have I. Let's go."

Two

Blaine

I STEP OUTSIDE, LOOKING ONE WAY and then the other, feeling more disappointed than surprised when I don't see him. I check my phone again, but it's just as silent as it has been all night. Well aware of the time, I feel no guilt when I find his number in my list of saved favorite contacts and push a call through. I listen to it ring until I'm dropped into his voicemail, and I mutter a curse under my breath before I end the call. I don't bother leaving a message.

"Hey, need a ride?"

I whip my head around as Dodger walks through the door. Having clocked out for the morning, he's in only his black slacks and a gray beater, his black button-up now draped over his shoulder. I offer him a half-hearted smile, my eyes admiring his bare arms in a fleeting glance. He's covered in ink, three-quarter-length sleeves decorating each arm. It suits him; though, the patrons who frequent the bar are none the wiser. Short sleeves aren't exactly part of the dress code around here.

"He comin'?" he asks, stopping beside me before gently nudging me with his elbow.

"He's not answering," I mutter, lifting my phone before dropping it into my bag.

"Come on. I'll take you home."

He shoves his hands into his pockets and then juts out his elbow, signaling for me to take it. I flash him another half smile as I loop my arm through his. We don't speak as we make our way along the quiet street, headed for his car. I appreciate his silence. More than that, I appreciate his lack of judgment. That's always been Dodger. Hard on the outside, rough around the edges, but warm, kind, and *gooey* on the inside. This isn't the first time he's offered to take me home after our late shift. Not the first. Not the second. And as much as I want to proclaim that it'll be the last, I'm sure it won't be.

If it wasn't so late, I'd walk to the Light Rail, which drops me a couple of blocks away from the loft—but it *is* late, and I've missed the last train.

"You scheduled for tomorrow?" he asks after we've both climbed into his blue, '99 Mustang.

I lean my head back against the seat rest and sigh. "Yeah. Same shift. Six to close. You?"

"Not until Thursday," he replies, adjusting the volume on his stereo.

"Lucky you. What are you going to get into?"

Shifting his eyes off the road for a moment, he grins over at me before he says, "Takin' Hope to see Bruno Mars tonight. It's a surprise."

"Seriously?" I ask, remembering how much his girlfriend loves Bruno.

He chuckles, offering me a slow nod.

"You deserve a high five for that," I insist, holding up my hand.

"Damn right, I do," he says, slapping his palm against mine.

"Now I know why you needed the next two nights off," I say teasingly.

Smiling at the windshield, he asks, "Why's that?"

"You are *totally* getting laid."

His smile stretches into a grin before he holds up his hand again. Laughing, I clap my palm against his in another high five.

"She's lucky to have you, Dodge. I mean it."

Glancing over at me, I notice his smile slip before he mutters, "That fucker's lucky to have you, too, B."

I press my lips together, turning to look out the passenger-side window. I don't come to Mateo's defense like I usually do. Not this morning. I'm too tired. Too fed up. Too disappointed to plead his case. It's always the same.

He's just a little eccentric. He's an artist. He's passionate. He gets lost sometimes—but he loves me.

Dodger and I don't say anything else to each other for the duration of our short trip, both of us content to let his music fill the silence. When he pulls up in front of my building, I throw the strap of my bag over my shoulder, turning to face him as I reach back for the door handle.

"Thanks, Dodger. I really appreciate the ride."

"I got your back, Blaine."

"Enjoy Bruno."

"No doubt," he says with a chin lift.

Offering one final wave, I hop out of his car before hurrying inside. I race my way to the fifth floor, anxious to get inside and get ready for bed. That's all I want right now is *sleep*. More than fighting with Mateo, more then demanding an explanation as to why he didn't pick me up like he promised he would, *again*—I just want sleep.

I pause when I reach my door, hearing his loud music through the barrier that separates us. Pressing my forehead against the cool surface, I force in a deep breath and let out a sigh before inserting my key. When I step inside, it takes all of two seconds for me to see him, standing with his back to me.

My loft—*our* loft—is really just one, big open room. It has a closed off bathroom, a laundry nook, and a couple closets on the far end of the space, with a kitchen/living room/dining room area beyond the front door—above which is a small loft that houses the bed. The view of downtown Denver, seen through the four tall, arched windows across from me, is *killer*. Inside, it's lots of concrete and brick with wood flooring, which is how I fell in love with it; and over the last couple of years, I've worked really hard to make it homey and inviting. When Mateo moved in, about six months ago, he decorated the walls with a few old pieces he had laying around that never sold. Outside of the television he had mounted on the wall, along with his art, and all of his supplies that live in the space I *used* to consider my dining area, he hasn't contributed much.

I look over at him now. His arms are folded across his chest, his focus glued to the canvas in front of him, and he doesn't hear me—not even when I slam the door shut behind me. It isn't until I turn the music off that he spins around to look my way. He smiles, as if he's happy to see me, but it only lasts a moment. I don't know if it's the blank expression on my face, or simply my presence that triggers his memory, but I don't care.

Dropping my bag on the kitchen counter, I speak not a word

before I start for the bathroom, in order to begin my nightly routine. I only make it halfway there. Mateo's arms stop me as he pulls me back against his chest, squeezing me tightly.

"I'm sorry, baby. I'm so sorry. I—"

"You forgot. *Again*," I mutter, shoving at his arms in an attempt to get him to let me go.

He buries his face in my hair, between my neck and my shoulder, holding me closer. "I lost track of time. You know how it is. I was working. I—"

"Mateo, I really don't want to hear it right now," I insist, pushing his arms once more.

He lets me go this time, and I spin around to face him. His shirt is covered in speckles of paint, and there's a smear of yellow on his light brown skin, just above his eyebrow. His shaggy, dark hair is pulled back into a tiny, disheveled ponytail at his nape; and for a moment, I remember. I remember how easy it used to be to get lost in his rich, brown eyes surrounded by his incredibly long, thick lashes. I remember how I used to think it was cute how he couldn't work on a piece without getting paint on his face. I remember how one simple *I'm sorry* accompanied by his arms wrapped tightly around me used to stir my desire for him. Yet, as much as I love him, none of that means anything right now.

"I don't mind you borrowing my car," I remind him. "You know that I don't. But when you say you'll pick me up from work, it's fucking *disrespectful* when you don't. I *called* you, and you didn't answer."

"I'm sorry, Blaine. I didn't hear—"

"You never do," I grumble, turning to continue toward the bathroom.

He stops me again, wrapping his arms around me once more.

Only this time, he slides one of his hands up over my left breast, slipping the fingers of his opposite hand under the waistband of my slacks.

That used to get me, too—his seemingly bottomless appetite for all things me.

"Let me make it up to you," he whispers into my ear.

"Yeah," I bite out, yanking his hand off of my chest. "Because *sex* will make it all better."

"Come on, baby. You've had a long night. I can—"

"Get your hands off me, Mateo. I just want to go to bed. Besides, you have no idea what kind of night I've had. You didn't bother to ask."

"Fuck, Blaine," he grunts, finally stepping away from me. "I'm trying to apologize. Don't be a bitch."

"Oh, yeah, 'cause saying no to your dick makes me a bitch?" I argue, spinning around to scowl at him.

"I said I was sorry."

"You *always* say that you're sorry. It's getting old, Mat. I swear to god," I groan, reaching up to bury my fingers in my hair. "*Sorry* doesn't pay the bills or put groceries in the fridge or put *gas* in *my car.*"

"Now this is about *money?*" he barks, his eyebrows shooting up in surprise.

I puff out a breath of air, dropping my hands to my sides as I declare, "All I'm saying is, I'm the one bringing in the consistent income. The least you can do is pick me up from work when you say you're going to!"

"Whatever," he mumbles, turning away from me.

I jerk my head back, appalled by his flippant response. As if there's no relevancy to what I've said. As if I'm not completely in the right. As if he's not sorry at all!

After glaring at his back for a full sixty seconds, I realize that he's got me so upset, there's no way I'll be able to sleep now. Not here, at least. Knowing that I need to get some rest so that I can be a functioning human being for my shift later tonight, I don't think twice before going to the closet to grab my overnight bag.

I have it packed in less than five minutes.

I'm in the kitchen, hooking my oversized purse over my shoulder when he finally notices what I'm doing.

"What the fuck, Blaine? Where are you going?"

"Someplace where I can sleep!" I answer, searching for my car keys. I find them discarded on the small table I keep beside the door and snatch them up without delay.

"Blaine!" he bellows.

I whirl around, giving him my best glare as I mutter, "This? This fight? I'm not doing this right now. I'm so sick and tired of having this argument, Mateo. All I want to do is go to bed. I don't want to yell until the sun comes up. I don't want to fuck until you've gotten off and feel better for being a dick and forgetting me—a-fucking-gain—I *just* want to sleep."

I open the door and step over the threshold into the hallway, calling back over my shoulder, "I won't be home before work."

"Real mature, baby! Just walk away!" he yells after I've shut the door.

I huff out an irritated breath.

The gall on that one! Like he didn't turn his back on the conversation first.

I pull in a deep breath, close my eyes, and will myself to calm down. I know better than to get behind the wheel angry as a raging bitch. By the time I've made it to the parking lot, I'm collected enough to think with a straight head. When I start my Chevy Cruse and glance at the gas gage, I tell myself that I'm not going to cry. All the way to the gas station, I try to remember that Mateo loves me. That he's not using me. That he's not some starving-artist-free-loader. That we've been together for almost two years, and this is just a season. It'll pass.

All seasons must come to an end.

I WAKE UP IN my old bed all alone, missing the warmth of Mateo beside me. Then I remember the argument we had in the wee hours of the morning—the argument that drove me to leave the loft—the argument that had me driving thirty minutes across town to my father's house—and I relish my solitude.

Flopping onto my back, I reach for my phone, plugged in and resting on the nightstand next to me. I roll my eyes at the ten missed text messages I got while I was sleeping, all from Mateo. Ignoring them for now, I note the time. Three o'clock. I'll have to leave for work in a couple of hours; but if I've slept through the entire morning, that means—

"Lulu? I'm home. You up? Like to know why my baby girl showed up in the middle of the night," dad calls from downstairs.

I smile, picturing him standing at the foot of the stairwell, yelling up at me—his voice floating down the hallway, just like old times.

"Give me a minute, dad!" I cry in return.

"All right," he grumbles, no doubt making his way to the kitchen.

Dad and I are on opposite schedules. It's been like that since I started working at the Lounge. I crashed this morning somewhere around three, but I know without a doubt that he was up and getting ready for his day a half an hour later. He's a Budweiser distributer. Has been for the last seventeen years. He spends his mornings stocking up grocery stores, and the early part of the afternoons hitting the liquor stores on his route. That basically leaves us a window of three hours during the day, plus the weekends I have off, to see each other. I don't see him as often as I'd like, but I do my best to drop by at least once a week.

As convenient and consistent as his schedule may be, I worry about him all the time. He's not as young as he once was, and I know his long days aren't good for his aging back. He'd never abandon the company, I'm sure of that. He's always quick to remind people of his loyalty to them after they showed him such kindness and flexibility when mom got sick. Of course, every time I bring up the idea of inquiring about an internal desk job, he huffs and puffs like I'm questioning his manhood or something. It's a battle I've yet to win.

Sure that if I don't get my ass out of bed he'll come hollering for me again, I slip from beneath the sheets and gather what I need for a quick shower. I'm in and out in less than ten minutes. After I towel dry my wavy locks, I dress in a pair of black, cotton shorts and a loose fitting, pale gray, graphic tank. The bold, black letters across the front read: *Whatever Sprinkles Your Donuts;* and the bright pink sports bra I have on underneath is visible beneath my arms.

I'm on my way out of the bathroom when I hear dad holler, "Lulu! My patience ain't as good as it used to be."

Laughing, I hurry down the short hallway, rounding the corner of the railing that leads to the narrow, wooden stairs. My bare feet carry me down quickly, and I stop on the second to last step, making me level with my father. He's got one arm leaning against the railing, his other hand curled into a fist that is propped against his hip, and he quirks an eyebrow at me when I smile at him. Leaning over his round belly so that I can reach his face, I kiss his scruffy cheek before I finish my descent.

"Hey, dad. Are you hungry? I'm starving. Want me to make you something?" I ask him, not waiting for an answer before I start past the living room to the kitchen.

"Brought some food home," he grunts, following after me. "Figured we'd eat together."

"That was sweet of you. But you know that I..."

My voice trails off, and I stop short when I see the bucket of KFC on the counter—along with three smaller containers I would bet my life are filled with mashed potatoes, gravy, and macaroni and cheese.

"Dad! You can't eat this shit," I grumble, turning to scowl at him. "Tell me you haven't been on a take-out regimen for the last week."

"I haven't," he says innocently, shrugging his shoulders.

I fold my arms across my chest, challenging him with my blatant, accusatory stare.

He furrows his brow playfully, pointing a finger at me as he asks, "Who's the parent here, huh?"

He squeezes past me, which isn't easy to do with his large, heavy frame, and I drop my arms, spinning to face him as I fight a pout. I succeed, barely, but my heart still wrenches in my chest as I think about *his.*

"Dad—"

"Baby girl, I'm not lyin' to you."

"You promised me. You've only got one heart, and I've only got one parent left, and the doctors—"

"Blaine Luella Foster, quit your worryin', get your little ass in here, and eat."

I hesitate only long enough for my stomach to remind me that I'm hungry, and then I join him in the kitchen, grabbing each of us a plate.

"I'm peeling the skin off of your chicken," I state resolutely.

"Jesus," he mutters under his breath.

He doesn't offer up any protest, but piles a couple pieces on his plate before sliding it in front of me. I grin victoriously as he makes his way to the kitchen table and plops down in his usual seat.

"So are you going to tell me why you were sleepin' under my roof all day?"

"Mateo and I got into it after I got home," I reply vaguely. "I was exhausted, didn't feel like hashing it out, and needed a place to crash."

"Not that I don't mind you being here, Lulu, but it's *your* bed he's sleepin' in. Shit goes down, it's his ass that should be tryin' to find someplace else to crash."

I bite the inside of my cheek, not saying a word as I carry both of our plates to the table. When my hands are free, I turn to go and grab us some silverware, but dad stops me, gently catching my wrist.

I twist my neck to catch his blue eyes, and he lifts a bushy, dirty blonde eyebrow at me, silently expressing his discontent. I wait for him to speak, but he doesn't really need to. I know what he's thinking. While he's always been friendly with Mateo, he was against us moving in together from the moment I broached the topic. It's like he saw the writing on the wall long before I could—like he knew, no matter how much we love each other, that maybe we weren't as ready as we thought we were to take our relationship to the next level.

I didn't listen to his advice. But John Foster is the best dad in the whole world. No matter how many times I've found myself fleeing from *my* home to seek the shelter of *his,* not once has he uttered the words *I told you so*.

Even still, I can see it in his eyes sometimes. Like now.

"Don't ever accept less than you deserve," he says instead. "*You* promised *me.*"

I nod, my love for him making my heart swell in my chest.

Tipping his chin, he lets go of my wrist and instructs, "Grab me a fork, baby girl. Tell me how things are going at work."

I do as he says, curling my legs beneath me when I return and make myself comfortable in the seat beside his. We chat for over an hour, and then I offer to clean up our meal while he makes himself comfortable in his Lazy-Boy, like he does every evening after work. He kisses the top of my head as he leaves me in the kitchen, and I load our used dishes in the dishwasher before I go about peeling off the fried skin of the chicken left in the bucket. When I get to the bottom, with one thigh remaining, I leave it untouched and bury it under the others, smirking as I stow the container in the fridge.

It's a few minutes to ten when I look up and see Mateo maneuvering his way through the Lounge, making his way toward me. I didn't respond to any of his text messages earlier, which I'm sure pissed him off, but I had nothing to say. Now that he's here, I still don't; but I can't deny that seeing him causes my affection for him to tug at my heart. When things are good, it's unheard of for us to go all day without speaking to one another.

"Hey," he murmurs, now standing across from me.

"Hey."

He looks down the length of the bar, noticing that we're a little slow at the moment, and then asks, "Can you take a break?"

I glance back at Irene, who's filling in for Dodger tonight, and she offers me a slight nod as she assures me, "I got it."

"Thanks," I whisper.

Mateo meets me on the far left side of the bar as I make my exit, immediately reaching for my hand. I don't pull away as he escorts me through the tables, leading me outside. The weather is cool, the absence of the sun taking with it most of today's warmth, and I reach up with my free hand to rub my arm in search of some heat. Mateo notices and tugs me against his chest, wrapping his arms around me.

I look up at him from beneath my lashes, and I relax against him when I read the apology in his eyes.

"You were right. I was a dick for forgetting you. I'm sorry. I won't let it happen again, baby, I swear." Before I can even think of a response, his lips are pressed against mine in a tender kiss. "I mean it, Blaine," he whispers, kissing me again. And then again. "I'm sorry, baby."

When he flicks his tongue out, tasting my bottom lip, I can't stop myself from opening up for him. He doesn't hesitate to make his move, filling my mouth with his tongue, and I totally cave. I'm not sure how long I let him kiss me, but I'm sure it's me who slows us down, easing away from him before capturing my lower lip between my teeth.

"I need you to know that I heard you last night," he goes on to say. "I know what it looks like. I do—but it's just a slow season for me. Things will pick back up. I've got some shit in the works.

You've got to trust me."

"I do," I murmur, fidgeting with the collar of his t-shirt. "It's just hard. I feel like I'm carrying a lot and—"

"I'm doing my best," he interrupts, giving me a squeeze.

I nod, not wishing to be too judgmental or too hard on him. I understand what it's like to fight for a dream. Most days, it takes everything I have in me to try and discover my own. I know chasing after them isn't always easy.

"Listen, I could really use the car tonight. I know it's getting late, but—"

"Wait," I mutter, pushing my hands against his chest. He doesn't let me go, but that doesn't stop me from putting some distance between us—enough to squint my eyes at him in confusion. "Did you come down here and say all of that so that you could convince me to hand over my keys?"

"Blaine. Come on, you know I meant—"

I shake my head at him, coughing out a humorless laugh as I shove my way out of his hold. "I can't believe you."

"Blaine, baby—"

"No. No! Don't *baby* me. One night. You couldn't go one night without figuring it out for yourself? You know how many times you've left me to *figure it out for myself?* God! I *seriously* cannot believe that's why you came down here."

"Fuck! That's not the only reason why I'm here. Did you not hear everything that I just said? I mean, *Christ,* how many times do I have to apologize?"

I shake my head at him, backing my way toward the door as I tell him, "I don't know. Maybe trying apologizing without feeling me up. Or, better yet, without asking for favors immediately after. Maybe then I'll be able to *hear* you." Turning away from him, I call out, "I'll see you at home, Mat. I have to get back to work."

Walking briskly through the bar, I head straight for the bathroom, pressing my back against the door as soon as I'm inside. I need a minute to breathe—to clear my head. I'm not really sure what just happened, or what's *been* happening. I think back on our kiss, tracing my fingers across my lips, wishing I felt the tingle that usually lingers after he showers me in affection. Wishing I felt better about his apology. Wishing I felt more hopeful—more optimistic.

But I don't.

And it hurts.

Three

Michael

I STEP INTO THE PROHIBITION LOUNGE with no expectations, and yet I still find myself surprised as I take it all in. It's a good sized space, while still managing to maintain a sort of intimate atmosphere. The lights are dimmed down a tad, making it inviting, and the dark furniture only adds to the ambiance. There are no tablecloths on the tables, but the silverware wrapped in white linen, along with the white cloth chairs pushed up to each place setting, gives the Lounge a crisp, clean, sharp look to it.

It's not particularly crowded, which isn't surprising for a Tuesday night at this time, and I wonder if their kitchen is still open.

"Good evening, sir. Table for two?" greets the hostess, pulling me from my perusal of the place.

I offer her a small smile, dipping my chin in a silent hello, and then search the bar. Noting that there are only a few patrons sitting at the long stretch of counter, I nod in that direction before

I inquire, "Would it be all right if I made myself comfortable at the bar?"

"Absolutely, sir. The bar is free seating."

"Thank you."

As I make my way past the hostess station, I hear Clay requesting a table near the door. I don't bother inviting him to sit with me, knowing already that he would decline. He always does—wishing to remain on the periphery of the room, watching my back. He's constantly on duty when he's with me. He never lets his guard down. While I don't always find it necessary, I appreciate his professionalism just the same.

I drape my jacket over the back of my stool and take a seat at the corner of the bar. Pushing up my already cuffed shirt sleeves to my elbows, I rest my forearms against the counter top and shift my focus toward the bartender currently attending to another guest. My gaze relocates when I notice another stepping behind the bar to join her. She spots me right away, offers me a small smile, and then casts her eyes down as she begins to close the distance between us.

I watch her as she approaches, noticing her shoulders rise and fall, as if she's taking a breath—not because she needs oxygen, but because she's attempting to prepare herself for something. Just before she stops in front of me, she lifts her head, straightens her neck, and plasters on a smile. Before she even speaks a word, I know the friendly expression on her face isn't genuine.

It's a shame, really. She's got a beautiful face.

Her eyes are hazel, more brown than green—though, perhaps it's the lighting that plays with the color, or her dark, wavy hair she wears loose; it frames her face, cut just short of her shoulders. Her milky skin looks soft and smooth—save the small mole she's got on her right cheek, a short distance away from her mouth. Thinking about her mouth makes me look there, too. Her bottom lip is fuller than her top one—and with my focus zeroed in on her lips, her forced smile becomes even more obvious.

"Hi, there. I'm Blaine, and I'll be taking care of you tonight. What can I get you to drink?" she asks, pulling my attention back up to her eyes.

"That depends, actually," I say, my stomach clenching in hunger. "Is your kitchen still open?"

"Sure is," she assures me, looking down in front of her. She reaches for a menu, placing it before me as she goes on to inquire, "Would you like a water while you decide on something?"

"Sure, thank you."

She offers me a nod and another forced smile, and I watch as she goes to fetch me that water. My curiosity getting the better of me, I don't take my eyes off of her, noting how her shoulders sag the minute she thinks no one is looking. Something tells me it's not just a long night she's having. Shoulders that heavy carry an invisible weight that only the bearer is privy to.

Shaking my head clear, I glance down at the menu. It only takes me a minute to decide what I'd like—my hunger driving my decision to disregard the late hour and go for what I crave. Even with my mind made up, I don't hesitate to engage the little brunette in conversation. If she's forced to wait on me whilst dealing with whatever it is that plagues her mind at the moment, the least I can do is be extra pleasant.

"Blaine, was it?" I ask before she can step away.

The corners of her mouth twitch up in what might be an almost genuine smile, and she nods, smoothing her hands down her fitted, black, button-up top.

"How's the burger here? I've had a long day, I haven't eaten since lunch, and I'd really rather not be disappointed," I tell her with a smirk.

Her smile grows a little more as she rests her palms against the edge of the counter and leans toward me. She shifts her focus down to the menu as she replies, "The burger is decent, but the steak?" She hesitantly reaches for the corner of my menu and turns the page, pointing at the item which she's in the process of recommending. "It's amazing. Well, if you order it medium rare. Julio is on deck tonight, and he can *kill* a medium rare cut. I'd also go with a side of the baked macaroni and cheese. It might sound a little elementary, but I swear by it."

She leans back, the curve of her lips growing bigger still, and I can't help but to return the expression. When she gives me a hint of her real smile, it's contagious.

"You know—if you like that kind of thing," she finishes.

"I do," I insist. I consider her recommendation for a moment, then flick my attention down to my wristwatch. Wishing not to disappoint her, I gently remind her, "It's a little late for a steak, though."

"True," she hums before pressing her lips together and tugging them to the side. I watch her, temporarily neglecting my hunger, wishing to distract her for a bit longer. Leaning toward me again, she flips back the page in front of me and points at something else. "How do you feel about crab? Our crab cakes are the best in at least four city blocks."

Chuckling, I point out, "That's a very specific radius."

She shrugs, meeting my eyes and offering me a shy smile. "Just being honest."

"So, the crab cake? That's your best offer?"

She glances down at the menu once more and then looks back

up at me, giggling softly before she straightens. I fight a grin, feeling as though I've just won a battle she didn't even know I was fighting.

"I swear I'm not trying to dig into your wallet," she murmurs, interrupting my thoughts. "But you haven't eaten since lunch, and I don't want you to be disappointed, either."

I peer down at the price of the crab cake dinner and smirk. Shutting the menu, I push it toward her as I finally place my order. "I'd love the crab cake with a side of steamed broccoli."

"Yes, sir," she says, speaking through a gorgeous smile.

"Blaine?"

"Yes?"

"Call me Michael. And I'll take a beer. Fat Tire, if you have it."

"Okay, Michael. Coming right up."

Blaine

"He's cute," Irene mumbles under her breath when I return to the register.

I add a beer to Michael's tab, hearing my friend without actually *hearing* her.

"Hmm?" I hum, turning to look at her as she leans on the counter beside me.

She grins at me slyly before she says, "Don't act like you don't notice. I have a fiancé—doesn't mean I can't appreciate a fine specimen of a man when he sits down at the far end of the bar."

My eyes flick across the distance separating us from Mister Tall-Dark-and-Handsome, who appears to be enjoying his beverage and scrolling through something on his phone. Returning my attention to the conversation at hand, I meet Irene's studious gaze once more.

She waggles her eyebrows, and I fight a laugh as I point out, "He's married. He's also got to be at least, like, thirty-four."

"Admit it!" she demands through her laughter. "You think he's hot." Turning her back toward him, she props her hip against the counter and grips her opposite side with her hand as she goes on to add, "The fact that he's potentially ten years older than you makes him that much more alluring. Only *men* can sport a five-o'clock shadow as well as he can."

I lean back a little, peering around Irene and sneaking another peek at Michael. The truth is, I didn't notice at first, my mind still trudging its way out of the scene that transpired between Mateo and me a few minutes ago. It wasn't until Michael asked my advice that I really *looked* at him.

I bite the inside of my cheek, shifting my focus back to the register, knowing that I don't need to stare to remember him. He's the kind of guy that's hard to forget. He's huge, first of all—his broad, sculpted shoulders and incredible biceps filling out his white button-up so perfectly, it's as if it was painted on him. He's got his top button undone, his blue tie hangs in a loose knot against his chest, and I swear I could see a hint of chest hair peeking out from beneath the collar of his undershirt.

I bet he's covered. I bet it's sexy as hell—the dark strands standing out against the pale skin of his massive chest…or what I imagine his massive chest would look like.

Irene chuckles mischievously, and I fight a smile, continuing my mental perusal of the image of Michael that's still at the forefront of my mind.

I see his strong, square jaw, covered in the dusting of facial hair Irene mentioned a second ago. I think about his pretty blue eyes, a few shades darker than dad's pale blue ones. And his hair—*good god*—it's thick, and dark, and curly. He wears it slicked back and neat on the sides. The top is a little longer; and with the way he parts and combs it, he's got one big curl that falls across the top of his forehead.

Like Superman.

"Okay," I say softly, lifting my eyes to meet Irene's. I know that if I don't fess up, she'll stare at me until I can't take it anymore. "I'll admit it. He's extremely easy on the eyes. But he's also *married* and—"

"Yeah, yeah, you're completely in love with Mateo. I know, girl. I totally get it. I love my man, too."

My smile falls when she walks away. As I listen to her check on her customers, I furrow my brow, feeling guilty that I wouldn't have finished my sentence the way that she did. I wasn't thinking about Mateo at all. I was *going* to say that since Michael is *married* and a *customer*, I really don't think it'll work in my favor to ogle. Not when I'm hoping he's a good tipper.

Yet, now that Mateo has worked his way back into my thoughts, the ache in my chest I felt fifteen minutes ago is back in full force. His half-ass apology really had me going for a minute, then he had to go and ruin it. Replaying his words in my head only gets me worked up, and I try to busy my hands, keeping myself occupied in an effort to shift my focus. It doesn't work, of course, but it gives me the chance to decide that I'm not going home tonight.

Dad might be right in that I should kick Mateo out on his ass until he can get his shit together, but I can't do that.

"Got a crab cake order," announces Austin from the wait staff, standing at the opening to the bar.

"That's me," I reply, hurrying over to grab it. "Thanks." He nods, and I grab a roll of silverware, stowed in a bin under the counter, before heading to the opposite end to deliver Michael's plate.

"Dinner is served," I tell him, trying to be jovial while simultaneously shoving thoughts of Mateo and our sleeping arrangements out of my head. "Did you want me to get you another beer?"

"No, thank you," he declines, unrolling his utensils.

"Okay." I offer him a feeble nod as he tosses his napkin into his lap, all the while keeping his eyes trained on me. "Well, if you need anything, give me a wave."

I force a smile, take one step back, and then pause as he furrows his brow at me and mutters, "You're giving me the liar's smile again."

"Um, excuse me?" I mumble, taken aback by his accusation.

He props his forearms on either side of his plate, leaning toward me as he softly clarifies, "The smile you gave me when I first sat down, it wasn't real—a lot like the one you just gave me. I thought I'd chased it away."

He shrugs and then finally looks at his plate. Still trapped in a state of confusion, I watch as he picks up his fork and cuts into his crab cake. It isn't until he takes a bite and looks up at me that I shake my head clear and ask, "You just met me. How do you know if my smile is real or not?"

He smiles as he chews, and I immediately wish I could take back my question. I know, without an ounce of doubt, that the curve of his lips is the reason behind the light in his pretty blue eyes. Only an idiot would question whether or not the closed-mouth grin he's giving me is genuine.

After he swallows, he pulls me back into the conversation and says, "Blaine, in my profession, lies have always been a factor with which I've had to contend. Most days, I know counterfeit when I see it."

Discarding my embarrassment for curiosity, I fold my arms across my chest and inquire, "What do you do? Are you a detective or something?"

He chuckles—the sound deep, warm, and enticing—and cuts another bite of crab cake. Before he puts it in his mouth, he informs me, "Not quite. I'm a politician."

Connecting the dots between *lies* and *politicians*, I can't silence the giggle that bubbles out of me as I reply, "I guess that makes sense. The Capitol building is only about a block away." He nods, and I find myself asking, "So what kind of politician are you? Not the lying kind, I hope. We've got enough of those."

He swallows another bite, spears a piece of broccoli, and smirks as he admits, "My constituents teasingly refer to me as *Honest Abe.*"

"Your constituents, huh? So you were voted in."

My eyes widen a bit when he squints at me and asks, "Are you registered to vote, Blaine?"

"Of course," I gasp, feigning offense.

"And the last time you found yourself at the polls was...?" His inquiry trails off, the silence an obvious invitation for me to finish it for him.

"Okay! You got me," I admit, throwing my hands up in surrender. "I've only ever voted in a presidential election. Two of them, to be exact. I don't even know when the others are."

"You should pay more attention," he insists, his voice not condescending but encouraging—almost *pleading.* "State elections are just as important. Your representatives do just that—represent your voice in higher sects of government. Voting in people you can trust is nothing to neglect—especially not for the younger generations."

I purse my lips together, fighting a grin. He's very passionate about politics, that's for sure.

"So, are you going to tell me what you do?"

"I'm your state governor," he answers nonchalantly, popping a bite of broccoli into his mouth.

I jerk my head back a little, totally buying his statement for a second, and completely appalled that I was recently checking out the Colorado State Governor. He said it so confidently—so *coolly.* It takes me a moment to shake off my surprise and come to the conclusion that he must be kidding. He knows that I am obviously uneducated when it comes to local government, and he's taking advantage of my negligence. I walked *right* into this.

My lips curl in a knowing, crooked smile, and I prop my hands against the edge of the bar before I say, "Yeah, right. Be honest. What do you do?"

He lifts his cloth napkin, and I try not to blatantly stare at him as he smears it across his lips before dropping it back in his lap. I'm not very successful, wishing not to break eye contact with him while I wait for the truth. Only, he doesn't break character. Not for a single second.

"I promise you that I'm not lying. Honest Abe, remember?"

My mouth falls open and words come flying out before I can think better of them.

"You must be joking. I've never known a governor as—" I manage to shut myself up before I say something irrevocably inappropriate; but I can tell by his quirked eyebrow that I've said enough to pique his interest.

"You've never known a governor as…what?" he asks, spearing another piece of broccoli.

I fight like hell to keep a rush of color from blossoming across my cheeks as my mind silently finishes my thought.

I've never known a governor as attractive as you are.

Clearing my throat, I blurt out the next thought that comes to mind. "As...*young* as you are."

"I'm not sure I'm as young as you think," he says, speaking around his broccoli. He swallows and then adds, "Would you mind a little history lesson?"

Relieved that I've managed to not completely embarrass myself, I shake my head in reply.

"The youngest governor to ever serve was sworn in at twenty-five. He was elected in the state of Michigan when it became a part of the Union. I won't bore you with the second and third youngest, but Bill Clinton was only thirty-two when he was elected into office in nineteen-seventy-eight. I'm not the youngest governor to ever be sworn in; but I must admit I'm the youngest holding the position currently—by a year."

I watch him eat another bite of his dinner, still a bit unbelieving that *this* man is essentially the leader of the entire state of Colorado. Aside from his looks, he doesn't strike me as—*ruthless* or unbearably *ambitious* as I always imagined the higher-ups of government have to be in order to reach such a status.

"You still don't believe me," he chuckles, reaching for his glass.

He downs the rest of his beer as I admit, "I don't know. You're just so...*nice.*"

He grins, setting aside the now empty glass, and tells me, "How do you think I got elected?"

"Now I know you're lying," I declare with a laugh. "*Nobody* gets elected by being *nice.*"

"I've got a few other qualities and qualifications that worked in my favor as well," he tells me before consuming the last of his crab cake.

"Mmmhmm," I hum. Pointing at his plate, I ask, "May I?"

"Please. And my check, if you don't mind. I should be going."

"Certainly."

I set his dishes aside and head to the register, wasting no time printing out his tab. When I set it in front of him, he doesn't even look at it before placing his card on top. I'm back at the register in less than thirty seconds, mindlessly completing his transaction. I'm so accustomed to it that I rarely think about it anymore.

By the time I return to his side of the bar, he's on his feet, shrugging his jacket over his immense shoulders. He signs the receipt, an absentminded smile on his lips as he does it, and then returns his card to his wallet. He slides out a bill and places it on the bar; only, I can't see what it is, as he doesn't lift his palm right away.

When my gaze collides with his, he murmurs, "I wasn't the slightest bit disappointed. It was a pleasure speaking with you, Blaine."

"You too, Michael," I reply, noting that the smile that tugs at the corners of my mouth is completely genuine.

"You have a good night."

"You, too," I repeat.

He dips his head in a final nod farewell and then lifts his hand, turning toward the entrance without hesitation. When I look down and spot the fifty-dollar bill, my lips part in a quiet gasp.

"Oh, and Blaine?" he calls out from the door.

I whip my head up to look at him. For the first time since he walked in, I notice the lone man in a suit at the front of the Lounge. He stands, buttons his jacket, and walks toward the door, his focus on Michael.

"If you still don't believe me, google it."

Then, without another word, he's gone.

"Wow," Irene mumbles. I jump, not having noticed her approach. Her gaze flicks down at the bar and then back at me as she says, "That's some tip."

Biting the inside of my cheek, I swipe the fifty and shove it into my back pocket without comment. She chuckles in reply.

Four

Blaine

I wake up to a quiet house, the sun shining through the closed blinds into the room. A year ago, when I first started working the night shift at the Lounge, I thought I'd have a hard time adjusting to sleeping when the sun was out. I learned pretty quickly that after seven and a half hours on my feet tending bar, a little daylight isn't enough to pull me out of my slumber.

Reaching for my phone, I check the time and find that it's a few minutes past one in the afternoon. I also find a text from dad, informing me that he's got plans with some of the guys at work, so we'll probably miss each other today. I'm only slightly disappointed. It makes me happy to know he still goes out with his friends a couple of times a week. I don't ever want him to get too lonely.

My phone is still in my hand when another text message comes through. It isn't until I see *My Artist* lit up on the screen that I realize, unlike yesterday, Mateo didn't blow up my phone this morning. He didn't even respond to my message last night, when I told him I'd be staying with dad again. My chest aches as I ask myself, *what's happening to us?*

Sliding my finger across the notification, I open the message and let out a sigh.

Come home. I love you.

Five words. Five words have never left me feeling so conflicted. A part of me is now afraid that he doesn't actually mean what he says; or maybe not so much that he doesn't mean it, but that the meaning behind the words is different than it used to be. Then there's another part of me that simply loves him, too; loves him enough to understand that every relationship goes through phases, and not every phase is easy—just like every phase won't be hard.

Trying my best to find some forgiveness in my heart, I type out my reply and hit send before I can change my mind.

I love you, too.

The truth is, I only packed enough underwear to stay at dad's one night. I *have* to go home this afternoon so that I can shower before work tonight. Except, rather than getting out of bed, I roll onto my side and burrow underneath the covers a little more, wishing to stay right where I am for a while longer.

I think back over the last thirty-six hours, not sure what to expect when I face Mateo again. Remembering how quickly things went sour last night doesn't leave me particularly anxious to return to the loft just yet. I close my eyes as a yawn comes over me, and that's when my thoughts see fit to remind me of another conversation I had last night.

My eyes pop back open, and I tug my bottom lip between my teeth as I combat my smile. Then I hear his voice in my head—*You're giving me the liar's smile again*—and I immediately free my lip. This time, instead of the sense of shock that washed over me at hearing his observation, my stomach tingles at the realization that he *noticed.* More than that, he made an effort to find my *real* smile. A complete stranger. An undeniably handsome stranger.

A kind stranger.

I flop onto my back as bits and pieces of our conversation bounce around in my head. I remember telling him that he was too nice to be our governor, and he told me to google it. I'm going to. *Right now.*

I open the app, type in *Colorado state governor*, and hit the search button. Two seconds later, his picture is right in front of my face. Not just one picture, either, but an entire thread of them. I swipe my thumb left, glancing at the ones that appear on my initial search page, and I can't help but laugh.

"Oh, my god," I mutter in amused disbelief, stopping on the last image available.

He's sitting at a table behind a propped up microphone, obviously in the middle of saying something. He looks serious, like a politician—a really, really *hot* politician. I know that it's ridiculous of me to think such a thing, but it's true. The look captured on his face isn't one I was graced with last night. His dark eyebrows are drawn together, and his eyes look like pools of angry water. It's obvious that whatever he was talking about in this moment, he was definitely passionate about it.

Now completely intrigued, I click on his Wikipedia link. For a second, I think about how crazy it is that I spent part of the night talking to someone who actually *has* a Wikipedia link, and then I start getting to know him.

His full name is *Michael Isidro Cavanaugh* and he's an American politician—more specifically, Colorado's forty-third governor. It's a title he's held for the last two years. He's a member of the Republican Party, born in Colorado Springs, Colorado, and he's a graduate of Harvard Law School—*holy hell!*

As I continue to read, I note that he's thirty-seven years old; he's been married for the last fifteen years, to a woman named Veronica Hernandez; and before he was elected governor, he was elected to the position of District Attorney—where he served for three years. Given this snapshot of his life, I admit that I was wrong. He's definitely got some sort of ruthless ambition. He's obviously worked really hard to get to where he is today.

Scrolling down to his family life, I learn that he's half Caucasian and half Latino. For some reason, that knowledge explains and justifies his incredibly good looks. Apparently, his dad was originally born in California, while his mom is from Ecuador. Douglas Cavanaugh is the senior pastor at a non-denominational Christian church, Mercy Hill, here in Denver. My eyes widen a little bit at that information. I've never been, but I've definitely heard of it and driven by it. They're very active in the community, and that place is huge.

I'm starting to read how he's one of three Cavanaugh children when a call starts to ring through, blocking his information from view. I grin when I see *Mommy's Pearl* lit up in front of me, and I don't hesitate to answer.

"Simone, hi!" I greet excitedly.

"Did I wake you, darling?" she asks instead of hello.

"No. I'm up."

"Good. Meet me at our spot. Thirty-minutes. I'll be waiting."

Before I can protest, complaining of how I'd prefer to head home and clean up a bit first, she disconnects. I shake my head, stifling a laugh as I climb out of bed. If Simone demands my presence, I try my best to never deny her. When I need her—night, day, sunshine, rain—it doesn't matter, she's there. Always. The least I can do is show her the same kindness.

Though, I'm not stupid enough to imagine that I could ever begin to repay her for the love she's shown me over the last few years.

After I hurry to the bathroom to brush my teeth, splash water on my face, and toss my hair up into a messy little bun, I race back to my room to change my clothes. With not much choice, I opt for my black work slacks and the matching, form fitting, cotton camisole that I usually wear underneath my button-up. I skip the work shirt, yanking my *Whatever Sprinkles Your Donut* tank over my head, and slip into the sparkly, black Toms that I often wear to the Lounge. After one last glance around the room, I race out the door—locking it behind me—not wishing to keep her waiting.

Our spot is this tiny place downtown that serves gourmet sausage sandwiches. Basically, The Über Sausage sells hotdogs on steroids. They're huge, delicious, and should be eaten with a knife and fork—but we never do. It's our thing. Messy hotdogs that leave us stuffed like—well—*sausages.* I can't really explain *how* it became *our spot.* It was as if our united grief drew us there. The outrageous menu distracted us somehow. We ate until we were too full to cry, and a couple weeks later, we found ourselves there again. It's been four years now, and it's still our favorite place.

By the time I find somewhere to park, I'm fifteen minutes late. I run down the street toward the shop, throwing open the door anxiously before stepping inside and looking for my friend. When

I see her, she's already looking at me. Seated in a stool at one of the high-top tables—one of the *awesome* high-top tables, with a glass surface that covers a bunch of random pieces of chopped wood resembling logs for a fire—Simone looks as gorgeous as she always does. Sitting up straight and poised, dressed in a pair of navy slacks, a silky, coral, sleeveless blouse, and a colorful scarf she's got wrapped around her neck and shoulders, she offers me that *all knowing* smile that I've come to recognize as hers.

It's been a few weeks since I've seen her, and I take her in, as is my habit. Her pale, brown skin looks smooth, beautiful, and *healthy*—her pallor not the least bit sickly. Her hair is still cropped short—buzzed almost bald, it's so close to her scalp. I know that she once had long, unruly curly locks, but I can't deny that she looks really good with her hair like it is. When my eyes finally return to her dark brown ones, she lifts an impatient eyebrow at me, and I giggle before picking up my feet. Closing the distance between us, I drop my bag on the stool across from hers as she climbs down. We wrap each other in a warm embrace, and I squeeze her delicate frame tightly.

Simone Deveraux—my mother's pearl. They met when they were both going through chemo, and they became each other's best friends. They understood each other in ways dad and I couldn't; they supported each other, encouraged each other, and *fought* for each other. Mom lost a lot of friends when she got sick. It was as if her cancer was too hard for them, too much for their friendships to bear. She told me once that Simone was her beautiful, black pearl—her treasure found within the dark, hard, ugly confines of their clam of a situation.

"What'll it be this time?" she asks, pulling away from me. "My treat."

Knowing better than to argue with her, I glance at the menu before I tell her that I'd like the *Colorado Buffalo* and a citrus pale ale—because after I turned twenty-one, I learned fairly quickly that Über's dogs were meant to be consumed with a cold can of beer. She nods, grabs her wallet from her purse, and goes to place our order. Since it's already after two o'clock on a Wednesday afternoon, she doesn't have to wait long. When she returns to the table, she's got a tray with our baskets and drinks sitting on top. I can tell right away that she ordered *The Tijuana* for herself, along with a side of tater tots for us to share.

I'm munching on a tot when she says, "John called. Things with Mateo are a little rocky?"

I stall, cracking open my beer before taking a long sip. I shouldn't be surprised that this is the reason she called me, or that dad called her and ratted me out—nevertheless, I'm not exactly prepared for this conversation.

"Blaine…"

Setting my drink down, I offer her a pathetic shrug and reach for another tot. Instead of eating it, I pull it apart and admit, "Sometimes things are great. *Amazing,* even. Most of the time, I like having him around. He's my boyfriend. He's *been* my boyfriend, and I wouldn't have agreed to us living together if I didn't love him."

"And other times?"

"I wonder if we rushed things."

She doesn't say anything right away, and I take advantage of the silence. Picking up my sausage, I take a big, completely unladylike bite. She does the same, and I know she's processing my confession.

When her mouth is empty, she asks, "Do you want him to move out?"

I swallow hard, looking at her with wide eyes. "Wouldn't that be, like, breaking up?"

"Perhaps."

My heart sinks at the thought. "No. I mean, I don't think so. Things suck right now, but I still want him. We have history—we've *built* something."

"Yes. All that is true; but are you hanging onto that history because it's scary to let it go, or because you can't imagine your future without him?"

"I haven't thought about a future without him," I state promptly.

"You haven't *thought* about it or you can't *fathom* it?"

I scrunch my brow, wishing I could throw a tater tot at her. I would if they weren't so delicious. *This—this, right here*—it's why dad called her. She's never afraid to ask the hard questions. She's never been shy about challenging me and my way of thinking, or hesitant about offering her advice or perspective. I hate it and love it simultaneously.

When I don't answer her, she nods her head as if I've shouted my response from the rooftop.

"I'm not here to tell you what to do, or how to think or feel. I don't even think that you need to know the answer today. I do, however, believe that you need to *consider* it. Open your mind and your heart to the question. Don't be afraid to look into the future and realize that it doesn't resemble your present. Don't be afraid of the unknown, the unfamiliar, and the uncomfortable.

"Relationships are work. If Mateo *is* in your future, if he *is* a piece of your happiness, then you must come to the realization that you cannot run away when *things suck.* You must stay. You must fight. It is how you keep the treasures in your life that are worth keeping."

I look down into my basket, offering her a silent nod.

"I wish only to see you happy, darling. It's what your mother wanted."

I force a small smile, lifting my gaze to meet hers. "I know."

"Eat," she demands, tipping her chin in my direction.

My smile softens into a real one as her small hand wraps around her overflowing bun. I mimic her stance before I obey.

It's almost four o'clock when I insert my key into the lock of my front door and twist it open. When I step inside, I find the loft empty. I'm not sure if I'm relieved, disappointed, or indifferent to being here alone. I don't bother thinking about it as I set aside my things and strip down for a shower.

I take my time shampooing and conditioning my hair before I soap down my body. After I've rinsed myself completely clean, I'm just about to turn the water off when the shower door opens. I don't turn around to watch him step in behind me. Neither do I speak a word of protest when I feel his hands graze down my sides before he flattens his palms against my stomach. I pull my bottom lip between my teeth as he brings me back against him, his erection pressing against the top of my ass.

"I missed you," he murmurs, his lips caressing the tip of my shoulder. "Tell me you felt it, too." One of his hands slides down between my legs, and I can't stop myself from melting into him, widening my stance. "Baby?" he asks, his fingers circling around my clit.

A quiet moan spills from my mouth as I twist my neck and tilt my head back. Reaching up to bury my fingers into his long hair, I gently tug him closer as I whisper, "*Mateo.*"

He grunts as he closes his mouth around mine, and then he fucks me.

He fucks me like he missed me.

Five

Michael

"GOVERNOR CAVANAUGH?" HEIDI KNOCKS on my open door, peeking her head inside of the office. I close the folder in front of me, looking up at her in time to see her smile as she says, "You're feeling better. Admit it. It's been a long forty-eight hours, but things are looking up."

"Marginally," I admit on a grunt.

"I'm headed home," she says, rolling her eyes. "I hope you are, too."

Flipping my wrist, I note that it's almost seven-thirty. I exhale a heavy sigh and dip my chin in a nod. "Right behind you. Have a good night."

"You, as well. See you tomorrow."

Before I start to gather my things, I pick up my phone to check for any missed messages. I notice that I have three texts from Veronica—the first of which was sent nearly three hours ago. I'm quick to open them.

I'm going straight from a committee meeting to my book club. I was planning on leaving dinner in the oven for you, but the afternoon got away from me. There're some leftovers in the fridge, but you might prefer takeout. I know how you like your salmon fresh.

Sorry I'll miss you. Should be home by nine.

Oh—and don't eat the cheesecake bites, sweetie. They're for the party.

I know how to cook. There was no way in hell my mother was letting any of her children leave the nest without the skills to cook a decent meal. *Arroz con pollo* was the first dish I ever remember learning how to make. Her favorite is *bolon de verde*, which is more of a breakfast food, and we all know how to put that together, too. My favorite has always been empanadas. They're simple, but they hit the spot. And while my Ecuadorean palate is quite defined, mom has her American favorites, as well; which basically means I don't *have* to resort to takeout.

It's been a while since I've found myself in the kitchen for any considerable amount of time. When I was dating Vee, I used to cook for her frequently. Now it's the other way around—or takeout. While working a long day is a poor excuse for avoiding the task of throwing something together for dinner myself, it's become a hard habit to break. I would blame it on fifteen years of marriage, but it's more complicated than that. In my household, we each have our roles to play—and I let Veronica play hers as she wishes.

As I shrug my suit jacket over my shoulders, my stomach growls, and I try to think of someplace close to stop before heading home. It isn't until I switch off the overhead lights that I remember the little brunette trying to convince me that I couldn't go wrong with a medium rare steak and a side of macaroni and cheese at the Prohibition Lounge. A small smile tugs at the corner of my mouth when I recall the look of disbelief on her face when I informed her of my current office. Now curious as to whether or not she ended up searching the internet for proof, I decide that steak and macaroni and cheese is *exactly* what I'd like for dinner tonight.

It doesn't occur to me, until I walk into the establishment with Clay, that the little brunette might not even be working tonight. When I spot her behind the bar as I approach the hostess station, it's relief that I feel spread across my chest at the sight of her. She looks different today—her hair pulled up into a little bun on top of her head, a couple lose strands dangling by her ears. I watch as she laughs with one of her fellow bartenders—a tall guy that I don't recognize from my last visit—and I'm immediately cognizant of the fact that whatever was bothering her the other night, she looks not to be concerned with it now. That, too, fills me with relief. I don't have an explanation as to why, other than the fact that I like her real smile better than her false one; and the look on her face now, as she grabs that guy's elbow and throws her head back with a laugh, it reminds me of how beautiful she really is.

My name is Blaine…

As if being in the atmosphere of the lounge is what I needed to trigger the finer details of our previous encounter, my memory plays back her introduction. Looking at her, I decide that hers is a name I doubt I'll let slip away. I shake a lot of hands and meet a lot of people in my line of work. I won't deny that some names are easier to forget than others. But hers—*Blaine's*—I doubt I'll be forgetting it anytime soon. Like her smile, it's not hard to remember.

Clay clears his throat before he mutters, "Governor," under his breath. I look back at him from over my shoulder. He jerks his chin and replies, "Where would you like to sit tonight?"

It isn't until he asks that I realize the hostess must have been trying to get my attention. Finally offering it to her, I smile politely before I inform her that I'd like to sit at the bar. Just like last time, I'm invited to occupy any available seat, while Clay stays behind to request a table for one.

Making my way over, I see that the front of the bar is almost full of patrons. On the far side, where I sat Tuesday night, there's only one man seated on the corner, while the three remaining stools are left empty. I choose to sit in the middle spot, draping my jacket over the back of the seat before I sit down. Blaine looks over at me as I'm getting settled, and I watch as her eyes widen before her cheeks warm in a blush. She then tries to disguise her smile as she drops her forehead into the palm of her hand and shakes her head.

I grin, certain of two things.

She googled me.

And steak for dinner was the right choice.

Blaine

My stomach tingles at the sight of him, and I bite down hard on my lower lip, willing the blush on my face to go away before I walk over and greet him. It isn't until this very moment that I realize I harbored a desire to see him again. That said, I had no idea he would be capable of making me blush like a little girl.

After a couple deep breaths through my nose, I free my lip, smooth my hands down the front of my black shirt, and stand up as tall as my height will allow. As I head to the far end of the bar, I find him grinning at me knowingly, and I do nothing to silence the giggle that spills from my lips.

Wishing to play off my moment of embarrassment, I offer him a shallow curtsy before I say, "Good evening, Governor Cavanaugh."

He chuckles, the sound doing mysterious things to my belly, and replies, "I do believe we can dispense with the formalities. If I remember correctly, you and I are on a first name basis." Titling his head in a subtle nod, he goes on to say, "Good evening, Blaine."

"You remembered my name," I blurt out stupidly.

"And you learned my last. It appears as though I have some catching up to do."

"You should actually be impressed with how much I know about our state's governor," I say teasingly, folding my arms across my chest.

Leaning back in his chair, he mimics my stance, folding his arms across his own chest. It makes the fabric of his shirt hug his muscles even tighter, and I can't prevent my eyes from admiring his sculpted biceps, his massive shoulders, and his now bulging chest. His shirt cuffs are rolled up over his forearms, and the top button of his collar is undone; but his pale yellow tie is barely loosened.

"School me," he insists, pulling me from my thoughts. My eyes snap back up to meet his, and I have to fight another blush. I was totally just checking him out. *Again*. Fortunately, he doesn't seem to have noticed, an observation I pick up on when he lifts one of his thick, dark eyebrows and smiles. "I'm ready," he assures me patiently.

Before I can utter a word, I hear Dodger guffaw from beside

me. I look up, surprised to see him there, but he doesn't pay me any mind.

"Well, I'll be damned," he says, as if in awe. "We don't get the political elite in here often, but that's never stopped me from imagining one day we might."

Dropping my arms, I look from Dodger to Michael, and then back to Dodger again. "You know who this is?" I ask, hooking my thumb at Michael.

Dodger coughs out a laugh, looking at me as if I've got two heads. "Of course I do. Don't you vote?" he answers.

I clamp my jaw closed, shooting a wide-eyed look at Michael. He catches my eye, laughing softly as he winks at me, and then shifts his attention back onto Dodger, who proceeds to introduce himself.

"Dodger," he says, holding out his hand. Michael reciprocates, and they exchange a handshake as Dodger goes on to tell him, "It's nice to meet you, Governor."

"You as well, Dodger," Michael says politely.

"I was at Coors Field when you threw the first pitch of the season for the Rockies. You weren't messing around. You ever play?"

Michael grins, shaking his head as he looks down at the bar. It's as if the question has taken him back, and he's allowing himself a moment to remember. He lifts his gaze with a nod, informing the both of us, "I did. In high school, and for a couple of years in college."

"Why'd you stop?" asks Dodger.

"I got hurt," Michael replies with a shrug. "I was disappointed at the time; but in a lot of ways, I see now that it was meant to be. Baseball was never my career path."

"Well, you're kicking ass in office. Looks like it worked out for the best. Anyway—I don't mean to hold you up." Dodger claps a hand on my shoulder and waves at Michael before he says, "I've got to get back to it. You're in good hands, Governor."

I watch him as he leaves my side to attend to his customers, wondering how it escaped my knowledge that he's into politics. We've been friends since I started working here. We met when I was in my last year of school, while I was working part time. Two years, we've been getting to know each other, and I had no idea my tatted up, seemingly liberal compatriot was a *Cavanaugh* supporter.

"I like him," says Michael, earning my attention. "An active participant in the liberties of democracy. Hang around him enough, you might learn a few things."

I press my lips together, fighting a smile. "Ha, ha," I jib mockingly, setting a menu in front of him. "What can I get you tonight?"

He slides the menu back toward me, and I assume I've been presumptuous in my assumption that he had an interest in the dinner menu. That is, until he tells me, "I hear the steak is good—so long as I enjoy my cut medium rare. I'd like to try it. With a side of macaroni and cheese and broccoli, please."

This time, I don't even attempt to hide my grin, returning the menu back behind the bar before I assure him, "Coming right up."

Michael

"ARE YOU *SURE* I can't get you anything to drink besides water?" she asks, clearing away my empty plate.

I check the time, noting that it's a few minutes after eight thirty, and decide that I can spare a few extra moments for a nightcap. I order bourbon, and she gives me another smile before she sets aside my plate for pick-up and pours my drink.

When she sets it in front of me, I remind her, "I'm still waiting for you to school me on Colorado's governor."

"Oh, that's right. I am a wealth of knowledge, you know?" she says teasingly, propping herself against her palms on the edge of the bar.

Enjoying the ways in which she banters with me, I raise my glass and insist, "By all means."

"Well, he's a Colorado native, which I appreciate. Who better to represent our state than someone who not only grew up here, but wished to come back after spending some time away. Which he did, by the way." She arches a knowing eyebrow at me, and I force my mouth to remain straight, as if I'm really learning something at the moment.

In a way, I suppose I am. She's completely endearing.

"He graduated from Harvard Law, which I assume means he's crazy smart. Also reassuring. Though, I learned just recently that he played baseball during his undergrad, which leaves a hole in his history. I don't recall reading where he got his undergrad."

Freeing a smile, I inform her, "Dartmouth."

She coughs out a laugh, rolling her eyes. "Of course. Because he's crazy smart and would obviously go to two different Ivy League schools."

I hum a laugh of my own as I tell her, "I'm sure your brain is equally impressive."

"Right," she scoffs through a grin. "What gave me away? The fact that I'm wearing a different black shirt than I was the last time you saw me? I know they look a lot alike, but they're different, I assure you."

"Hey," I scold, pointing a finger at her. "Personal hygiene is a very important key to success." She smirks and rolls her eyes at me again. Chuckling, I smooth my forehead of my playful scowl and mutter softly, "You're young. Something tells me this is not all you'll ever be."

She tugs her lips to one side of her mouth as she self-consciously sweeps a loose strand of hair behind her ear. Nodding, she replies, "You're right—but we're not talking about me."

She waves her hands in front of her as if waving off the topic of *her future*. A part of me is disappointed that she has no interest in discussing such dreams. I'm curious to know what she keeps hidden—what *plans* she treasures so much that she holds them close—but I let it go. When she resumes her biography lesson, I listen intently while I sip at my liquor.

"Did you know that our governor is a conservative Christian and a Republican? His dad is the founder of a really big church here in town."

"Not always conservative," I correct. "But keep going. I'd like to know more."

"Well, his mom is from Ecuador, which makes him half Ecuadorean. Verdict is still out on whether or not he's bilingual."

Now grinning from ear to ear, I reply, "*Lo estás haciendo muy bien. Lo estoy disfrutando.*[1]"

Her eyes widen in excitement, and I watch as another gorgeous smile slowly pulls at the corners of her mouth. Shaking her head at me, she mumbles, "Crazy smart." Then, leaning toward me, she lowers her voice to a hushed whisper and asks, "What did you just say?"

Leaning toward her—as if what I'm about to translate is some

1 You're doing very well. I'm enjoying this.

sort of secret—I rest my elbow on the bar and whisper back, "You're doing very well. I'm enjoying this."

I notice the light blush that colors the tops of her cheeks as she rights herself behind the bar and offers me a shrug. "I hope it doesn't disappoint you to find out that's where my wealth of knowledge ends. I can't remember anything else. History was never my best subject."

"Ouch," I mutter jokingly, lifting my hand to cover my heart. "Was that a dig at my age?"

Laughing, she shakes her head insistently in response. "No! Not at all. But that reminds me—the youngest governor in the United States is thirty-seven."

I lift the last of my bourbon in a silent toast before downing the rest of it. Setting my empty glass on the bar, I commend her for her research. "You did your homework. I'm impressed."

"This crazy smart guy told me I should pay more attention. I thought I'd put in a little effort," she replies with a crooked smile. Pointing at my glass, she asks, "Would you like another?"

"No. Thank you," I murmur in reply. Remembering that Veronica will be home any minute now, I reach for my wallet. "I guess it's about time I headed home."

"Sure. Let me grab your check."

She doesn't take long. When she returns, I already have my card ready for her. As she completes my transaction at the register, I thumb through the bills in the center of my wallet. The last time I was here, I dropped her a fifty-dollar tip. Truth be told, I didn't anticipate coming back again so soon. If I'm not careful, I'll break the bank on tips alone in this place.

I find two twenties and begin to ease them out, hesitating for only a moment. I remember the brief look on her face when she eluded talk about her future—thinking of whatever it is that she dreams of doing that'll get her out from behind this bar. It's been over a decade since I remember feeling that way; like I wasn't yet equipped with what I needed to progress in my desired career field. Wishing only to encourage her, I don't think twice about slipping her a forty-dollar tip.

"Thanks for stopping in tonight, Michael. I hope you enjoyed your meal."

"The steak was exceptional," I admit, signing my receipt. "And the company just as enjoyable as the last time."

"Glad to hear it."

I tuck her tip into the check holder and fold it closed before standing to my feet. Shrugging my jacket back over my shoulders, I dip my chin farewell. "You take care, Blaine."

"Foster," she blurts out, hugging the check holder against her chest. I furrow my brow in confusion, and she goes on to say, "I don't have a Wikipedia link or anything. Really, it's mostly just useless information—but my last name is Foster. Now we're even."

My lips curl into a lopsided grin, thinking back over our conversation and all that she knows about me. It's a hell of a lot more than my last name, but her admission isn't as useless as she realizes. In fact, it actually sounds like an invitation of some kind—an invitation that leaves me intrigued.

"Not even," I reply, backing my way toward the door. "But getting there."

I offer her a friendly wink, and her face lights up just the way I like. When she lifts her hand and wiggles her fingers in a delicate wave, I make a mental note to drop by the bank in the next couple of weeks. I'll need the cash when I come back.

Six

Michael

The mansion is quiet when Clay and I enter through the garage. That's what I call it. That's what I've always called it, much to my family's chagrin. My mother insists that it's a home I've worked hard for—a home I've *earned.* She thinks to title it *the mansion* makes it seem like a cold, unwelcoming place. My sister just thinks I sound like a pompous ass when I call it as such, but I can't help it. The truth is, it's my house, but it's not *home.* While I endeavor to remain in the good graces of the people of Colorado long enough to serve them as governor for a full eight years, I doubt this place will ever feel like home. *Home* doesn't come with an expiration date. Not to mention, a good part of the mansion is open to tourists. There's even a team of curators who work hard to ensure that the history of the place stays intact.

No—this isn't home. However, I have earned it, and I respect what that means, regardless.

The absence of Veronica's town car means that she and Noah are still out, most likely back at the church finishing up her clothing drive. I make my way up to the bedroom, kicking my shoes off before propping myself up against the pillows at the top of the bed. I then turn on the television mounted on the wall across from me.

It's not often that I find myself alone in front of the television. If it's not work keeping me busy, it's Veronica. Every once in a while, I can convince her to sit down and watch a movie with me, but I know her. I know she'd rather be flitting about, making sure everything is *just right.* The older we get, the harder it is for her to relax. I always thought it was supposed to be the other way around, but she's tenacious in her resolve to be everything she promised me she would be on our wedding day—and *more.* Sometimes, I swear, my election was also *her* election; as if the position of *First Lady* is just another opportunity for her to step up and show me that while she can't give me *everything,* that doesn't mean she can't give me *more.*

I wish she knew that she didn't have to work so hard to keep away my resentment.

I've never resented her. Not ever.

I must doze off unknowingly, because when I feel Veronica's lips pressed against mine, I'm startled out of sleep. I open my eyes and draw in a deep breath, catching sight of her smiling face before I look around the room to get my bearings. When I notice that the light pouring in through the windows is dimmer than it was before, I wonder how long I was out.

Veronica snatches back my attention again when she kisses me once more before she tells me, "It's a quarter to five, Mike. We need to leave in a half hour if we're going to be on time."

"Quarter to five?" I grumble, scrunching my brow at her. "Are you just now getting home?"

"No," she answers simply, shaking her head as she reaches up to run her fingers through my hair. "I got home around two. I didn't want to wake you. I know you've had a long week."

"Mmm," I grunt in agreement, sitting up straight. "I better get a quick shower."

"Okay."

It isn't until she stands that I notice what she's wearing. It's a long-sleeved dress made of some kind of light-weight material that moves whenever she does. The front dips down low, showing off a bit of her cleavage, and the two sides of the dress appear to be clasped somehow at her waist on her left side. The material is navy blue with white, lavender, and peach flowers printed all over it. There's also a generous slit that opens up around her left leg when she steps the right way. It's not a dress she'd wear while making a public appearance at my side, but tonight is about family. Tonight, she's wearing this dress for me, and it doesn't go unnoticed.

Climbing off the bed, I catch her around the waist and pull her against my chest. She melts into me immediately, her full breasts even more obvious now that they're smashed against me. My pants grow a little tight when she smooths her hands over my back, holding onto me as she gives me her deep brown eyes.

"Hi," I murmur, my gaze dancing around her face.

"Hi," she whispers through a grin. "Did you enjoy your game of golf this morning?"

I think back to my morning with Lawrence, followed by our discussion over brunch at the club. It was a productive meeting, one I've been anxious to have. Lawrence has always been able to provide insight on the climate of the business world and the banking industry. He's a very wealthy man with connections in high places, his hand dipped in more than a few pots. He was a major contributor during my campaign, and I'll always be grateful for the introduction to him when I was working as the DA.

But with my dick at half-mast, Lawrence and golf are the last things I want to discuss right now.

Running my fingers through Veronica's thick, black hair, I inform her, "Not exactly what I want to talk about right this second."

Chuckling, she presses against me tighter and tells me, "I can *feel* that—but we don't have time, sweetie. Half an hour, remember?"

"I like this dress," I mutter, ignoring her reminder. I slide the hand that's not in her hair down and around her ass, giving her a squeeze.

"It's new," she says on a sigh. "I thought a wrap-dress would be fitting for the party. I mean, I know we're not getting into the pool, but—"

I cut her off with a kiss, bringing both of my hands to her waist before I ask, "Wrap-dress? Does that mean I can unwrap you right now?"

"Mike," she laughs into my mouth as my hands feel around her middle, trying to figure out how to get this thing off. Just when I think I've figured it out, she pushes her way out of my arms and holds up a finger. "We can't be late."

I look down at my crotch, my dick now fully erect and pressing against the zipper of my pants. Glancing at her with a knowing smirk, I ask, "And what are we to do about this?"

Stepping toward me, she reaches down and grips me through my pants, causing a groan to spill from my mouth.

"I promise I'll take care of it later." Her grip tightens as she tilts her head back and presses her lips against the underside of my jaw. "Right now, I think a cold shower might be in order." She kisses me again before she lets me go completely. "And a shave."

I free a disappointed sigh as I watch her exit the room.

"Twenty-five minutes, Mike!" she calls from the hallway.

Scrubbing a hand down my face, I start for the shower.

My parents became empty-nesters almost fifteen years ago. It wasn't until Abigail graduated from college that they decided to move out of our childhood home. Only, instead of *downsizing* like we all expected, they invested in something bigger. At the time, when Gabriel and I were seriously questioning whether or not our dad was indulging mom during a mid-life crisis, my mother insisted that she needed five rooms and six bathrooms with a pool and big backyard so that she could accommodate all the grandchildren she intended on having.

Nine and a half years and five grandchildren later, no one can deny that there was a method to her madness.

Dad met mom while he was spending the summer in Ecuador on a mission's trip. It was the summer after his freshman year in college. He was nineteen, she was seventeen, and when she graduated from high school, he brought her to the States and married her. Twelve months after that, Gabriel was born, and I followed two years later. They waited a while before they tried for Abigail. It was during those five years that dad started his ministry at Mercy Hill Church. How they managed to stay together, start a church, and have three children within the first ten years of marriage is still a mystery to me—a miraculous, grace-filled mystery. There's no doubt in my mind that God has his hand on their union, which is why we're all gathering tonight.

Their fortieth wedding anniversary was last year, but dad was out of town—preaching at a conference in India. He travels quite a bit every year. It's been that way for at least three decades, and we're all used to it—mom more than any of us. She told him she didn't mind, that she knew the reality of being a preacher's wife all too well, and that she had no intention of holding it against him. Of course, that didn't stop dad from telling her she could go all out and plan a party for their forty-first anniversary.

As we walk up my parents' long driveway, I balance the container full of cheesecake bites in one hand while Veronica holds my other. "I think I'll bring a plate out for Clay after we start eating," she tells me, glancing back over her shoulder to the town car we just exited.

"He's stubborn as a mule, that one," I tease.

"He's professional," she insists with a grin, patting my chest with her free hand. "Can't fault him for that."

"Won't argue with you there."

I let go of her hand, after we step onto the front porch, not bothering to ring the bell before I open the door and allow Veronica to precede me inside of the house. I follow after her, the sound of music and chatter immediately filling my ears. We make our way toward the voices, which leads us straight to the kitchen. Standing around the island, my mother is busy putting together some sort of platter, while my sister-in-law, Tamara, attempts to help. Abigail is with them, too, but her hands are full—her two-year-old, Isabella, perched on her hip.

"Unka Mike!" she cries at the sight of me, throwing her hands up in the air.

"Oh, god, trade me," Abigail insists, practically launching her toddler at me. "She's so freaking *clingy* today."

I happily exchange the cheesecake bites for my niece, whose

little arms circle around my neck before she smacks a kiss against my cheek. "*Hola, niña hermosa*[2]," I murmur, holding her against me snuggly.

"*Hola!*"

When she makes no sign of wanting to let me go, I return my attention to the other women in the room. Abigail, having already discarded Veronica's treats into the refrigerator, leans around mom, who is currently still saying hello to Vee, and tries to eat off the platter mom was fussing with. I shake my head, muffling my laughter in Isabella's hair, already knowing what's about to happen.

My mother has eyes in the back of her head. That's fact.

"Abigail," she starts to say, turning just as my little sister shoves half a *llapingacho* in her mouth. "*Tú, mi pequeñita, fuera!*[3]" she demands, pointing for Abbie to leave the kitchen in order to join the others.

"*Pero tengo hambre, mamá,*[4]" she replies, complaining of her hunger even as she stuffs the rest of the appetizer into her mouth.

"Oy," mom sighs in defeat. Turning her back on my sister, her face softens, a smile lighting up her eyes when she sees me. "*Mi gobernador.*"

I chuckle, shaking my head at her as she closes the distance between us. She calls me *her governor* every chance she gets. I never tire of it. Not because of my pride, but because of *hers*.

She reaches up, taking hold of my face, and I lean down so that she can kiss my cheek. "Are you hungry? Your sister has already decided to help herself to the appetizers. There's more food outside."

"I'll make the rounds and say hello first," I reply as she frees me from her hold.

---

2 Hello, beautiful girl.

3 You, my little girl, out!

4 But I'm hungry, mama.

"It's *you* that should be making the rounds and eating, mom," pipes in Tamara. "It's your party, after all."

"Yes. Go, get out of here," Veronica insists, placing a hand on my mother's back, as well as my own. "Take her, Mike. We've got this."

"*Ok, Ok, está bien.*[5]" She throws her hands up in surrender, shedding the apron from around her waist. Tamara is quick to take it, and I drape my arm across my mother's shoulders as I lead the way out into the backyard. "Oh, empanadas are in the oven keeping warm. Bring those too, *mis hijas.*[6]"

Smirking down at her, I ask, "You made my favorite?"

"I made everybody's favorite," she informs me matter-of-factly.

My smirk softens into a small smile, and I gaze down at the wonderful woman at my side. It doesn't surprise me in the slightest that she spent all day slaving in the kitchen to ensure that each of her children could have their favorite dish at *her* party. That's who she is. That's who she's always been. That's why, when we step out onto the deck at the back of the house, we're greeted by at least fifty more guests, all of whom are here to celebrate the loving couple I get to call my parents.

"*Feliz aniversario, mamá,*[7]" I tell her before I let her go.

Looking up at me, she replies, "Thank you, Michael." She then looks out over the yard, searching for my dad. I know when she spots him because her whole body relaxes as she sighs happily. "I'm ready for forty more."

5 Okay, okay, fine.
6 My daughters.
7 Happy anniversary, mama.

I look down at my wife's bare legs as she kicks her feet lazily in the pool water. Her dress is gathered above her knees, and I'm half listening to the conversation she's having with my brother while simultaneously thinking about when I get to strip Veronica naked and satiate the hunger she ignited earlier.

She laughs at something Gabe says, leaning into my side, and I lift my gaze to her face. When her amusement fades away and she again talks around me to my brother, she doesn't pull her body away from mine. I don't mind; rather, I take another swig of my bottled water and watch as my oldest nieces—ages seven and nine—fool around in the pool, completely oblivious to the party happening on dry land.

"Hey, word on the street is you signed another bill this week," Gabriel announces, nudging me with his elbow.

"That I did, big brother. All in a day's work."

"God," he groans, shaking his head at me. "Sometimes I don't know whether to be proud of you, or completely annoyed when you say stuff like that."

"*Tell me* you're not talking shop," Tamara begs as she comes up behind us. Gabriel tilts his head back as his wife affectionately runs her fingers through his hair. I chuckle when I note the look on her face reads more like a *warning* than an expression of love.

"No new laws were discussed. I promise."

Her warning stare turns to one of suspicion as her eyes shift from Gabe to me and then back again. He distracts her and changes the subject.

"Where's Josiah?" he asks, speaking of their youngest.

She laughs softly as she replies, "Charming all the ladies with grandma."

"Figures. The little flirt."

At four, Josiah has already learned the power he wields with his big, green eyes and long, thick lashes. I don't envy his parents for the trouble he'll bring home when he's older.

"Anyway, Abbie said she and Graham have some sort of gift for mom and dad. They're trying to gather everyone around the deck. You've all been summoned."

"A gift?" He tosses me a frown before looking back up at Tamara. "We all went in on the gift together. I thought the plan was that we'd present it to them at the end of the party?"

"Yeah, well, I'm fairly certain you had *nothing* to do with this gift. Come on. Help me get the girls out of the pool."

Shrugging, he simply drops his focus onto his daughters before he calls out, "Everly? Isla? Come on out. Time for a break."

They whine in protest, but obediently trudge their way out of the water as Tamara and Gabe grab them each a towel. Standing to my feet, I don't bother to unroll my navy khakis. Instead, I help Veronica up before we make our way toward the deck for Abbie's mysterious announcement. We situate ourselves near the front of the crowd, and I pull Veronica against my chest, wrapping my arms around her middle.

It doesn't take long before the guests that remain have all gathered in an anxious silence. Abigail stands with one hand wrapped around Elliana's little fingers, who waits as patiently as a four-year-old can, while her other hand is hidden behind her back. Graham holds Isabella in his arms, who rests her head tiredly against her father's shoulder.

"Okay, you've left us all in suspense," says dad, rubbing his hands together in excitement. "We're ready when you are."

Abigail beams over at our parents before bending down and whispering something in Elliana's ear. She nods and holds out her hands, then Abigail gives her an envelope that she rushes to my mother.

Mom's quick to take the delivery, and gasps loudly when she sees what's inside. "Another grandbaby!" she cries out in excitement.

The moment the words fall from her mouth, I feel it as Veronica's body goes rigid in my arms. I give her a reassuring squeeze, pressing a kiss against her temple, but she doesn't respond. I allow her a moment, watching the scene unfold before me as everyone exchanges hugs and congratulations with the expecting parents. I long to be up there as well, celebrating with my family, but I won't go without making sure Veronica is all right.

"Babe?" I murmur into her ear.

She blows out a breath, as if she'd been holding it this whole time, and then spins around to face me. I can see right through her smile as she insists, "I'm fine. This is great news!"

I don't get a chance to remind her that it's okay—that she doesn't have to lie to me—because she's out of my grasp and on the deck with my siblings before I can stop her. Then, by the time I've managed to offer my own congratulations to Abbie and Graham, she's nowhere to be found.

"I know what you're thinking," says dad, gripping hold of my shoulder and grabbing my attention. "Just let the news settle. She'll be okay."

I nod, giving up my search long enough to chat with my father. Being the man of the hour, he's pulled away from me after only ten minutes, but I don't mind. Intent on finding my wife, I slip inside to take a look around the house. I discover her in the kitchen, her hands busy as she appears to be cleaning up and storing leftover food.

"Babe, what are you doing? Come back outside with me."

"You know, it's such a mess in here!" she says, not bothering to look my way. "I'd hate for your mom to have to deal with all of this after the party. You go ahead. I'm going to stay in here."

"Vee—you don't need to do this by yourself. I'm sure—"

"I'm fine, Michael," she insists, her tone sharper than it was before.

I furrow my brow at her, wishing she would quit using that damn word. As if she can feel my stare and hear my thoughts, she finally looks up at me and tries offering me a small smile.

"Please, sweetie. I want to help. Let me help."

With our eyes locked, we remain unmoving in a silent standoff. Knowing that this is a battle I always seem to lose, I don't say another word before I turn on my bare heel and leave her in the kitchen.

It's true that I've never resented Veronica. I'm not heartless. I'm aware of the pain that she feels knowing that she cannot give me what we both once dreamed and hoped for. Nevertheless, I cannot deny the disappointment that eats away at me every time she shuts me out—as if it isn't my broken dream, too.

Our ride home is a silent one. Veronica only came back to the party when Tamara went to get her, informing her that we were about to present my parents with our joint gift—a five day Caribbean cruise. Not five minutes later, she expressed her desire to go home, complaining of being tired. I didn't deny her request, and we said our goodbyes before joining Clay and starting for the mansion.

As always, she thanked him for escorting us before we went

to our room and he went to his. Now, as we both stand in the closet, undressing for bed, I can't seem to take my eyes off of her. It's not lust I feel, but a deep sense of responsibility. It's important to me that Veronica never feels as though she's somehow *less* of a woman because she can't bear children. I know it's something she struggles with from time to time, but that's not something with which I've ever crowned her identity. In my eyes, she's the woman God created her to be—nothing more, nothing less.

Furthermore, she's my wife. Her body fits with mine, which I intend to remind her of tonight.

Once I'm down to my boxer briefs, I don't bother putting on any other clothes. She's slipping on a dark purple negligee when I walk toward her. I press my chest to her back, my hands immediately reaching for her breasts. They sit heavily in the silky material, and I massage them gently, silently expressing my intentions.

"Mike," she murmurs, her tone not the least bit inviting. "For me or for you?"

I hold her tits firmly, pulling her against me even tighter, and then dip my head so that my lips graze over the tip of her bare shoulder. "For *us*," I reply between kisses.

She sighs, gently taking hold of my fingers and prying them away from her chest. Squeezing my hands, she admits, "I'm sorry, Mike—I know I promised, but—"

I shake off her hands, gripping hold of her waist, effectively cutting off her refusal. Not wishing to push it, I turn her around and pull her against me before I insist, "Fine—then *talk* to me. Tell me what you're feeling."

"You know what I'm feeling," she says, avoiding eye contact with me as she tries pushing out of my arms.

I tighten my grip around her and confess, "No, Veronica. I *don't* know what you're feeling. That's why I'm asking."

"You do," she argues, lifting her head and allowing me to see the pain in her gaze. "You're just making it worse by humiliating me and making me say it out loud."

I blow out a scoff, my arms loosening from around her as I take a step back. "Are you joking? Asking after the well-being of my wife is now somehow *humiliating* for her?"

"That's not—that isn't—" She shakes her head, clearly at a loss for words. When I drop my arms completely, she steps toward me, circling hers around my waist as she tries to apologize. "I didn't mean that. Can we please just drop it?" She hugs me closer, smashing her chest against mine as one of her hands slides down my back and over my ass. "I'm sorry. Let's just have sex. I shouldn't have said no."

"Yeah, well, you did," I mutter, removing her arms from around me. "Forget I asked."

When I leave her alone in the closet, she doesn't stop me. I'm at my sink in the bathroom, brushing my teeth, when she enters to do the same at her own sink. I keep watching her in the reflection of the mirror, but she doesn't ever look up to catch my eye. The longer I stare at her, the more frustrated I become. It's been ten years since we found out that the chances of Veronica ever being able to carry a child to term were basically nonexistent. After *ten years*, I've managed to convince myself that nights like this don't have to end in an argument. The fact that she continues to prove me wrong makes me wonder if we'll ever be able to move past it.

We finish in the bathroom at the same time, both of us heading straight for the bed. We turn down the sheets together, and I hit the lights before climbing in with her. She doesn't attempt to touch me, and I don't make the effort, either. I listen to the sound of her breathing, waiting for her to fall asleep; but I can tell she's as restless as I am.

An hour later, when my eyes finally start to grow heavy and I begin to doze, I feel it when she reaches for my hand. She squeezes my fingers once before she lets me go and turns onto her side, facing away from me. As sleep pulls me under, I'm unsure if I hear her whisper *I'm sorry,* or if it's only in my dreams.

Seven

Michael

It's been a week since my parents' anniversary party. Veronica and I haven't made love in all that time. In some ways, that's not unusual. However, over the last seven days, the absence of our intimacy isn't a result of our busy schedules—it's a statement. It's a message that my sister's announcement has ripped open an old wound that Veronica simply refuses to discuss. Last Sunday, on our way to church, she broke the silence that had existed between us all morning, took my hand in hers, and said that she was *fine*; that what she was feeling would pass.

That's all she gave me.

That's all she ever gives me.

No es suficiente—never enough.

Now, as we stand in the lobby of my father's church, chatting with my siblings before we all go our separate ways for the day, the look in her eyes doesn't go unnoticed. I can't explain what it is that she tries to hide behind those brown irises—*jealousy? Inadequacy? Anger? Sadness?* It's a combination of things—an emotional cocktail for which I don't know the recipe. It's her best kept secret. Between the look she's giving me, and the expression she's trying to hide as she talks to Abigail and Tamara, I decide that my attention is best focused elsewhere.

I've got Josiah in my arms, and I shift my gaze from my wife to my nephew. He's getting a little big to be held, but I can never refuse him when he insists that he needs to be closer so that he can show me something. Currently, he's explaining the art project he made in children's church, his little fingers pointing at various aspects of the paper he holds in front of us. I listen intently, until Gabriel says that it's time for them to be getting home.

After I set Josiah on his feet, my family and I make our exit together. The parking lot is busy, with people leaving the first service of the day while others pull in for the second. We call out our goodbyes, and as soon as Veronica and I are alone, the tension that's been between us becomes more obvious. Frankly, it's starting to get exhausting. Not wishing to turn our mediocre morning into a heated one, I continue to avoid the subject she doesn't wish to discuss and ask her what she plans on doing with her day. Just like every other day this week, she answers with a long list of tasks. I don't remind her that it's Sunday or that I'll be back in the office tomorrow; I don't imply that I think she could make time for me. I say nothing at all.

I CONTEMPLATE COMING up with one excuse or another to get out of the house all afternoon. It isn't until after dinner—a meal shared with my wife, filled with mindless chit-chat—that I decide I need a break from her charade. After my food has settled, I go knock on Clay's bedroom door. He answers almost immediately, and I ask if he wouldn't mind going on a run.

"I'll meet you outside in ten minutes," he says in reply.

I dip my head in a nod, sure that he doesn't realize how much I appreciate his service. I know he's paid to be my shadow, but that doesn't make me any less grateful that I'll have a willing companion on my run. We don't usually talk much during our exercise, but at least I know his silence isn't weighed down with some sort of hidden heartache I'm not privy to.

"Where are you going?" asks Veronica as she enters the room.

I don't bother looking up from where I sit, on the bench at the foot of the bed, lacing up my tennis shoe. "Out for a run."

"Now? It's nearly eight."

"Yeah. Now." My laces tied, I slip my phone into my pocket and walk past her toward the door. "I'll be back in an hour or so."

She doesn't speak a word of protest; then again, I don't give her a chance. When I step out through the side door, I find Clay already waiting for me. We don't waste any time before we start down the driveway.

We've been running before the sun is in the sky for so long, as we jog out of the neighborhood, I find myself paying more attention to our surroundings. Wishing to switch things up a bit and lengthen our track, I suggest we circle our way around to my office and weave through the downtown area. He agrees, indicating that with the late hour on a Sunday evening, there shouldn't be too much activity to worry about.

It takes us twenty minutes to reach the building that houses my office, and I run right by it, letting my feet take me where they will. A few minutes later, as we turn down a recently familiar street, I slow my pace when I catch sight of the little brunette from the Prohibition Lounge. She looks to be standing just outside of the establishment, her phone pressed to her ear. My pace shifts from a jog to a walk as I draw closer to her, approaching with the intention of saying hello. It's uncanny that our timing would have us on the same sidewalk at the same time. Remembering the invitation she extended the last time I was with her, a small smile tugs at my lips as I draw closer—Clay falling behind a step.

Foster, she had told me. *My last name is Foster.*

It isn't until I'm almost right next to her that I realize that *Blaine Foster* is crying.

Thinking back on the first false smile she ever gave me, on the disappointment I felt and the determination I held to find her *true* smile, it never occurred to me how much more it would bother me to see her cry.

But it does—it bothers me a great deal more.

Blaine

He promised me.

He promised me he'd be here.

We had a good week. We had one of those weeks where I was reminded of all the reasons why I love him. Last weekend, I had a couple days off, and we spent all of that time together. We stocked up on groceries—and he paid for half. He took me to this free, outdoor art expose on Sunday afternoon, and then we hit a couple breweries with some mutual friends of ours. Still feeling guilty about our fight, he offered to drink light so that he could be our ride home at the end of the evening, and he kept his promise. I had so much fun, I kept him up all night to show him how much I appreciated the weekend he had shared with me.

Our bliss spilled into the days that followed. On Tuesday, he got a call about a commission piece he'd been hoping for—a mural for the Denver School of the Arts. His meeting was on Wednesday. When I offered to let him borrow my car, he declined and assured me he'd find his own way. It put me at ease, knowing that he had heard me; grateful that he was making an effort to address the aspects of our relationship that worried me.

But then Friday came.

I got home from work a little after two, as usual, only Mateo wasn't home. I called him what must have been five-hundred times, but he never answered. Even though I was exhausted as hell, I couldn't go to sleep, restless from wondering where he was or if he was okay. When he stumbled through the door after four in the morning—drunk and high, and mumbling some lame-ass excuse about losing track of time with *his clan*—I was so irritated that it took me another hour to fall asleep.

Yesterday, I had the pleasure of waking up to a very *hungover* boyfriend, who decided that I didn't deserve anything more than a mumbled apology that I barely even heard. Of course, *that* started a fight, where he proceeded to throw in my face the two nights I slept at dad's house and didn't return any of *his* messages. I argued the point that the situation was *completely* different, but he wouldn't budge on his version of the truth. Up until this morning, I wasn't sure when the hurt feelings of our disagreement would go away—but when I climbed into bed after returning home from work, he pulled me into his arms and just held me, offering me an apology that I was too tired to question.

This afternoon, when I was getting ready for my short, four-hour shift, he asked me if he could borrow my car. He told me he needed it to pick up the cans of paint he'd be using when he started his project tomorrow. He promised me that it would only take an hour or so, and that he'd be by in time to pick me up with no trouble.

After all—the store is only open until five, and I was scheduled to work until eight.

Now, it's nearly eight thirty, and all three of my phone calls, along with my four text messages, have been met with radio silence.

And I'm so tired.

So tired of fighting with him.

So tired of being disappointed by him.

So tired of being *forgotten* by him.

When tears of frustration start to blur my vision, I'm grateful that Irene isn't here to see me cry. I told her I was sure I didn't need a ride—that Mateo would be here any minute—that he promised.

He fucking promised.

I pull my phone away from my ear, cutting off the sound of Mateo's voicemail greeting as I end the call.

"Blaine?"

Startled, I jump a little at the sound of my name. When I turn and see the owner of that familiar voice, my cheeks grow warm in embarrassment as I quickly wipe away my tears.

"Michael? I mean—Governor, what are you—?"

I shake my head, trying to gather my wits about me. Except, seeing him like he is now—in a pair of gym shorts and a sweaty t-shirt—collecting myself is not exactly the easiest thing in the world to do. If it's even possible, he looks bigger in his casual attire—or maybe it's the fact that there's no *bar* between us at the moment.

"Blaine, are you okay?"

His brow is furrowed in concern as he looks down at me, and I will myself to get it together.

"Yeah," I reply with a sniffle. I hurriedly shove my phone into my purse before running the pads of my middle fingers underneath my eyes, rubbing away the last of my tears. "I'm okay. What are you doing here?"

He ignores my question and asks one of his own. "Would you mind telling me why you're crying?"

"It's not important," I assure him, folding my arms across my chest.

Feeling overexposed underneath his penetrating stare, I break eye contact with him and look down at my feet. I don't know what's wrong with me, but I suddenly feel completely out of sorts. Maybe it's because he caught me during a low moment I hadn't anticipated him to see. Though, that doesn't exactly explain the warmth that spreads through my chest knowing he's concerned about me.

I shake my head at myself, realizing how ridiculous it is for me to even care about such a thing. He's a decent human being, and I was crying. He's just being kind.

Seriously—standing this close to him is overwhelming.

"Hey," he mutters, taking a step closer to me.

I suck in a quiet breath when I feel one of his fingers tap the underside of my chin. I lift my head immediately, meeting his gaze. The soft expression I see in his dark blue eyes makes my stomach tingle.

"Whatever it is, it's important enough to make you cry."

When I bite the inside of my cheek, still not sure that I want to confess my boyfriend problems, he nods his head in understanding. I'm grateful. Seeing as the issues he is called to address in his current position affect literally *millions* of people, I can guarantee that explaining the reason behind my tears would just be humiliating.

"Well, do you need a ride home or something?"

His use of the word *home* pulls a trigger deep inside of me, and my bottom lip starts to tremble. Against my greatest efforts, my eyes well up at the thought of *home*. These days, I feel like my home isn't mine anymore. It's not my happy place; it's not my *resting* place; and tonight, when I walk through my door, I know the turbulence of the current state of my relationship with Mateo will make my sanctuary an environment I don't even want to enter. It hurts my heart to admit it. Not simply because I've worked so hard to make the loft my home, but because I really thought that Mateo and I could make it *our* home.

"Angel, you're killing me right now," Michael mumbles. I almost don't make out his words, as he speaks them from behind his palm while he runs his hand down his face.

"What?" I squeak out, not certain that I've heard him correctly.

"I'm trying to help, I *want* to help, but I need you to help me help you."

I hesitate for a moment, still stuck on what he said before.

Did he just call me angel*?*

I draw in a deep breath, reaching up to run my fingers through my hair, and discard the question. Even if he *did*, I'm sure he didn't mean it; or, at the very least, he didn't mean anything by it. Nevertheless, I'm so caught off guard, I don't think as I tell him, "My boyfriend was supposed to pick me up from work. He forgot or something. I don't know. He's not answering his phone. It's been happening a lot lately and—god, I don't even know why I'm telling you this. It's okay. I'm fine. I'll be fine."

He stands a little taller, his expression seeming to lose a bit of its softness at my use of the word *fine*. My suspicions are proven correct when he mutters, "Right. Fine. Okay."

For reasons I don't feel need explanation, I'm quick to amend my statement. "I just mean that I'll be all right; that I'll find my way home." His shoulders relax a little bit. Relieved, I go on to say, "Thank you. Thank you for stopping and checking on me. You didn't have to." My eyes dart over to the man I see standing a few paces away from us. I recognize him as the companion that's come to the Lounge with Michael. Given that I now know his occupation, I'm guessing he's the governor's full-time bodyguard.

"How will you get home?" Michael asks, stealing back my attention.

"Um, the Light Rail is only a couple of blocks from here. I live in Washington Park. It's not that far."

"I'll walk you."

My lips part open in surprise, and it takes me a second to collect enough words to form a complete sentence in response. "You don't have to. Really. I know how to get there."

"Good. I don't." He extends his hand in front of him, signaling for me to lead the way. I hesitate for so long, he takes it upon himself to point out, "The sun is all but gone. I'm here, on foot, and I don't mind. You shouldn't make it a habit, walking around at night downtown on your own."

I bite down on my lower lip, fighting a smile before I remind him, "It's Sunday, and it's not even nine o'clock."

My amusement gives way to something else—something not at all *innocent* when he shakes his head and says, "*Es tan terca como es hermosa.*"

I don't have any idea what he just said, but I don't care. The look on his face when he said it is enough for me. This time, when he extends his arm, signaling me to show him the way, I readjust my bag on my shoulder and start walking.

Michael

I HADN'T MEANT to call her *angel*, it just slipped out. Even on the verge of tears, her hazel eyes—more green today than brown—shone with a sweetness that only pulled at my heart strings even more. The term seemed fitting, even if I didn't mean to say it aloud. Besides, it got her to open up to me a little about her situation. Now, as we walk side by side toward the nearest rail stop, I can't silence the curiosity that fills my mind with questions about this boyfriend of hers.

"What's his name?"

"Who?"

Smirking down at her, I clarify, "Your boyfriend."

"Oh. Mateo."

Remembering the way her eyes grow wide every time I speak to her in Spanish, I furrow my brow at the sound of his name. Knowing it's ignorant to be presumptuous, I inquire, "Hispanic background?"

"He's a bit of a mutt. His dad's Cuban, I think; but his mom is half Chicano and half Italian."

"Does he speak any Spanish?"

She coughs out a humorless laugh, shaking her head at me. "No. He's more proud of the Italian blood in his veins than the Latino blood. Though, he doesn't speak Italian, either."

I hum my response, my impression of *Mateo* not improving with this information.

My eyes are quick to admire her profile when she catches my attention, reaching up to tuck a bit of hair behind her ear as she softly asks, "Do you mind if we don't talk about him?"

"We can talk about whatever you'd like."

"Okay," she murmurs.

We walk a little in silence, and I'm afraid her preference is that we don't talk at all. I'm beginning to miss her voice before she finally speaks again.

"So, um, how was your weekend?"

I furrow my brow, instantly feeling the desire to change the subject. However, wishing to stay true to my word, I reply honestly and admit, "Mediocre." I pause for a beat and then add, "Until now."

She scoffs and rolls her eyes at me as she says, "*Yeah*—'cause walking the abandoned barmaid to the Light Rail is *so enthralling*."

Tilting my head to the side, I study her profile in fascination. This isn't the first time I recall her putting herself down, and it makes me wonder why such a beautiful woman would have a reason to do such a thing.

"You shouldn't do that."

"Do what?" she asks, confusion tugging her eyebrows together.

"Talk about yourself like that. Is it so hard to believe that your conversation is anything *less* than enthralling?"

She shrugs, looking away from me as she readjusts her bag on her shoulder. "You're a pretty important man, Governor. I imagine you hold much more worth-while conversations every single day."

"I won't deny that some discussions are accompanied with various degrees of significance, for that is true. However, just because you tend bar for a living doesn't mean that whatever you have to say doesn't hold its own value; it doesn't mean that our conversation doesn't have its own significant worth."

"Is that right?" she asks with an unbelieving smirk. "And what is our conversation worth?"

"Well, Blaine, that depends."

"On what?"

"On whether or not, by the end of it, I can make you smile."

She stares up at me in shocked silence for a second before she throws her head back and laughs. I don't know what she finds so funny, but I can't help but chuckle right along with her. This isn't the first time I've seen her laugh so hard; but when I last saw it, it hadn't been *me* that made the joyful sound pour from her lips. Knowing that I can take ownership this time makes the grin she bears even better.

If I thought she looked like an angel before…

After she's gained control of herself, she tells me, "You're quite the charmer, aren't you? I'm beginning to think you had more than one tactic up your sleeve on the campaign trail—*Honest Abe.*"

"Perhaps," I reply teasingly, offering her a wink.

"My, my, Governor Cavanaugh—are you flirting with me? I read the other day that elections for your office aren't for another year or so. Don't use all your ammo on me. Pretty sure you've already got my vote."

My smile slips as her question filters through my mind, and I miss most of what she's just said. I'm too busy wondering if there's any truth to her jest to come up with an appropriate quip in response.

What is it they say about jokes? They're always rooted in a foundation of truth.

I don't realize that we've arrived at her stop until she places a hand on my arm. Her touch is cool, but I'm certain the goosebumps that spread across my skin have little to do with the temperature of her fingertips.

"Hey," she murmurs, catching my attention.

I look down at her hand, trying to remember if she's ever touched me before. It seems a silly thing to question, as I don't think I'd forget a touch like hers—but I don't get a chance to dwell on it. She removes her hand from me almost immediately. I then watch as a blush creeps into her cheeks.

Shaking her head at me, her eyes grow wide in panic as she insists, "I was just teasing about the flirting. I—I'm sorry. That was a really inappropriate joke. I didn't mean—"

"It's okay," I interrupt her, wishing to put her at ease. I berate myself for the forced smile I give her while clasping my hands behind my back. For reasons I can't explain, I think it best that she remains out of reach.

I stare at her for longer than what seems normal, the silence stretching on between us growing uncomfortable and strained. Somewhere in my brain, I know that it's my turn to speak, but I'm too busy trying to process how we managed to get here. Not *here,* at the rail stop—but *here*, where our playful banter has somehow escalated to the level where it may be misunderstood. Or, perhaps, not misunderstood at all. Yet, what really leaves me speechless is the disturbing reality that there's a part of me that gets a thrill from the awkward limbo we've managed to stumble into.

"Shit," she whispers under her breath. Dipping her head, she hides her face from me as she rakes her fingers through her hair again.

I'm barely cognizant of my actions when I extend my arm across the distance that separates us and use my finger to tap on the underside of her chin, much like I did earlier. Her head snaps up, her gaze instantly finding mine, and the fraudulent smile I wore a moment ago transforms into a genuine one as I read her plea for forgiveness in her expression.

"Undoubtedly enthralling—and worth every minute spared."

When she bites the inside of her cheek, in an attempt to hide her smile, I wish I could rub the side of her face with the pad of my thumb and get her to give me what I've craved from her since day one. Taking a step closer, I know I'm about to cross an invisible line as I contemplate giving action to my thoughts. Before I have a chance to make another move, the sound of an approaching train distracts us both.

Each of us shift our focus toward the vehicle that will now carry her home, watching as it slows to a stop behind her.

Looking up at me once more, her shoulders rise and fall with a sigh I cannot interpret.

"Um, so, I guess this is goodnight," she stammers, taking a step away from me.

"It appears that way."

We stand staring at each other as the train comes to a full halt. There aren't but a few people on the platform, and it's not long before she's the only one left. Accepting the grace of perfect timing, I dip my chin in a final farewell and back away from her even more.

"Goodnight, Blaine."

Without a word, she spins around and hops onto the train. The doors shut behind her not even a second later. Before she speeds off, she lifts her hand in a small wave. I watch her go, feeling equal parts relieved and disappointed. Rather than entertaining the question of what the hell just happened, I turn toward where I know Clay is standing. Silently, he starts to jog back in the direction from which we came. I catch up with him, allowing him to guide me home—to *my wife*.

Eight

Blaine

By the time I get home, Mateo and his negligence are the last things on my mind. All I can think about are the fifteen minutes that I spent with Michael. The way he touched me. The way he laughed with me. The way he *stared* at me. Maybe it was just the natural light of the setting sun playing tricks on me. Or maybe it was my stupid heart, trying to latch onto someone who acted like they *gave a shit* about whether or not I made it home safely after work. Whatever it was, those blue eyes trained on me had never been so captivating.

Then I went and acted like a complete idiot!

The look on his face when I said that joke made me feel so stupid, and small, and childish. Except, when he spoke, it was as if he wasn't sure—like he was contemplating whether or not what I said was inappropriately funny or inappropriately accurate. As I walk up the stairs to my loft, I can't help but wonder what might have happened had the train come a minute later. He looked like he wanted to *say* or *do* something, but then he didn't get the chance.

Or maybe I have it all wrong. Maybe he just felt sorry for me. I was practically crying on the side of the road when he found me.

Even as I think the words, there's a hope that exists inside me—a hope that dares to dream that I have it all wrong. That it wasn't *pity* he felt, but attraction. That it wasn't *human kindness* that he was bestowing on me, but something more reckless than that. Something deeper. Something heavier. Something resembling the feelings that have my mind racing as I enter the loft, not even the slightest bit concerned with where Mateo might be.

My head is so muddled, I don't realize what I'm doing until the counter is covered in boxes, bags, and containers of familiar ingredients. Deciding that my heart is what brought me to this place, I don't question it. I'm feeling anxious, and doing something familiar, something that always brings back comforting memories, it seems exactly what the moment is calling for. I pull my hair up into a little messy bun on top of my head and then wash my hands, double checking the counter to make sure I have everything that I need.

Honey Nut Chex. Wheat Chex. Pretzels. Cashews. Pecans halves. Almonds. Peanuts. One egg. Butter pecan maple syrup. Ground cinnamon. Chipotle powder. Chili powder. Salt. Cumin. Cayenne pepper.

I've had the recipe for *the Foster Girls' Mix* memorized since I was nine years old. That's when mom and I perfected it. There's no sense in counting the number of batches we made as I was growing up—or the batches I've made since we lost her. That said, it doesn't take any time for me to get lost in the motions. I pre-heat the oven before I take out my baking pan, spraying it down with oil and covering it in parchment paper. After I mix together the cereal, the nuts, and the pretzels in a large bowl, I grab a smaller bowl to mix the wet ingredients and spices together. I then drizzle the syrup mix over the dry ingredients, stirring it until everything is coated. By the time I've spread the combined ingredients evenly over my baking sheet, the oven is ready, and I pop them inside.

It takes an hour for the mix to crisp up, and I shuffle the pieces around every twenty minutes, until I'm satisfied with the golden brown color of the snack. I clean up the kitchen and change out of my work clothes between stir times, then mess around on my phone for a while. I'm pulling the finished product out to cool when the front door rattles, Mateo inserting his key into the lock. I freeze for a second, realizing that I've been home for over an *hour* and I haven't received a single call or text from him explaining his whereabouts.

"Hey, baby," he says as he enters, his tone completely casual.

I frown at the snack mix in front of me as I ask, "Where have you been?"

"Oh, after I went and got the paint, I decided to stop by the school and start priming the wall that I'll be working on," he replies. I hear it as he deposits a few things on the dining room table, his usual spot. "Then one thing led to another, and I fell into the pocket. I couldn't stop. I got a lot of work done. They'll be surprised when they show up tomorrow morning. It'll still take me the rest of the week to finish, but I might be able to get it done a day early."

Appalled that he's telling me all of this as if he hadn't broken his word to me, I still don't turn to look at him when I ask, "Did you have your phone with you?"

"Yeah. Shit—I turned it off. Were you trying to reach me?"

I feel him at my back now. When he presses a quick kiss against the side of my neck, it takes a great deal of effort for me to not jerk away from him.

"Yes," I answer, feigning a sense of calm. It doesn't take long before my head is filled with the memory of my journey home; a memory I would never have made had Mateo been around to pick me up. Biting the inside of my cheek, I try and ignore the way my stomach tingles at the thought of Michael. When I manage to suppress the feeling a little, I find my voice and say, "It's fine. Glad you got some work done."

"Me, too."

He kisses my neck again and then reaches around me, his fingers hovering over my snack mix. Instantly, I dart my hand out and smack his.

"This isn't for you," I insist.

The words are out of my mouth faster than I can comprehend what I'm saying or *why* I'm saying it.

He only mutters a lame *whatever* before smacking my ass and walking away from me. "I'm getting in the shower."

When he's almost reached the bathroom, I finally look at him. Watching as he disappears behind the closed door, I take a deep breath and then shift my attention back to the cooling snack in front of me. It wasn't until Mateo tried to take some that it hit me. I didn't make the mix for me. I certainly didn't make it for Mateo. And with my head still swirling with thoughts of Michael, that only leaves one other person.

Biting down on my lip, I look to the dining room table, wondering if Mateo has left out his phone. When I see it laying amongst some of his art supplies, I hurry toward it and power it on. Anxiously looking over my shoulder, I wait impatiently for the lock screen to appear. As soon as it pops up, I type in his code and find our thread of text messages. I delete the four I sent him earlier, and wipe his phone of any record of my voicemails, too. That done, I then power off his device and put it back where I got it.

I tell myself that it's for the best. I convince my conscience that I've just prevented another argument. If there's one thing I'm sure of, it's that I'd rather not get into it with Mateo *again*. I compile a list of reasons why what I did wasn't deceitful but *smart*, all the while avoiding the real reason I erased the evidence of his forgetfulness.

I don't want to tell him how I got home.

That memory is mine, and I don't want to share.

WHILE MATEO REMAINED blissfully ignorant of the anger I felt toward him last night, that didn't stop me from preventing him from using my car today. I told him that I needed it. That I had some errands to run. It wasn't a lie. Not exactly.

Except, I don't know if unsuccessfully stalking the governor actually counts as an errand.

My stomach is in knots as I pace back and forth in front of the statue that sits before the Colorado State Capitol Building. I'm sure that any minute now, some huge security guard in a state patrol uniform is going to come out here and arrest me for looking suspicious. My imagination fills with scenarios where they confiscate my purse and test my *Foster Girls' Mix* for traces of poison or something. I've been here for nearly a half an hour, and I'm sure I'm starting to look shady as hell.

The truth is, I have no idea what I'm doing here. Yes, I want to see Michael. I want to thank him for his kindness yesterday by showing him a little of my own. I thought about it all night. I couldn't *stop* thinking about it. While I know that I probably shouldn't be here, and I probably shouldn't want to see him as much as I do, I have to know. I can't wait. I need to see if everything that happened between us last night was a fabrication of my imagination or if it was real.

Only, it wasn't until I got here that it dawned on me that I can't just *walk* into the Capitol and ask for an audience with the governor. So while I do want to see Michael, I'm pretty sure it's not going to happen. Why I'm still pacing outside of the building like I'll somehow be able to think of a way to get inside is not something I can explain. My false hope is making me stupid. Yet, I can't make myself leave. Not yet.

Instead, I readjust my purse on my arm, I look up at the old, stately building in front of me, and I continue to pace—like the stupid little girl that I am.

Michael

I'M RETURNING FROM a lunch meeting with the Adjutant General and Assistant Adjutant General of the Department of Military Affairs and Public Safety when my phone alerts me to a message. I pull it out of my pocket and find a text from my sister, Abigail. When I open it, I see that it's a group text, reminding the whole family that Elliana's birthday party is this Saturday at two o'clock. Sure that everyone will start chiming in, I turn on the *do not disturb* feature and slip my phone back into my pocket.

I won't forget my niece's birthday party. Even if I do, Veronica will make sure that I remember.

Clay clears his throat, effectively pulling me from my thoughts as he mutters, "Sir?"

I look over at him to find he's got his attention focused elsewhere. Following his line of sight, I stop in my tracks when I spot her. She's not wearing the usual black attire in which I've grown accustomed to seeing her. As she paces around the statue, I take her in from head to toe.

Her hair is loose, framing her face and brushing the tops of her shoulders—which are covered in a white t-shirt. When she turns her body in my direction, I can see that there's bold, black font on the front. Squinting, I make out the words: *You Gotta Risk It To Get The Biscuit,* and a smirk pulls at the corner of my mouth just as she turns and gives me a view of her back. She's got her shirt tied into a knot at the side of her hip, and the pastel printed skirt she wears hugs the little curve of her ass and slim legs, stopping mid-thigh. My eyes trail down to her feet, tucked into a pair of flat, canvas looking shoes—doing nothing for her height. When she makes another turn and faces me once more, she looks up at the Capitol Building and purses her lips to one side of her face.

She's probably biting the inside of her cheek, too.

She's adorable when she's nervous.

I frown at the thought and mentally take a step back, forcing myself to remember where I am; to remember *who* I am. Trudging my way back to reality, I wonder what she's doing here.

"Sir?" Clay repeats.

This time, when I shift my attention in his direction, I find him staring right at me.

"What do you want to do here?"

His question begs for another. The fact that he's asked, the fact that he thought it prudent to point her out to me, when I'm sure

I would have waltzed inside of the building without noticing her, it makes me question if what happened between Blaine and I last night was more significant than I was willing to admit when I bid her goodnight. *That* question breeds more questions—questions that have me rooted in this spot, trying to justify a few minutes alone with the little brunette who has seen fit to step foot on my territory this time.

I look down at my wristwatch, taking note that I have a meeting with the Lieutenant Governor in less than a half an hour. While that doesn't leave me with much time, it's enough to ask a few more questions. My mind made up, I tip my chin in her direction before doling out my instructions.

"I'm going to my office. Get her through security."

"Yes, sir."

Blaine

LOOKING DOWN AT myself for the fourth time, I curse my outfit choice.

I should have just worn my work clothes.

While they aren't exactly *business* attire, they're a hell of a lot closer than what I've got on. I barely manage not to pout as Michael's security guard leads me past another group of men huddled in conversation, all of whom are in suits. Even the women who eye me suspiciously have plenty of reason, every single one of them dressed in their professional attire.

And if the people who do *belong here weren't enough to remind me that I* don't, *the absolutely gorgeous interior design of the grand facility makes it crystal clear.*

I think about turning around and running out of here as quickly as possible, but then my escort stops abruptly. Halting a couple steps behind him, I look around the room. It's quite spacious, a fully-occupied desk with a vacant chair situated by the window. Then, what looks like a living room plucked out of some wealthy estate designed in the turn of the century—the turn of the *twentieth* century—takes up the rest of the space. Hearing a woman's voice, I peek around Michael's guard and realize that we must be in the governor's reception area. I come to this conclusion when I see Michael standing in an open doorway that I assume is his office.

I stop thinking entirely when he looks up from the stack of papers the woman is explaining to him. His eyes meet mine, and I know immediately that my imagination hasn't been playing tricks on me. When he smiles, the knots of anxiety in my stomach give way to something else—something much more pleasant and tingly—something that makes me smile at him in return.

"Heidi, I'm going to need a moment," he informs her, interrupting whatever it is she was saying.

"Governor?" she asks, looking up at him in surprise.

"I have a guest I must see to." He tilts his chin in my direction, and she turns to look at me.

Her gaze is unassuming, but still obviously one of appraisal, and it takes a great deal of effort not to cower behind the man in front of me. She's older than I am, but I wouldn't guess that she has more than a few years on me. She's very attractive, in a strikingly *understated* way. She wears makeup, but only just enough for you to hardly notice. Her pencil skirt and ruffled blouse make her look classy, and the stiletto heels on her feet give her that contemporary flare that suits her. For a second, and for reasons that don't seem rational, I'm jealous of her and her station.

Returning her focus toward Michael, *Heidi* reminds him, "You have a meeting—"

"Yes," he says, interrupting her. "In twelve minutes. If I'm still occupied with Miss Foster when the Lieutenant Governor arrives, offer my apologies, tell him I won't be but a moment, and then ring my phone. However, I don't anticipate that will be necessary."

My stomach drops as he doles out his instructions, my anxiety returning in an instant. Seeing him in his element, listening to him speak with such authority, it makes me feel *arrogant* and *naïve* for coming here today. Not only am I interrupting what is probably a meticulously planned out schedule, but his certainty that he won't need more than a few minutes with me before he's finished leaves me questioning him all over again. While I would never, *ever* deem myself important enough for more than five minutes spared during his work day, I can't silence the doubt that creeps into my thoughts.

Have I managed to confuse his kindness for something else? Is he indulging me? Am I about to be disappointed? Is disappointment what I want? It definitely feels like a much safer and *appropriate* outcome.

Fuck—what am I doing here?

"Miss Foster?"

It isn't until he says my name that I realize he's now standing alone in his open doorway. Heidi is on her way back to her desk, and Michael's guard has stepped aside to allow me to pass. Feigning a semblance of confidence, I close the distance between us and step into his office. He murmurs something I don't hear behind me, and then the door clicks closed. Feeling nervous, my eyes bounce around the room, taking in various details.

The walls are made of intricately carved wood, giving the room dimension while at the same time speaking of the history of the building. The floors are also made of wood—as is the large desk in the middle of the room, making the space very masculine. The two windows behind his desk offer enough light to brighten the place up, and the heavy drapes remind me of another time and another era. The Colorado state seal hangs on the wall between the windows, and there's a chandelier—a *chandelier*—hanging above the desk.

"I'm sorry I don't have more time to give you." His smooth, deep voice is closer than it was a moment ago, and I whip my head around just in time to see him as he walks by me. He props himself up against the front of his desk, setting aside the folder full of papers he was discussing when I was escorted into his presence.

"You're busy. I understand. I didn't mean to—I mean, I'm sorry for just dropping by. It was rude and—"

"Blaine…" He smiles at me, his blue eyes glowing with both warmth and amusement. "We don't have much time. Don't waste it with unwarranted apologies. Please—sit," he invites, holding his hand out toward one of the two wing-backed chairs situated in front of his desk.

I tighten my fist around the straps of my bag and shake my head at him, anxiously explaining, "It's okay. I really just wanted to drop by and say thank you. I, um—well…"

Coughing out an embarrassed laugh, I reach inside of my purse for the heavy, blue mason jar full of *Foster Girls' Mix*. I furrow my brow, appalled that I'm actually doing this, and then take a step toward him as I thrust the jar out for him to take. I don't look him in the eye, suddenly feeling stupid. It's hard to stand in this room—full of so much history, and significance, and a sense of power that I'll never fully understand—while offering him *cereal snack mix* without feeling like an idiot.

"For me?" he asks, taking the jar from my grasp.

I chance a look at him. While he cradles the gift in his hands, his eyes are still focused on me.

"It's a family recipe," I start to say, his steady gaze encouraging me to speak. "My mom and I must have made hundreds of batches before we decided that this was the one we'd call *ours*. I make it a habit to always have the ingredients on hand, just in case. I know it might seem like a silly gift offering, but it's one of the fondest memories I have of my mother. Anyway, I just wanted to thank you. For last night."

His eyes *still* not looking away from mine, he doesn't speak for what feels like a full minute. Much like at the rail stop, I feel uncomfortable in our silence. Not because it's unsettling, but because it's heavy with all that we *aren't* saying. I've never experienced something so *terrifying* in all my life.

"Chex Mix. You came all the way down here to give me Chex Mix?"

My cheeks heat in a blush as I whisper, "Foster Girls' Mix."

His lips twitch with a small smile as he sets the jar on the desk before standing to his full height. Taking a step toward me, he amends, "You came all the way down here to give me *Foster Girls' Mix*."

"Yeah," I breathe. He's standing so close to me now, I have to tilt my head back to keep eye contact with him.

"Is that all?"

My heart is thumping so hard that I can hear the rush of blood in my ears as it races through my veins. I have *no idea* how to admit to him what I'm feeling, or what I was feeling last night. I don't know how to tell him that I haven't been able to stop thinking about him since we said goodbye. So, like a coward, I clamp my lips closed tight, pulling the nub in my cheek between my teeth.

"That's not all," he says.

As he answers his own question, he reaches up with one hand and gently takes hold of my face, easing the pad of his thumb from the corner of my mouth to the side of my cheek. My lips part in a gasp, and his gaze drops. Not a second later, his thumb traces along my bottom lip, and I can't breathe.

"Have dinner with me."

My eyes widen in astonishment at the same time that my stomach clenches in excitement, and my feet guide me a step closer to the stunning man in front of me.

"Michael," I hardly manage.

He shakes his head, taking another step toward me. He frowns, looking almost *angry*, but then lifts his other hand, slipping his fingers into my hair as he holds the back of my neck.

"You didn't just come here to give me Foster Girls' Mix."

I shake my head, and the crease in his brow intensifies.

"Have dinner with me."

Feeling like one of us needs to state the obvious, I remind him, "You're married."

"You have a boyfriend," he counters.

My gut wrenches, and I feel guilty for thinking of his wife before thinking of Mateo. Yet, at the same time, I can't make myself pull out of his hold. He feels good—his hands feel *good.* Plus, the way that he *smells*—like cologne and something else, something else I can't put my finger on—it makes me wonder what he tastes like. I know that what I'm feeling is wrong, but I can't help it.

"Have. Dinner. With. Me."

His insistence almost makes me moan, and I can no longer pretend to deny him. "When?" I murmur, taking a step closer to him.

I can now feel the warmth of his chest, and his grip in my hair tightens a little as his eyes dance around my face.

"Saturday," he replies. "Guard and Grace. I'll get us a private table. Eight o'clock."

My stomach clenches again as I pull my bottom lip between my teeth. Even though I usually have every Saturday off, it's not unusual for me to pick up some extra hours or trade my bi-monthly Sunday shift with someone. My mind all cloudy and distracted, it takes me longer than it should to remember that I'm free Saturday night. When I offer him another nod, I'm sure that I've never felt this giddy and this guilty all at once.

"Michael?"

He's just getting ready to respond when the phone on his desk starts ringing behind him. We break apart immediately, and he doesn't waste a moment before reaching for the receiver.

"Cavanaugh," he answers. He pauses a beat and then replies, "I'm finishing up now. Thank you." After he hangs up, he runs a hand down his face and lets out a heavy sigh. I can feel a blush heating my cheeks when our gazes align, but he doesn't falter. "Clay will escort you out," he informs me, giving name to his guard.

"Okay," I nod, turning to take my leave.

I barely make it two steps before I feel his hand pressed lightly against the small of my back. When we reach the door, he grasps the handle, pausing long enough to earn my attention.

"Saturday. Eight o'clock."

"Guard and Grace," I whisper.

Finally opening the door, he allows me to cross over the threshold as he calls out, "It was a pleasure visiting with you, Miss Foster."

Miss Foster. Until today, he's never addressed me so formally.

Fifteen minutes ago, I would say that he was simply addressing me in a respectful manner, given where we are and who he is. But now? Now it feels bigger than that. It feels like a secret. It feels like he's playing a game.

Wishing him to understand that I want to play, too, I reply, "Goodbye, Governor Cavanaugh."

Michael

The look in her eyes when she says goodbye stirs a desire inside of me that I didn't know I had. Forcing myself to let her go, I shift my attention to Clay and nod. He interprets the silent command accurately, standing to escort Blaine back through security.

Spotting my Lieutenant Governor waiting patiently, I smooth a hand over the front of my jacket and extend another for him to join me. "George," I greet before returning to my office.

It isn't until I reach my desk that I remember the jar of snack mix that Blaine brought me. Picking it up, my mind yanks me back to a few minutes ago. Instead of the cool glass in my hand, I feel the warmth of her breath against my thumb when I grazed it across her lip. I feel the silky texture of her hair when I cradled her head, bringing her closer to me. I feel my heart racing even now, remembering how our close proximity made me want to forget *everything* but her.

What was I thinking, asking her to dinner? God—what am I doing?

As soon as I ask myself the question, I realize that I don't want the answers. The longing that fills my chest, knowing that I won't see her again for another five days, is stronger than my doubt. I can't explain it anymore than I can deny it. The way I am drawn to her creates an unyielding pull that lets me know—no matter how wrong this might be, I'm going to Guard and Grace Saturday night. It's already done. I won't stand her up.

"Governor? Are you all right?"

I pull in a deep breath through my nose and look beside me. George is now standing in the place where Blaine just left, and I shake my head clear.

"My apologies." I walk around to the opposite side of my desk, stowing the full jar in my bottom left drawer, next to the bottle of unopened bourbon. "Please, have a seat," I instruct, taking a seat myself. "Let's get started."

Nine

Michael

It's been an excruciatingly long week. If I wasn't arguing over budgets at work, I was tiptoeing around my wife at home. She's still pretending as though she's *fine*, even when I know that she's not. I haven't attempted to broach the topic of my sister's pregnancy, of Veronica's feeling on the subject—*or mine, for that matter*—since our initial argument. Undoubtedly, it would only stir up another one. As the days drag on, my patience grows thin. I'm not sure that I could keep an even temper like I did last week.

Then there's Blaine.

My week has been so full and exhausting, by the time I've donned my suit, I barely have a moment to spare a single, fanciful thought for the rest of the day. Yet, in the morning, before the dawn, when the air is still cool and the roads are quiet—when all I hear is the sound of mine and Clay's feet hitting the pavement, our breaths coming in rapid succession—that's when I get lost, counting down the moments until I'll see her again; wondering *why* her? I don't know what it is about her that makes me curious. Makes me reckless. Makes me dare to be...*unfaithful.*

Unfaithful.

It's a disgusting word, one I never thought I'd fear. Now, I'd be lying if I said that I wasn't afraid. Only, it's not Veronica that frightens me. It's not even Blaine. It's *myself.*

I fear the man who closes his eyes while he's in the shower and finds himself thinking of another woman. The man who imagines what it might be like to sit across from her, not because he's a paying customer, but because he's intentionally getting to know the woman behind that gorgeous smile and her angelic laugh. I'm afraid of the man whose appetite is changing—who hungers for something more than what he's been consuming for the past two decades.

I'm frightened of what he's capable of.

What I'm *capable of.*

It's not just lust that I feel. While it's been nearly two weeks since I've seen to my wife intimately, that's not what makes me stubbornly adamant about seeing Blaine again. No matter what excuses my common sense manages to come up with, there's a part of me that will *not* be denied. A part of me that needs the exposure to whatever it is that Blaine posses. It's not simply *carnal.* It's—ironically—more innocent than that.

"Mike?" Veronica calls out to me as she enters the bathroom, effectively shifting the direction of my thoughts. "I won't have time to stop at the cleaners this afternoon," she goes on to say, speaking loudly enough that I can hear her over the water pouring down on my head. "I put the dry cleaning ticket in your wallet. Please make sure you stop and pick up your tux—or send someone after it, if you must."

I stop soaping down my body as I try and make sense of her request. "Why was my tuxedo taken to the cleaners? What use do I have of it today?"

"Sweetie, neither of us has time to argue about what you'll be wearing tomorrow night. I'd like you in the tuxedo. I already told you that; and we won't have time to drop by the cleaner's tomorrow. We have the birthday party at your sister's. I imagine we'll have to leave early in order to come back and get ready for the gala, so it needs to be picked up today."

"The gala?" I mutter, frantically searching my memory for any sort of remembrance as to what she's talking about.

"Mike, please tell me you're joking," she huffs. "Have you been listening to a *thing* I've said to you at all this week?"

Turning off the shower, I ignore the suds of soap that still cling to my chest as I step out of the stall and grab my towel. Wrapping it about my waist, I frown at Veronica and explain, "I have plans Saturday night."

"Yes. I know," she states, propping her fists against her hips. "You have plans *with me.* The gala, at the Civic Center—I'm giving a *speech!*"

I cough out a sigh as I look away from her, at a loss for words. If I'm attending this gala tomorrow night, that means I *won't* be going to dinner with Blaine. I only have a moment to be disappointed—certain that the last thing I want to do with my weekend is attend another public event where I'm expected to be *the governor* for my wife. Before that reality even settles, I realize that I don't have Blaine's phone number. We didn't exchange them during our short encounter. We were interrupted prior to the thought even crossing my mind.

"Michael!"

My head snaps up, and I don't attempt to mask my scowl—unappreciative of her tone. Reading my face accurately, she drops her hands away from her hips and breathes in deeply before she speaks.

"I'm sorry. I didn't mean to raise my voice. I'm under a lot of stress—which I know is not a valid excuse. Nevertheless, right now, I'd really appreciate it if you would *listen* to me so that I'm sure that we're on the same page for the rest of our weekend."

As I stare at her, I try and think back over the last few evenings. I can admit that with the unspoken tension that exists between us as of late, and the long days that have had my mind occupied, I didn't bother to dig deeper into what's been going on with her. I know how she gets when she's in charge of a major event. My negligence has led to forgetfulness, and I'm man enough to own that. How I'll get word to Blaine that I'm no longer available tomorrow night is something I'll have to figure out this evening. For now, I have to see to other obligations.

"My tuxedo is at the dry cleaners. I'll arrange for someone to pick it up this afternoon. We'll leave Elliana's party early to attend your gala. I've got it."

"Thank you," she breathes, as if relieved. "In the morning, I'll be out early, seeing to last minute details. I'll be back in plenty of time to get ready to leave for your sister's with you."

"Okay."

She offers me a small smile as she closes the distance between us. Wrapping her hand around my wrist, she pushes up onto her tiptoes and kisses my cheek. "I know you have to be off soon. I'll leave you to it." Turning to leave, she looks back over her shoulder and informs me, "You forgot to shave."

Running a hand over my scruffy jaw, I mutter a curse before stepping back into the shower.

Blaine

"Yo, B—you on tomorrow?" asks Dodger as I wipe down the bar one last time.

My mind fills with memories of Michael—honing in on the ones where he's touching me—and my stomach clenches in excitement. I have to clear my throat and shake my head, scattering my thoughts before I reply, "No. I have the weekend off."

"What are you getting into?"

Finished with the counter, I turn to see him closing the recently emptied glass washer before pulling his black shirt from out of his pants. While he unbuttons the front, as if he can't stand to be in the garment a second longer, I shrug and tell him, "Hanging out. What about you? You working?"

I don't know why I feel so relieved when he takes the bait, allowing the conversation to shift in his direction. He doesn't know that I'm hiding anything from him. *Nobody* knows that I've spent the last week constantly thinking about a man who isn't my boyfriend. *Nobody* knows that I've seen Michael outside of the Lounge. *Nobody* knows that I'm carrying a secret that's both terrifying and thrilling.

Nobody knows—which means that nobody is suspicious; which means, I shouldn't be surprised when Dodger believes me when I tell him I haven't got anything special going on with my weekend. The fact that I am is only proof that I harbor a sense of guilt that I can't seem to ignore. Nevertheless, I have every intention of being at that restaurant tomorrow night. I've been looking forward to it since before I agreed to go. Even if I wasn't, even if I changed my mind, I don't have any way of getting in touch with Michael. My meeting him on Monday happened by chance. The likelihood of that happening again is slim to none. I've already come to the conclusion that no matter how you look at it, I have to show up. It would be rude not to.

"Blaine," Dodger calls out, yanking me from out of my head. Quirking an amused eyebrow at me, he asks, "You comin' or what?"

"Yeah. Shit, yeah," I mutter, exiting the bar in haste. "I just need to grab my purse."

"I'll wait."

It only takes me a minute to run to the back employee room and get my bag from out of my small locker. Like he so often does, Dodger follows me out, escorting me to my car.

"See you Monday night," he says, walking backwards in the direction of his own vehicle as he gives me a salute goodbye.

"Bye," I reply with a wave. "Tell Hope I said hey."

"You got it, B."

Glancing at the clock on my dashboard, I see that it's a quarter after two. It's *Saturday*, the day I've been looking forward to all week. I haven't mentioned to Mateo that I have plans tonight. I figured I'd bring it up if *he* brought it up. As of now, our weekend seems as though it's going to be a quiet one, which doesn't exactly surprise me. He finished his commission piece early yesterday afternoon—but he's been so focused all week, working long hours trying to create his latest masterpiece, that he's been cool with laying low recently. The last few nights, he hasn't waited up for me, and he's long gone by the time I wake up. I can't say that I mind. It's been kind of nice, each of us consumed in our own routine.

It doesn't take me longer than ten minutes to get home. When

I enter the loft, the only light on is the one Mateo leaves lit for me above the stove. I quietly go about readying myself for bed, hoping that I won't have any trouble falling asleep. As the week has worn on, I've been growing more and more anxious. Sometimes the thought of going to dinner with Michael Cavanaugh seems *unreal.* Not because he's the governor or because he's married—not for any of the reasons that make what we're doing *wrong.* No, it's a lot simpler than that.

Michael Cavanaugh is a gorgeous man with a brilliant mind, and it gives me butterflies remembering the way he looks at me—like he wants me. All that he is, all that he's accomplished, and an evening in my company is a crazy risk he's willing to take.

It seriously blows my mind.

After I shut out the light in the kitchen, I tiptoe my way to the spiral staircase that takes me up to bed. Quietly as possible, I ease my way between the sheets. Just as I start to close my eyes, Mateo shifts behind me. With a low, sleepy groan, he gathers me into his arms, pulling me back against his front. My eyes now wide open, I stare into the darkness, trying to decipher if he's asleep or awake—the erection I feel against my ass leaving me unsure.

He doesn't move right away. I think I'm in the clear until he slides a hand underneath my tank top and palms my naked breast. Not exactly in the mood, I try and protest.

"Mateo—I'm really—"

"I'll be quick, baby," he assures me as he starts to pull down my panties. "Haven't felt you all week. Need to dip my dick." As he says the words, he rolls me onto my stomach, his fingers grazing over my entrance from behind.

My body doesn't take long to respond to his touch, and my heart wrenches. Awash with guilt, I let him touch me—my self-reproach tugging me further from my reality and deeper into my sinful truth. With my cheek pressed against the pillow and my eyes sealed closed tight, I let him fuck me. Yet, like so many other moments this week, I'm not thinking about Mateo. As I grow slick with arousal, it's not Mateo I see in my mind's eye. And when I come, milking him dry, I wonder if I'll ever know the weight of Michael on my back.

Michael

I FEEL SICK. As I stare out the window of the town car, watching as the sun begins to set on the city, I know that Blaine is on her way to the Guard and Grace. I know that she will approach the hostess, who will in turn tell her that I will not be joining her this evening. I wonder if she'll stay. I wonder if she'll accept my apology or my offer to cover her check should she decide to dine. I know that I am an asshole for not offering her more—but that's all I could manage.

I started to call the Prohibition Lounge a half a dozen times yesterday; but, as if the world was against me, I was interrupted at every attempt. When I called this afternoon, I was informed that she was not on the schedule. I guess I shouldn't have been surprised. Nevertheless, the rising sense of regret and panic had me pacing the floor, trying to think of what I could do. Phoning the restaurant where she was to meet me seemed like my best option at the time—but now I feel sick.

I think about how disappointed I am. Instead of sitting across the table from a beautiful, engaging woman that sends a forgotten thrill through me, I'll be attending yet another function. Anymore, they often times all feel the same. Tonight, however, will be different. Worse. Tonight, I'll have an angel on my mind.

I imagine the look that will cross her face when my vague message is delivered. I regret that I won't get so much as a glimpse of her—of what she's wearing, or what she did with her hair. I won't get to touch her; and after tonight, I may have ruined my chances completely.

While I should feel relieved, as if this is an opportunity to do the right thing—I'm anything but *relieved.*

"Mike?" I only hear Veronica after she takes my hand and gives my fingers a squeeze. "We're here, sweetie. Are you okay?"

I nod my head curtly as I reply, "I'm fine. Let's go."

Blaine

I DON'T KNOW what it says about me and my lying skills that I managed to leave the loft, looking like I do, after only claiming an impromptu *girl's night* with Irene. Mateo simply eyed me down, told me I looked hot, and then turned his attention back to the television. Much like the rest of the week, we didn't do much today. He stayed in bed with me until I was ready to get up, and then we hung around the loft all afternoon. I'm not exactly sure what I imagined his response would be after I finished getting ready, but I thought I'd have to try a lot harder to convince him of my plans. I think I may have even hoped he was a little jealous.

Stupid. So stupid.

Deep down, if I'm honest with myself, I was hoping Mateo's reaction to the way I'm dressed tonight would give me a hint of what I might expect from Michael. I want him to be impressed.

He's only ever spent a considerable amount of time with me while I'm behind the bar in my black slacks and button-up. What I wore to his office was definitely more *me*—but tonight is different. Tonight, we're stepping into uncharted territory, and I wanted to dress the part.

While my black, leather, bodycon dress is simple, it's always one that's made me feel sexy. It's sleeveless and extents only until the middle of my thigh. It has a high neckline, so I don't wear a necklace with it. Instead, I've styled my hair into a messy chignon, and I wear a pair of dangling gold earrings, which tie in the gold of my shoes. The heel and sole of my stilettoes are black, but the straps—beginning across my toes and stacked all the way up and over my ankles—are a metallic gold.

It takes me a little effort to find parking downtown, but I still have time to freak out after I've found a spot. I'm so nervous, I have to rub my hands over my cloth seat a couple of times to try and dry my sweaty palms. When I can stall not a moment longer without being late, I flip down my visor and take one last look at my face. I took my time with my makeup earlier, something I rarely do. I went with a dark, smoky eye tonight. The reminder of my handiwork instills me with the confidence to get out of the car and walk the block that spans between me and the restaurant.

When I arrive, pulling open the front door and stepping inside, my eyes scan around the room. It looks pretty crowded, but I remember Michael saying that he could get us a private table. I wonder where it is and if he's already here.

"Hi. Welcome to Guard and Grace. How many will be in your party?"

The host who greets me is tall and slim, his generous amount of blonde hair slicked back stylishly. He smiles at me, and I manage to find the bravery to smile back as I inform him, "There will be two of us. There should be a reservation. The name is—" I stop short, not sure *what* name the reservation is under. It seems obvious that to use the name *Cavanaugh* wouldn't be the smartest choice. Deciding to take a chance, I murmur, "It might be Foster."

"Oh. Yes. Here you are," he says, his attention focused on the tablet he cradles in his arm. He takes a step, as if he's about to come out from behind his station, and then he retreats. He frowns, studies something for a moment, and then casts me a sympathetic glance. "I'm sorry, it looks like you'll be dining alone tonight."

My stomach drops, my lips parting open in surprise as my brow furrows in confusion. "Pardon?"

"It says that the guest who made the reservation called earlier. He won't be joining you, but has offered to cover the cost of your check if you'd like to stay."

Oh, my god.

He changed his mind.

Pressing my clutch purse against my stomach, I try to process what's happening.

Michael's not coming.

"Shit," I mutter, disappointment hitting me square in the chest.

No—it's not disappointment.

It's humiliation.

I can barely think when I turn and flee from the scene—the place where I had intended to spend an evening on a date—or whatever the fuck—with a man who is not mine. I knew. I knew when I got in the shower, when I slipped into this dress, when I picked out my shoes—I knew that I was doing it for a married man. I *knew*, and yet I did it anyway.

I lied to my boyfriend, I got into my car, and I drove here—not because I'm some heartless bitch, but because Michael makes me smile when I feel like crying. Because he walks me to the Light Rail when the sun is going down. Because when his hands are on me, all that I can think about is him. I came here because I thought he liked to make me smile. Because I thought he enjoyed my company. Because I thought he might have *wanted* me.

But he's *married.*

He's *married,* and I am a fucking *idiot.*

When I close myself into my car, I'm breathing so hard, it's as if I ran all the way here. Maybe I did. I can't remember now—I'm too busy combating my angry tears. I'm not even mad at him. How could I be? He made the right choice, and I didn't.

I'm mad at myself.

I can't believe that I came. Not just that I came, but that I came hoping. The guilt, the embarrassment, the anger, it makes me want to go home and shower. I want to wash away every bit of evidence that this night even existed. I want to scrub away every thought and fantasy I've had of him all week.

Except, I can't go home. I just left. If I went back, I'd have to think of another lie to tell Mateo.

Fuck. I'm a liar.

Maybe I am heartless.

Thinking fast, I gnaw on my lip as I pull out my phone and send Irene a text. While I wait for her response, I try to remember if I saw her name on the schedule for tonight. When my phone pings with her reply five minutes later, I hold my breath and ask if she wants to grab a drink with me. The relief I feel when she agrees to meet me in an hour—telling me to name the place—it's a fuck of a lot more than I deserve.

Ten

Michael

I WORK UNTIL EIGHT O'CLOCK—NOT because it's critical that I stay well past the end of the day, but because I want to ensure that Blaine is at the Prohibition Lounge when I arrive. I'm not sure what time her shift starts, or if she's even working today, but I've never dropped in early. So long as I have anything to do with it, I won't miss my opportunity to see her this evening. If that means working late, so be it.

I was distracted all weekend, riddled with guilt. While I smiled at all the appropriate times, engaged in conversations that required my attention, and was altogether *present* where I should have been, my mind still found ample time to be at war over what I am in the midst of doing. *Doing* being the operative word. I have not changed my mind about what I want—about what I feel *drawn* to.

Who I feel drawn to.

On the one hand, I'm well aware that *life* has seen fit to offer me an *out*. My obligations Saturday night brought me to a fork in the road. I've been standing between the two roads for two days now, recognizing that each path comes with its own set of consequences. Yet, try as I might to make sense of how it is that I got here, or how it is that I've managed to find myself questioning which direction I should travel when the answer seems so obvious, all I see at the apex of my present station is *Blaine*.

I'm the one who asked her to dine with me. I practically insisted on it. I cannot even begin to imagine what she felt like on Saturday night when she showed up at the restaurant and I wasn't there. I won't insult her by taking away the significance behind her choice to meet me anymore than I'll take away the significance of me asking her to be there. We're both adults. We know the score, here. That said, it's entirely possible that she won't want to see me at all after the way I stood her up; but I owe her an explanation, if nothing else.

Though, if I'm to admit the truth, my intentions this evening are to offer more than an apology. Whatever it is that exists between us—whatever it is that tempts me in her direction—it's greedy. I was robbed of an opportunity on Saturday, not *rescued* from it. No matter how much I think on it, I cannot squelch the desperation I feel to make it up to her.

At eight o'clock sharp, I stand from my desk. Draping my suit jacket over my arm, I slide my phone into my pocket and exit my office. Clay stands when he sees me, and neither of us says a word as we take our leave. It isn't until we're in the car and he's started the engine that I inform him of my plans.

"I'll be making a stop at the Prohibition Lounge before we go home."

"Yes, sir," he answers simply.

It takes us less than five minutes to arrive at our destination. Clay makes a move to get out of the vehicle, but I stop him. "I'll only be a few minutes," I insist, placing a steady hand on his shoulder.

He looks back at me, nodding reluctantly, and then I head inside to the bar. Anxiety makes my chest ache as I step inside of the establishment. I don't realize I'm holding my breath until I see Blaine behind the bar. Relieved, I free the air from my lungs. Not even pausing to address the hostess, I march right up to my usual spot at the far end of the long stretch of counter. I don't sit. I won't be staying long.

I'm only waiting a second before Blaine notices me. The frown that tugs at her brow makes me think that she's angry, but the blush that tints her cheeks speaks of something else. *What*, I'm not sure—but I intend to find out.

Blaine

WHEN I LOOK UP and see Michael standing at the end of the bar, all the air *whooshes* out of my lungs at once. I can feel my confusion as it makes itself evident on my face, along with the humiliation that colors my cheeks. I can't believe that he's actually *here*. In fact, I'm a little pissed that he is. Yesterday totally sucked. While I somehow managed to salvage my Saturday night, Irene obliviously lifting my spirits, my Sunday was spent trying to forget every moment I'd ever spent with *the Governor*. Except, in my attempt to forget, I only burned into my memory every single moment we'd ever shared. I went to bed thinking that maybe I wouldn't be able to forget him, but at least I wouldn't have to see him again.

Except, now I'm looking right at him. He's here. In the freaking flesh.

I swallow hard, trying and failing to combat the relentless fluttering in my belly as I slowly close the distance between us. I don't read into the way his eyes dance around my face. I don't try and guess why he's here. I'm too busy fighting with myself as I attempt to beat down the ridiculous sense of hope that seems to be rising up inside of me. It's a task that takes up so much of my mental capacity, I don't even bother speaking when I come to a stop in front of him.

"Do you have your phone on you?"

I stare at him blankly, caught off guard by his question. I have no idea what I thought he was going to say—no idea of what he *should* say after what he did to me Saturday night—but I certainly wasn't expecting *that*.

"Blaine. Your phone, do you have it on you?"

Pulling the side of my cheek between my teeth, I manage to nod my response.

"May I see it?"

It isn't until he asks for it that it becomes glaringly obvious that he doesn't have my number. I feel stupid, not having thought about that until now. Of course, I *knew* that he didn't have any way of getting a hold of me any better than I had a way of getting a hold of him. Even so, in all the excitement of Saturday night, it never occurred to me that his rejection might have been something else; only, he had no way of letting me know.

Now, against my better judgment, I stop the fight against my hope as I stare into his dark blue eyes—eyes that seem to be pleading with me. Now I *do* read into the way his gaze dances around my face. My heart beats faster, wondering why he's here, asking for my phone.

"Blaine," he speaks, his voice hardly above a whisper as he leans against the bar, extending his hand toward me, palm up. "There are things I wish to say, things I'd rather ensure stay between you and me. Your phone, please."

My eyes widen at the implication behind his words, and I don't hesitate a second longer. Pulling my phone from out of my back pocket, I unlock the screen and discreetly slip it into his hand.

"You're going to take a break in a minute. If you have customers you need to see to, I suggest you do so now."

Warmth spreads through my chest in a way that it shouldn't in response to his bossy tone, but I don't combat it. Neither do I deny my lips the smile that tugs at my mouth as I do as he says, checking on the patrons that are under my care at the moment. By the time I've seen to them—refilling a couple of drinks and putting in an order to the kitchen—Michael is no longer standing at the bar. I look over and see that he reached down and set my phone on my side of the counter. I hurry toward it, snatching it up just as Dodger returns from his dinner break. When my phone starts ringing in my hand, I jump and look down at it. *Michael* lights up the screen, and my stomach clenches in excitement.

"Hey, you good?" asks Dodger, nudging me with his elbow.

I shake my head clear, suddenly aware that I've stopped dead in my tracks in the middle of the galley. As I look up at him, he furrows his brow in concern and asks, "Is everything okay? Do you need to take that call or something?"

"Yeah. I mean, yes, everything is fine. But yes," I stammer. "I do. I do need to take this call. I'm—I'm going to go on a quick break, okay?"

"Yeah, B. We got it."

"Thanks," I murmur, rushing out from behind the bar. I swipe my finger across the screen, picking up before Michael is dropped into my voicemail. I'm halfway down the hall, headed toward the small employee lounge in the back as I answer, "Hello?"

Michael

I REACH UP and run my fingers through my hair, letting out a sigh at the sound of her voice. The phone rang so many times, I was afraid that she wasn't going to pick up. As I stand on the sidewalk, just beside the town car, I stare down the street at the bar, imagining her tucked away in some corner as she graciously offers me her attention.

"I'm sorry," I tell her, wishing I could look her in the eyes as I say the words. "I wanted to be there Saturday, but something came up. I had an obligation to see to, one I couldn't back out of easily."

There's a pause on the line before she tells me, "I thought you changed your mind."

The vulnerability in her admission causes an ache to gnaw at my chest, and I regret ever making her feel such doubt. It isn't lost on me that our situation is complicated, or that her agreeing to meet me in the first place was not a simple decision. This wasn't some minor misunderstanding. What we're entertaining between the two of us is as delicate as an intricately crafted time bomb.

"No, angel," I murmur, hoping she takes me at my word. Right now, it's all I have to give her. "I haven't changed my mind."

"Okay," she whispers.

"I want to make it up to you. I want to see you. I owe you a better apology than this."

There's another long pause on her end, and I bury my fingers in my hair once more, feeling out of sorts without her here in front of me.

"Are you sure?" she finally speaks. "Maybe everything that happened was the universe's way of keeping us apart."

Frowning down at my feet, I ask, "Do you believe that?"

"I don't know."

"Are you turning me down, Blaine?"

Another pause.

"Blaine?"

As I wait for her response, I'm forced to process what I'm asking of her. I'm forced to come to terms with how selfish my request truly is. Leaving the ball in her court, leaving her to choose whether or not she wants to explore whatever it is that exists between us—the *pull* that I feel toward her in spite of our circumstances? It's not fair; and yet, it is her choice, for I have already made mine.

"I don't want to turn you down," she replies, her voice soft and low. "But I don't want to be stood up again, either."

"Saturday. Let me make it up to you."

"Where? What time?"

"I don't know yet. I have to work some things out," I tell her, my mind already racing as I try to think of something we could do, something special for her. "I'll let you know as soon as I can."

"Okay." She sighs, before she reminds me, "I'm at work. I should probably go."

"Of course. I don't mean to keep you. I'll be in touch."

Blaine

I BITE DOWN ON MY cheek and try desperately to hide my smile, knowing that *being in touch* is a figure of speech, and I'm totally immature to think otherwise.

Not to mention totally in the wrong for wanting to feel his touch as much as I do.

Nevertheless, I find myself saying, "Talk to you soon."

"You will. Goodnight, Blaine."

"Goodnight."

When I pull my device away from my ear, I stare down at it and hold my breath until I can't hold it anymore. Blowing out a huge sigh, I let the reality of what just happened sink in a little bit. Everything that I was feeling yesterday was based on a misunderstanding. Now, not only do I have tentative plans this weekend, but I have Michael's phone number.

I have the governor's personal cellphone number.

Tapping on his contact information, I smirk to myself as I go to edit his name. I know that it's silly, the way that I save numbers to my phone, but the important people in my life aren't just saved under their names. Whatever is going on between Michael and me might be new, but it's not *nothing*. Besides—it feels safer, giving him his own code name. Well, *sort of.*

After typing in *The Governor*, I hit save, slide my phone into my pocket, and get back to work. I then spend the rest of the night hoping that our next attempt at a date will result in the two of us being in the same place at the same time.

Michael

As soon as I disconnect from the call, I return to the backseat of the town car. Clay catches my eye in the rearview mirror, and I signal him with a nod before he begins the short drive home. When I enter the mansion, I head straight to the kitchen. I open the refrigerator, and my stomach growls at the sight of the spaghetti and meatballs my sister packed up for me on Saturday.

I'm sure she makes the best meatballs in at least five counties, a fact the whole family can agree on without argument. Though, I think Elliana likes to slurp the noodles more than anything else. Whatever her reasons, she requested the dish for her birthday dinner, and I'm content to indulge in the meal right now. Popping the lid on the Tupperware container, I slide it into the microwave, all the while replaying the conversation I had with Blaine not ten minutes ago.

I haven't a clue where I'd like to take her Saturday evening, but I intend to go out of my way to make it a night that she'll remember. I'm not always the most romantic guy in the world, but I have my moments. I'd like to cash one in this weekend. The look on her face when I walked into the Lounge tonight, the sound of her voice when she admitted that she thought I had changed my mind—I don't like being responsible for it. I've seen her hurting before. I've witnessed her tears, and I know that I don't want to be that guy. I don't want to be that guy who disappoints her.

It doesn't make any sense. I barely know her, but I feel *protective* toward her. Maybe it's the way she puts herself out there—the way she allows herself to be vulnerable with me, even if just for a moment. Whatever it is that draws me to her, I feel damned if I do and damned if I don't explore it. It's the hunger—it's the thirst for that instant connection that I've found with her that has brought me to this place.

I don't bother sitting down while I eat, too preoccupied with my thoughts. Halfway done with my late dinner, I'm on the cusp of formulating an idea when I feel a pair of arms circle around my waist.

"Are you sure you should be eating that so late? You know how you respond to pasta when you don't give it the proper amount of time to digest," Veronica says before pressing a kiss below my shoulder.

Shoveling another bite into my mouth, I simply reply, "I'm hungry."

Laughing, she kisses my back again before patting a hand against my chest and letting me go. "I'll leave the Tums out for you."

A pang of guilt hits me in the gut. The woman at my back has been there—*at my back*—for over twenty years. She knows just about everything there is to know about me, including the indigestion I'm sure to wake up to in the morning after my spaghetti dinner. Yet, I can't stop my thoughts from thinking about a little brunette, whose laugh sounds a lot different than that of my wife's, with a smile I missed out on two nights ago.

Frowning down into the dish before me, I inform her, "I won't be home Saturday evening. I have a dinner engagement. I hope that doesn't conflict with your schedule."

"I don't think so," she says unassumingly. "I'll have to double check; but if you have something going on, I'm sure I'll manage just fine without you."

"Good."

"Hey, Mike?"

She leans against the counter next to me, her gaze trained up at me when I look over at her. Offering me a guarded smile, she hooks two fingers into the waist of my pants before she continues.

"I know that I haven't really been myself lately."

I wait for her to say more, for her to stop pretending like she can carry the weight of her sorrow all on her own without any help from anyone. I wait for her to acknowledge how pushing me away also means ignoring *my* loss, as well—but then she shrugs and begins tracing her fingers back and forth between my shirt tail and my pants.

"I know I haven't been fair to you, and I'm sorry. I was hoping you'd let me try and make it up to you tonight."

"You want to have sex?" I ask bluntly, for clarification.

My cock might be feeling a little neglected, but our lack of physical intimacy hasn't been the issue at hand lately.

"Yes," she replies with a knowing grin. Giving my pants a playful tug, she scoots closer and whispers, "I miss my husband."

Staring down at her, I realize that I want to tell her no. Not simply because when I close my eyes, it's not *her* that I see—but because for the last several days, when my eyes are *open* and I'm looking *right at her*, she hides from me. Yet, in spite of that truth, I know that admitting it won't make her open up to me anymore than she has for the last decade. Furthermore, to deny her now would lead to questions of *why*, which would only make way for another argument. Not wishing to force us back into the never ending cycle of what we've already been through the last couple of weeks, I simply nod my head in agreement.

"All right." I lean down and press a quick kiss against her lips, earning me another smile as I tell her, "I'll meet you upstairs in a bit."

"Don't take too long," she insists, pressing up on her tiptoes to kiss the smooth skin of my cheek.

I agree, looking down at my leftovers as she leaves the kitchen.

Running my hand over my face, I free a heavy sigh.

My head at war, I try to decipher what it is that I feel for Blaine. The unknown answer is a stark contrast juxtaposed with the question of why my wife is no longer the one who temps me.

My appetite lost, I cover up the rest of my spaghetti, stow it in the fridge, and head upstairs.

Eleven

Blaine

Coors Field. 7pm. Baseball attire optional.

I GLANCE DOWN AT THE TEXT MESSAGE once more and then peer out of my windshield. I've checked the Rockies' game schedule at least half a dozen times since I received Michael's text, and every single occurrence yielded the same answer.

There's no baseball game tonight.

The fact that I was able to find street parking only a couple of blocks from the stadium is further proof that something else is going on here, and I'm not sure what. Knowing that I won't receive any answers unless I get out of my car, I step out, lock up, drop my key into my bag, and start walking.

While I'm feeling less nervous this time than last time, my small ounce of *calm* comes from the fact that I didn't have to lie to Mateo before leaving the loft. He and some of his buddies hit the road this morning, headed for Blackhawk. Set on celebrating his birthday in true wild fashion, his friend Wilson decided he wanted to spend the day gambling and drinking. Someone suggested they turn the whole thing into a guys' weekend of sorts, and they won't be back until tomorrow afternoon. I'm sure Mateo could care less where I am right now. He's never really been one to obsess over my whereabouts. He trusts me.

Though, apparently, he shouldn't.

I know that lying by omission is still lying, but I shove that thought out of my head when I reach the final stop light between me and my night at Coors Field.

Looking across the street, I think I see someone standing right outside the entrance, and my stomach clenches in anxious anticipation. With a few seconds remaining before the light turns and I'm able to cross, I assess my outfit. I don't have any baseball attire, so I went with a mix of casual, cute, and sexy. Deciding to stick with my old-faithfuls, I tucked my feet into my favorite, worn pair of red Toms. The skirt I have on is short and high-waisted, the form fitting, cream colored material accented with a lace overlay, hitting just shy of mid-thigh. I paired it with a deep V-neck cut, fitted t-shirt that I wear tucked in. It's a washed-out red color, and the front reads: *I'm sorry, did I roll my eyes out loud?* I skipped the dangling earrings this week and opted for a simple, pendant necklace instead.

Smoothing my hand over my stomach, I look up in time to see the walking man appear in front of me. As I draw closer and closer to the wide, empty entrance of the stadium, the figure I spotted across the street becomes clearer and clearer. Michael stands alone as he waits for me—though, I'm sure he's not *really* alone. I've never seen him without Clay. In any case, with no one around to watch me, I don't stop myself from drinking him in.

He's dressed casually, in a pair of dark-washed jeans and tennis shoes. The baseball t-shirt he wears—and, *god,* does he wear it—has green sleeves and a white body. *Dartmouth* is in bold print across his broad chest. He's got the sleeves tugged up over his elbows, a detail I only notice because his biceps deserve my attention, and he's wearing a wristwatch—like always. The hat he's got pulled on over his head full of hair is black, with a Rockies emblem on the front, and I'm sure I've never seen anyone make a hat look as sexy as he does. I can't make out his eyes from where I am, but the smile he flashes my way encourages me to walk faster.

It isn't until I'm standing right in front of him, my heart racing, that it truly hits me.

He came.

"Hi," I murmur, my voice barely above a whisper—as if every word exchanged between us tonight is meant to be a secret.

"Hi," he replies, his voice almost just as soft.

From my current vantage point, I can see into his eyes. The longer I stare, the more certain I become that I could drown in his blue irises.

"Are you hungry?"

"Yes," I answer with a nod.

He narrows his gaze on me suspiciously before he asks, "What's your take on hotdogs?"

In a failed attempt to stifle my giggle, I make some sort of weird hiccup noise. A blush blossoms across my cheeks before I admit, "I love hotdogs."

His face lights up as a grin pulls at his lips, and my breath catches in my throat.

"Come on, angel."

He nods his head toward the stadium, and I follow him without question, trying to concentrate on keeping my heart from beating out of my chest. Suddenly, the expression: *be still my beating heart,* seems to make a whole lot more sense. That's the third time he's called me angel. I don't know why he does it, but I like it. *A lot.*

As I follow him, he leads me past the row of turnstiles and over to a swinging gate. Just as I suspected, Clay stands on the other side. He pushes it open for us, not speaking a word as we pass. For a second, my feet slow my progress as my mind comes to terms with his presence. He has been a witness to every encounter I've had with Michael. He might have been standing at a distance, or waiting in another room, but he knows. If not before now, then *definitely* now—he knows what this is.

"Hey."

Michael slides his finger under my chin in order to lift my head. It isn't until I peer up at him that I notice I've come to a complete stop.

"Are you okay?"

"Will he tell?" I whisper, hoping that Clay can't hear me.

Michael's eyes flicker behind me, connecting with his security detail for a fraction of a second before he focuses all of his attention on me. Taking a step closer, he moves the hand from under my chin, gently grazing his fingertips along my shoulder and down my arm. A shiver climbs up my spine, and his lips twitch in a smirk.

Leaning down, so that the bill of his hat almost connects with my forehead, he whispers, "He saw you first."

Confused by what he's trying to tell me, I shake my head a little as I ask, "What?"

"At the Capitol. I would have kept walking. I had a lot on my mind, and I wasn't paying attention to my surroundings. Clay saw you. Clay pointed you out to me."

My lips part open, forming in the shape of an enlightened *Oh*, but I'm not sure if I utter the word or not. I don't think on it too long. The next thing I know, Michael has my hand in his as he explains, "No one is better at their job than Clay is. He's professional to a fault. Our secret is safe, okay? Trust me."

Trust.

Pulling the nub on my cheek between my teeth, I admit to myself that while it doesn't make sense—while it's completely ass backwards—I do trust Michael. In the midst of his lie—*our* lie—I trust him enough to be here, and I don't regret it. At least not so far.

"God," he practically groans. Reaching up with his free hand, he smooths his thumb over my cheek, just beside my lips, causing me to lose hold from inside of my mouth. "You're adorable when you do that."

Nope. No regrets.

Feeling more bashful than I ever thought possible, I shift my eyes away from his. The view of his massive chest doing nothing to help my current state, I peek up at him from beneath my lashes, hoping that he'll put me out of my misery and take me to those hotdogs he mentioned.

As if he's somehow managed to read my mind, he winks at me before he starts making his way further into the stadium. Tugging on my hand lightly, he encourages me to follow while simultaneously wordlessly explaining that he has no intention of letting me go.

Five minutes with the man, and he already has me feeling giddy.

What will he have me feeling like in an hour?

Recognizing that I'll soon find out, I give his hand a squeeze and softly call out, "Michael?"

"Yes?" he replies instantly, glancing down at me.

My stomach tingles wildly as I whisper, "I'm glad you came."

Michael

I DON'T REMEMBER the last time I felt like this, or if I've ever felt like this. The thrill of this chase is unlike any other. It's true that the secret nature of what we're doing plays into the feelings I have—that is unavoidable. But it's more than that. It's the look in her eyes. Her gorgeous, dark green, hazel eyes. It's the way she responds to my touch. It's the sound of her whisper when she stands close to me. It's her little hand wrapped in mine, sending a *zing* up one arm and down the other, making my free hand tingle. It's as though I'm buzzing with the promise of what this night could hold. It makes it easier. Her smile, that blush, the way she bites the inside of her cheek, it all makes this lie, this *secret,* easier to swallow.

And I haven't had my fill. Not even close.

"So, when do we get to the part where you explain to me what we're doing here on a night where there's no baseball?" she asks as I lead her up the stairs.

"Have you ever been here before?"

"Yeah. My dad's a big sports fan. He's brought me a couple of times."

"Is that right? Which sports does your dad like?"

She laughs as she tells me, "Uh, any sport with a ball or a puck about covers the list. Hockey is his favorite, though."

"What about you?"

"Me?" she asks as we climb up yet another flight of stairs.

"Yeah. Did you inherit any of his love for sports?"

"On the contrary," she says teasingly, shaking a finger at me. "I inherited my mother's abundant *tolerance* of sports. It might not ever get my blood going, but I know enough to understand what's happening during a game. Mom always taught me to pay attention so that when dad got into a fit, I could join in on his outrage when he recapped the game later.

"Anyway, I'm glad I listened. I'm an only child, so it's not like my dad has any boys to talk sports to. Then, when we lost mom, dad and I spent a lot of time watching different games and yelling at the outcome. It was a good distraction. I know it's kind of stupid, but it helped us get through the first couple of months without her."

Stopping at the landing on the level of our destination, I give her hand a squeeze. I had no idea that she was without a mother. When she talked about her *Foster Girls' Mix*, it never occurred to me that the woman she spoke of had passed away. Now knowing that to be the case, her gift means even more than it did before.

"I'm sorry to hear about your mother."

"Thank you."

"What happened to her?" I ask softly.

As soon as the words leave my mouth, I lose her eyes. Understanding that this is a topic of conversation I may not have a right to, I attempt to gain her attention back cautiously. I let go of her hand, reaching up to tuck a bit of her hair behind her ear. With that one touch, I'm reminded that I'm already familiar with her soft, silky strands. I don't hesitate to sink my fingers into her wavy locks, gently holding the back of her neck, and she lifts her gaze to align with mine. For the first time since I laid eyes on her, I notice how young she looks—the honesty in her expression giving her away.

Before she has a chance to respond, I assure her, "We don't have to talk about it if you don't want to."

Stepping closer to me, she rests her palms against my stomach, and my muscles tighten, enjoying the feeling.

"I was twenty," she begins, her voice low and subtle. "She got sick when I was nineteen. It was my third semester in college, and she was already at stage four when they found the cancer. I withdrew from all of my classes and took off the rest of the year. She was gone less than nine months later."

"God, that's awful," I mutter, sliding my arm around her waist and pulling her closer.

She gasps softly, her fingers closing around the fabric of my shirt before she relaxes against me. I watch as her throat moves with a hard swallow before she stammers, "Yeah. Yeah, it sucked pretty bad." Shaking her head, she coughs out an airy laugh and goes on to say, "Not to ruin the moment or anything, but it's very hard for me to—like—think clearly with you, um…"

I pull her against me tighter, unable to restrain myself. She gasps again, louder this time, her eyes growing wide as she stares up at me. I like the way she feels pressed against me. She's not like Veronica. She's not curvy and familiar. She's slight and new. She's soft and delicate. Not to mention, the way she responds to being in my arms—her breaths coming in short, shallow spurts—it causes a heady feeling I hadn't quite anticipated.

"Michael," she says on a sigh.

My dick jerks, enjoying the way her voice wraps around my name, and it makes me want to kiss her.

No, it's more than that—greedier than that. I want to taste her.

Sure that if I don't let her go soon, I'll cross a line I'm not sure either of us is prepared to cross, I decide to hold onto her for one more question. In spite of our bodies reactions to one another, I haven't lost sight of what she's just informed me. Her mother died when she was twenty, but I have no idea how long ago that was. I've never thought to inquire about her age, until now.

"How long has it been? Since you lost your mother?"

"Four years."

Twenty-four.

Dipping my head in acknowledgment, I finally let her go, stepping back to give her space to breathe. As I do, I run a hand down my face, wondering if what we're doing could be even more wrong than it was a moment ago—when I was blissfully unaware of the thirteen years that span between us.

Twenty-four.

It seems as though I've lived an entire life since I was twenty-four. I was still at Harvard. I hadn't even begun to step foot into my career. I was a newlywed—now, I'm not. What's worse? I've been with Veronica almost as long as Blaine has been *alive.*

"Don't. Don't do that," she insists, stepping toward me as she pinches her eyebrows together.

Drawing in a deep breath, I reach up to rub the back of my neck as I ask, "Don't do what?"

"Don't look at me like that—like I'm off limits because I'm too young." Stepping even closer, she takes hold of my free hand, staring straight at me as she declares, "I'm not a kid. I stopped being a kid a long time ago. I'm not standing here in front of you because I'm some stupid little girl who was somehow coerced into coming. I'm standing here in front of you—I'm standing here *with* you—as a woman capable of making my own choices."

I was wrong before. I don't just want *to taste her—I* need *to taste her.*

Clenching my jaw to keep myself in check, I offer her a curt nod before turning toward our destination, pulling her along with me.

Blaine

He's holding my hand so tight, I can feel my pulse as my blood rushes through my veins. As he leads me into the stands, I follow after him, unable to take my eyes away from our connection—partly because his legs are longer than mine, and he's taking the steep, narrow steps faster than I can manage without concentrating; but also because I enjoy the feel of his hand swallowing mine. It isn't until he comes to a stop, motioning for me to step into a particular row, that I take in the grandness of our surroundings.

The stadium lights illuminate the field, and the empty stands are lit up, too. Having been here before, seeing the place filled with bodies, I knew that it was huge. What I didn't know was that being the only two people here would make it seem five times larger, and yet so incredibly private at the same time.

As I obediently take a seat in the middle of the row he's chosen, I ask, "Okay, *now* must be the part where you tell me why we're here, right?"

Reaching into the row behind us, he grabs a large, square, insulated bag and then takes the seat beside me. Grinning, he simply replies, "We're here for dinner."

I cough out a laugh, nudging his shoulder with my own. He chuckles, ignoring me as he reaches into the bag and pulls out what I assume is a hotdog wrapped in aluminum foil. He hands it to me before tossing a box of Cracker Jacks in my lap, and a giggle bubbles out of me.

"Michael!"

"Ketchup and mustard?"

I don't answer him right away, my disbelief and the innocent look on his face making me giggle even more. Finally, I tell him, "Mustard, please."

He nods, handing me a couple packets, and then proceeds to take out two hotdogs and a box of Cracker Jacks to put in his lap.

"Hey, why do you get two?" I tease, lifting an eyebrow at him. "What makes you think I can't out-eat you?"

Raising both of his eyebrows, he counters, "Is that a challenge? I've got two more hotdogs in here."

Fighting a smile, I seriously contemplate whether or not I'm hungry enough to scarf down two hotdogs. Deciding that it's the principle of the matter, I hold out my hand expectantly.

"Damn, I like you," he mutters, reaching back inside the bag.

Even though he said the words in jest, his statement still makes my stomach clench in excitement. I don't hold back my smile as he hands me another hotdog. He then sets aside the insulated container and reaches behind us again. This time, I hear him pop open a lid before pulling out two beers.

"Hope you don't mind beer. We're at the ball field—it's the only way to go."

Shaking my head, I assure him, "I don't mind at all."

He opens them both, placing them in our respective cup holders, and I thank him as I doctor one of my hotdogs. Taking my first bite, I decide that this—the two of us eating junk food in the middle of an empty stadium—it's so much better than anything I imagined. It's fun and random and private; even more, it's the complete opposite of the fancy restaurant he was going to take me to last week. I appreciate the contrast more than I thought possible.

After swallowing my bite, I watch him chew his mouthful as I tell him, "I don't know how you did this—or *why* you did all of this—but I wanted to say thank you. This is awesome."

He stares at me contemplatively as he finishes chewing. He then replies, "I know a guy. That answers the how."

Remembering who he is, I accept his vague response before ask, "And the why?"

"I owed you an apology. I told you I wanted to make it up to you, and I meant it."

"Oh," I murmur.

Thinking back a week, on all the thoughts that were swirling around in my head as I fled from that restaurant, it becomes very clear that I was incredibly wrong about what he was feeling. I'm so flattered, I don't even know what to say. No one has ever gone out of their way to make me feel as special as he is in this exact moment.

"Thank you."

A small smirk tugs at the corner of his mouth before he informs me, "You already thanked me, Blaine. Now I want to see you polish off both of those hotdogs."

"I wouldn't underestimate me, Governor," I warn before consuming a big bite.

"Mmmhmm," he hums, taking another chunk of his dinner into his mouth. "We'll see."

"So I take it you're still totally into baseball?"

He stops chewing, looks around us, and then quirks an eyebrow at me.

"Right," I say, speaking through a laugh. "Do you get to come here often?"

He shrugs and swallows. "I like to catch a handful of games each season. I usually come with my brother."

"Oh, yeah. I think I read somewhere that our governor is one of three children. Where do you fall in the pecking order?"

"I'm in the middle."

"*Yikes,*" I mumble, pretending to feel bad for him. "Isn't it the middle child who always has the most issues?"

He barks out a laugh before he asks, "And what do they say about people like you? What do they call it, only child syndrome?"

Joining in on his laughter, I remind him, "We're not talking about me, we're talking about you. So, is your brother older or younger?"

While we both work our way through dinner, we talk about each other's families. I can tell by the look on his face as he tells me about his relatives that he's very close with them and loves them immensely. Listening to him talk about his nieces and nephews is sweet, and the respect he has for his parents is evident. I, in turn, tell him more about dad, sharing a little bit about Simone, too. They're all the family I've got, but I wouldn't trade them for more.

While we munch on our caramel popcorn, I prop my feet up on the seat in front of me, and we discuss a bunch of random things. Just like at the Lounge, conversation is easy and playful between us. He makes me smile in that way that seems unique to only him—like it's somehow his duty. I certainly don't mind. When I smile, he smiles right back, and it's an expression he wears extremely well.

When I'm out of popcorn and I've polished off my second beer, I manage to take my eyes off of Michael long enough to notice the change in the atmosphere. The sun is long gone, the moon high in the sky, and the lights shine down on the field even brighter than before.

Suddenly feeling more daring, Michael making me completely at ease in his company, I turn to him and ask, "Do I get something for exceeding your expectations and consuming two whole hotdogs?"

Admittedly, I wouldn't normally eat as much as the mountain of a man sitting next to me—who happened to stop after two dogs, too—but I wasn't lying about my love of his dinner choice. Except, now I'm totally stuffed, and I'm hoping that what I have in mind will help with that.

Chuckling, he inquires, "Perhaps. What are you thinking?"

I tug my bottom lip between my teeth, looking out at the field before I focus my attention on him once more. "This guy you know…will he let us out onto the field?"

Grinning, he replies, "I thought you'd never ask."

Michael

Blaine helps me gather the trash, and I carry the small cooler and meal bag as we leave the stands. It takes us nearly ten minutes to get to the belly of the stadium, where I abandon my supplies and she leaves her purse. Then I grab her hand. She walks so close to me, her arm brushes against mine almost constantly, and it's as though I can feel her excitement as we traverse our way through the tunnels that will take us to the field.

I had to make a number of phone calls and pull a lot of strings in order to make this happen. So far, it's been worth the effort. I haven't been to a dinner this fun in ages. Honestly, I don't know who's to blame for that. If I really think about it, I'm not even convinced that there's any one place for blame to be assigned. Is it even possible to experience the high I'm feeling now with all the history that exists between my wife and I? Furthermore, I'm learning that Blaine and Veronica simply aren't comparable.

I brought Blaine here because a night at the ball field is

something that I will always treasure. It reminds me of a time in my life that I won't ever get back. I'd *hoped* that she'd be up for it—that she'd enjoy herself and appreciate what I had planned. I wanted to offer her a grand apology, and this was the first thing that came to mind. That said, I wasn't sure if this would be her taste or not. I took a risk. Walking into this evening, I was certain of one thing only—that Veronica wouldn't find hotdogs and Cracker Jacks the least bit romantic. She outgrew her tolerance for anything to do with the sport of baseball immediately after I stopped playing. It's nothing I hold against her, it's just a fact.

"Are we almost there, yet?" asks Blaine, pulling me from my assessments.

Shoving aside all thoughts of Veronica, I remember where I am and the good time that I'm having. I then give Blaine's fingers a light squeeze. Jerking my chin toward the double doors ahead of us, I inform her, "Right through there. You ready?"

She flashes me the biggest grin and then nods her head enthusiastically. We hurry down the corridor and push through the doors before climbing a few steps and stopping just beyond the dugout. I hear it as she blows out a breath, and then I get lost in my admiration of her. Watching as she takes it all in, I see the reverence clearly etched into her features. She's a woman who isn't shy about expressing her thoughts and feelings—*that*, or she's incapable of hiding them. Either way, I appreciate the trait. Especially now.

When she finally settles her gaze back on me, her hazel eyes sparkling, my chest swells, causing a tightness in my lungs that almost aches. Then she giggles, drops my hand, and races out onto the field, heading straight for the pitcher's mound. For a second, I can't move. I know that if I do, that if I chase after her, it'll be for one reason and one reason only. I know that I won't be able to resist anymore. My desire is too strong. My greed is now undeniable.

Si salgo, la voy a besar, y no sé si seré capaz de parar.[8]

I clench my fists, the ache in my chest making it impossible for me to think.

"Michael!" she calls out, waving for me to join her. I can see the smile that lingers on her lips even from here. While I continue to hesitate, she cranes her neck back, turning in a slow circle as she takes in the view from the mound.

After she's spun around in a full rotation, she realizes that I've yet to make my way toward her. This time, she doesn't call out to me. Rather, she extends her arm, her hand opened in invitation. Staring at her, it dawns on me that this is not the first invitation she's offered me.

Foster, she had told me. *My last name is Foster.*

Taking my first step in her direction, I wonder if this was always inevitable. If the door to this moment was opened so long ago, that there was no stopping it. After my second step, I wonder what will become of us? I wonder where can we possibly go from here? By my third step, I've graduated to a steady jog. As I close the distance between us, my mind already made up, I acknowledge that I have no answers—only this desire, this *hunger* that's been eating away at me for weeks. Whatever it is that exists between Blaine and me, it's created a craving that won't be satiated by anyone other than her. Wrong as it may be, I'm blinded by my need.

I slow my steps when I've reached the dirt of the pitcher's mound, but I don't stop. I don't stop until my chest is pressed against hers—until I've got my arm wrapped around her waist, pulling her flush against me. I don't stop until my hand is cradled around the side of her face and my lips are pressed against hers.

---

8 If I go out there, I'm going to kiss her, and I don't know if I'll be able to stop.

Blaine

I CAN'T BREATHE. He's literally stolen all of the oxygen out of my body. When he finally made his way toward me, as soon as I could interpret the look in his eyes, I knew that things were about to shift between us. What I didn't know was how he would forever alter the axis of my entire world when he pulled me against him and pressed his lips to mine.

The kiss he's giving me is soft and chaste. He lingers for a long moment, and my head grows faint. My eyes open slowly when he severs our connection and looks down at me. His irises are so dark, it's like I'm staring into a violent storm in the middle of an ocean. Without a word spoken, I know that he's asking for more. I know that he's telling me that he's shown me what he wants, and now it's time I do the same.

Still unable to catch my breath after that one, simple kiss, I come to an easy conclusion. I rationalize that the only way I'll possibly be able to breathe again is if I take back the breath that he stole. Pushing myself up onto my tiptoes, I circle one of my arms around his neck. I then reach for the bill of his baseball cap and gently slide it from over his thick, dark hair. I'm just getting ready to kiss him when he grows impatient and kisses me first. Only, unlike the first time, this one is not soft. It's not soft at all.

I gasp, my lips parting open as he uses both arms to crush me against him. My heart pounding and my stomach clenching, I cling to him, wanting every single feeling he's giving me. When the tip of his tongue grazes my bottom lip, I whimper, opening my mouth wider as I beg him for more. He responds in kind, and the next thing I know, his tongue is tangled with mine. I drop his hat, needing both hands to bury my fingers in his unbelievably soft curls, and he groans.

I'm lost.

All there is is Michael. I don't feel the cool, night air. I don't sense the vastness of the stadium. I don't remember what day it is or what color underwear I'm wearing—only that he's making them wet. His whole body—hard and warm and *perfect*—it consumes me. His hold around me is unrelenting; and I don't know if I can hardly breathe because he's crushing my lungs, or if it's because I've offered him my air supply in surrender, but I don't care. I don't want him to stop. I don't want him to let go.

When he slides a hand up and buries it in my hair, holding my head as he tilts his and deepens the kiss even further, my nipples pebble, and I can feel my clit begin to swell. My pulse makes itself known between my legs when he groans a second time. The sound is deep, rumbly, and desperate, making me crazy. I graze my teeth over his bottom lip, holding it captive while I taste it with my tongue, and he holds me tighter *still.*

Michael

"*MICHAEL,*" SHE WHIMPERS AS I tug my lip free only to trace the tip of my tongue around her mouth's entrance.

My dick throbs, pressing against the confines of my jeans, and I wonder if she can feel it—feel what she does to me—*with one damn kiss.*

She moans softly, tugging on my hair, pulling me closer, her impatience getting the best of her. I smile as I bring my lips back to hers, turned on by her zeal. She sweeps her tongue through my mouth, tasting me as she circles her arms around the back of my neck. Hugging me as tight as she can manage, I swear she's trying to meld her body with mine. When another whimper spills from her mouth, it's as if I'm swallowing her desperation, and I know I'm in over my head.

Her lips are soft, but her kiss is hungry.

Her body is slight, but her hold is unyielding.

Her chest heaves against mine, and I get the feeling that she's struggling for breath as much as I am, but neither one of us pulls away. This kiss is unstoppable, as I knew it would be.

No. Not as I knew it would be.

More *than I imagined it* could *be.*

I can't stop.

I'm hooked.

Blaine

I DON'T WANT to stop. I know, the moment we do, I'll wish we hadn't. But if I don't take a break, I'll pass out from a lack of oxygen. Bringing my hands around to his cheeks, I hold his face with every intention of slowing us down. Before I get the chance, he does it for me. Only, rather than slowing to a stop, the strokes of his tongue become gentle and languid. In an instant, all thoughts of breaking away from him are nonexistent.

When he closes his fingers in my hair into a fist and lightly tugs my head back, another moan crawls from out of me, my jaw falling open as if I'm too distracted to shut it. While he drags his lips away from my mouth and down the column of my neck, my eyes roll into the back of my head. Then he tastes me, leaving a trail of wet kisses up and over my chin before his lips reconnect with mine.

My panties are soaked.

Undeniably soaked.

And still—I cannot make myself stop.

I'm hopelessly strung out on his kiss.

Michael

"*Mierda*," I mutter, forcing my lips away from hers.

Both of us breathless, we stare at one another in awe and wonder. Her wide-eyed gaze does nothing to help calm the stiffness of my cock—neither does the sight of her swollen, pink lips. When she tugs her plump bottom lip between her teeth, I groan, leaning down to press my forehead against hers.

"Michael?" she whispers hesitantly.

Sucking in a deep breath through my nose, I contemplate my next move. I wasn't finished. Even now, feeling her hot, shallow exhales against my skin, it makes me want to kiss her again. I know that if I look into her eyes, I won't be able to resist, so I don't. Instead, I touch my temple to hers, my lips grazing her ear as I whisper in return, "What is it, angel?"

She shivers against me, her fingers curling around the front collar of my t-shirt as she presses her forehead against my chest between her fists. My hand still buried in her hair, I massage the nape of her neck, wishing I could stand here all night—oblivious to the reality that waits outside of the stadium.

"Was that…" she starts and then she stops. Tilting her head back, she forces me to look at her as she asks, "Was that so unexplainably amazing because we shouldn't have done it? Or because we should have?"

Hearing her give voice to the truth that she was as enraptured by that kiss as I was only feeds the hunger that I have for her; the hunger that feels even more insatiable now than it did before.

Shaking my head, I give her my honest answer and reply, "I don't know."

"Me neither."

Her gaze drops from my eyes down to my lips, and mine follow suit. Bringing my mouth to hers once more, I kiss her softly. Then, murmuring between her lips, I confess, "I want to find out."

Nodding, she lifts up onto her tiptoes, kissing me again before she admits, "Me, too."

I squeeze her around her waist, reminding myself that it's getting late. Even thinking about saying goodbye to her and going home to Veronica makes me feel unsettled—unbalanced and confused. I know that I should feel guilty, but so long as I hold Blaine in my arms, all I'm capable of thinking about is *her*.

"When can I—god, I can't *not* see you again," she says pleadingly.

"I know. We'll figure it out."

"Okay."

Touching the tip of my nose to the tip of hers, I reluctantly inform her, "We should get going."

"Yeah."

When she doesn't let me go right away, my chest swells as a smile plays at my lips. That heady feeling returns, and I don't stop myself from kissing her one last time—stealing a taste of her before I pull away completely. I take a step backwards, my foot tapping my fallen baseball cap, and I'm quick to pick it up. Dusting it off a little, I slide it on over my head and then hold out my hand. Blaine takes it without hesitation, clinging to me as we make our way off the field.

"I need to stay behind," I announce when we've returned to our discarded bags. "I'll walk you out, and Clay will escort you to your car while I make sure the place gets shut down and locked up."

She nods her head, following my lead without a word. When we've ascended to the main level, I stop her before Clay comes into view. Holding the side of her neck, I allow my eyes to devour her gorgeous face, not sure how long it'll be before I see her again.

"I'll call you," I promise.

"Okay," she murmurs, a small smile lighting up her eyes.

The next thing I know, she's up on her tiptoes, pulling me closer. Touching her lips against the scruffy side of my cheek, she whispers, "Best date ever."

Then, without another word or glance, she's gone.

Twelve

Blaine

After closing my front door and twisting the lock, I press my back against it and shut my eyes. The moment I do, I see him. *More* than that, I *feel* him. I remember what it felt like to be held by him. He's built differently than Mateo. *A lot* differently. Even merely thinking about his strong bulk surrounding me makes my stomach clench with desire. And the way he touched me? His hands insistently holding me where he wanted me—*shit*—it makes me short of breath and turns me on even now.

I let my purse slide from my shoulder, down my arm, and to the floor as my body continues to revel in the memory of Michael. I can almost *taste* him, and it makes me long for the chance to taste *more* of him. Not just his mouth, but all of him. Squeezing my legs together, I can feel the dampness of my panties, and an undeniable urge to relieve myself of the sexual tension that still consumes me has me hiking up my skirt.

My eyes still closed, not wishing to lose sight of Michael, I push my underwear down my legs. Once I've stepped out of them, freeing my ankles, I trace my fingers up the inside of my thigh before sliding them through my slick center. I'm still sopping wet, and I shiver, thinking of the man who made me this way.

Swirling my fingers around my clit, I pretend that he's in the room with me—that he wants me to touch myself; that he wants to watch me come. I whimper as I fill myself with two fingers, coating my hand in my arousal. As I begin to stoke the passion that was awakened in me tonight, I reach up and palm one of my breasts over my t-shirt and bra. Frustrated that I'm still wearing so many clothes, I stop what I'm doing to yank the shirt off of me. I drop it to the floor, discarding my bra as well, never once opening my eyes.

Pressing my back against the door, I imagine how turned on Michael would be if he saw me like this—if he could know how hot he makes me. Continuing to stroke myself with one hand, I pinch and pull at one of my peaked nipples with the other. I'm still so worked up over that kiss, it's not long before I can feel my orgasm start to rise to the surface. I pump my hand faster, the heel of my palm grazing my clit, and I moan loudly.

I come remembering the way he kissed and licked my neck, my body shaking with the most powerful release I've ever managed to find on my own.

"Oh, god—*Michael,*" I whisper, the walls of my sex tightening around my fingers.

It isn't until my body starts to relax that I become fully cognizant of what I've done. My eyes fly open, and I stare into the darkness of my apartment, looking up at the moonlight pouring in from the windows and casting a spotlight on my empty bed—the empty bed I share with a man whose name is *not* Michael. The desire that swam in my belly a moment ago gives way to something else—something close to guilt, but more painful.

Shame.

I suck in a sharp breath, my eyes welling up with tears as the truth settles in my heart. Like my body's climax has shattered the illusion that I've been lost in all evening, *reality* washes over me like a tidal wave.

I'm a cheater.

As I quickly gather my clothes from the floor and hurry toward the bathroom, all I can think about is cleansing myself of the evidence of what I just did. I start the shower before rushing into my closet to deposit my clothes into my hamper. When I've returned to the bathroom, I don't even bother checking to make sure the water is hot before I step under the spray. My heart aches as I think about Mateo. The entire time I scrub my body, I think of how oblivious to this whole night he is. My lie weighs heavily on my shoulders, and I feel awful.

I hate knowing that the consequences of my actions will cause Mateo pain. I'm fully aware that if the situation was reversed, I'd feel betrayed and heartbroken. To go behind his back, to hide from him—I cannot deny that it's wrong. I'm aware that in this moment, I don't deserve to feel sorry for myself, but I cry anyway. The pain that's tangled up inside of me, it's unlike any that I've ever felt before. It's messy. Complicated. *Confusing.*

I thought I loved Mateo. I'm sure that I did. Yet, I believe with my whole heart that you don't cheat on someone that you love. Except, I don't know when I stopped loving him. Maybe I haven't. Maybe life isn't as black and white as I once believed. The ache that I feel, the *regret* that mingles with my guilt, it speaks of a tenderness I still have for him. My boyfriend. He's my *boyfriend.*

The worst part is, while I'm ashamed of myself for what I've done, I'd be lying if I said that I regretted a single second of my night with Michael. I wouldn't take it back. Not any of it.

Is it possible to regret the pain you're sure to inflict but not regret the actions that caused that pain? How can I regret that kiss? How can I regret the most incredible moment I've ever shared with another human being in my entire life?

Burying my face in my hands, the spray of the water beating on my back, I close my eyes and see *Michael.* I want *Michael.* As awful as I may feel, as shameful as my actions might be, and as fucked up as this entire mess is, I'm certain of one thing—*I can't* not *see him again.*

DAD GRUMBLES AT the television, but I don't hear what he's saying. As I sit with my legs stretched out along the sofa, ignoring the plate of food in my lap that I've barely touched, I stare at the screen.

I'm lost.

Watching the camera pan out across the outfield, I wonder if I'll be able to look at a baseball game the same *ever* again. Every time I try to focus on what's happening during the inning, I remember sitting next to Michael in the empty stands of a different stadium. There were no awkward silences as we ate—only stories, and laughter, and that feeling that comes when you know there's no place else you'd rather be. We both felt it. I'm sure of it. If I harbored any doubt, that kiss destroyed it.

"Dammit, Lulu," dad grunts.

I only hear him because the TV is now muted—something he *never* does during a game. I turn my head and find him scowling at me from his recliner. His plate now resting on his side table is empty, as is his water. I think about getting up to go get him some more, but he speaks before I can move.

"What's the matter with you?"

"What? What do you mean?" I ask dumbly, reaching up to sweep a nonexistent stray hair behind my ear.

"You've been mopin' around since you walked in the door. You're playin' with your food, even though I know your mother taught you better than that, and now you're ignorin' me when I call your name."

For a second, I feel like I'm ten years old again.

"Sorry. I didn't hear you."

"Well, shit, Lulu—I know you didn't hear me. I'm tryin' to figure out why the hell not."

Biting the inside of my cheek, I mentally kick myself for being so transparent. Though, after the restless night I had, I'm surprised he didn't ask what was wrong with me as soon as I arrived.

My phone pings from where it sits on the cushion beside my leg, and I jump as it jars me from my thoughts. I reach for it without delay. Except, before I can turn it over to see who it is that's texted me, my guilt and shame tangle my stomach in knots. Setting the phone down with a frown, I fight the urge I have to see who it is. Avoidance is my best option right now. To look would only open the door to disappointment. Admitting that I don't know *whose* name I'd wish to see makes me feel like a terrible person, so I pretend like I'm not interested in conversation at the moment.

"Baby girl, if you don't start talkin'…"

I suck in a breath, shifting my focus back onto my father. I had forgotten that we were in the middle of a conversation. Now, his raised eyebrow and impatient stare let me know that I just had an audience for my little show, too. Our gazes locked in a silent standoff, I make up my mind to confide in my old man. At least a little. I'm struggling right now, and I could use some of his fatherly wisdom. Without mom around, he's the best I've got. While no one can take mom's place, he's pretty damn good and certainly nothing to scoff at.

Drawing in a deep breath, I move my plate onto the coffee table and shift so that my legs are curled up beneath me. As I lean my elbow against the armrest, I fidget with my fingers, avoiding dad's gaze as I try and think of what to say.

"Now, Blaine, you're tryin' my patience."

I shrink back a little at his use of my first name. He so rarely uses it. When he does, I know he's about to be stern with me. Not sure how to ease my way into the topic, I blurt it out instead.

"Did you ever think about cheating on mom?"

He flinches, his eyes growing wide in disbelief before his brow scrunches in offense. "Tell me you didn't just ask me what I think you did," he grunts.

His response makes my chest ache, and I wish I hadn't said anything. The last thing I need right now is for my dad to judge me. I've pretty much got that covered on my own. Not knowing where to go from here, I don't say anything at all.

"*Blaine Luella—*"

"God, dad, I didn't mean anything by it," I murmur, staring down at my hands. "I know you would never hurt mom. I *know* that. Just—forget I asked."

Acknowledging that my father is a good man, who only ever showed respect to the woman he loved, causes me to feel like a failure and a disappointment all wrapped into one. Remembering what I did last night, unable to deny that I'm craving Michael's kiss even *now*, it makes me want to cry.

"Baby girl, look at me."

When I don't, I hear it as he leans forward in his chair before he growls, "Did Mateo—"

I don't allow him to finish, knowing it's not fair that I let him drag Mateo's name anywhere *near* the mud when *I'm* the one at fault. "I met…someone," I whisper. My nose tingles as my eyes grow blurry with tears, but I force my next words out anyway. "I don't know what to do, dad."

"Lulu, baby," he says on a sigh. "I think you do."

I shake my head in disagreement, not ready to admit that he's right.

"Baby girl, you *do*." He leans back in his chair, and I hear it as he scratches at his scruffy cheek. After another pause, he goes on to say, "You asked me if I'd ever thought about cheating on your mom. You didn't have to do that, Lulu. You know good and damn well I loved your mother with all my heart. Wasn't another woman out there as beautiful as her. Inside and out. I didn't need to go lookin' for greener pastures 'cause I'd already found mine.

"Now, I won't condone cheatin'. It's not fair to anyone. There's no sense in it, baby girl. If Mateo gives you reason to stray, it's okay to let him go."

I gasp, surprised by the sob that suddenly fills my throat. Tears now streaming down my face, I continue to keep my gaze down as I murmur, "I love him, dad. Or, at least, I thought I did—or, I don't know. I'm so confused"

"Lulu, would you look at me, dammit?"

Swallowing hard, I dry my cheeks and stifle my tears before obediently meeting my father's eyes. He studies me for a long time before he speaks again.

"I don't want to know the details. It's not my business. But we made a deal, you and me."

"I know," I assure him.

"I get it. I understand that it's hard to let go of something just because you've had it for a long time. But if you're settling—I won't stand for that."

"I don't want to hurt him," I squeak, my tears returning.

"Staying with him because you don't want to hurt him is not the same as loving him. You do him a disservice by believing that shit. Hell, you do yourself a disservice by believing it. Now, I don't know who this other guy is, but I know *you*. I trust *you*. You're my baby girl, I love you, and I raised you right. If someone's caught your attention, it's because Mateo wasn't holding onto it. That goes against our deal."

Rubbing my knuckles underneath my eyes, I blow out a frustrated breath as I tell him, "I don't deserve excuses."

"Maybe you don't. Now, I won't claim to be an expert on the matter, but nobody thinks about cheatin' for no reason. Means there's a lack. You either choose to address it with the man you're with, or you let him go. You're young, Lulu. You've got a lot of life left to live. You're not always going to get it right—but you sure as shit are not going to do it with a man by your side who has you runnin' over here when you fight, and wishin' you were with someone else."

I laugh, not because I'm amused, but because it's ridiculous how simple he makes it seem when I feel like this is anything but simple.

"Easy as that, right?" I mutter flippantly.

"No. I didn't say that," he says softly, his pale blue eyes speaking of his empathy. "Right and easy are not the same thing. Rarely are."

I nod as I sniffle, the truth of his statement making me feel better and worse at the same time.

In need of a reprieve from our conversation, I ask, "Do you think we could just...watch some baseball?"

He picks up the remote, but doesn't unmute the television right away. Instead, he lifts his eyebrows at me and grunts, "You heard what I said?"

"Yes, dad. I heard you."

"All right, then."

He lifts and points the remote, then the room fills with the sound of the game. I notice that the opposing team scored during our chat at the same time as dad. He grumbles something unintelligible, and a small smile teases my lips. There's something about the familiar that offers me comfort in this moment, on a day where *comfort* feels so far out of reach.

Remembering that I have an unread text message on my phone, I hesitantly reach for the device and flip it over to see who it's from. My heart sinks when I see *My Artist* lit up across the screen. Just like that, I know where I stand. The disappointment that makes me feel unsettled has nothing to do with the conversation that awaits me when I get home. The truth is—

I'd hoped it was Michael.

Michael

My father is a great pastor. He's smart. He's got a business mind but a servant's heart. Half the reason his church is successful is because he understands that in a changing world, the church must adapt. While the message is always the same—the gospel of Jesus Christ being the foundation of my father's calling—he knows how to draw people in. He knows how to build a team of leaders who help him strategize and connect people, both within the walls of this establishment, as well as outside of it, in the community. I respect him for all that he's accomplished through his ministry, and I admire him for his faith.

I don't come to Mercy Hill because my family's name is attached to it. I don't come because my dad is the one standing behind the pulpit week after week. I come because it's a choice that I made a long time ago—this church with this congregation is where I feel at home. I was raised here. I was married here. It's where Veronica and I decided to plant our feet. This morning, I feel no different about whether or not I belong here. Yet, I feel uncomfortable. I'm distracted. I swear, I didn't hear a word of my father's sermon, my thoughts consumed with memories of Blaine.

I know that I should feel convicted. Everything that I've been taught about the sacrament of marriage leads me to believe that what I did last night was wrong. I should be seeking God for forgiveness and confessing that the desires of my sinful nature are becoming more than I can control on my own. However, it's not the memory of last night that makes me feel uncomfortable. While there is guilt in my heart, my shame cowers in the presence of my longing. I've never felt a pull toward another person this strong before. I can't explain it. I can't shut it off. After that kiss—I no longer feel like the man I was yesterday morning.

I feel uncomfortable being in this place not because it is the Lord's house and I am a sinner—for we are all sinners, welcomed into His house—but because my wife is on my arm, and all I can think about is how much I want another woman.

"Hey. You okay?" Gabriel steals my attention, nudging me with his elbow as we stand in the noisy lobby, waiting for the rest of our family to join us.

Glancing beside me, I see Veronica is talking to Graham, which means Abigail and Tamara have gone to pick up the kids from children's church. I didn't notice when they broke away from us after exiting the service.

"Michael?" Gabe claps a hand on my shoulder and gives me a small shake. "What's going on, Mikey?"

I blow out a sigh and shake my head, willing myself to remain in the present. "I've got a lot on my mind, is all."

He studies me a moment, a slight frown tugging at his brow. If there's one person in the Cavanaugh clan that has always been able to see right through me, it's Gabe. It's like he's got a gift or something. Even after fifteen years of marriage, my brother can read me better than my wife. Then again, he's known me my entire life, which is why I'm not at all surprised when he squeezes my shoulder and lets me go before reminding me, "I'm here if you need to talk."

It's a standing offer; one that goes both ways. Over the years, nothing has been able to wedge a gap in our bond. Not when I went out of state for college, not when either of us got married, not when he started having kids—nothing. With that truth in mind, I know I can trust him with the conflict that weighs heavily on me today. I can't say for sure how he'll take it or what advice he'll offer, but I could use someone to talk to right now.

Deciding to take him up on his offer, I ask "Got any plans tonight?"

"Sounds like I'm about to."

"Yeah."

He nods at the same time that we both hear, *"Daddy!"* before Isla comes crashing into his legs. He smiles down at his youngest daughter, speaking his own soft greeting as he affectionately sweeps her hair out of her face. I feel a pang of regret and jealousy as I watch their exchange, but I ignore it as my brother shifts his attention back on me and resumes our conversation.

"Old Chicago? We'll grab some pizza and beer? Six o'clock?" he asks, naming a familiar spot.

"I'll meet you there."

When I arrive at the restaurant, Gabriel is already seated in a booth on the outskirts of the bar. As I make my way toward him, Clay breaks off and heads to one of the high-top tables, giving me my privacy—as always.

"Is this all right? I didn't want to wait to be seated in the dining room," Gabe says in greeting as I slide in across from him.

"This is perfect. Thanks for meeting me."

"Please," he scoffs, waving his hand in dismissal. "Thanks for giving me an excuse to eat pizza. Tamara started one of her clean eating kicks again last week. The only thing resembling pizza in my house for the next couple of months is sure to be made with some cauliflower crust or some shit."

"That's not pizza," I chuckle.

"My point exactly," he replies with a grin. "I already ordered. *Magnificent Seven*. The waitress should be back around any second to grab you a beer."

I nod my acknowledgement and then pick up the beer menu to peruse my options. This place is known for their wide selection, and I usually like to switch it up whenever I get the chance. While I try and decide, I ask Gabe about work. He obliges me, giving me a second to work up the nerve to tell him about what's going on with me. I know he's onto my tactics. I can't ever fool him, and I appreciate the easy conversation for as long as it lasts.

As soon as my beer is set in front of me, he's quick to shift gears.

"Okay. Enough small talk. What's going on? Why are we here?"

I cough out a nervous laugh, feeling far from amused, and try to figure out where to begin. Memories from last night flood my mind, and all I see is Blaine's smile. Then I look across from me and see a man who has been married, a man who has never strayed from his wife in the last fourteen years. Even before that, when they were dating, he remained faithful. The only reason they got married after Veronica and me is because Tamara spent the last two years of her undergrad studying abroad in France.

They were a world apart, but their love was unbreakable. It still is. In fact, I'd even go so far as to say that it's stronger now than it's ever been. Gabe is a carnivore, through and through. He'll talk shit about cauliflower pizza, but if Tamara puts it in front of him, he'll not only eat it, but he'll praise her for her efforts and mean every single word he says.

"How do you do it?" I mutter, my voice so quiet, not even I can tell if I meant for him to hear me.

"Do what?"

"Love your wife. And don't tell me it's easy because she's Tamara. She's great, and I love her like the sister she is to me, but I'm talking about something else. I'm talking about something deeper. I'm talking about—"

"Dirty love," he interrupts. His face set in a serious, contemplative expression, he props himself up on his forearms against the table and says, "The kind of love you drag through the dirt when things are hard. The kind of love that pulls you through those times when it feels like you're covered in sweat and blood and tears because you've been through a war fought in pitch black darkness. The kind of love that says—*I choose you still* and *we're getting out of this together.*"

His description about knocks the wind out of me, and I sit back in my seat and shake my head at him. The fear that's been tormenting me the last couple of weeks settles in my gut, and I wonder when I became this man? When did I become the husband who isn't sure if he has the endurance to survive another war fought in the pitch black darkness?

"What's going on up in that head of yours, brother?"

"God, I don't even know," I moan, rubbing my eyes with my thumb and forefinger. When I drop my hand in my lap, my gaze goes with it. "I'm changing," I admit. "I can't explain it. I can hardly understand it, it just—I don't feel the same."

"Can I be honest with you about something?"

I brace myself for what he might say next, and then lift my eyes to connect with his.

"I wondered when you'd come to me."

My eyebrows shoot up in surprise, as I was not excepting those words. Not entirely certain that I catch his meaning, I mimic his stance, propping myself up on my forearms as I ask, "What do you mean?"

"I see you, Mike. You're the politician in the family. You've always been able to bullshit a lot of people, but you can't bullshit me. You and Vee—you haven't had an easy go of it. Yeah, okay, on paper, you look really good. To the people of Colorado who watched you on your campaign trail, Veronica should be First Lady of the *White House* for all they know. But I've been around for a stretch. I've seen your ups and downs. I've watched you both change—and I wondered when you'd come to me."

"It's not that I'm unhappy. I'm not miserable. She's a good woman."

"And you're a good guy. That's not the point here, is it?"

"No," I agree on a sigh.

"So what's going on? I know Abigail's news must have hit you both pretty hard. Is this about kids?"

"No." My answer falls from my lips before I even think about it. As soon as I speak it, I furrow my brow, suddenly wondering if that's not exactly true. "I mean, maybe—but not in the way that you might think."

Gabriel stares at me, silently waiting for me to elaborate. I don't talk about this stuff very often. Veronica's infertility is a sensitive subject. I learned at home *not* to talk about it. Now, with the issue hoovering between us, I don't know what to say.

When Vee and I first found out that she couldn't conceive, Gabe took me out for a beer. He knew already what a conversation with dad would be like for me. He knew that it would be full of encouragement and faith. He was right. Dad reminded me that God doesn't do anything on accident. He quoted scripture about women in the bible who conceived in the most unlikely of circumstances. He insisted that whatever happened from that point on, Veronica and I had chosen each other; we needed to stay true to our marriage, put our faith in God, and move forward. Gabe, on the other hand, had something different to say.

He never once told me to abandon my marriage. However, he wasn't afraid to ask some bold, hard questions. He asked me what I wanted and what I was willing to sacrifice given our situation. At the time, he wanted to know how deep my love went, and if I was prepared to fight for it. Back then, I was. Now—now it's not about our lack of children. Rather, it's about what our lack of children has done to us.

"It's like our marriage is a house," I tell him. "There are rooms everywhere. Every door leads somewhere, and every door is unlocked…except for one."

"And?" he prompts.

"And it's frustrating. She has full access—and for whatever reason, my security clearance doesn't exist. Half the time, she wants to pretend like the door isn't even there. She's so *busy* trying to distract me from it…" My voice trails off when I grow tired of talking in analogies. "I don't even know if it's about that. Or maybe it is and I don't want to point fingers but—"

"If what's about that?"

I glance down at my beer, wondering if I can admit the truth while looking my brother in the eye. Then I remember the way Blaine moaned into my mouth when I kissed her. I remember the way she clung to me like she was afraid I'd let go. I remember the hard-on I had to hide from my wife and stroke out in the shower before I got into bed last night, and I decide that this is too big. The weight of this truth is too heavy for me to be a coward about it.

"Gabe," I start to say, lifting my gaze once more. "There's someone else."

He blows out a heavy breath as he rakes his fingers through his hair. Staring at me in a state of shock, he mutters, "Whoa."

"Yeah."

"I—I—I don't even know—wow," he stammers. "You were Mikey and Ronnie at sixteen years old. Maybe I shouldn't be surprised? I don't know, man. God…"

I don't speak, waiting for my announcement to sink in. He takes another second to process what I've said, and then he asks, "Have you—I mean, how serious is this? Have you slept with her?"

Both of us go mute when our waitress arrives with our pizza.

After setting it down in the middle of our table and asking if we'd like anything else, she leaves us for another group of customers. Neither Gabe, nor I, reaches for a slice, his question still lingering unanswered.

Finally, I confess, "No. But I'd be lying if I said it hasn't crossed my mind."

Rubbing his hand over his chin, he grunts, "*Mierda*, Mike."

"I know. Okay? I know."

"Do you?" he asks, casting a worried look my way. He speaks in a harsh whisper as he says, "Remember who you are, Michael. I'm not judging you, you know I would never do that—but what you're talking about, it could destroy you. Not just your marriage, but your *career*."

"You don't think I've considered that?" I argue, the ache in my chest catching me off guard. "God, Gabe—I know this is crazy. I *know*. But I want her."

"Is this about sex? I mean, is Veronica—"

"No. I told you. I haven't had sex with her. I'm still getting to know her. It's just—sometimes I feel like she's all I ever think about."

He leans back in his seat, blowing out another heavy sigh. "I have to tell you, Mike, I wasn't expecting this. I want to say something, but I don't even know where to begin."

"I probably shouldn't have told you," I mutter, realizing how selfish and unfair it is of me to ask him to keep this secret. "I'd appreciate it if—"

"I'm not going to say anything. You know that. I love you, and I want the best for you. I want you to be happy. But you need to be smart, man. You *have* to think this through. Don't be impulsive and stupid—and for the love of God—whatever you do, *don't get caught*."

I nod. He's right, and I know it. Yet, still, I can't ignore the pull that I feel even now. I haven't been able to stop thinking about her all day. My phone feels like it's burning a hole in my pocket.

"Michael," he pauses and leans toward me. "I won't pretend that I know what you're going through. I'm not arrogant enough to sit here and tell you what to do. Just don't lose sight of the man that you are. Don't become someone you can't face in the mirror. And if you need me, I'm here for you. *Tienes mi apoyo, pase lo que pase. Confío en tu corazón.*[9] Always."

I relax a little, my shoulders feeling a lighter knowing that I'm not carrying the weight of this secret all on my own. Yes, I know it's selfish, but that doesn't make me less appreciative of what my brother is offering me. His love with no judgment.

"*Yo también te quiero, hermano.*[10]"

"*Mierda,*" he says in a huff. "Let's eat this pizza."

---

9 I've got your back, no matter what. I trust your heart.

10 I love you too, brother.

Thirteen

Blaine

I SIT IN MY CAR, OUTSIDE OF THE LOFT, for ten minutes. I'm sick to my stomach. There's no way that this is going to end well. While I know what I need to do, I don't know that I'll ever be prepared for the fall out. I'm about to end a relationship that I've been holding onto for two years. It's the longest relationship I've ever had. Mateo is the first guy I got serious with after mom died. My heart is breaking even now just *thinking* about my choice.

I force myself out of my car and try not to throw up as I make my way to the fifth floor. I can hear music from the other side of the door, and my palms start to sweat as I unlock the knob and let myself in. Mateo is in the corner, focused on a canvas he's working on. Like always, he doesn't even notice my presence.

I stop and stare, trying to remember when it all started to fall apart. As I watch him, I realize that dad was right. This isn't all about Michael. There were fractures in my relationship with

Mateo—cracks in our foundation that allowed me to *see* Michael. While I shouldn't have gone behind Mateo's back this weekend, while I'm no more right in this moment of realization than I was yesterday, it doesn't change the fact that we're broken. We've been *breaking* for a little while now.

Walking into the kitchen, I shut off the music and set my bag on the counter. Mateo turns his head as the apartment is blanketed in silence. He then lifts his chin in a subtle nod as he says, "Hey, baby. Thought you'd be home sooner."

He doesn't wait for me to respond before he returns to his painting. I rub my hands on my shorts, trying to find the nerve to speak.

"Mateo, can we talk?"

His back stiffens, but he doesn't face me when asks, "Talk about what?"

"Us..."

I know I have his full attention when he sets down his paintbrush and turns to look at me. "That sounds ominous. Should I be worried?" he asks, folding his arms across his chest. "What's going on?"

For a second, I start to question myself, wondering if I'm really doing the right thing. Then I hear dad's voice in my head.

Staying with him because you don't want to hurt him is not the same as loving him.

My vision grows blurry with tears, and I struggle to find the words I need to say.

"Okay, what the fuck?" he asks, dropping his arms as he closes the distance between us. "What's wrong?"

When he reaches up to hold the back of my neck, I don't stifle my cry as I touch my forehead to his chest. Not sure where to begin, I blurt out the truth and tell him, "I think we should break up."

I feel it when he goes stock-still, but he doesn't let me go. Instead, he takes a deep breath and presses his lips against the top of my head. I don't move, waiting for him to reply.

"Baby, where's this coming from?"

Pressing my hands against his stomach, I lift my head to look into his eyes. My tears now flowing steadily, I allow myself to be honest with him—honest with *myself*—for the first time in weeks.

"We're not the same as we used to be. We fight more since you moved in than we've ever fought before. It doesn't feel good, Mateo. I don't think—"

"Blaine—we're transitioning. We knew moving in together would be different. Every couple goes through shit when they take the next step. This is normal."

"Normal?" I mutter, scrunching my brow in disbelief. "Sometimes I don't even *want* to come home. That's not normal, Mat. That's not us being happy."

Dropping his hands away from me, he scoffs and asks, "So that's it? You just want to give up? After two years, all I get is—*I think we should break up?* Are you fucking kidding me right now?"

Fidgeting with the hem of my t-shirt, I murmur, "It's not working out the way I thought it would."

"Baby—" He exhales an exasperated sigh before reaching up to sink his fingers in his hair. "You can't just say shit like that and walk away. If we're having problems, you need to talk to me."

I jerk my head back in surprise, suddenly feeling irritated. "I've tried talking to you. Over and over again! How can you stand there and think otherwise? That—*this*—it's part of the problem. You don't *listen*. You don't *hear* me. And let's not get into how many times you've flat out *forgotten* me."

"Fuck, Blaine, are you going to hold that over my head forever? How many times do I have to tell you I'm sorry?"

I brush my fingers across my cheeks, wiping away my tears, surprised that the hurt I felt a minute ago has given way to something else. Now I'm *angry*.

"I'm sick and tired of hearing you tell me that you're *sorry*. I don't *want* you to tell me that you're sorry. I don't *want* you to be sorry. I *want* you to stop doing things that require an apology."

"What kind of fairytale expectations are those? Huh? Nobody's perfect. You think if you kick me out, you'll find someone who is? Well, you're wrong."

"I'm not asking for perfection. I've never wanted that from you," I argue, folding my arms across my chest.

"Then what do you want, Blaine?"

Unexpectedly, my answer comes in the form of a memory. I close my eyes, and I'm in the middle of a baseball diamond. Only, Michael isn't with me—not yet. I'm on the pitcher's mound by myself, and I see *everything,* and it's *beautiful.*

Opening my eyes slowly, I look up at Mateo and whisper, "Everything. I want *everything*."

He looks at me incredulously, and I can tell that my words mean nothing to him. He's *listening* but he doesn't *hear* me. There's a disconnect, one that I can no longer ignore. As I stare back at him, I see that he's pissed, but that's all. I don't recognize an ounce of desperation is his brown eyes. There's no pain or longing. There's no violent storm in the middle of a dark blue ocean. It's in the midst of my epiphany that I decide it's time I told the whole truth.

"I kissed someone last night."

"Excuse me?" he practically growls.

"I'm not proud of it, but it happened. I didn't do it to hurt you or get back at you—I just wanted to feel good, and it felt good."

"You wanted to *feel* good? What the fuck is that supposed to mean? Are you trying to tell me that I don't satisfy you? My dick isn't good enough for you now?" Taking a step toward me, he mutters, "I know an orgasm when I feel one, baby, and I'm pretty sure I satisfy you *just fine.*"

"This is not about sex," I argue, pushing him away from me.

"No?" he challenges, taking hold of my hips. He pulls me against him and touches his forehead to mine. "You let some other fucker put his dick in you and you're going to stand here and tell me this isn't about sex?"

"I didn't *sleep* with him, Mateo—we only kissed."

"Great. Fine. If it was only a kiss, then we can fix this. It's supposed to be you and me, Blaine. I'm here," he grunts before pressing his lips against mine. "Right here."

My tears return when he pries my mouth open with his tongue. His kiss is hard and aggressive. It's possessive and not the least bit persuasive. I kiss him back not because I want him, but because he deserves this goodbye. The truth is, I can't taste his love. I can't feel it. I can't find it in order to get lost in it. I don't know how I got used to this. I don't remember when we stopped being *us*. All I can think about is how different it felt when I kissed Michael.

Thinking about how he stole my breath with one brush of his lips—it causes me to break away from Mateo. I push myself out of his arms and cover my mouth with my hand, swallowing my guilt. Between my shame, my heartache, and my frustration, I can hardly stand to be in my own head. This whole thing feels so fucked up, and yet I know that it's the right thing to do.

Taking another step back, I grab my purse and loop the straps over my shoulder as I meet Mateo's cold stare. "I'm going to step out for a while. Will you please just go?"

He shakes his head, scowling as he mumbles, "I can't believe you're doing this to me."

A sob rises in my throat as regret joins my solemn party of emotions. Backing my way to the door, I wish that this had gone differently. I know that he deserves more, that we both deserve more, but this is all I have to give.

"I'm—I'm sorry. I really did love you. I just—can't anymore. I'm sorry."

Without second guessing myself, I head straight for the door and don't look back. I hear him yell *son of a bitch* when I press my back against the barrier that now stands between us, and my heart sinks even lower. I can hardly wrap my head around what just happened. It feels surreal. In this moment, absolution is the last thing that I can grab hold of, my hands marred with a loss I know not how to comprehend.

As I start toward the steps, headed back to my car, I reach for my phone. Before I can bring up my list of contacts, a call comes through. I stop my descent immediately, staring at *The Governor* as my ringtone echoes in the stairwell. I want so badly to answer and to hear his voice, but I can't. Not right now. Not after what just happened.

God—I'm such a bitch.

I let the call ring through to my voicemail as I hurry to my car. Once inside, I pull up my contacts and find the one I was originally after. *Mommy's Pearl* answers on the second ring.

"Hello, darling. How are you?"

I blow out a tearful sigh before I tell her, "I broke up with Mateo. I made a mess. A really big mess."

"I'll meet you in thirty minutes."

She hangs up without a goodbye, but I don't complain. Like

always, Simone is headed to our spot without hesitation. She's constantly there for me, exactly when I need her.

Michael

"THANK YOU FOR your time, Governor, it was a pleasure having you on today's show."

"The pleasure was mine."

I hang up the phone and Heidi smiles at me from where she sits on the other side of my desk. Standing just enough to reach for the file in front of me and hand me another, she says, "One down, one to go."

I nod, flipping my wrist to check the time before looking down at the notes that were prepared for me. In her poised, practice manner, Heidi briefs me about what I can expect on my next radio interview, scheduled for ten minutes from now. Try as I might, I'm only half listening while I mentally sort through the rest of my day. After my upcoming call, I have a cabinet meeting, which will take me into the late afternoon, followed by another meeting with the mayor of Denver.

Coming to the conclusion that now is probably the only window of time I have until the day is over, I glance at my watch once more, interrupting Heidi as I murmur, "I'm sorry to cut you off, but I need a moment. Five minutes. I have a personal phone call to make."

"Yeah, sure," she replies, hopping out of her seat in an instant. "Five minutes. I'll be back."

I watch her take her leave and then draw in a deep breath as she closes the door behind her. Pulling my personal phone from my pocket, I don't waste any time bringing up Blaine's number. I haven't heard from her since Saturday, when she kissed my cheek in farewell. I tried to call her Sunday but got no answer. I told myself not to read into it—but that was three days ago. Now her silence makes me wonder if she's changed her mind about us; if she's having second thoughts, or maybe she's feeling guilty after our evening together. Whatever it is, I need to hear her say the words.

When my first call rings through to voicemail, I shake my head and call back again. I want to believe that the feeling in my gut is worry over her well-being. I want to believe that she wouldn't ignore me on purpose, not after our time together. I don't want to admit that I'm starting to feel desperate. What happened on that ball field was not one-sided. I know that I can't be the only one thinking about that kiss and craving another. I can't be the only one who misses the sound of her voice, and the way her face lights up when she giggles. I can't be the only one going crazy.

I don't leave a voicemail when she doesn't pick up for the second time. Instead, I pull up Veronica's number and hit *dial.* When she doesn't answer, I'm relieved—so much so that I don't have room to feel ashamed of myself for what I'm about to do.

"Vee, it's me. I wanted to let you know that I'm going to be late tonight. Don't hold dinner, I'll eat out. I hope to be home around eight or so. Love you." The words fall out of my mouth without thought, and my speech falters for a moment. Sure that I don't have time to think about what those words mean these days, I conclude my message with a goodbye and hang up.

Upon entering the Prohibition Lounge, I don't bypass the hostess and make my way to the bar. Switching up my routine, I ask for a table for two—requesting a seat with a view of the bar, in case I want to check the score from tonight's game.

"Sir?" Clay questions me quietly as we're escorted to our table.

"You'll be my dinner companion tonight. I hope you don't mind."

"No, sir. Not at all."

While I know it probably irks him to have his back to the room, Clay doesn't protest when I take the booth-side seat against the wall. He's a smart man, and I doubt he's ignorant of why we are here, or that the score of tonight's game is the last thing on my mind as I focus my attention across the room.

I go unnoticed, a circumstance that doesn't bother me. It gives me an opportunity to try and get a read on her. Since the moment that I met her, I've been able to *see* her. That is who she is. She doesn't hide from the world—at least not very well. Tonight, I can see that while her smile may be genuine, it is not *whole*.

It isn't until after our dinner orders are taken that I pull out my phone and send my first text. I'm not even certain that she'll answer. I'm sure it's against the rules to text while she's behind the bar, but it's worth a shot. It takes her nearly five minutes to even check her device, but my concerns in regards to her desires are put to rest when she unknowingly gives me her back, facing the register as she types out her reply.

Have you changed your mind?

No. Shit, Michael, I'm sorry. Sunday was…horrible timing. This afternoon, you called while I was still sleeping.

Still sleeping? At two in the afternoon?

She steps away from the register before reading my reply, but I know when she feels her phone alert her to my text from inside of her pocket. Her smile hitches a little higher as she tends to a customer, causing a smile of my own to play at my lips. I patiently wait for her answer, which comes after she mixes two drinks and closes out someone's tab.

Don't judge. I work until 2am. Besides, I've been having trouble sleeping lately. Anyway, I'm sorry. I haven't changed my mind.

…I miss you.

My chest swells as I read her text twice. When I glance back up at her, I find her still situated at the register, waiting for my response. Knowing she won't be able to linger long, I'm quick to send her my reply.

I need to see you.

Me too. Schedule sucks this week. Here late every night until Friday. Covering a shift Saturday. Traded my Sunday, though.

She shoves her phone into the pack pocket of her slacks the same time that our dinner arrives. I frown down at my plate, counting the days until Sunday. Practically speaking, I don't see how any sooner would be possible. Nevertheless, I feel impatient at the thought of waiting. That's what she does to me. I haven't felt this anxious about being with a woman in what feels like a lifetime. Even simply being in the same room as her has calmed my nerves.

I laugh to myself, realizing how crazy that makes me sound.

Looking across the table, I watch Clay cut into his steak before I ask, "Would this constitute as stalking?"

He jerks his gaze up at me, his face impassive. His eyes speak of his alarm, until he realizes I'm joking. He then quirks an eyebrow at me and mutters, "In my experience, sir, there's a fine line between *stalking* and *pursuing*. I'll keep you abreast if I feel as though you've crossed into dangerous territory."

All teasing aside, I let my smile fade away as I offer him a nod, silently expressing my gratitude—not just for his comment, but for his discretion. Acknowledging that I owe him more than a *thank you*, we spend the rest of our meal in conversation. Clay has a history of being private and professional, but a cordial companion at all times. We don't discuss anything personal, keeping to sports and the news, our rapport as comfortable as always. Then, all too soon, our empty plates are cleared from the table and we're served with the check.

It isn't until our waitress goes to process my payment that I reach for my phone again to send Blaine another message.

Sunday. My office. The Capitol will be a ghost town.

Just tell me when.

5pm. Front doors.

Okay.

After I've settled the bill, I send one last text, hoping she'll see it before I leave.

I missed you, too. Had to see you. The crab cake isn't quite the same without your company.

I wait a moment after pushing *send* before I stand and start for the door. When I reach the threshold, I chance a glance over my shoulder, and look right into her eyes. The shy smile she gives me makes tonight's dinner bill completely worth it. Then, five minutes later, when I'm halfway to the mansion, my phone alerts me to one final message.

Is it Sunday, yet?

Fourteen

Blaine

I TRY NOT TO LOOK SUSPICIOUS AS HELL as I climb the steps leading to the Capitol—but I'm nervous, it's Sunday, and I know I don't belong here anymore *today* than I did the first time I came. While Michael assured me there wouldn't be a bunch of important people roaming the halls in suits, that didn't stop me from upping my dress game a little. The short, white summer dress I'm wearing has a pink rose floral pattern printed on it. It's strapless, and the ruched bodice hugs my torso before the skirt drapes comfortably around my narrow hips. I paired it with a denim jean jacket and my white Keds.

Okay, so, not exactly business casual—but I work at a high-end bar with a strict dress code. It's the best I could do.

When I reach the second flight of stairs in front of the building, I see Clay sitting at the top. My stomach knots up at the sight of him, his presence reminding me that I'm only moments away from being with Michael again. It's been a week since we last got to spend any time together, but it feels like much longer. The last several days have been long and draining, and I've been looking forward to this evening since we set the date.

Before I have a chance to hurry up the steps, Clay stands and hurries down them. "Ms. Foster, follow me please."

I do as I'm told without question and follow him to an alternate entrance. It doesn't take much for me to guess why he's sneaking me in some private, back doorway, and my nerves go up a notch at the thought of being caught. Even with the silence that trails after us, my heart beats faster, and I try not to breathe—not wanting to make a sound until we step foot into a familiar room.

The reception area outside of Michael's office is only lit from the little bit of sun that shines through the window. The absence of the overhead light reminds me, once again, that we really are *alone* in here, and I have nothing to worry about. When Clay comes to a stop in front of me, he turns and motions for me to proceed. The nerves in my stomach turn into something else. Knowing Michael is only a few feet away has my heart racing for entirely different reasons.

"Thank you," I whisper as I walk past Clay, heading toward the governor's office.

I find him pacing the floor, which makes me smile for some reason. It's cute, seeing him frazzled. Michael Cavanaugh is a man of *power* and political *prowess.* He exudes a confidence that he's earned—not just because he's worked so hard to get to where he is today, or because he's an elected official that basically makes him the president of Colorado, but also because he's a *man* who has walked this earth for almost forty years. Yet, his anxiousness over this moment reminds me that regardless of how far apart we are on the spectrum of *life,* and in spite of the fact that this is new and undefined—whatever *this* is—we're in it together.

Taking advantage of this opportunity to give him a proper look, I don't cross the threshold as I drag my eyes up and down the man who has been occupying my dreams. He's wearing a navy blue button-up shirt and a pair of black jeans. His shirt is untucked, the collar undone, and the sleeves are rolled up his forearms. Fully aware that I've only really ever seen him in dress shirts or a t-shirt, I must conclude that there's something about the way his button-ups hug his muscles that makes me weak at the knees.

When I close the door behind me, the *click* that sounds as the latch slides home causes Michael to stop and look my way. My stomach clenches as his gaze collides with mine, and I'm overwhelmed with the slight sense of absolution that lifts a weight I've been wrestling with all week. Being here with Michael, the desire I have to run into his arms right now, it's proof that breaking up with Mateo was the right thing to do. Even if what's going on between us ends up being a huge cluster-fuck, I want it—I want *him* more than the relationship I let go.

Neither of us speaks for what seems like an eternity, both of us appreciating the other from afar. Then, skipping over hello, Michael's hushed, raspy voice commands, "Come here," and I don't hesitate.

Dropping my bag into one of the chairs in front of his desk along the way, I walk straight into his chest. He wraps me in his arms as if I belong there, forcing me on my tiptoes as he lifts me up for a kiss. I don't hold back, resting my arms across his broad shoulders while I tangle my tongue with his. If I thought for one second that our first kiss was some epic, one-time only occurrence—*this* kiss proves me wrong.

Michael takes his time, reacquainting himself with my mouth.

I give as good as I get, trying to express how much I've missed him.

"I missed you," I practically whine when he finally pulls away from me.

Shaking his head, his eyes dance around my face as he breathes, "You have no idea, angel."

He presses another quick kiss against my lips, and I slip my fingers into his hair as he pulls away. Having him in my arms—being crushed by his—it almost makes me forget the week that I've had. *Almost.* Yet, as long as it was, as I stare into his eyes while we both work to catch our breath, I concede to the reality that it was worth it—even if for just this stolen moment. Only, now that I'm here, I have to admit that I'm in this, wherever it's going.

"I have to tell you something," I murmur, afraid to let him go.

"Okay."

With one arm still holding me close, he reaches up and traces a finger along my face, tucking a few strands of hair behind my ear. I swallow hard before I confess, "I broke up with Mateo. Sunday—right before you called—I ended it."

He freezes, his fingers still at my ear, and I find myself holding my breath as I wait for his response.

"Blaine," he mutters, his brow furrowed as he retreats, letting me go. "I'm sorry. I didn't—"

"Don't apologize," I insist, taking a step toward him.

Shaking his head, his blue eyes expressing his worry, he goes on to tell me, "It wasn't my intention for you to—"

I don't let him finish, pressing my hands to his stomach as I plead with him, "*Don't* apologize. It was my decision."

He sighs and runs a hand down his face. Clenching his jaw, he stares at me for a second before he mutters, "I could use a drink. You want a drink?"

"Uh," I stammer, my eyebrows shooting up in surprise. "Sure?"

The word comes out more like a question than an affirmative answer, but he nods and steps away from me anyhow. I watch as he goes behind his desk and pulls open the bottom, left-hand drawer. As he sets out a bottle of bourbon and two tumblers, I have to bite my lip to keep myself from laughing. The fact that he has liquor hidden away in his desk seems so humorously cliché.

"What are you smirking about?" he asks me, breaking the seal on the bourbon.

A blush blossoms across my cheeks. Having not realized that I was smirking, I look down at my feet as I admit, "It just, I don't know—seems like something out of a movie. The straight-laced governor with a bottle of bourbon in his desk."

"And his mistress in his office?"

I suck in a breath, my amusement evaporating into thin air as I lift my eyes to meet his. Hearing him say it like that, hearing him put a *label* on it, makes it feel more real. Joining him behind his desk, I wrap my hand around one of the empty glasses and push it toward the bottle.

"I could use that drink now."

He pours us each two fingers of bourbon before he stows the bottle away and sinks down into his chair. I take a sip, the brown liquid warming me from the inside out as I prop my backside against the edge of his desk. We stare at one another, the truth exposed in the last two minutes hanging between us.

I swallow another shallow drink of the strong liquor before I break our silence and explain, "I know that it's hard to separate the two—the beginning of…whatever *this* is and the end of my relationship with Mateo, but they don't go hand in hand." Staring down into my tumbler, I go on to say, "We were together for two years. Somewhere along the way, it became more convenient than anything else. I didn't notice until, well…"

"Until when?" he asks, his voice soft and rumbly.

Peeking at him from beneath my lashes, I whisper, "Until someone better came along."

He nods his understanding, but I can tell by the crease in his brow that he's still rattled by my news. When he looks away from me and takes a sip of bourbon, I realize what it is that he's feeling. *Guilt.* At first, I don't understand it. Sure, he didn't know that much about Mateo and me. He wasn't privy to the dynamic of our relationship, but he'd somehow managed to see me during a couple of our low points, which means he knew we weren't perfect.

"Blaine," he mutters, pulling me from my thoughts. I study him, watching as he reaches up to rub the back of his neck before he says, "I've been with my wife since I was—"

"Oh, my god!" I gasp, suddenly understanding his confliction.

Setting aside my glass, I hop up onto his desk, holding onto the edge as I lean toward him.

"Please don't think that I expect you to, like, reciprocate or something. I might be young, but I'm not dumb. I also read your bio, remember? I know how long you've been married. You've known me for a millisecond. I don't know where this is going, but—*god*—I do *not* expect you to make any sudden movements. Honestly. I swear." I pause to take a breath and then hold out my hand for him to take. When he curls his fingers under mine, I hold on tight as I promise him, "I broke up with Mateo for me. You—you're just who I'm hoping for."

Michael

I WON'T DENY that hearing her tell me she broke up with her boyfriend filled me with a shocking amount of relief. I never met the guy, but I didn't like the way he treated her. I can't claim to know a lot about their relationship—if anything—but what I saw convinced me that she deserves better. It's laughable to think that *I'm* somehow better, but I want her. There's a part of me that likes knowing that whatever we share, she won't be going home to give herself to someone else. It's selfish, hypocritical, and shameful. I'm fully aware. Yet, that doesn't make it any less true.

At the same time, upon first hearing the news, I was afraid that she had skipped ten steps ahead of me. To think that she expected me to make some sort of bold declaration—it filled me with a sense of panic. We've barely just begun. I don't want what's happening to end because of expectations that are too daunting for me to even wrap my head around. Except now, after what she's just said, my relief is of a different sort. We're on the same page.

Almost.

I readjust our hands so that my fingers are laced between hers. Then, after setting aside my half empty glass, I move my chair so that I'm sitting directly in front of her. Reaching up to take hold of her hip, I graze my thumb against her in slow circles as I bring my eyes level with hers.

"I want to get to know you. I want to see where this goes."

She squeezes my fingers, and I squeeze back, moving my opposite hand up to her waist.

"It's not fair. It's not fair to you—hell, it's not fair to anyone—but I can't..." I sigh in defeat, leaning forward to press my forehead against the bare skin of her chest, just above her dress. I inhale deeply when she buries her fingers in my hair, and my eyes fall closed as she tickles the nape of my neck. "I can't stay away from you," I confess on a whisper.

"I don't want you to."

Her declaration has me dropping her hand so that I can wrap both arms around her hips. She sucks in a breath when I pull her closer to the edge of my desk, her knees now straddling my sides. When I lift my head, she drops hers immediately, touching the tip of her nose to the tip of mine. The feel of her hot, shallow breaths against my lips makes my dick jerk, and the bourbon I smell on her makes me want to taste her—so I do.

Sinking my fingers in her hair, I pull her closer, until her lips are pressed against mine. The instant I flick my tongue across the seam of her mouth, she opens up for me, moaning softly as she leans into our kiss. It's not long before the soft whimpers coming from her throat have me so hard, I'm starting to feel uncomfortable. I stand, hoping a shift in position will help alleviate some of my ache.

It does nothing of the sort.

As Blaine tilts her head back, so as not to break our connection, she hitches her legs around me. With a groan, I plunge my tongue into her mouth, kissing her deeper as I ease her across my desk. The bulge in my pants connects with her center perfectly. When she digs her heels into the back of my thighs, beckoning me closer, I know she feels it, too.

I don't think as I grip one of my hands around her side, holding her as I sweep my thumb along the slight curve of the underside of her breast. She arches her back, sighing into my mouth, and I can't stop myself. I palm her small breast through her dress, and her legs grow tighter around me.

"*Michael*," she moans, rolling her hips.

Certain that I should stop, that it's imperative that we slow down, I drag my lips away from her mouth and kiss along the side of her neck. She smells amazing, like flowers in springtime, and I don't deny myself a taste. I deliver one wet kiss, then another, and then she's reaching for my wrist. She drags my hand away from her chest, down her stomach, and in between her legs. I lift my head abruptly, seeking out her eyes, and find them hooded in lust.

"I'm so wet," she pants. "I want you to see. I want you to know how much I want you. Every time I think of you. Touch me, Michael. Please."

I can't tell her no. I cannot reject her. Not like this. Not with her laid out beneath me across my damn desk—I cannot deny her when she's looking at me the way she is now. So I lift her dress and touch two fingers against her panties. My eyes fall closed of their one volition, my jaw going slack as I feel my self control slipping away from me.

She's soaking wet.

I don't know how it happens. I can't explain how it is that I don't recall moving aside the drenched fabric of her panties. All I know is that when I slip my fingers inside of her, she shudders beneath me as her hands begin frantically pulling at the buttons of my shirt.

And I don't stop her.

As I coat my fingers in her arousal, something happens in my brain.

Suddenly, I only have five senses.

I *feel* it when her hands greedily paw at my bare chest.

I *hear* it when my belt buckle clinks as we both unfasten it.

I *smell* it when the sweet scent of her arousal begins to fill the room.

I *see* it when her face relaxes into a state of bliss as I fill her.

And I *taste* it—the sound of her moan as I close my mouth around hers.

Blaine

I THOUGHT *KISSING* Michael was amazing.

I thought the feel of his hands on my body was enough to set me on fire.

And then he filled me with his big cock, and now I feel frantic and voracious and absolutely out of control.

I hadn't anticipated that this would happen. I didn't agree to meet him because I had some sort of agenda—and I believe in my heart that he didn't, either. Then he moved my panties, and it was like we both hopped on a freight train traveling a hundred miles an hour, and there was no stopping it. Now, if he stops, I'm sure I'll never recover.

I'm so wet, I can hear the sound of my arousal soaking his dick over the noise of our panting breath. I'm without a doubt that I've never been so turned on in all my life. Maybe it's because I've never had illicit sex before; or maybe it's because I've never had sex on a desk before—or maybe it's because I've never had sex with *Michael* before. Whatever the reason, I don't care. I'm too busy enjoying it to care.

When I start to sweat, I try wiggling out of my jacket. Michael's quick to help me, sliding a hand against my back and lifting me off of the desk. After I blindly toss my jacket somewhere behind me, he doesn't lay me back down. Instead, he grabs my right knee, lifting it as he holds on and pumps into me faster. My breath catches as

I grab the open flaps of his shirt and tug him closer. He brings his lips to mine without further instruction, and neither of us close our eyes as we tangle our tongues together.

For reasons I can't explain, I find that incredibly hot, and I sense it as my orgasm starts to bloom inside of me.

"*Como me haces sentir,* angel—*No puedo parar. Mierda, no puedo parar.*"

I have no idea what he just said, but the sound of his voice makes me moan anyway.

"Michael, I—" My breath hitches and my head falls back as I climb higher and higher toward my release. I let go of his shirt and slip my hands up his sweat soaked neck and into his hair. Gripping two fistfuls, I feel my body start to lock up as I whimper, "I'm gonna come. Shit, Michael—*don't stop!*"

He growls, fucking me harder, his arm around my waist holding me so close, I'm not sure we'll ever be able to pry our bodies apart. Then it hits me and my jaw falls open. The euphoria that bursts inside of me is so intense, I can't even make a sound. I'm still lost in my own orgasm when he buries his face in the side of my neck and groans deep and long. He thrusts into me twice more, and then we're both still—neither one of us letting go.

Michael

My dick twitches inside of her, and she relaxes in my hold, her hands still tangled in my hair. For a moment, I can't sense anything except for her warmth enveloping me. Then my conscience starts to awaken, and I realize what we've just done.

"*Mierda,*" I curse. "*Mierda, mierda, mierda.*"

I loosen my grip from around Blaine as I start to free her, but she clings to me, refusing to let go. When she leans back and gives me her beautiful hazel eyes, I find myself at a loss for words. My heart is at war—my mind lost somewhere between regret and longing. For the first time in my life, I've had sex with a woman who is not Veronica.

As a married man, something in the back of my mind tells me that I should feel disgusting. Something tells me that I should feel remorse and shame. In my mind, I know that what we just did was wrong. It was impulsive and stupid. In my mind, I know that the consequences of our actions are more than we could possibly measure in this moment—and I should let her go.

But then she reaches up and lightly traces her fingertips across my forehead, quietly and gently smoothing out my frown. Her eyes grow glassy as she cups my cheek in her hand and whispers, "I don't know what you're thinking, and maybe I don't want to know, but I just want to ask one thing."

She pauses for a second, long enough to bring her lips a hair's breadth away from mine before she breathes, "*Don't regret me.*"

I don't hesitate. I close my lips around hers and I kiss her ardently. I know not how else to express that she is impossible to regret.

It isn't until after we've both straightened ourselves up that my lust haze begins to fade. I think back, not merely on *what* we've done, but *how* we've done it.

"We didn't use a condom," I mumble, combing my fingers through my hair. Coughing out a dry laugh, I add, "I haven't used a condom in over a decade. I didn't think. I—"

"I'm clean, I swear," Blaine interrupts, taking a hesitant step toward me. "I'm also on the pill."

I nod my acknowledgement and inform her, "Veronica and I have only ever been with each other. I'm clean, too."

Her lips part open as she stares at me with what looks like a mix of shock and worry. Not wishing her to feel either one of those things, I gather her in my arms and seek to reassure her that what we've started is not a mistake, regardless of my history. More than that, it is merely our beginning. I meant what I said to her before, that I want to get to know her, and I intend to.

"I'd like for us to be more careful in the future."

"Yes. Of course," she agrees, leaning into me as she curls her fingers around the front of my shirt. "I'll—I'll pick up some condoms on my way home. It's probably better." Dropping her chin, she lowers her voice and says, "Your wife would suspect something if you came home with a box."

"Blaine, look at me," I insist, sliding a hand around the back of her neck. She lifts her eyes to meet mine, and I lean down to brush a kiss against her lips before I ask, "When can I see you again?"

Pressing up on her tiptoes, she gives me her slight weight, her gaze locked with mine as she whispers, "Not soon enough."

I kiss her again, and when she slips her tongue into my mouth, I know that she's right.

"You work every night this week?"

"Not Wednesday," she says hopefully, her eyes searching mine for a response.

"Wednesday then."

She grins up at me, and my hold around her tightens as she whispers, "You could come over. I could make you dinner."

"I'd like that," I admit softly, tracing my nose alongside hers.

Sliding her hands up my chest and wrapping them around my shoulders, she tilts her head back, signaling her desire for another kiss before she replies, “Me, too.”

I take my time with our next exchange, making it slow and sensual, knowing it’ll be our last for a few days. She follows my lead, and we stay lip-locked until my dick starts to harden. Reluctantly, I pull away, touching my forehead to hers.

“We should go.”

“Okay.”

“Clay will walk you out.” She nods, and I give the back of her neck a gentle squeeze, hating that I can’t take her home myself, like a gentleman.

“Wednesday. I’ll text you my address,” she says, retreating from my arms.

“Wednesday,” I repeat with a nod.

She grabs her bag and hurries to the door, turning to look at me from over her shoulder before she whispers, “Goodbye, Governor.”

Smirking, I wink at her and call back, “Goodbye, angel.”

As soon as I step foot into the mansion, I head straight for the shower. I’m relieved when I manage to submerge myself under the spray of hot water without being stopped or questioned by Veronica. Nevertheless, as I wash away the scent of Blaine, I do so regretfully. It makes me feel like a bastard to admit it, but it’s not the smell of our intimate encounter on my skin that I regret, but the fact that I have to wash it away so soon. As awful as the truth may be, the anticipation that consumes me as I look forward to Wednesday evening makes it hard for me to hold onto any sort of self-degradation.

I've never been both fully cognizant of my actions and yet entirely confused by them at the same time. While there's a part of me that has no idea what I'm doing, there's another part me—the *primal* part of me—that knows exactly what I'm doing. Not only that, but as I rinse my body of soap, I make up my mind that I don't want to fight this war anymore. It's been weeks since I first met Blaine; weeks since the catalyst for what happened not even an hour ago on my damn desk was sparked. There are still more questions riddling my mind than there are answers—but the answers I *do* have are the only ones that I care about.

I know that she desires me as much as I crave her.

I know what it feels like to hold her in my arms.

I know how her skin tastes after she's come on my cock.

I know that she wants more—and so do I.

It's already been decided. We're in this together, and I won't fight it. I won't justify it. I won't condemn it. Rather, I intend to enjoy it, like any journey worth traveling.

"Mike?" Veronica calls out, yanking me from my thoughts as she enters the bathroom. "Hey, I didn't hear you come in."

"Yeah. Got in a minute ago," I reply, not moving from beneath the spray of water.

"Did you get the work done that you needed?"

My mind fills with the memory I now hold of Blaine's face as I slid into her hot, wet center, and I look down at my dick as it starts to fill with blood. Clearing my throat, I answer, "It was a productive evening."

"Good. I'm glad. Are you tired? Do you need anything?"

"I'm okay, babe. Thanks."

She hums in response, and then I watch through the steamy glass as she takes her leave. Glancing back down at my semi-hard cock, I'm sure Wednesday can't come soon enough.

Fifteen

Michael

I FIND MYSELF GLANCING AT THE DOORS I bypass as I ascend to the fifth floor. The neighborhood where her building is located seems safe enough, and I don't notice anything noteworthy as I make my climb. When I reach the landing of the top floor, I count four other doors—each one facing the stairwell—and spot Blaine's to my right. Anxious to be in her company, I don't linger in the hallway, but move toward her residence and knock without hesitation.

A faint trace of music sneaks out from beneath her door, and I listen for her footsteps as she approaches. Just as she twists the deadbolt, I hide the bouquet of flowers I picked up on the way over behind my back. When the barrier that stands between us is swung open, I breathe deeply, an uncontainable smile stretching across my face as I take her in.

Her hair is pulled up into a little, messy bun on top of her head, a few loose strands hanging against the sides of her neck. She's in a pair of holey, blue, cut-off, jean shorts that show off her slim legs, and a black t-shirt she wears tucked in that reads: *Stay Home. It's Too Peopley Out There.* Her feet are bare, but she's got a thin chain that hangs around her ankle, and a toe ring on her left foot. Dressed the way she is, she appears far younger and more carefree than I can ever remember being—but more than that, she looks *gorgeous.* There's something so unapologetic about her, with no makeup and no frills; something that screams—*this is me on purpose*—and I admire that about her.

"I'm extremely overdressed," I mutter, looking down at the suit I wore to work today.

She bites the inside of her cheek, tugging her pursed lips to one side of her mouth as her eyes give me a once over. She then blushes and tells me, "I could change."

Grinning, I step toward her, leaning down so I can greet her properly. My lips a breath away from hers, I assure her, "I was only kidding."

I feel her smile as I kiss her hello, and she leans into it, making my chest swell and my dick twitch. Then she grabs hold of my tie and pulls me closer while simultaneously backing into her apartment. I don't resist, but bring my arms out from behind my back and wrap them around hers as I taste her lips. She opens up for me as if to deepen our kiss, but then the rattling of the plastic wrap around the flowers distracts her. Craning her neck, she twists to look over her shoulder, hanging onto my arms to keep her balance. Upon catching a glimpse of my gift, she turns around completely, putting her back to my front, and takes hold of the bundle.

"Are these for me?"

Chuckling, I grip the sides of her waist and ask, "What do *you* think?"

She leans against me, lifting the flowers to her nose to get a whiff of their scent. I remain still, content to bask in her unabashed reaction to my simple gift. Looking up at me, she replies, "I think you're super hot and you brought me flowers, which means that I should definitely check on dinner because you deserve a meal that's *not* burnt."

"Then I suppose I better let you go," I mutter, giving her sides a squeeze.

"Only for a little while," she replies with a bashful smile before twisting out of my hold. I watch her as she closes the door behind me and then makes her way into the kitchen. "You can sit or look around or whatever you want. Oh, um—" She spins and faces me, now clutching an empty mason jar against her chest as she insists, "Just ignore the mess in the corner. I'm—*rearranging*." She shrugs and turns away from me once more, and I take in the details of her place.

To my right, I spot three doorways—one with a door, two without. The door furthest from me appears to be her bathroom. I'm not sure about the other two spaces, but I'd guess at least one of them is a closet. Deciding that I'm more interested in what I *can* see, I shift my attention to the main part of her loft apartment.

Her kitchen is to the left of the front entrance—her refrigerator sharing the same wall and stationed next to an industrial, metal shelving unit, which appears to serve as an open pantry. On the adjacent wall is her stove and oven, kitty-corner to her sink and dishwasher—the extra counter space along the back of the sink doubling as a low breakfast bar, of sorts. She's got butcher top counters and stainless steel appliances that are a strikingly attractive contrast to the exposed brick backdrop of the whole apartment.

Beyond the kitchen, her dining table is situated to be a sort of focal point, the black square surface surrounded by four wooden, backless chairs that match her counters. To the left of her dining area is her sitting room. She's got a navy blue sofa, with a pale gray throw blanket over the back, pushed up against the wall. It sits on top of a large, light blue area rug, along with a low set coffee table covered in magazines and coffee table books.

On the opposite side of her dining room is a spiral staircase that leads up to her loft space. Her bed—which looks remarkably like a golden yellow, chain-link fence constructed into a contemporary, edgy, sleigh bed of some kind—sits between two small nightstands. Her white bedding with navy and gray throw pillows ties in the colors she seems to like best, and I wonder if she's not so young as she is charmingly sophisticated.

"Your place is amazing," I tell her, not bothering to mask the awe in my voice as I slowly walk further into the room.

"Thank you. I've worked really hard to make it my home."

"I can see that." Shrugging off my jacket, I make my way toward the staircase to drape it over the railing, stopping short at the piles of books I find scattered all over the floor. "What happened over here?"

"I thought I said to *ignore* the mess," she says, amusement laced in her tone.

I toss my jacket over the railing and unfasten my cuffs, rolling up my sleeves as I glance over at her. When I quirk a curious eyebrow, she rolls her eyes and continues arranging her flowers in the mason jar now filled with water before she mumbles, "One sec."

After quickly peeking into the oven, she brings her flowers to the dining room table and then comes to join me. Pointing at the now empty bookshelf pulled out a few inches from the dark corner under her loft, she informs me, "That is a *bitch*. I thought if I took all the books off that I could move it. I moved everything else," she declares, pressing her fists on her hips. "I probably grunted and cursed more than I should have, but I managed. Anyway, I want this shelf in that corner." She points to the empty space beside her couch and the wall, then shrugs. "It escaped my memory that I wasn't the one who put that iron bitch there in the first place."

Fighting a grin, I fold my arms across my chest and inquire, "Why is it that you were so adamant about moving around your furniture all on your own?"

With a sigh, she casts her gaze down at her feet and admits, "I wanted it to be different. I didn't want to look around and be reminded of the missing pieces of Mateo."

I let her words sink in for a moment. It doesn't escape me that regardless of whether or not she felt it best to end things with her boyfriend of two years, the absence of him must still be felt. It might seem like a simple confession to someone else, but I appreciate her telling me her intentions.

When she doesn't lift her gaze, I reach my hand out and tip up her chin. Tracing the pad of my thumb across her plump, lower lip I murmur, "I'll move it after dinner."

"Really?" she breathes, her hazel eyes growing wide in excitement.

"Really."

Pursing her lips to the side, she steps toward me and asks, "Are you hungry?"

I smile down at her, thinking about how much I've been looking forward to tonight—recalling every moment I got distracted day dreaming about her over the last couple of days. Sometimes, I'm sure I'm going crazy, my carnal nature never having been so greedy before. Now that I'm here, now that the *pull* that I feel toward her seems to ease just being in her presence, I'm not sure she could even begin to understand that she's already satisfying my insatiable hunger merely breathing the same air as me.

Dragging my thumb over her lip and down her chin, I then drop my hand to my side and admit, "I'm starving."

Blaine

SURE THAT OUR DINNER will burn if I don't break away from his heated gaze, I bite my tingling lip and hurry around him. Honestly, I've been an anxious mess all day, preparing for him to be here. As soon as I woke up, I started cleaning. I'd been rearranging the loft for a couple of days, trying to decide where I wanted to put things, and I had stuff everywhere. As soon as I was satisfied with my current set up—excluding the bookshelf, of course—I hopped in the shower and then started preparing dinner. Now that Michael's here, the sound of his dress shoes against the hardwood floor as he looks around heard over the music I've got playing low, my anxiety has given way to excitement.

He likes it here—and I like him *here.*

"Can I ask you a personal question?"

After taking another look into the oven and seeing that the flatbread is ready, I grab an oven mitt and answer, "Sure."

"You do all right living here without the help of another income?"

Placing the baking sheet on top of the stove, I glance over and see Michael, now sitting in a stool on the opposite side of the breakfast bar. I can tell by the expression on his face and the tone of his voice that he's not trying to be nosy. He wants to make sure I'm okay.

Propping myself up next to the sink, I offer him a nod and explain, "Mateo actually never really contributed much. He only lived here for six months. I've been here for almost four years. When mom passed, dad insisted that I take the majority of her life insurance policy money. He helped me invest some, and then I put a decent down payment on this place—enough to make my monthly mortgage payments manageable. I've always made a decent amount of money at the Lounge, so I'm good."

His eyebrows shoot up in awe as he asks, "You own this place?"

"Working on it," I reply with a giggle.

"*Es tan sabia como es hermosa.*"

Smiling, I lean across the counter, shortening the distance between us as I ask, "What did you just say?"

His eyes dance around my face before he murmurs, "I like you."

I sense it as a blush fills my cheeks at the same time that my stomach clenches tightly. Feeling bashful, in that way that only seems to happen in Michael's presence, I admit, "I like you, too."

He winks at me, sending another flurry of excitement right through me, and then he asks, "What did you make? It smells delicious."

"Right. Dinner!" I straighten, clasping my hands together at my chest as I inform him, "I made honey mustard chicken salad with avocado and bacon, along with something called California chicken flatbread—also with avocado and bacon—topped with chipotle ranch. I can hold the ranch if you don't like it. I've had it, though, and I promise it's better with the ranch. Oh, and I hope you like avocado. Shit, I didn't think to ask. I love it and—"

"Blaine," he interrupts softly. He then coughs out a laugh,

smiling at me warmly as he goes on to say, "It sounds amazing. You didn't have to go to so much trouble for me, but I'm excited to try it. How can I help?"

After instructing him to grab the two bowls of salad I prepped just minutes before he arrived from out of the fridge, I plate the flatbread and join him at the table. I sit for only a second, and then jump up, remembering that we need silverware. When I return with forks, knives, and napkins, I sit once more before I notice I forgot something to drink.

"Dammit," I laugh. "Did you want something to drink?" I start to stand, but he takes hold of my hand and gives my fingers a squeeze.

"Let me. Tell me what you've got and where to get it. You've outdone yourself already."

"Um," I start to say, using my free hand to sweep a stray strand of hair behind my ear. "Well, I've got water or wine. I wasn't sure if you liked wine or not."

"Wine is good."

"Okay. It's on the counter. Glasses are to the right of the stove."

"Got it."

I watch as he gets up and makes his way into my kitchen. He finds my stemless wine glasses without trouble, and then the bottle of wine. When he asks after the corkscrew, I tell him where he can find it, and then proceed to stare as he uncorks the bottle. For reasons that I don't know how to explain, watching him do something so simple sends a warmth through my chest and straight down do my core. Maybe it's because I like the way he looks in my kitchen; or maybe it's because I've missed him these last couple of days; or maybe it's because since having sex with him in his office, I've imagined having sex with him in a variety of other places—including my kitchen.

Shaking my head clear of my lustful thoughts, I thank him when he sets my wine in front of me, and then we both dig into our meal.

"You've one-upped me," he says, holding up a slice of flatbread. "Tastes even better than it smells. Definitely beats a hotdog."

"Thank you," I reply on a laugh. "But don't knock the hotdogs. I wasn't lying about how much I love them. When I'm home, though, I try to keep it pretty healthy. You'd be surprised with how many low-carb, healthy-fat recipes I've got in my repertoire that include *bacon*."

"Oh, yeah?" he asks with a grin before taking another bite of the flatbread. "I'm surprised. I didn't take you for the calorie counting type."

"I'm not," I mutter around my mouthful, dismissing the thought with a wave of my hand and a playful scowl. "Definitely not." He looks at me, obviously curious for more of an explanation, and patiently waits for me to swallow before I continue. "My dad—he's the reason I got into cooking. I mean, I'd help mom out a little when I lived with them, but right after she died, dad's health kind of took a turn.

"He had a heart attack. It scared the shit out of me. We knew he had high cholesterol and that he needed to be careful about what he ate, but he was grieving, not thinking about his diet. Anyway, we made a deal. He has to watch what he eats, and I help out as often as I can. He's really good about eating leftovers, so I like to stock his fridge a few times a month."

"I take it he likes bacon?" he asks, spearing his fork with his next bite of salad.

My eyes grow wide, and I nod my head enthusiastically as I reply, "More than you could possibly imagine."

"I like him already," Michael chuckles.

While we finish our meal and enjoy our wine, I talk a little bit more about dad, and he tells me more about his parents, too. He fills me in on his day, and I tell him about mine, and it's nice—just like our first date. One conversation flows into another and then, before I know it, we're both finished with our food. He helps me clear the table, and as I refill our glasses of wine, he moves my bookshelf across the room.

I'm not sure watching him move a shelf should be sexy—but it totally is.

To my surprise, as soon as he has the bookshelf where I want it, he starts picking up my books. "Are these stacked in any particular order?" he asks, both of his hands full of paperbacks.

Setting our wine down on the coffee table, I shake my head and join him. "No. I'm sure a different kind of book lover would go insane knowing that I have no rhyme or reason to how I store my books, but I like it that way."

"You've got quite the collection," he says, picking up another stack. Tilting his head to inspect the bindings, he reads off, "Tolstoy, Fitzgerald, Woolf, Austen—you like the classics."

"I've got a little of everything." I grab a copy of *The Girl with the Dragon Tattoo* by Stieg Larsson and *The Reader* by Bernhard Schlink, holding them both up for him to see. He smirks at me when his eyes fall to the next book on my stack, *Warm Bodies* by Isaac Marion sitting right on top. "See?" I giggle.

"I do," he replies, headed back toward the shelf.

"There's something about classic lit," I concede, filling my arms with another stack. As I slide the books alongside the others, I go on to explain, "They talked differently. It's like their words held more meaning or maybe that the author had a relationship with words different than we do now. I can't really explain it."

"It's been a while since I read for pleasure. Even longer since I read a piece of *fiction* literature for school—but I remember books like *Moby Dick*. God, I hated that book."

I can hear the smile on his face even before I look up next to me and see it with my own eyes. His attention still focused on my collection of books, he goes on to tell me, "I always justified stories like those, stories that seemed to last forever with such vivid details, with the time in which they were written. No television. No cell phones. Go back far enough, they didn't even have radios. Can you imagine? Long, slow evenings with nothing to do but sit in the house and let the hours pass. I figured, books like these were great entertainment back then."

"Yes. Exactly. I bet that each reader hung on every word."

His phone chimes from within his pocket, and the small sound seems to break our moment. I bite the inside of my cheek, waiting for him to check the device, suddenly realizing that I can't have him all night. He's been here for over an hour already, and I'm not sure how much time we have. When he lifts his hand from his side, I don't expect him to reach for my chin, and my eyes meet his as his thumb rubs across my cheek, causing me to lose hold of the nub inside of my mouth.

"How much longer can you stay?" I whisper, afraid of the answer.

"A while," he replies, not even bothering to check the time.

"Okay." Bringing a hand up to touch his waist, I find my manners and say, "Thank you. For your help, I mean."

"You're welcome."

My eyes drop down to his lips and stay there. Even though he said he could stay a while, I know that anything short of all night won't be long enough. Every moment we have together is stolen, and I don't know when I'll get to see him again. The more I get to know him, the longer the days in between our visits seem. Something tells me that after tonight, I'll be well acquainted with a new longing in the morning.

"Michael?" I say softly, taking a step toward him.

"Hmm?" he hums in return, his hand sliding to hold me around the back of my neck.

With my gaze still trained on his lips, I press my chest against his and pleadingly echo, "Michael?"

He groans quietly, leaning down to touch his forehead to mine before his voice rumbles, "God, angel—if you say my name one more time—"

"*Michael,*" I breathe, *aching* for him to kiss me.

A low growl vibrates his chest as he crashes his lips against mine, causing me to free a whimper. Immediately, I push myself up onto my tiptoes, circling my arms around his neck as my entire body begins to buzz in anticipation. He leans into me, engulfing me in his arms, and I'm certain I've never wanted to give myself to a man the way I want to give myself to him. Then he flicks his tongue against my lips, sending a shock of tingles to my belly, and I open up in invitation. When he hums into my mouth, I squeeze him tighter, wanting him closer, and I can feel any and all sense of self-control slipping away from me.

Just like the other night, all that exists is his touch—his kiss.

All I desire is Michael.

"I want you," I practically beg between kisses.

"*Te deseo,*" he mumbles in reply. He pulls away from me enough to look into my eyes, and I know that no matter what he said, we're on the same page. He confirms it when he grunts, "Bed."

Nodding my emphatic reply, I sigh, "Yes."

"Condoms."

Breathless with excitement, I don't even try hiding my smile as I inform him, "Nightstand."

"Now."

Giggling, I push myself out of his arms, taking him by the hand as I start toward the spiral staircase. "Yes, sir."

Michael

She doesn't let go of my hand as we hurry up the steps to her bedroom space. When we've reached the highest point of her loft, I'm barely cognizant of the fact that there's still plenty of ceiling above us—enough where I can stay fully upright as I kiss Blaine and reach for the sides of her t-shirt, pulling it from out of her shorts. I'm too busy concentrating on undressing her, *needing* her to be naked, for me to worry about anything else.

The last time I was inside of her it was hurried and desperate. While I'm feeling no less anxious to have her now, I do intend on taking advantage of the privacy of her place—the comfort of her bed—and every single second I've stolen to be with her tonight.

Blaine's got my tie undone by the time I've untucked her shirt. She slides it from underneath my collar, and I feel underneath the fabric on her back, my hands gliding up the soft skin at her sides and squeezing her waist. When her hands are free, she pulls her lips from mine and reaches for the hem of her t-shirt.

"*Faster*, Michael," she begs on a sigh.

My dick grows even harder hearing her repeat my name with so much fire. As she uncovers her chest, exposing her sheer, lacy, black bra, I can't get undressed quickly enough. Looking away from her only so that I can see the buttons that stand in my way, I get half of them undone before I give up. Reaching behind me, I tug the fabric over my head. It hits the floor at the same moment that I begin toeing my feet from out of my shoes while loosening my belt buckle. My trousers fall to my ankles, and I'm quick to discard my undershirt before I stop to catch another glimpse of Blaine.

I freeze at the sight of her. She's standing completely still—her arms dangling at her sides, her lips parted open, and her eyes wide in wonder. Her thin bra and matching lacy panties are still covering her up, and my hands itch to touch her. She's stunning. Her curves are subtle, her shape narrow and petite. Her breasts are small, her belly is flat, her legs are toned, and her skin is without blemish. I want to know every inch of her. I want to *see* all that she is. The *unknown* that stands before me calls to the primal man that lives inside of me, and I *hunger* for her fervent passion. I *thirst* for the woman who laid across my desk and pleaded with me to touch her.

"You're—you're beautiful," she breathes, interrupting my lustful thoughts.

"As are you, angel."

Peeking into my eyes shyly, she runs her teeth over her bottom lip before she says, "I want to see all of you."

I step out of my pants, sliding my socks from over my feet before closing the short distance between us. She sucks in a breath when I pull her against me, my stiff cock pressing against her stomach as she brings her hands up against my chest. Without a word, I unhook her bra, and she hesitantly moves to drop the scrap of fabric at our feet.

"God, I'm shaking, I want you so badly," she murmurs, smashing her small tits against me. I feel the tremor in her hands as she feels her way over my pecs, her fingers grazing my chest hair. "I know this isn't our first time, but it sort of feels like it, you know? I'm a little nervous. Do you feel that? I mean—have you seen you? 'Cause, I mean—"

I cut her off with a kiss, sweeping my tongue through her open mouth. I kiss her long and hard, and she moans as she presses her body tighter against mine. It's not long before she's no longer thinking about her nerves. I know this when she skims her hands down my sides and into my boxer briefs. She gropes my ass, eliciting a groan from me, and drags one of her hands around to my front.

"*There's my girl*," I mutter against her lips as she curls her fingers around my cock. "Don't be nervous. I want you, too." She grazes her thumb over the head of my shaft, and I jerk in her hold. "*Maldita sea*—I want you *right now*."

Casting her gaze down her cheeks, she manages a deep breath before she pulls my underwear down to my ankles. Rising back up to full height, she then reaches for her lacy panties and wiggles her way out of them. I watch as she climbs across her bed and pulls open the drawer of the furthest nightstand. After taking out a condom, she rips the package open with her teeth and makes her way back toward me on her knees.

Sitting back on her heels, she removes the condom and then looks up at me. I step toward the side of the bed, my dick jutting straight out, and she reaches for me, carefully rolling on the thin layer of rubber.

"We don't have much time." As soon as she speaks the words, her cheeks heat in a blush. Frowning, she shakes her head, as if reprimanding herself for reminding us both exactly what it is we're doing here. "I just meant—"

"I know what you meant, Blaine," I assure her, crawling toward her, easing her onto her back, and settling myself between her legs.

She wraps her arms around my shoulders as her gaze locks with mine.

"I don't want to waste another minute with you, either."

Blaine

No sooner are the words out of his mouth, and his lips are on mine as he slides his stiff length along my center, nudging my clit with his head. He feels so good—his magnificent physique all around me, making me feel small and completely at his mercy. I shudder as he teases me while tangling his tongue with mine. When our breaths grow heavy and he starts grinding down on me harder, he grunts before reaching between us to position himself at my entrance. My legs fall open wider as he thrusts into me urgently, and I suck in his exhale as I stare up at him.

His eyes are stormy, the dark blue of his irises and his dilated pupils speaking of his current state. He groans as he pulls out of me slowly, and then he thrusts forward—sure and deep. I gasp, holding onto his huge biceps for leverage as I arch my back and lift my hips to take as much of him as I can hold.

"*Angel,*" he sighs.

I whimper as he begins to set a steady pace, easing out carefully before returning determinately. Never once does his gaze stray from mine, and I'm breathless as I get lost in all that is *him*. His cock fills me up and stretches me open in a way that makes me feel blissfully full. I hold onto him as he coaxes my orgasm, my arousal just as abundant as it was the last time we were together. Except, unlike our illicit moment on his desk, I sense that there's a part of him that he's holding back. It's like he's here, but he's also someplace else. I don't know how I know. I can't explain it—but the fire in his eyes doesn't match what his body is giving me, and I want all of him. I want us to be lost *together.*

"Mike," I mumble, lifting my legs and hooking them around him.

He grunts, jerking into me a bit harder, and a spark of excitement flickers inside of me.

"*Michael,*" he says on a growl.

"What?" I sigh, temporary distracted.

He kisses me, rolls his hips, and then mutters, "When I'm inside of you, you call me *Michael.*"

Something about his demand makes me giddy, and I smile as I say, "I'll call you whatever you want me to. *Michael. My lover. The Mighty Governor.*"

Chuckling, he thrusts into me again, running his nose along mine before he whispers, "Just Michael."

I nod, reaching up to sink my fingers into his hair. Then, remembering why I called his name in the first place, I tighten my legs around him and plead, "*Michael?*"

"Hmm?"

"Whatever it is you're holding back? *Stop*. I want all of you." I close my eyes, feeling both shy and needy all at once, and then lift my head to kiss his lips. Without pulling away, I insist, "Fuck me, Michael. Fuck me *harder.*"

Michael

A SENSATION THE likes of which I've never known races up my spine at her command, and my hands fist the blanket beneath her as I try to control myself. Then she forces her tongue into my mouth, and I realize *control* is exactly what she's asking me to let go of. I wasn't even aware that I was being gentle with her, stifling the raw urge I harbor to possess her in her bed the way I did in my office—when I wasn't thinking, just *feeling*.

"Michael, *baby*, I need you to *move!*" Blaine begs, squeezing her legs around me.

Her voice yanking me out of my thoughts, I look down at her and remind myself that she is not my wife. She's *my angel*, and she wants to *fuck*.

"Baby," I grunt as I prop myself up on my hands. Her grip in my hair falls away as I begin to pump in and out of her, holding nothing back. "I like that, too."

She reaches for my waist, her small hands clinging to my sides as she stares up at me—her lips parted in ecstasy. She moans, the sound making my balls ache, and I pound into her harder.

"Yes—yes—*yes*," she sighs.

With every stroke of my cock, I can sense her heightened sense of arousal. Her heat welcomes me as she grows slicker with desire, and I glide in and out of her with ease. Wanting to feel her skin—longing to touch her everywhere—I move one of my hands from beside her head and cup my palm around her breast. She pulls her bottom lip between her teeth, her brow creasing in desperation as I roll her nipple between my fingers.

"That feels so good," she breathes, closing her eyes as she presses her chest into my hand.

Releasing my hold, I slide my arm underneath the small of her back, keeping her lifted as I dip my head to take her opposite breast into my mouth.

"Oh, my god—*Michael*," she whimpers, frantically jerking her hips and digging her fingernails into my sides as I suck on her hardened bud.

Every single noise she makes spurs me on, and I want more.

"Touch yourself, Blaine. Come on my cock."

She doesn't hesitate, and I watch as she slips her hand between us, pressing her fingertips to her clit. Rubbing firm, quick circles around herself, it's not long before she's gasping, her body trembling beneath mine. She cries out, and I groan as her climax causes her core to clamp down around my dick. I pull out before she's finished, certain that I won't be able to keep a reign on myself for much longer. Replacing my shaft with my fingers, I pump in and out of her as she rides her release.

As soon as she starts to relax against the mattress, I bring my lips to hers and mumble, "On your hands and knees, angel."

"Okay, baby," she pants as she begins to flip herself.

I sit up on my knees, watching as she lands on her stomach before lifting onto all fours. When she peeks back over her shoulder at me, her hazel eyes smoldering, I'm overwhelmed by how much I want to bury myself inside of her until I come. It's more than her body. It's more than the way she's looking at me right now. It's her *obedience*—her willingness to do as I wish, no questions asked.

"Michael?"

Her voice breaks through my thoughts, and I don't waste another second before I position myself at her entrance. I slip inside of her center slowly, curving my body around hers as I rest my hands on top of her hands. She flexes her fingers, causing mine to fall between hers, and then we both hold on tightly.

Bringing my mouth to her ear, I lick her earlobe. I feel her shiver as I groan, "If I get too rough—"

She twists her neck, cutting me off with a kiss before she reminds me, "*All* of you, Michael—*please*."

Blaine

He doesn't disappoint.

He bucks his hips and rides me like he's trying to penetrate my *soul,* and it's *awesome!* Our bodies are now hot and coated in sweat, and our joined hands slip further up the bed, causing me to lean forward and bend further. His growl lets me know that he likes it, and I lick my grinning lips as he continues to drive into me.

He then takes me by surprise when he gently twists one of my arms, then my other, and pins my hands together above my ass in his solid grip. I rest on my cheek, breathless as he continues to fuck me. It only takes me a second to relax and surrender to him completely. I close my eyes, acknowledging that I feel safe at his mercy. More than that, I'm *turned on* by it. There's something about having a big, strong man at my back that excites me—so much so that it's not long before our new position has me on the brink of another orgasm.

"*Don't stop!* Oh—*baby,*" I moan. Twisting my face so that my mouth is covered, I free a muted cry into the blanket as my climax rushes through me.

Seconds later, Michael stills, his fingers squeezing my wrists even tighter. A guttural groan resounds in the rafters of my loft as he twitches with his release, filling the condom. When we both start to come down from our heightened state of passion, he frees my arms and folds his body over mine, grazing his lips along my shoulder. The weight of his bulk is better than my most vivid dreams, and I sigh, feeling sated and happy.

"*No sé de dónde saliste,* angel—*pero eres mía. Dios, tienes que ser mía,*" he mumbles against my skin.

"Wh—what? What does that mean?" I stammer, my mind a muddled mess.

It's hard to concentrate with him on top of me, his heavy legs tangled with mine, and the hair of his chest tickling my back.

Burying his face in my neck, his hot breath fans across my skin and his voice rumbles in a low, sexy tone as he tells me, "That was amazing. *Mierda*, I don't want to let you go."

I don't say anything in return. I'm not entirely convinced that he's translated what he said—but that's not what keeps me silent. It's knowing that, one day, he might actually let me go that weighs heavily on my heart. After all, I *am* the other woman. Yet, as stupid and naïve as it may be, I want so much more with him. It's true that we've barely scratched the surface with each other, but already I'm sure that my life will never be the same because of him. I thought he was pretty spectacular *before* he made me come twice in one round. Now?

Now, I can hardly believe that I spent two years with a man who didn't make me feel a fraction of what Michael is capable of making me feel in *two hours.* Now, I wonder how I lived this long without him. *Now,* I wonder if I'm crazy for the rate at which I'm falling for this man.

Most of all, I don't want him to let me go, either.

He kisses the side of my neck before he hoists himself off of me, swinging his legs over the side of the bed. My heart jump starts into a gallop, and I flip around to face him in a panic.

"You're leaving?" My voice comes out with a tremble that surprises even me, and he's quick to twist around to face me. At first, his brow is creased in a worried frown, but then I watch as his expressions softens at the sight of me.

"No. Not yet," he assures me, giving my hip a squeeze. "I just wanted to get out of this condom."

"Oh," I whisper, my cheeks heating in embarrassment. I hadn't thought of that.

He leans over to kiss me before he mutters, "I'll be right back."

True to his word, he's only gone long enough to go to the bathroom and come straight back. My eyes connect with his as soon as he reaches the loft, and he smiles at me before he returns to the bed. While he was gone, I draped the lightweight blanket at the foot of the mattress over my nakedness, but he's quick to discard it as he gathers me in his arms. Giggling, I don't protest, but snuggle up against his chest.

His smile transforming into a smirk, he tucks a fallen strand of hair behind my ear and tells me, "I love the sound of your laugh."

My stomach clenches and I try to press against him even closer. Grazing my fingers through the fine, dark hairs that cover his pecs, I murmur, "I love *this*."

"I'll keep that in mind," he chuckles, dipping his head to touch his lips to mine.

When he pulls away, his smile falls as his eyes dance around my face in that way that is characteristically *Michael*. I absentmindedly bite the inside of my cheek as I wait for him to speak, somehow knowing that he's going to.

"I want you to understand that this is not just about sex. I don't want you to ever feel as though I'm using you. I'll never get myself off and then leave—that's not what this is."

"I understand," I assure him with a nod. His words bring me comfort, filling me with the confidence to ask, "When will I see you again?"

"Soon, I hope. I don't know, though. It's Fourth of July weekend. I have a couple of events that I must attend—work and family. It's not ideal. I'm not sure I'll be able to get away."

I try to hide the fact that I'm disappointed with his answer. The rational part of me knows that it's not fair to ask him to make concessions for me; but I won't deny that there's a selfish part of me that simply wants to be in his company sooner rather than later.

"I'll call you. We'll work something out." I nod my reply, and he presses a kiss against my lips before touching his forehead to mine. "I feel like a bastard for asking but…"

"But what?" I prompt.

"Would it be all right with you if I took a shower before I left?"

"Oh," I sigh, taken aback by his request. I don't know why I am. He certainly can't go home smelling like *me*. Gently easing my way out of his arms and sitting up, I start to climb out of bed as I tell him, "Yeah. That's fine. Let me get you a towel."

I slip back into my underwear and throw my t-shirt over my head before making my way down the stairs. Michael's not long behind me, his belongings gathered in his arms as he follows after me to the bathroom. When he closes himself inside, I stand in the middle of my apartment, momentarily at a loss. Spotting our forgotten wine on the coffee table, I decide that I could use a drink right about now.

I sit on the couch with my legs curled up beneath me, sipping at the dry red liquid as I come to terms with my situation. Up until now—the *end* of our night—the reality that he's not mine felt distant; so distant, in fact, that I could almost pretend that he *was* mine. Now that our time together is drawing to a close, one word seems to be circling my brain around and around and around again.

Affair.

He's having an affair. *We* are having an affair.

While I'm no longer lying to my boyfriend, that doesn't make this anymore right than it was before. His wife is still a factor in all of this. She's why he's in the shower, rinsing off all evidence of me while I try not to be disappointed that he has to go. Yet, while my brain knows the score, my feelings for him are already stronger than my desire to do what's right. What's *right* would be to tell him to not come back, and I can't do that. I *can't*. So while it sucks that I don't know when I'll see him again, and while I hate that when I climb into bed tonight, I'll smell him but he won't be there to hold me, I'll find a way to endure. For now, it's the best either of us can do, and I know that.

When he emerges from the bathroom, he looks almost as crisp as he did when he arrived. I stand to meet him halfway, setting aside my now empty wine glass on the breakfast bar as I pass. He takes my hand when I'm in reaching distance, and we walk the couple steps it takes to reach my front door. I know that it's nearly eleven, and our borrowed time is up, so I do my best not to pout.

"Thank you for dinner. It was perfect," he says, pulling me into his arms.

"Thank you for coming."

"I'll be back." He seals his promise with a kiss, and I press up onto my tiptoes, returning his affection.

He lingers for a little while, and I follow his lead when he pulls away. Taking a step back, I whisper, "You better go."

"I'll call you," he tells me once more, his tone adamant and sure.

"I look forward to it, Governor."

His gaze trained on my lips, he reaches up and gently grazes the back of his knuckles against my cheek as he murmurs, "Michael."

I give him a smile, leaning into his touch before I reply, "Goodnight, Michael."

"Goodnight, Blaine."

After pressing one last soft kiss to my lips, he opens the door and steps into the hallway. Ridiculous as it might be, I miss him almost immediately. He's barely even made it to the stairwell before my chest starts to ache with a dull sense of restless anticipation—all the while, the soreness between my legs that he's caused makes my core yearn for the next time I get to be with him.

"*Michael*," I call out in a mock whisper, peeking my head into the hallway.

He stops his decent, looking up at me from where he stands on the stairs.

There's a tingling at my wrists as I remember the way he held them while he fucked me with all the power and strength I'd practically begged him for. Now, I bite my lip coyly, hoping that what I'm about to say leaves him as impatient for another round as I feel.

"You're welcome to bind me any time. Just make sure you BYOR."

A smile plays at his lips as confusion tugs at his eyebrows.

Laughing softly, I whisper, "*Bring your own rope*," and then I shut the door closed, locking it behind me.

Michael

I CAN'T WIPE the grin off of my face as I hurry down the stairs, her words on repeat in my head. The fact that she even suggested such a thing only confirms what I felt before—it's as if she was *made* for me.

I have sexual desires that have never been satisfied in my

marriage bed. I didn't always struggle with a need for such dominant control; but over the years, my tastes have changed, becoming more wild in nature. The things I said to Blaine are true. What's happening between us, it's not about sex. However, the fact that after one night in her bed, she was able to tap into a fantasy I've often ignored for the sake of Veronica's preferences—it makes my sated dick jerk.

Running a hand down my face as I approach the waiting town car, I breathe in a deep breath as I literally attempt to wipe away my smile. When I climb into the vehicle, I slouch into my seat, propping my head against the seat rest as I let out a heavy sigh.

"*God*—what am I doing?" I mumble.

"Was that a rhetorical question, sir?" Clay asks as he starts the engine.

I bark out a dry laugh, certain that the truth is the furthest thing from what I want to hear right now. I don't want anything to spoil the memory of this night.

"Yes. Don't answer that, I beg of you. Let's just go home."

Sixteen

Michael

Much like last year, the holiday celebrations kicked off on the third of July. Thursday evening, Veronica, my parents and I made our way down to Civic Center Park for the Independence Eve Fireworks show. Then this morning, the whole family geared up for the Liberty Run and Firecracker Kids Fun Run. Decked out in our patriotic gear, dad, Gabe, Graham, Tamara, Clay and I hit Washington Park for the four-mile distance trek—the proceeds of which benefited our veterans. After our run, we joined the others and walked with the kids for their firecracker festivities.

The location of the event made it nearly impossible for me to keep my thoughts from drifting toward Blaine every two minutes. Being only a few blocks away from her place left me at odds with my conscience. Two days without her and the reality of my responsibilities as a husband, as a son, as a brother, even as a *governor* left me wishing that I could shed it all off of me so that I could indulge in my responsibilities as a lover—*Blaine's* lover.

I was a kid when I met Veronica. Twenty-one years ago, the excitement that comes with any new romantic relationship felt a lot different. While I'd be stupid to discard the truth that the forbidden nature of my feelings for Blaine play into my temptations and my desire to be with her, it would be equally unfair and outright dishonest to say that there isn't something about her—just *her*—that makes my chest swell with emotions I had forgotten existed.

Everything is new with her, and I don't simply mean that in the sense that *she* is new to *me*. The whole *world* seems different now. Every day, as I walk through my routines and live my life, there's a new filter in my thoughts. When I pick out my tie in the morning, I wonder if Blaine would like it. When I'm on my morning run, I wonder if Blaine enjoys the outdoors. Just yesterday, a new bill crossed my desk, and I wondered what her opinion might be on the matter. I asked myself if the topic would be something she even cared to discuss, and if *I* cared if it didn't interest her at all.

Now, as I stand beside my brother in his backyard, watching as he rotates hotdogs and flips burgers on the grill, I can't stop myself from picturing the look on Blaine's face when she sat next to me at Coors Field, asking me why she was only given one hotdog. There was a twinkle in her hazel eyes that night, one that I'm already quite fond of. I can't say for certain when I'll get to see her again, but after the last two days, I know that I don't want to wait much longer.

The thought crosses my mind to sneak away and give her a call, if for no other reason than to hear her voice, but then Gabriel's voice pulls me back to the here and now.

"You're still seeing her."

I look behind me, beyond the deck and out into the grass, holding my tongue until I see Veronica. She's sitting on a blanket, spread out on the lawn. My mother is with her, holding Isabella in her lap as she blows bubbles with Josiah.

"It's just you and me up here, Mikey," says Gabe, nudging me with his elbow.

I clear my throat, sliding my hands into the pockets of my khaki shorts as I finally speak. "Yes," I answer simply.

"*And?*"

I study his profile, his attention still focused on the grill, and sense only curiosity in his inquiry. Nevertheless, what Blaine and I now share is far more intimate than it was the last time I confided in my brother, and I don't intend on laying out all the details.

"And what?"

He twists his neck to look over at me and lifts his eyebrows as he replies in a hushed voice, "*And* what's going on? What's going through your head? Give me something, man. I'm worried about you."

I free a sigh, mentally kicking myself for treating my brother—my only confidant—like he's some sort of gossip when I know that he's not. I offer him a shrug, shaking my head as I try and think of what to say.

"I like her."

"Yeah. I got that much."

"No, I mean—" I reach up and grip the back of my neck, thinking about the other night. It was so easy being in her space. It felt natural. It felt *good.* Then we got caught up in the moment, and it got better. "Gabe, I could fall for this girl."

"What are you going to do then, huh?" he asks, turning to address me directly.

"I don't know."

"I told you to be smart. How long have you known this girl? A few *weeks?* And you're over here talking about *falling* for her?"

I take a step toward him, feeling suddenly defensive. I lower my voice as I hiss, "You think I'm doing this for kicks? You think this is easy for me? It's not. I'm somebody's husband. I've been somebody's husband for so long, it's a part of my identity. And while my wife, the woman I've loved in one way or another for more than half of my life is sitting across the yard, my *head* is across the city, in an apartment—in the home of a woman who can make me smile like some dopey teenager when she's not even here. I don't know what to do with that, Gabriel. I *don't.* I have no answers, okay? Not yet."

He stares at me for a long time, his jaw locked shut as he keeps his thoughts to himself. Finally, he draws in a deep breath, shaking his head at me as he turns back to man the grill. I think he's silently dropped the subject all together, but then he asks, "She knows you're married?"

"Of course."

"She in as deep as you?"

"Pretty sure."

"I don't envy you, brother. I do not envy you."

Blaine

I'm fresh from a shower, a towel wrapped around my naked body, and my damp hair dripping onto my shoulders as I emerge from the steam-filled bathroom. Glancing at the clock across the room on my stove, I note that it's just after two o'clock, which means I need to move my ass if I plan on being to dad's house by three. I'll only get to hang out with him for a couple of hours before I have to head into work, but I don't want to miss out on seeing him on a holiday.

I step one foot over the threshold of my closet when my phone starts to ring, and I freeze immediately. I haven't heard from Michael since he left my apartment the night before last. It's entirely possible that it's not him trying to reach me right now, but just the thought that it *could* be has me racing toward the stairs. I curse myself for leaving my phone on my nightstand, then curse again when I slip and bang my knee. I hobble as quickly as I can up the rest of the steps, throwing myself across my bed as I lunge for the still ringing device. My towel comes undone in the process, but I don't even care—not when I see *The Governor* lit up across the screen.

I make a mental note to change that, knowing he prefers I not call him by his stately title, and slide my finger across the screen to pick up the call.

"Hello?" I answer breathlessly.

"Blaine?" he asks, his voice barely above a hush. "Are you all right? You sound—"

"Like I ran across the apartment, and then tripped up the stairs, and then lost my towel, leaving me naked, all because I thought it might be you trying to reach me? Because that's about right." Sucking in a deep breath, I curl onto my side. I stare through the railing of my bedroom loft, not actually seeing the rest of my apartment, too excited to hear his voice. "*Hi*," I sigh wistfully.

He's silent for a moment before I hear the quiet rumble of his low chuckle. "Are you sure you're all right?"

"I am now."

"Are you really naked?"

I laugh, glancing down at myself before I murmur, "Yes. I was just getting out of the shower when you called."

"Are you cold?"

"No." I utter the word with a smile playing at my lips, irrationally happy that he thought to ask, and amused that he thinks I could be anything but *warm* with his voice in my ear.

"Stay naked. That is, if you have a minute to talk."

Did I say warm? I meant hot.

"I do, and I will," I concede bashfully.

He blows out a slow sigh and then confesses, "I miss you, angel."

My stomach clenches, and I curl into myself even more, a zing racing down my spine at his words. It feels good, knowing that no matter how difficult and complicated our situation might be, I'm not in this alone.

"I miss you, too."

"I don't have a lot of time, but I needed to hear your voice. I'm sorry it's taken me so long to call."

"I know you're busy."

We both pause, as if each of us is coming to terms with the consequences of sneaking around. Before either of us gets too lost in our thoughts, he breaks the silence and asks, "How are you celebrating today?"

"Oh, nothing crazy. I'm going to hang out with my dad and then I've got work."

"No fireworks?"

"Dodge and I snuck out back to watch the fireworks at Civic Center Park last night. We had a pretty good view from behind the Lounge. That's good enough for me."

"I guess we were watching together, then."

"You were there?"

"Yeah. We went with my parents."

I nod, even though he can't see me, and then think about what he means when he says *we*. Another round of silence is exchanged between us, and I gnaw on my bottom lip. It only takes me a few seconds to remind myself that as much as it sucks that I found this great guy who is part of a *we*, his marital status is part of our deal. For now, this is our plight, and I won't hold it against him—it's not fair of me. Furthermore, the last thing I want to do is kill any chance we have of getting to know each other by acting standoffish when he's just calling to chat.

"So," I say, interrupting our silence, "What about you? What are you doing to celebrate?"

While I listen to him tell me about his morning, I let the sound of his voice soothe the ache I've felt over the last couple of days, not knowing when I'd see or hear from him again. I also can't deny that it's sweet, hearing how much time he's spent with his family for the holiday. I'm learning how important his family is to him, and it's just another detail that I appreciate. While my family isn't nearly as large as his, I love my people, and it's something we have in common.

"I should probably go. I'll be missed, soon," he tells me.

"Yeah. I need to get going, too," I mutter, thinking that I'm definitely going to be late to dad's now.

"I won't be able to get away to see you this weekend. There's too much going on; plus, it's a holiday. I can't use the excuse of work."

"Next week, then?"

"Monday. I don't think I can wait longer than that."

My face breaks out into a grin, and I cover my eyes with my free hand, beside myself at his transparency.

"I can work in an hour for lunch. I know it's not much, but—"

"Come over," I interrupt. "I'll be here. I don't work late on Sundays, so I'll be up."

"Don't cook. My treat."

"Okay," I say, still speaking through my smile.

"I'll see you in a couple of days."

"Can't wait."

"You have no idea, angel."

"Happy Fourth of July, Michael."

"You, too."

By the time Monday rolls around, I'm so excited to see Michael that I can hardly keep still. I tried my best to stay busy over the weekend, but it didn't stop me from thinking about him. The more I thought about him, the more I missed him. When he called late last night, we got to talk for nearly an hour, and it eased my impatience as much as it heightened it. Now, as I sit in the corner of my couch with a book in my lap, I find myself reading the same two sentences over and over again, too distracted to actually *comprehend* what I'm seeing. It also doesn't help that, every so often, I'll look across the room and smile at the sight of my flowers, still situated on the dining table. It makes my heart flutter, remembering his thoughtfulness.

My phone sounds with a text alert, and I'm quick to discard my book in order to see who it is. I snag the nub on the inside of my cheek, resisting the urge to break out into a giddy grin when I see *My Lover* lit up across my screen. His message informs me that he'll be here in five minutes, and I'm quick to hop up from the couch as I race for the bathroom to take one last look at myself before he arrives.

The denim shorts I have on are frayed at the bottom, the tips of my pockets peeking out from beneath the edge. On top, I've got on one of my favorite sweatshirts. The gray fabric is lightweight and fitted, with a pocket on the front, like a hoodie. The best part is the collar—which looks more like a pair of sweat*pants*. I wear it off my shoulders, the drawstring pulled tight enough to keep it up around my chest and strapless bra. I've left my hair down, the tips of my wavy locks tickling my bare shoulders; and I've kept my makeup light, as usual, wearing just mascara and a little lip gloss.

When a knock sounds at the door, my heart leaps in my chest, and I'm practically running on the balls of my feet as I go answer it. Knowing our time together is limited, I don't waste a second before opening up. I swear, I almost swoon at the sight of him standing on the other side of the threshold. He's not wearing a suit jacket, and his pale blue button-up, hugging him just the way that I like, is opened at the collar. Instead of a tie, he's paired his navy blue pants with a vest, which shows off the tapered cut of his waist.

It takes everything I have in me not to jump into his arms.

"Blaine?" he asks on a chuckle.

"Hmm?" I hum, snapping my gaze up to meet his.

His beautiful blue eyes smile down at me as he inquires, "Are you going to let me inside?"

"Oh, my god. Yes! Sorry," I stammer, stepping aside.

He walks right by me, and I watch him as he deposits a paper bag on my kitchen counter. He then turns back and closes the door I didn't realize was still open before gathering me into his arms. I gasp in delight, my own arms circling around his shoulders as he takes full advantage of my parted lips and greets me with his tongue.

My stomach clenches, and I swear, I'm wet in a matter of seconds.

I tighten my grip around him when he frees a soft moan into my mouth. Then I kick my legs up, hooking them around the back of his thighs. With a grunt, he drops a hand to grab my ass and effortlessly hoists me up higher. I squeak in surprise and excitement, adjusting my legs around his hips as he continues to kiss me. I'm barely aware that we're moving until he sets me on the counter beside my sink. His hands slide down and around my waist, and he gives me a squeeze before pulling his lips away from mine.

His chest heaves with his labored breaths as his eyes dance around my face. I feel my way over his shoulders and down his chest, greedily clinging to his vest as I press my knees into his sides. I want *more.* How he found it within himself to stop, I have no idea. I tug on him a little, my gaze trained on his lips—red from our fervent hello—and he leans toward me, pressing his forehead to mine.

His hands clench around me, and I sigh in want, tilting my head back in an attempt to reach his mouth. He groans before mumbling, "If we don't stop, we won't eat."

"Are you hungry?"

He coughs out a laugh, running his nose alongside mine. "That's currently a surprisingly complicated question, angel."

Tugging him even closer, I brush my lips over his as I whisper, "*Un-complicate* it."

Speaking into my mouth, he all but growls, "I don't have *time* to have you the way I want, and I made you a promise."

Closing my eyes, I pull my lips away from his, burying my face in his neck. He smells so wonderful, I lose track of my thoughts for a second, and I can't recall which promise he's referring to. Then his hands skim up my back, gently holding the nape of my neck, and my heart swells in remembrance.

I'll never get myself off and then leave—that's not what this is.

Nodding my head in understanding, I take a deep breath, kiss the underside of his jaw, and then force myself to let him go.

"Let's eat. What'd you bring me?"

While he reaches for the bag beside us, I try and ignore the throbbing between my legs. It's not easy, especially not when he tells me that he brought me a salad—in an attempt to keep it healthy—but that if I wanted part of his sandwich, he'd happily share.

"Half and half?" I ask hopefully.

"You got it."

He steps out from between my legs to grab us some plates. I hop off the counter to open the salad and unwrap the sandwich, trying not to think about how much I like that he remembered where my plates are stored. When our lunch is divided, I set the food on the breakfast bar, and he takes a seat on one of the stools while I get us each a small mason jar of water. As soon as I sit beside him, he rests a hand around my bare thigh, affectionately earning my attention.

His perfect irises seem a tad bit lighter today, reminding me of a calm, deep blue sea, and I can't help but lean toward him a little as he looks at me. Speaking through a panty-melting smile he says, "Hi."

"Hi," I murmur in reply.

He pecks my lips with his own before picking up his sandwich and explaining, "I believe I rudely skipped over that before."

I laugh, reaching for my fork as I assure him, "If *that* was you being rude, feel free to show up on my doorstep and be rude as often as you'd like."

"I'll see what I can do," he chuckles.

"So, how's your day going?"

"Busy, as per usual," he mutters, speaking around a mouthful. He chews and swallows before he goes on to say, "Some days it feels like I'm being pulled in a million different directions. This morning was a lot of meetings. The forecast for the afternoon doesn't look a whole lot different. Then again, it's Monday."

"Why do you do it? I mean, what is it about politics that makes you excited to get up and go to work everyday? Well, assuming you *are* excited to get up and go to work everyday."

"Most days I am. I consider it an honor and a privilege that people have put their trust in me to fill my office. It's not without its challenges. Actually, I think that's what I like most about it—by nature, the job *is* a multitude of challenges that must be addressed head on every day. That's the beauty of democracy. Opinions matter, and it's my job to try and make sure that the people are heard. I'd like to think that this is the most effective way for me to express how much I care about my fellow citizens. I know people have their doubts about democracy, about our government as a whole, and the way that it's run; sometimes, I can't blame them. No system is flawless, but it's a politician's job to make it the best it can be."

I can't contain my grin as I listen to his reply. Hearing the passion in his voice reminds me of the first couple of times that he came to the Lounge. It's quite apparent that he's doing what he was made to do.

"What are you smiling about over there?" he asks before taking a bite of salad.

Giggling, I confess, "I like how geeked out you get whenever you talk politics."

"Yeah? And what makes you *geek* out? What's your dream job?"

I shrug, looking down at my plate. In all honesty, I hate it when people ask me that question. At twenty-four, I feel like I should know the answer by now, but I don't. After mom died, it was all I could do to finish college. I did it knowing that she'd have wanted me to. She always taught me to *never* quit, and I wasn't about to let her down. Then I started working at the Prohibition Lounge, and it felt like a good enough place for me to settle while I got my shit together. Apparently, I haven't quite worked it all out yet.

"Hey," Michael says softly, reaching over to playfully pinch my knee.

I force a smile as I look at him, and he creases his brow at me. I can tell without him having to say a word that he's not impressed with my *liar's* smile, which makes me laugh a little.

"It's kind of annoying how you do that."

"Do what?"

"See through me," I murmur with a slight blush. He smirks, and I pretend not to be affected by it as I try to offer him an explanation as quickly as possible. "Anyway, to answer your question, I don't know. I'm sure I'm not the type who could be happy sitting behind a desk all day. Hospitals freak me out, and I don't think I could survive anymore school, so anything in the medical field is a *no*. Kids are great, but trying to teach a classroom full of them sounds a little bit like torture, so teaching isn't my thing either. I can figure stuff out on the computer easily enough, but I'm no techy. I just—" I shrug once more, shaking my head as I repeat, "I don't know."

"I think that's okay," he replies nonchalantly.

Surprised to hear him say such a thing, given that he's the freaking *governor* of Colorado, I lamely ask, "You do?"

"I do," he reiterates. "When did you graduate from college? A year ago?"

"Year and a half," I reply, tucking a bit of hair behind my ear. "I finished early."

"That's not so long ago. You have plenty of time to figure out what it is that makes you happy and then go after it. There's no rule that says you have to graduate from college with some master plan. Hell, these days, even if your generation *does* have a plan, the workforce spits it out without batting an eyelash."

"My generation, huh?" I ask teasingly, nudging my knee against his. "Careful. You're starting to sound like my dad."

He scowls at me playfully before he grunts, "I'm not *that* old."

Giggling, I lean toward him and press a kiss to his cheek. "You don't have to convince me," I whisper into his ear. "I'm well aware of how *virile* you are."

He sucks in a slow, deep breath, turning slightly to press his cheek to mine as he whispers back, "Don't start, Blaine. Finish your lunch."

Pursing my lips together in an attempt to hide my grin, I straighten in my stool before I murmur, "Yes, sir."

Michael

I'M NO STRANGER to the term *sir*. People have been calling me that for years—as far back as when I held the office of District Attorney. Yet, for unexplained reasons, Blaine is certainly the first person who has ever made my cock swell when using the term. *Polite* is not how I would describe her intentions—neither would it be an appropriate way to articulate the things I want to do to her when I hear the word pass her lips.

It's not long before our lunch is gone. When we're both

finished, Blaine gets up and clears our plates. After rinsing and stowing the dishes in the dishwasher, she props herself against the counter, biting on the inside of her cheek before she asks, "How much time do we have?"

I flip my wrist to check my watch, noting that our borrowed moments are slipping away faster than I'd like to admit. "Twenty-five minutes," I inform her. She nods, looking about as disappointed as I feel, and I jerk my chin as I insist, "Come here."

She's quick to respond, walking around the counter as I stand from my stool. When she's in reaching distance, I take hold of her hand and lead her to the couch. I sit in the corner, lifting my arm in invitation for her to join me on the other side, and she snuggles against me without hesitation. It boggles my mind how natural this is—how good it feels, and how she seems to fit against me like she's been burrowing herself in my arms for years instead of days.

"Can we do this again?" she asks on a whisper, tilting her head back to look at me.

"I'd like that."

Sliding her arm around my waist, she relaxes into me further as she murmurs, "Soon?"

"I could make Friday work."

"Just tell me when and I'll make sure I'm up."

I assure her that I will, and then dip my head to seal my word with a kiss. I don't mean to linger, aware that we're running out of time, but then she sneaks a taste of my lips and I can't resist. It doesn't take long for us to escalate from light, teasing affection to hot, fervent touching. Remembering what it feels like to have her naked body beneath mine makes my hands greedy, and I'm all over her—but it's *her* all over *me* that has my throbbing dick pressing against the seam of my pants. I groan when she shifts and straddles my lap, grinding down on my erection as she sighs into my mouth.

"Blaine," I warn.

I know my tone means nothing when I've got a hand molded around one of her breasts, my lips leaving a trail of wet kisses along her bare shoulder, but it doesn't hurt to try.

"I want you so badly," she whimpers, pressing down on me again.

Sure that I won't be able to hold on to my self control much longer with her on top of me, I grip my hands around her waist and move her to the cushion beside me. Before she can protest, I shift my body and plant a knee between her legs, leaning over her until she's laying flat on her back.

"*Me provocas más allá de los límites de mi control,*[11]" I mutter, reaching for the buttons on her shorts.

"What are you—what are you saying?" she asks breathlessly.

Once I've freed the last of three buttons, I grab hold of the hem and tug. She lifts her hips, helping me to rid her of the garment as I semi-translate, "I can't deny you."

She grins, wiggling her legs as I strip her panties off, and then she starts to sit up and reach for me. I brush away her hands, shaking my head at her as I remind her, "We don't have time, angel. Lay back."

Capturing her plump, lower lip between her teeth, she does as I say immediately. After I sit, I take hold of her legs, lifting her hips as I hook her knees over my shoulders. She gasps as I bring my face to her bare, naked pussy, and I smile down at her before I take my first taste. The second my tongue glides over her wet entrance, she moans, and I know I'll never be the same.

She tastes good. *Amazing*. Better than anything I've ever had

---

11 You tempt me beyond the limits of my control.

before, and I can't stop myself from devouring her. I thrust my tongue inside of her, lapping up her arousal, and then lick my way to her clit. She rolls her hips as she whimpers, her legs locking around my neck, and I love every second. I don't pull my mouth away from her as I blindly reach underneath her shirt and unhook her bra. Understanding what I want, she rips the thing off, tossing it onto the floor, and I take each of her breasts into the palms of my hands.

"Fuck, Michael," she pants, arching her back and bucking her hips.

A deep growl reverberates from my chest, my cock now painfully hard as I suck on her clit and pinch her nipples. She mewls softly, taking hold of my wrists and holding on tight.

"*Don't stop*," she begs as I flick her sensitive nub with the tip of my tongue. "Please, don't stop! I'm—" She loses her words as a deep groan spills from her lips. She arches her back, pressing her thighs down on my shoulders for leverage as her body trembles with her climax. I suck her harder, drawing out her orgasm until she shudders, her hands frantically feeling up and down my arms.

I gaze at her face while I lazily lick the evidence of her release. She sighs contentedly, her eyes closed and her lips parted as her muscles start to relax. When I've had my fill, I gently lift her legs and lower her body onto the couch. She sits up instantly, reaching for my face before crashing her lips against mine. She kisses me ardently, tasting her own arousal while simultaneously making my balls ache.

As if she can read my mind, one of her hands leaves my face to find my groin. She squeezes the bulge in my pants, and I groan as I sever our kiss.

"I have to go," I mutter reluctantly.

"How much time do we have?" she whispers, her hand still at my crotch and her lips still grazing mine.

I lift my wrist and look around her, sighing in defeat as I inform her, "Five minutes."

"Okay. Be ten minutes late."

"Blaine—"

"Let me take care of you," she pleads, pressing her forehead to mine. "Let me taste you, baby, please?"

"*Mierda*," I curse, reaching for my belt.

As I work to quickly free myself, she stands to her feet and tugs off her last piece of clothing. My dick jerks in my hand at the sight of her, and I regret that I don't have time to bury myself inside of her the way I've been fantasizing about for days. That regret is shoved to the side when she kneels between my legs and replaces my hand around my shaft with her own.

My jaw goes slack when she licks the pre-cum from my head, her hazel eyes staring straight at me while she does it. I lose sight of them when her lids fall closed as she slowly takes me into her mouth.

"*Angel*," I moan. Her hot, wet mouth is heavenly, and I can think of nothing else but the beautiful woman before me as she begins to suck and lick me to her heart's content.

She starts off slow, as if to get a feel for my length. Gradually, her confidence begins to surface. She sets the perfect pace—bobbing her head and pumping her hand in tandem. I sweep some of her hair from out of her face, and she's quick to tuck it behind her ear, giving me full view of her profile. I know I'm not going to last long, not with the sight of her nakedness before me and the sexy as hell sounds she makes as she consumes my cock.

Taking me by surprise, she eases up a little before carefully taking me deeper. My balls start to draw up when the head of my dick hits the back of her throat. It feels so good, I lose the grip on my restraint. I fist a hand in her hair and buck my hips, fucking her mouth as I chase after my release. She sucks me harder, hollowing out her cheeks, and I don't even have time to think about pulling out before I'm coming down her throat.

After I've spilled my release, she pulls away from me, licks the head of my cock, and then tucks me back into my boxer briefs. While I'm still trying to catch my breath, she wipes her mouth off and then crawls back into my lap, straddling me before bringing her lips to mine. Instead of kissing me, as I expect, she murmurs, "I don't want lunch on Friday—I want *you. All* of you."

I sit up, wrapping my arms around her as I palm one side of her naked ass. Her mouth smiles against mine, making me grin. "You got it," I mutter before delivering one more kiss.

She doesn't protest when I pull away, but hops out of my lap and begins putting on her clothes. I stand to my feet, closing my pants and tucking my shirt back in, watching her as she dons her shirt without bothering with a bra. I decide to hold onto that image to carry me through the rest of my day.

"Thank you for lunch," she murmurs as I take her hand and walk her to the door.

"You're welcome."

"Call me?"

"I will," I promise, leaning down for one last kiss.

We exchange our final goodbyes, and I hurry out of her apartment and down the five flights of stairs. Checking the time as I emerge from her building, I note that I'm ten minutes late—on the dot. Mentally sorting through what I can remember of my afternoon calendar, I'm sure I'll be paying for my tardiness for the rest of the day.

As I slide into the backseat of the town car, and Clay shifts to reverse out of the parking space, I'm certain that I don't regret it. Not even a little.

Seventeen

Blaine

I sit alone, nervously waiting to see Simone walk through the door. Of course, it's not Simone herself who has me feeling anxious, but the decision I've made to finally confide in my friend. For the last couple of weeks, it hasn't been something that I was ready to do. Then, three days ago, when Michael left my apartment to head back to the Capitol, all I wanted was to tell someone about this *amazing* guy that I had in my life. It was then that it hit me—I hadn't told anyone about Michael because we were new, *not* because we were a secret.

Sure, I've always been well aware that we're keeping our affair unknown for obvious reasons, but I hadn't thought about keeping the truth from anyone other than his wife, his family, and my dad. Now, our relationship may still be in the beginning phases, but what exists between us isn't fleeting. I'm not a fling, and he's not a rebound. I can feel it in my heart. I can sense it in the way that he kisses me—in the way that he touches me—in the *promises* he makes me.

Nevertheless, the nature of our secret hit me in a way that it hadn't before. The reality that our situation makes it pretty difficult to acknowledge that he exists in my life, at least where other people are concerned, it's crippling. I know how dramatic that sounds, but it's true. As the days have passed, my feelings have grown too much for me *not* to confess them. I can't tell Simone everything; and for Michael's sake, I don't want to. I would never purposefully compromise him or his career in any way. Yet, at the same time, if I don't tell someone—not *one* soul—that I'm falling for him, I'll question whether or not it's actually real.

I jump, startled out of my thoughts at the feel of a hand on my shoulder. Simone smiles at me suspiciously, and I stand to greet her properly. She returns my hug, adjusting her purse on her shoulder as we pull away from one another.

"You sounded good on the phone. You seem…*preoccupied* in person. Is everything all right?"

"Yeah. Let's get lunch."

"Mmhmm," she hums, eyeing me studiously.

"Come on. What are you going to get today?"

I link arms with her, and we make our way to the register together. She orders *The Greek,* and I opt for *The Club.* While we wait for our order, I ask her how she's been since I saw her last. As usual, she indulges me, telling me about work and how she spent her Fourth. By the time I'm all caught up, we're seated at a table with our food making my mouth water.

I'm just savoring my first bite when she asks, "What's going on, darling? You've never been good at keeping things from me, and your conscience is showing."

Holding up a finger, I stall while I finish chewing. It may be true that I've made up my mind in regards to telling Simone about Michael, but I haven't exactly figured out the best way to do it. By the time I've swallowed my mouthful, I'm no closer to having a game plan, so I start with the easy truth.

"I've met someone."

Her eyebrows shoot up in surprise as a smile tugs at the corners of her mouth. "So soon? Do tell."

And here's where it gets awkward.

"Actually, I kind of met him before—I mean, before I broke up with Mateo."

She pops a tater tot into her mouth, cocking an eyebrow at me, and words start spilling from my lips.

"He came into the bar about a month ago. At first, it was nothing, you know? I served him and we talked a little. Then we sort of ran into each other one night when Mateo was—being Mateo. Anyway, I didn't have a ride home, and he walked me to the Light Rail. We had a moment of sorts and, one thing led to another, and we went on a date two weeks later."

"*While* you were still with Mateo?"

Tucking my hair behind my ears I admit, "I'm not proud of it, but, yes."

Another tater tot is tossed into her mouth before she says, "Go on."

"He kissed me." Just saying the words takes me out onto that pitcher's mound, and I don't realize how wide I'm smiling until I start to speak again. "That's all it took. One kiss and I knew that regardless of what happened between him and I, Mateo wasn't enough for me anymore."

"I like him already," she murmurs, her face proving her

sentiments true. I relax a little, and she points at my forgotten sausage. "Take a bite, I'm going to need a lot more."

I do as she says, and we both fall silent for a moment as we eat. No sooner have I swallowed, and she insists I go on. "What's his name? What does he do for a living?"

"His name is Mike," I reply, deciding that the abbreviated truth is good enough for now. It's his *occupation* that has me pausing for a second. "Um—*political science*," I blurt out, proud of myself for being quick on my feet. "He teaches political science."

"Wow. Impressive. I'm assuming he's…*older?*"

"Yup," I nod. She doesn't get a chance to pose her follow up question before I shove another bite of my lunch into my mouth, but it's unescapable nonetheless.

"How much older?"

"He's thirty-seven," I mumble around my food.

Her eyes bug out of her head as she leans against the table and whisper-shouts, "Thirty-seven? Darling, he's two years younger than *me*."

With my mouth no longer full, I smile at her teasingly before I ask, "You aren't calling yourself *old* are you?"

"We're not talking about me, Blaine—we're talking about *him*. That's quite an age gap."

"Age is just a number. Simone, if you were on the receiving end of the sexiest smile you've ever seen in your life, and he was thirteen years older than you, would you care?"

"No," she concedes. "No, you're right. I wouldn't. It's just my tendency to be protective. I worry about his intentions."

"He's a good guy," I assure her, beseeching her to hear my truth. "He's kind and funny and romantic. He's good at what he does, and he's *passionate* about it. He's worked really hard to get to where he is today, and he's smart. So smart. He's got a big family, and he loves them dearly. I just—I like him a lot already. He's sweet to me, and intentional and—I can't stop thinking about him, Simone. I don't know if I've ever felt like this before."

"This is good. I like what I'm hearing." She extends her arm across the table, offering me her hand. I slip my fingers around hers, and she holds on tight as she goes on to say, "I'll admit that it seems fast, but I would never hold your moving on against you. I want you to be happy. Your mother would want you to be happy—and if he makes you—"

"There's one more thing," I interrupt, not wanting for her to finish her well wishes if in the end she'll have to take them back. "Before I tell you what it is, I need you to promise not to look at me any differently than you are right now."

Squeezing my fingers, she declares, "I love you, and I would never think ill of you."

I draw in a deep breath and let out a heavy sigh before I confess, "He's...married."

True to her word, her face doesn't even flinch. Instead, she simply asks, "*How* married?"

"Married to the point that I can't tell anybody about him, except you. And he can't tell anyone, either."

"Take a bite, dear," she insists, letting go of my hand. "Give me a moment to swallow this."

I give her longer than a moment. While I consume two more bites, chewing slowly, she processes what I've told her. My stomach is in a knots as I try and get a read on her—but her face gives away nothing. I hold my breath when her brown eyes meet mine and she prepares to speak.

"You're glowing." She shakes her head, as if she can't believe that she's about to say whatever it is that's on her mind. "I have my concerns. It's my responsibility to hold such concerns—but you're glowing. I remember when you first met Mateo. I remember thinking how relieved I was that you were interested in taking that step in your life after the passing of your mother. I remember you telling me about your fist kiss. Darling, I remember it all. If life has taught me anything, it's to remember as much as possible and cherish every moment.

"If Mike is responsible for your glowing smile—a smile I've not seen since your mother walked this earth—then I will not be the voice that condemns your relationship."

"Seriously?" I breathe, my whole body slumping in relief.

"Seriously. But Blaine, I need you to tell me that you understand your future with this man has special obstacles it's up against—variables that you wouldn't have to face if the situation was different."

"I know. I know that this could all blow up in my face and break my heart—but, honestly, that could happen with anyone."

"Yes, but—"

"I hear you. I do. I also understand your concern. If I thought he was someone I could walk away from, I would have done it already. I can't. It's hard to explain, but he's a risk that I'd always regret *not* taking—and if life has taught *me* anything, it's to live with no regrets."

She smiles at me softly, reaching across the table to cup her hand around my cheek. I lean into her palm, silently pleading with her to understand.

"I hear you too, dear." Pulling her hand away from me, she reaches for her sausage and murmurs, "Tell me about your first date."

I grin, grabbing a tater tot and dropping it into my mouth before I begin.

Something came across my desk that won't wait. I'm sorry, angel, I can't do lunch today.

I'll make it up to you.

I check my phone one last time, confident that I haven't missed any new messages, but still holding onto hope that I'm wrong. I'm not. As I return my phone to my back pocket and exit the employee lounge, headed for the bar, I try to perk up a little. When I initially got his text, informing me that he wouldn't be joining me this afternoon, it felt like a reality check. All the excitement that came with telling Simone about him yesterday, as well as her acceptance of us, it didn't *change* the fact that I can't see Michael whenever I want.

Given our interrupted plans, I don't even know the next time I'll get to see him. It's frustrating, but I can't conceive any way around it. It's like Simone said, what's going on between Michael and me comes with a different set of obstacles than what's normal. He's worth it, though. Every moment we've ever spent together has proven that to be true, and there's so much more that I want to know about him and experience with him. I just have to put my big-girl pants on and deal.

"Hey, you good?" asks Dodger as I walk by him on my way to the register.

"Yeah. I'm okay," I reply, keying in my code to clock in for the night.

"We haven't really had a chance to hang since you and Mateo split. You've seemed cool, but I know you were together for a long time."

The smile that pulls at my lips is genuine, and I reach out to give his elbow a squeeze. "I'm good, Dodge. I promise. Thanks for checking on me."

"Yeah, well, I kinda like you," he teases with a shrug. "Say, what are you doing tomorrow night?"

"Uh—no plans yet. You?"

"I get off at seven. Hope and I were going to check out this new pizza place downtown. I guess it's been pretty wild over there, and people are raving about it. You should come."

I scrunch my face, totally reading into his pity invite. "Dodge, I don't want to be the third wheel on your date. I appreciate the invite, but—"

"Oh, come on. You wouldn't be the third wheel. We're all friends. Just come—eat pizza, have some beer; I think there's even a live band there, too. It'll be fun. If it makes you feel less awkward, I'll tell Hope to invite some tagalongs."

"Ah, so I'm a *tagalong* now?" I joke through a grin.

"Shut up. You're coming. I'll text you the address." He abandons our conversation to go help a customer, and I laugh softly as I get to work myself.

Being that it's a Friday, the night passes by pretty fast. I'm grateful for the distraction, but it doesn't go unnoticed that I don't hear from Michael during my shift. When Dodger walks me to my car after closing, we say our goodbyes and I drop into my seat behind the wheel before checking my phone one more time. It's stupid, but I can't help myself. I read our short text exchange from earlier and contemplate sending something to let him know I'm thinking about him. It only takes me a second to think better of it. As I drop my phone into my purse, I admit to myself how bad it would be if his phone went off at two in the morning. He's probably in bed with his wife, and waking her up is *not* a good idea.

All the way home, I try not to think about Veronica, or the fact that she gets to sleep beside Michael tonight. It's a struggle, but I manage to make it to my destination without getting lost in jealousy. I then hurry into my building, hoping that after a night of rest, tomorrow will look brighter.

My steps slow down when I reach the top of the stairs and see a thick, padded envelope leaning against my door. The postage on the front leads me to the assumption that the mailman must have been late today—though, I don't recall ordering anything. I knit my eyebrows together in confusion when I bend over to pick it up. Sure enough, my name and address are on the front. As I work to unlock my door, I try and figure out what the return address says, but that yields no clues, either.

I flick the lights on when I enter the loft, absentmindedly closing and locking my door behind me before I head to the kitchen. I drop my bag on the counter and immediately rip open the top of the package. When I realize what's inside, my jaw falls open as a laugh bubbles out of me. Pulling out the cords of navy, satin rope—complete with fancy tassels on each end—I'm suddenly awash in giddiness. I hug the envelope to my chest, my eyes flitting about my apartment before I look up at my bed. Instantly, my imagination is running rampant with images of me tied down—Michael having his way with me. Blushing, I take the ropes up to the loft, threading them through one of the links on my headboard, all the while hoping that I get to use them soon.

When I fall into bed a few minutes later, I do so knowing that even if Michael isn't here with me, he's still thinking of me. For now, that's enough to make the wait bearable.

Michael

Working on Saturdays is something I usually try to avoid. I don't, by any means, think that my job falls into the category of your typical nine-to-five, but every man needs his downtime. However, lately, it's been a good excuse for me to get some alone time. I'm in the mansion's office looking over some numbers when I'm alerted to an incoming text on my phone. After I see Blaine's name lit up across the screen, a pang of disappointment hits me square in the middle of the chest.

Canceling our lunch plans yesterday put me in a sour mood for the entire afternoon. Aside from the fact that I think about her frequently throughout my day, stirring a longing within me the likes of which I've never known, we hardly get to see one another as it is. Backing out of any precious time with her is frustrating—to say the least. Not knowing when I'll have another opportunity to see her makes it even worse.

When I open her message, a victorious smirk tugs at the corner of my mouth. I stare at the picture she sent—nothing more than an image of her ankles bound together by the satin ropes I had mailed to her. Her feet are bare, save one of her toe rings, and the implications behind her message makes my dick twitch in excitement. As another text message comes through, I have to stifle the groan I feel deep within my chest.

Can't wait to play. Missing you.

Before I get a chance to type a response, there's a gentle knock at my door. I blackout the screen on my phone, setting it down as Veronica pops her head inside of the room.

"Hey, sweetie. How's it going?"

"Fine, I suppose."

"Do you need anything before I go?"

Her departure coming as a surprise to me, I don't hesitate to ask, "Where are you going?"

"I told you yesterday, I'm going to do some shopping and then I'm meeting up with Francine for dinner," she says, speaking of our mayor's wife.

Frowning, I try and recall this information. I know for a fact that I would remember being told that she was to be out for a good few hours this afternoon and evening. "When? When did you tell me?"

"You were in the shower. You responded, so I assumed you heard me."

Shaking my head, I'm already thinking about the possibility of seeing Blaine tonight as I mutter, "I don't recall."

"Okay, well, I'm going out. There are leftovers in the fridge if you don't feel like making anything."

"I might go out, too," I start to say, trying to think of something that'll keep me out late. "There's a game on tonight. I think I'll go someplace to watch it."

"You should—you deserve a break," she tells me, nodding toward the paperwork scattered across my desk. "I'll see you tonight." She blows me a kiss before she turns to leave, calling out over her shoulder, "Love you."

"You, too," I mutter distractedly, checking the time.

Noting that it's just after two, I decide to put in a couple more hours of work before cleaning up and heading over to see Blaine. Ideas of how I'd like us to spend the evening cloud my thoughts, making it difficult for me to concentrate. I pretend to be productive until around four, and then it hits me—how I'll make up for disappointing Blaine yesterday afternoon. Wanting to put my plan in motion, I abandon the office and make my way to the bedroom to have a shower.

GATHERING THE GROCERY bags off of the seat beside me, I move to get out of the car, hoping that my surprise visit won't turn out to be a horrible plan. If Blaine isn't home, I don't know what I'll do. Truth be told, I wouldn't be above waiting for her to return. I need to see her. I need to feel her—to touch her—to *taste* her. It's been too many days. In spite of my growing sexual appetite, I haven't touched Veronica all week. She's not the woman I want. She's not the woman I *crave*, and I don't want to wait anymore.

Looking out into the parking lot, I realize that I don't even know what her car looks like in order to get a clue as to whether or not she's here. I make a mental note to ask her, and then I move to get out of the backseat. With one foot out the door, I pause to address Clay.

"If I'm not out in five minutes, you don't have to stay. You could come back."

"You know I can't do that, sir," he states matter-of-factly.

"I don't know how long I'll be."

"I'll be fine, sir. I always am."

I hesitate, looking up at the building. I'm well aware that Clay spends most of his days following my movements. Furthermore, this won't be the first time that he's brought me here only to *wait* for me to return. That said, it doesn't make me feel any less guilty to know that I'm here to indulge myself while he's left to keep watch when I'm sure there's no need for a watchman.

"Governor," he says, turning to address me over the seat. I give him my full attention. He stares at me pointedly and dips his chin in a nod before he insists, "Enjoy your evening."

I can't explain why—perhaps it's the look in his eye, or the lack of judgment in his expression—but it seems as though he not only understands why I'm here, but he *gets* it, too. I find myself wishing I had the time to inquire further into what he's thinking, but I know the moments I have are stolen, and I have a woman to see.

"Thank you, Clay," I mutter with a nod of my own.

I don't linger, but step out and close the door behind me, hurrying inside. Pulling out my phone as I make my ascent up the stairs, I find Blaine's contact information and push through a call. She answers on the second ring.

"Hello?"

"Hi," I reply, unable to keep the smile off my face at the sound of her voice. "How are you?"

"Good. Well, mostly good. I miss you. How are you?"

"Dying to see you. Are you home?" I ask, rounding the top of the staircase and taking the last few steps to her door.

"Yes. Why?"

Smiling mischievously, I end the call, slide my phone into my pocket, and then knock on her door. At the sound of her hurried footsteps, my smile turns into a grin. Then she's standing in front of me—wide-eyed and adorably marvelous.

Her hair is up in a messy bun on top of her head, and she's got a rolled up, white bandana tied in the front—though, that doesn't stop a few strands from falling around her gorgeous face. She's wearing a pair of black jeans that sculpt her legs perfectly, and a loose fitting, light pink tank top that dips low, showing off the top swells of her little breasts. I laugh when I read the front, which says: *Feed Me and Tell Me I'm Pretty.*

Stepping toward her, I wrap my free arm around her waist, pulling her against my chest as I dip my head. I graze my nose along hers and murmur, "I've come to make you dinner—and I think you're beautiful."

Bracing onto the back of my biceps, she leans into me and gives me her slight weight as she whispers, "Holy shit. Are you serious?"

I press my lips to hers as I chuckle, slowly backing her into the apartment. "I wouldn't lie to you, Blaine. I told you—I had to see you."

A whimper spills from between her lips, and she presses up on her tiptoes, circling her arms around my neck as she kisses me. "I'm so happy you're here," she mumbles into my mouth.

"You have no idea, angel."

Eighteen

Blaine

I HEAR THE DOOR SLAM SHUT, but I don't see it happen.

I'm lost.

Unabashedly, I cling to him, kissing him greedily. As I tangle my tongue with his, I seek to express two things. The first of which is that I've missed him more than my pathetic text messages could possibly convey. The second is that I have no intention of allowing him to break away from this exchange until I can no longer *breathe*. When I hear the plastic bags he holds in his hand rustle and fall to the ground, I know we're of the same mind right now. He brings his freehand up and around the back of my neck, holding my head in place as he tilts his and deepens our kiss.

I fucking love it *when he does that.*

I tell him as much with an honest moan, and he grunts his reply.

His surprise visit is by far the best thing to happen to me all week, and I can hardly believe he's here. Holding me. Kissing me. *Finally*.

"Mm," I hum in protest, burying my fingers in his hair and keeping him close as he tries to slow us down. "I'm not done, baby," I pant against his lips.

"*Creo que nunca me cansaré—nunca tendré suficiente,*" he mumbles before nibbling on my lower lip. I don't get a chance to question his meaning before he goes on to say, "Take as much as you want, angel." He then plunges his tongue into my mouth, and I instantly forget we were using our words at all.

We kiss until I can no longer stand the feel of his erection pressed against my belly without going insane. As much as I want him, I haven't forgotten that he promised to feed me, and that's something I don't want to miss. When I pull my lips from his and seek out his eyes, I find his stormy blues and melt even further into his arms.

"I love the way you look at me," I whisper, still incredibly breathless.

He gives the back of my neck a gentle squeeze before his chest rumbles with his voice as he asks, "How do I look at you?"

I sense the blush that creeps across my face as I bite my cheek, not having expected his follow-up question. His eyes seem to trace every surface of my face as he waits for my reply, and my stomach clenches in giddy excitement. I decide that underneath *his* stare, I am capable of holding nothing back. I want him to know how much I'm in this, even though sometimes it's frustrating as hell. I imagine it'll only get worse, but I don't care—not so long as he'll hold me just like this.

Speaking softly, I finally tell him, "Like you think I'm just as wonderful as I think you are; like you want to hold onto me as much as I want to hold onto you; like you missed me..."

He lowers his lips to my ear before he says, "I wouldn't be here if you weren't as wonderful as I believe you are. I'm enjoying getting to know you, and I want more—more of all that there is of you. And I've more than *missed* you. I've been aching to hold you since we last said goodbye. I don't know what you're doing to me, Blaine—but I don't want you to stop."

His words make me all tingly, and I shudder in his arms as I bury my face in his neck. From the very beginning, he's been upfront about what he wants from me and about how he feels. It's one of my favorite things about him. He's not a boy playing games, but a man who knows what's at stake. I don't have to be anxious over his intentions because they mirror my own.

"Are you hungry?" he asks on a mumble, pressing a kiss against my temple.

"Oh, dammit," I gasp, pushing my way out of his arms. I dig into the back pocket of my jeans, were I shoved my phone a few minutes ago, and quickly pull up my message thread with Dodger.

"Is everything okay?"

"Yeah, it's fine. I made plans tonight, and I almost forgot. I need to cancel them."

He's silent as I type a quick apology to Dodge, asking for a raincheck while assuring him I'm not merely bailing on his invite. I don't wait for his response, since I know he doesn't get off work until seven, but look back up at Michael.

"I apologize. I should have called. It was rude of me to—"

"To drop by unannounced, promise me dinner, and then kiss my face off?" I giggle as I shake my head at him. "We seriously need to have a talk about what you consider *rude*."

He smirks at me, and I'm instantly reminded of my damp panties. In need of a distraction, I grab the abandoned grocery bags from off of the floor. Holding them up, I ask, "So you cook, huh?"

"Not often, but yes."

"Well, I'm starved," I tease, extending my arm as I gently thrust his ingredients at him. "What are you going to make?"

He takes my hand instead of the bags, pulling me against his chest again before taking his supplies. "Choriqueso empanadas. They're not healthy, but I'll be making a creamy avocado dip to go along with them, and that's green. That counts for something, right?" he jokes.

"I love avocados," I murmur, resting my hands at his sides as I press up on my tiptoes in anticipation of all that he's mentioned.

"I know."

My breath catches in my throat, my whole body seeming to respond to the fact that he remembered I like the fruit. *No*—not just that he remembered I like it, but that he thought to make it a part of dinner for me.

"I *really* like you," I blurt.

Chuckling, he leans down to press a kiss to my lips as he mumbles, "The feeling is mutual." He kisses me one last time before stepping away from me and pointing at my breakfast bar. "Sit. I've got work to do."

"I could help," I offer.

"All I require is for you to tell me where things are as I need them."

Thrilled at the prospect of ogling him at work in my kitchen, I don't protest. Instead, I make myself comfortable, perched on one of my stools, and watch him unload his bags.

"I don't know that I've ever had an empanada before. I've *definitely* never had one that's homemade."

"Mmm," he hums, frowning over at me. "In that case, I'm sorry for cutting corners. My mother would kill me if she knew I bought the dough premade from the store—but dinner is not the only thing on our docket tonight. The dough takes over an hour to make."

I purse my lips together, fighting a grin at the thought of what else could be on our *docket* for the evening. Delicately clearing my throat, I insist, "I'm sure it'll be delicious anyhow. I can't wait."

Mateo never made dinner for me. Not unless you count heating up a frozen pizza—and he definitely didn't look as sexy as Michael while doing it. Even fully clothed, he looks delicious. The white V-neck t-shirt he has on shows off a little bit of his chest hair while simultaneously clinging to his broad shoulders and strong arms. His khaki shorts show off his sculpted calves and hug his amazing ass. I find myself trying to memorize his every detail as he moves about my space, wanting to lock away my memory of him for safe keeping—for when I'm forced to go days without him. How I manage to keep from drooling as I watch him at work is unexplainable. All the fantasies I already had floating around in my head of the two of us having sex in the kitchen are now even more vivid than before.

For the hundredth time, I swear—*he's way too hot to be a governor.*

While I'm not too busy gawking at him, he tells me about how his mom taught him and his siblings how to cook. Apparently, while they were growing up, when they were old enough, they each had a night where they were responsible to help her with dinner for the family. I also find out that even though his mother speaks perfect English, he has been bilingual since he first learned to talk. To this day, he says that so long as everyone at the dinner table can speak Spanish, that's the language they use while they dine.

"I like it when you speak to me in Spanish, even if I don't know what you're saying. Although, I'll admit, I wish I knew what you were saying," I confess.

Looking up from his task—he's stuffing the dough with filling now—he tells me, "Sometimes I feel like what I mean makes more sense in Spanish. When I'm passionate about something, it resonates deeper in my mother's tongue."

The thought of him being passionate about me makes me feel bashful, and I look down my cheeks, unable to keep eye contact with him. He does that to me—makes me want to be bold and daring one moment, and then he says something like *that* and I'm uncharacteristically shy. It's like he's got me on a rollercoaster. The thrill of the ride gives me a high I want to enjoy for as long as I can.

Michael

"Oh, my god—that was so good. How do you not eat those every day?" she asks, resting her hands on her belly.

Chuckling, I look down at myself and then back at her, quirking an eyebrow as my response.

"Right," she laughs.

"It's a treat. That's how it remains my favorite." I wink at her before I start to stand, reaching for her empty plate.

She slaps my hand away and shoots up to her feet, scowling at me as she scoffs, "You are *not* about to do the dishes. I sat on my ass while you cooked, and then stuffed my face—it's your turn to keep me company."

"While you clean up my mess, you mean?"

"Precisely."

I watch her without argument as she piles our silverware on top of our plates and then takes a dish in each hand. Before she turns to head toward the kitchen, she looks up at me and puckers her lips. Smirking, I lean down and kiss her.

"Thank you for dinner. It was amazing."

"I'm sorry I had to cancel yesterday. I wanted to make it up to you."

She stares at me a moment, running her teeth over her lower lip before she says, "You know what? I can do the dishes later."

My face breaks out into a grin as she sets the plates down and then circles her arms around my waist. I don't question her desire as I curve my hands under her chin. I like it—her willingness to drop everything just to be in my arms. When I stare into her warm, hazel eyes, I know she's not worried about the mess that'll need to be attended to later. She's not thinking about anything other than the fleeting moment that exists right here. There's no *to-do* list in her head. There's just us. There's just now.

I press my mouth to hers, softly at first. We start this kiss slowly, unlike the one we shared when I first arrived. She sighs sweetly, opening up for me when I run my tongue along the seam of her lips. I savor the taste and feel of her, moving my hands around the back of her neck as I kiss her deeper. Her small arms tighten around me, and my dick jerks in anticipation. I want her—I want her so badly. I feel as though I've been enchanted; like she's too good to be true, and she'll slip through my fingers if I'm not careful. I groan, kissing her harder and keeping her close.

I don't want to lose this. As wrong as it may be, I don't want to let her go.

She's awakened a dormant part of me that I'm sure was meant to be alive all this time.

"*Michael,*" she breathes, sliding her hands over my chest before wrapping her arms around my shoulders. As she clings to me, her lips still connected with mine, she begs, "I need you to touch me. Please?"

"Is my angel ready to play?" I murmur, resting my forehead against hers.

She nods as she steps away from me, her eyes smoldering with desire. My cock begins to stiffen as she walks around me, dragging her fingers across my stomach as she passes. I don't hesitate to follow after her. When we've reached her loft, she turns on her bedside lamps and then stands before me, as if waiting for instruction.

I don't say a word as I reach for the hem of her tank top, slowly peeling it off of her body. I help her out of her jeans, next. When she's completely naked, I untie the bandana from around her head and ask her to let her hair down. She does so without question or complaint, raking her fingers through her messy, wavy locks. Watching her has me so hard, I'm wondering how I've lasted a week without being inside of her. She's gorgeous, and I can't take my eyes off of her.

"Where's the rope, angel?"

Her eyes widen in excitement as her cheeks turn rosy, and my chest swells. This is something I've wanted to try for years. I've looked into it before, more than a few times, but Veronica has never been willing to try. Watching Blaine turn to one of her nightstands to retrieve my purchase from earlier this week has me anxious to begin. I can feel my fingers start to twitch, my own excitement barely containable.

After she hands me the satin cords, I instruct her to lay down on her back. She's quick to follow my lead, and her readiness only makes me adore her more.

"Hold your wrists together so that your elbows are touching."

"Like this?" she asks meekly.

"Yes. Just like that." Taking one of the long pieces of rope, I start to walk through the motions of a tie I've previously seen executed. I go slowly, wanting to make sure I get it right, and she watches me patiently.

"Michael?" she whispers.

"Hmm?"

"Have you—have you ever done this before?"

"No. I've wanted to, but I've never had the opportunity. You?"

"No." She shakes her head, her gaze still trained at her wrists as I continue to bind her.

When I'm finished, I take the end and string it through one of the links on her headboard, causing her to stretch her arms over her head. It doesn't escape me how the pace of her breathing has increased. I study her for a moment, trying to get a read on her before I continue.

"If ever you feel uncomfortable—"

"I'm not," she interrupts insistently, shaking her head once more. "Baby, I'm so wet. Hurry."

I clench my jaw, fighting a growl as I pick up the second navy cord. Quickly, I wrap it around her left ankle before attaching the other end of the rope to the far side of her footboard. She bends her right knee, planting her foot on the bed, leaving her pussy on full display, her eyes pleading with me to bring her the relief she so obviously yearns for. Seeing her so worked up only heightens my already amped up state of arousal, and I wonder how I'll be able to control myself.

My nostrils flare as I draw in a slow, deep breath, remembering that with Blaine—*I don't have to keep myself under control.*

Nevertheless, I intend to enjoy every single second. This is a first for both of us. It's not lost on me, the significance of being able to share something so intimate with her.

Standing at the end of the bed, I remove my clothing—keeping my eyes trained on her the entire time. Watching her squirm as I reveal my nakedness gives me a high I can't explain. Once completely bared to her, I give my cock a squeeze and a stroke, needing the touch. She moans pathetically, pulling at the ropes that bind her wrists, and I know already that tonight will be a night neither one of us ever forgets.

Kneeling on the foot of her mattress, I skim a hand along her left leg. She sighs, as if that one simple touch brings her pleasure, and I wonder how far I can push her—how high I can take her.

I lean over, pressing a kiss to the inside of her thigh, just above her knee. A long groan spills from her lips as I drag my tongue from her knee, all the way to the crease of her hip. She tastes sensational, and I can feel the pre-cum gather at the head of my dick as I tease us both. When at long last I flatten my tongue over her entrance, I feel it as her whole body convulses, fighting against her constraints. Using her right leg, she tries to lift her hips, seeking more. I chuckle mischievously, pulling my mouth away as I look up at her.

"Michael—Michael, *please!*"

Teasing her, I keep my gaze trained on hers, licking the opposite crease of her hip, taking hold of her right leg behind her knee. I push her thigh back, leaving her completely at my mercy, and she whimpers.

Lifting my head, I mutter, "You get what I give you *when* I give it to you. Understand?"

Her eyelids droop down low, her eyes hooded in lust as she breathes, "Yes, sir."

This time, I don't silence the growl that reverberates through my chest. I free it as I bury my face between Blaine's legs, devouring her with as much greed as I feel. The sounds she makes as I plunge my tongue in and out of her send a zing up my spine as my dick grows harder, still. Knowing that she's completely at my mercy—that she cannot touch, but only feel—it's a heady feeling. It's better than I imagined it would be, and we've barely just begun.

"Michael! *Shit!*" she yells, holding nothing back.

I suck on her clit, flicking the sensitive nub with my tongue, and she begins to shake with her cries. I don't stop. I *can't* stop. I want more of her. I'm *thirsty* for it—and I need her to come.

"Oh, god—oh, god. Baby!"

She comes on a scream, her pussy pulsing as she floods my mouth with more of her arousal. She's shaking so hard, I have to tighten my hold of her leg as I lap up the evidence of her orgasm. Once I've had my fill and she begins to relax, I proceed to kiss my way over her belly and toward her breasts.

"Fuck, I want to touch you so badly!" she whines as I suck on her nipple.

I grin against her tit, letting go of her knee and giving her the freedom of one leg. She doesn't hesitate before she wraps it around my waist, desperately expressing her desire for *touch*. By the time I'm done with her other breast, her back is arched and she's panting.

Licking my lips, I move further up her body, propping myself up above her. Our gazes collide, and the fire I see in her eyes stokes the fire within me. I dip my head to tease her lips with the tip of my tongue, and she flicks hers out with a whine.

"*Please*, Michael," she begs, her voice so soft I can hardly make out her plea.

"Please what, angel?"

Shaking her head, she says, "Kiss me. Fuck me. *Something!* I need you."

"You need this?" I grumble, grinding my hard length over her clit.

"You know that I do."

I touch my lips to hers in a feather light kiss before lifting myself off of her. Sitting on the edge of the bed, I reach into her nightstand for the stash of condoms I know she keeps there. After ripping open a package and sheathing my shaft, I glance back at her from over my shoulder. She looks so vulnerable. So wanton. So unbelievably gorgeous. Sure that I've denied us both for long enough, I position myself between her legs once more and submerge myself in her wet heat. Once I'm planted as deep as I can go, I pause, bringing my mouth to hers—needing her to know—

"You're so much more—so much more than I could have ever imagined."

Blaine

I'M SO RELIEVED to have him filling me, I don't bother whining when he doesn't move. Rather, I tug against my restraints, unable to help myself, and try lifting my head enough to steal the kiss that belongs to me. I moan my delight when our lips connect and he doesn't pull away. No—he *consumes* me, kissing me wild and hungry, making me crazy.

Crazy never felt so fucking good.

His groan mingles with my moan when he severs our lips and begins to move his hips. My eyes roam over every piece of him that I can see—every part of him I'm longing to *touch* and *taste.* The muscles in his arms bulge under his weight as he props himself above me, and his chest heaves as he plunges in and out of me with fierce determination. The veins in his neck pop out from exertion—and the look in his eyes, his deep blue eyes, it's so full of fervent passion, it's like watching a fire blaze across the surface of the ocean.

Never has anyone looked at me with so much yearning. It almost makes me want to cry—

But then I feel it…

I feel the budding of another orgasm as he continues to take me, and I surrender to it. I surrender to *Michael.* His power, his dominance, his control. It's breathtaking. I yank my hands again, the rope just as unyielding as it was a moment ago, but my desperation much stronger. The warmth that spreads from my core as my orgasm starts to bloom makes me freaking *unstable.* My hands start to tremble, then my arms—my legs—and as he drives into me harder, I'm shaking uncontrollably, unable to hear anything but the ear piercing scream that fills the rafters above us as I come.

And I come hard.

Everything grows muffled as my body milks Michael's dick of his own release. The sound of his roar seems far away, even with him being so close. It isn't until a few seconds later, when he gives me all of his weight, that my ears begin to lose that plugged up sensation. I relish in the sound of his heavy breaths and the feel of his sweaty body plastered on top of mine. He only stays but a moment, and then I lose him from inside of me as he begins to untie the rope from my ankle. When he loosens the knot around the headboard, I don't even give him the chance to release my wrists before I attack him.

I loop my arms around his neck and pull him on top of me before rolling us until he's on his back. His hands hold my waist, keeping me steady as I straddle him, but I'm not worried about my balance. My lips are everywhere—his face, his neck, his shoulders, his hairy chest. After I've kissed every inch of him that I can reach in this position, I fill his mouth with my tongue and kiss him until my lips are swollen and I can no longer manage a breath.

Forced to stop for the sake of my lungs, I press my forehead against his, panting as I murmur, "That was—that was—*god,* that was—"

"The best sex I've ever had in my entire life," he says, finishing my sentence for me.

I lift my head, only enough to look him right in his perfect blue eyes as I whisper in awe, "You felt it, too?"

"Yeah, angel," he mutters. Sliding a hand up the length of my spine, he gently grips the back of my neck as he draws me closer—right where he wants me. Before he touches his lips to mine, he grunts, "I felt it, too."

He kisses me tenderly, almost as if he's *thanking* me, and then rolls us over, putting me on my back.

"Let me untie you," he says with a smirk at the sight of my slight frown.

He dips his head from between my arms as I lift them, and then he frees my wrists. Even though the rope is soft, there are still red marks on my skin from being bound. I bite the inside of my cheek to hide my smile. I know they'll be gone in a few minutes, but I like wearing the evidence of what we just shared for a little while longer.

When Michael starts to climb out of bed, I'm quick to stop him, grabbing at his arm and giving him a tug. "Don't go," I insist.

I can't explain why, but the thought of him leaving me alone in this bed for even a minute—it makes me feel vulnerable and disappointed.

"Blaine, I'll be right back. I need to—"

I don't give him a chance to finish, my eyes darting down to his soft dick. Without even a hint of hesitation, I reach for the condom, slipping it off of him before tying it in a knot and dropping it on the floor.

"We'll toss it later. Please—please don't go."

He studies me for a second, the expression on his face something akin to concern. The next thing I know, I'm stretched out on the bed, half of my body draped over his as he holds me. I relax against his chest, sure that this is what I need right now. After being so restricted and unable to touch him, I'm not ready for him to be out of reach. As I graze my fingers through the fine hairs on his chest, I realize that him being *out of reach* isn't just something that worries me in this very moment. It goes deeper than that.

My feelings for him go way *deeper than that.*

Maybe it's stupid and naïve, but I'm here. I'm the other woman who is falling for a married man. From the very beginning, we've both been in this for more than just sex. There's so much about him that I admire; and the more I learn, the more I appreciate the man that he is. Despite our age difference, he's easy and interesting to talk to. He makes me laugh, and he's fun to be around. The sex—the sex just makes the prospect of losing him that much scarier.

Snuggling closer, I find the courage to ask, "Michael? What's Veronica like?"

I sense it when his body flinches in surprise, but I wait patiently for an answer anyway.

"Why are you asking me that?" he inquires, his voice low and guarded.

I lose what little bit of confidence I have at the sound of his tone. Then he tightens his arms around me and presses a kiss on top of my head before he murmurs, "Blaine?"

Sealing my eyes closed tight, I brace myself for his response as I admit, "I'm scared, okay? I'm scared of what we're doing. I'm scared of how quickly you've become important to me. I don't want to be blindsided if you decide not to choose me. I just—I'm up against your *wife,* and that's a lot to live up to. I want to know what she's like. Why you're here—why you think you need to be here. One day, you might not need whatever I give you that she doesn't, and I just…"

My voice trails off when I become fully cognizant of all that I've blurted out. I didn't really know that I was hanging onto all of that so closely. Of course, I've always known that his wife was what Simone would call a *variable* that we're up against, but I didn't know how much it worried me until just now. Maybe it was the mind blowing sex. Maybe it was his home cooked dinner. Maybe it's just *him* and the way he makes me feel simply by *holding* me. Whatever it is, my feelings are out there now.

When he remains silent, I decide I've already made a big enough mess, and I might as well finish it. I fold my arms across his chest and prop myself up until I'm staring down at him. "We have enough lies surrounding us," I whisper. "I don't want us to lie to each other. I want us to be honest about where this is going. I…" Shifting my gaze down my cheeks, I murmur, "I'm not ready to lose you."

The silence that stretches on between us feels heavy, and I'm worried that I've ruined our whole night with my big mouth. Then he reaches up and buries his fingers in my hair, tugging on the strands gently until my gaze is locked with his.

"A house full of open doors," he breathes—his voice softer than a whisper.

I shake my head, not understanding what he's saying. "What?"

A squeak bursts out of me as he rolls himself on top of me, making room from himself between my legs. I hook my calves over the back of his thighs as he rests on his elbows, situated on either side of my head. Tenderly, he traces his fingertips along my hairline, sweetly sweeping a few strands out of my face.

"You are extraordinary."

"Michael..."

"It's not about what she lacks. It's not about what you give me versus what she gives me. I wasn't looking for you. I wasn't trying to fill some sort of void—that's not who you are to me. You came out of nowhere. Blaine," he pauses, furrows his brow in frustration, and then goes on to say, "Veronica is not your competition. I know that it probably feels that way, and that's my fault. I'm sorry. I don't know how to do this. I don't know how to walk away from twenty years. I don't have any good answers. I know that's not fair, but—"

"Nothing's fair," I declare, sliding my hands up his chest and around his shoulders. I hold on tight as I repeat, "Nothing's fair, Michael. It's not fair for you to be here with me behind her back. It's not fair that in a little while, I'll have to say goodbye to you so you can go sleep in her bed. And I know—I know it's not fair for me to ask you to make a choice right now. None of it is fair. I'm not asking for you to apologize to me. I'm in this with you. I walked into this with my eyes wide open. I just—I want...*you*."

"I'm right here, angel." He presses a soft kiss to my lips before he pulls away and promises, "I'm right here. I've *been* here. So many times, my mind has been here with you even when I'm someplace else. When I tell you that I don't know how to walk away from twenty years with my wife, understand that I'm thinking about it. Because while I have history with her, I imagine what my life would look like without you, and I don't like it, Blaine.

"She may be my first love, but you—you make me feel things that I've never felt before. Everything is new with you. *I* feel new with you. I'm not ready to lose you, either. You're important to me. I hope you know that. I hope you believe that I would not be here if that were not true."

I nod, allowing my heart to latch onto his words and all of his unspoken promises. I nod, reminding myself of the risks he's taking to be here with me. I shove aside my insecurities and circle my arms around his neck as I tell him, "I'm really glad you're here."

"Blaine," he rumbles, running the tip of his nose along the side of mine. "There's no place else I'd rather be."

We kiss and cuddle for the next hour, and it's perfect.

It isn't until he gets up to take a shower that I realize, along with ingredients for dinner, he bought a bottle of his body wash to keep in my bathroom. Maybe it's stupid, but when he closes the door behind him, I can't keep the giddy grin off my face. Tonight, a bottle of soap is another unspoken promise—and I won't take that for granted anymore than I'll take for granted our stolen moments.

I'm halfway finished cleaning up the dishes from dinner when he emerges from the bathroom. I look at the clock, noting that it's almost eleven, and I try not to be too disappointed that he has to leave.

"I'll call you tomorrow, and I'll see you soon," he assures me as he walks me to the door.

"Lunch this week?"

"For you? Absolutely." I smile up at him as he curves his hand around the side of my neck, tracing his fingers across my nape. "I'll make it work at least one day this week."

"Okay," I whisper. "Thank you for dinner."

"You're welcome."

"Tomorrow?" I ask, pressing my hands against his chest as I lean into him, needing to hear him say it again.

"Tomorrow," he mumbles before leaning down and delivering a scorching hot kiss.

I get so lost in it, I don't know if he's saying hello or goodbye—that is, until he pulls away. When he reaches for the door handle, I don't stop him, sure that if he doesn't go soon, I won't let him.

"Goodnight, Michael."

With one foot out in the hallway, and one foot in the doorway, he reaches for one last kiss, making me giggle. He pulls away with a grin on his face, and he winks at me as he murmurs, "Goodnight, angel."

Nineteen

Three Weeks Later

Blaine

"BLAINE? IT'S ME! I COME BEARING GIFTS," Irene calls out from the other side of the door after knocking three times.

I peel myself from off the couch, shuffling my feet against the floor as I slowly make my way across the room. My whole body aches, and I'm sure I look as great as I feel—which is like shit. That's why, when I reach my destination, I lean against the barrier that separates us with no intention of opening up so long as Irene's on the other side.

"Thank you so much, Irene. I seriously owe you one," I mutter lamely. "I don't want you to even chance catching this shit, so you can leave the bag out there. I'll grab it when you're gone."

"Okay, hon. I hope you feel better soon! We've totally got you covered at work for the next few days, so don't worry about that, either."

"You guys are the best," I call out, managing a weak smile.

"Call or text if you need anything else."

She knocks twice more, signaling her departure, and I wait until I can no longer hear her footsteps on the stairs before retrieving her care package from my doorstep. Looking inside of the bag, I find everything I asked for. Four cans of chicken noodle soup, a box of saltine crackers, and some sleepy-time tea. I haven't eaten all day, so I force myself into the kitchen to make myself some soup before I lay back down.

The flu came at me from out of left field. I knew that I was feeling a little under the weather yesterday, but when I went to bed last night, I thought I could sleep it off. Even after sleeping in late, I woke up feeling awful. I hated to call into work, because I know nobody likes to cover a Sunday evening shift, but there was no way anyone would want to buy a drink from my sniffling ass.

It doesn't take me long to heat up my meal, and I manage to consume one bowl before I decide I need to lay down again. I make it halfway to the couch before I look up to my bed, my chest filled with longing. I want so badly to climb under my covers with my laptop and fall asleep watching countless episodes of *Suits*. Except, the thought of tackling the stairs when I just had an entire bowl of liquid, which will inevitably make me have to pee—meaning a trip back *down* those stairs—has me trudging my way back to the sofa.

I curl underneath my blanket and close my eyes. Sleep starts to tug me under its spell, and just as I surrender, my phone rings. Groaning, I lethargically reach for the device, my heart sinking when I see *My Lover* is calling. It isn't until this very moment that I remember that tomorrow is Monday. Monday afternoons have become *ours*. It's the one lunch hour that he promises me every week. He's built me into his day, and it's a standing date I look forward to. Sometimes, if our schedules mesh, he'll come over after work when I have the night off, but that didn't happen last week. He was busy this weekend, too. Now I'm sick—which means we'll miss our Monday lunch date, and I don't know when I'll see him again. I'm so disappointed, I forget to answer the phone.

Snapping out of my thoughts, I call him back immediately.

"Hey," he greets warmly after only one ring. "I thought I was going to miss you."

"Sorry, I'm really out of it today."

"What's wrong, angel? You don't sound like yourself."

I smirk at his kind way of telling me that I sound awful. "I caught the flu, which means you shouldn't come over tomorrow, which makes me hate the flu even more than I already did."

"I'm sorry you're not feeling well. Do you need anything? We're having dinner at my parents' house tonight, but I could sneak away before that and drop by."

"That's really sweet of you, baby, but you can't get the flu. You've got a state to govern. Anyway, Irene just left. She brought me some soup and tea. I'll be okay."

"All right. Listen, I don't want to keep you. Especially given that you need to rest. I just called to hear your voice."

"I miss you," I whisper.

"And I you. As soon as you get better, we'll go out."

"Out?" I ask, lifting my eyebrows in surprise. "We haven't been out since—"

"I know. Our first date."

My stomach tingles hearing him say *our first date*, my mind filling with memories of our time at Coors Field.

"I'll think of something."

"Maybe something that will give me an excuse to wear a little black dress?"

Chuckling softly, he replies, "Well, now I want to see you in a little black dress, so yes."

"Okay," I murmur through a grin.

Only Michael could make me smile when I feel like death. I'm so gone for him.

"Get some sleep. I'll call you soon."

We say our goodbyes, and even though I wish we could have talked for longer, I hold on to the happiness I feel having been promised a *real* date. When I drift into a deep sleep, I do so with a small smile still lingering on my face.

Michael

It's a quarter to one when I arrive at Blaine's apartment. I hurry to the fifth floor, aware that my trip to two different stores shed more time off of my scheduled lunch than I had anticipated. With only forty minutes left before I need to head back to the office, I don't plan on wasting another second outside of Blaine's company. I haven't seen her since last week—flu or no flu, there was no way she was going to convince me to stay away.

I knock twice with no answer. I lift my fist to knock a third time, but the door swings open, revealing my sick angel. She's got dull circles under her eyes, and her nose is red and raw. Her wavy hair is loose, a little messier than usual, and tucked behind her ears. Her legs are bare, save the skimpy, bright pink, cotton shorts she's got on; and her white t-shirt—which reads: *NOPE. Not Today*—covers her obviously bra-less tits. She's as disheveled as I've ever seen her, and yet I still want to kiss her.

"What—what are you doing here?" she stammers, shaking her head in disbelief. "I thought—"

"You thought I'd miss the one day this week that I've made sure I can see you?" Stepping toward her, I grab hold of the back of her neck and press a kiss on top of her head. Speaking into her hair, I mumble, "You thought wrong, Blaine."

"Michael, what if you get—"

Interrupting her once more, I assure her, "I got the flu shot a few months ago."

"Okay, but that doesn't mean—"

"My God, you are so stubborn," I say on a laugh. "Let me in, angel."

She doesn't move her feet, but tilts back her head to look up at me. After a stare down she has no chance of winning, she seems to lose energy before she whispers, "Hi."

"Hi," I say, speaking through a knowing grin. I press a kiss against her warm forehead and then decide it's time for me to start doling out instructions. "Go lay down. I brought you something."

"'Kay," she finally concedes, turning to leave me at the door.

"Have you eaten?" I ask, closing us in and heading straight for the kitchen.

Her voice soft and tired as she makes her way up to her loft, she tells me, "A little while ago. I'm not hungry."

I nod my reply, even though she doesn't see me do it, and set out on my task. I pull out the bouquet of flowers I bought first. It only takes me a minute to find her big mason jar, and I fill it with water before unwrapping the stems and setting them in their new home. Pushing the arrangement to the corner for her to discover later, I find her tea kettle—which was conveniently already left on the stove—and boil some water. Less than ten minutes later, I'm carefully climbing the stairs to her loft with a steamy hot toddy.

"What's that?" Blaine asks as I set the drink down on her nightstand.

She's laying under the covers, curled up on her side, looking from me to the mug in curiosity.

"Whiskey," I reply with a smirk, toeing my shoes off of my feet. "Try some. I swear it'll make you feel better."

With a frown of disbelief, she pushes herself up to sitting and reaches for the mug. Before she takes her first sip, she mumbles, "I can't believe you're here."

"Why wouldn't I be here? It's what any self-respecting boyfriend would do."

Her eyes grow wide for a second, and then she peers down into the mug and says, "You shouldn't see me like this."

I ignore her comment, watching as she drinks. "How is it?"

"Kind of gross. Kind of good."

"It'll get sweeter. There's extra honey at the bottom."

She drinks some more as I settle myself beside her, stretching my legs out on top of her blankets. When she looks over at me, I raise an arm, silently inviting her against me. I see it as her shoulders slump in surrender before she turns her back to me and leans into my side. I rest my arm around her hips and she sighs contentedly.

"Better?"

"Yeah."

Neither of us speaks as she consumes her hot toddy, but I don't mind. It's a natural kind of silence, and I enjoy being able to bring her as much comfort as I can manage in her current state. Once she's finished with her drink, she hands me her mug, and I set it on the nightstand beside me. With her hands free, she pulls up one of her extra blankets to her chin and shifts her body until she's curled up and burrowed into my chest.

"You called yourself my boyfriend," she says, her voice softer than a whisper.

It takes me a moment to recall. After I do, I kiss the top of her head, speaking into her hair as I recognize, "I guess I did." The thought crosses my mind to make a joke about it, something snarky about being exclusive—but then I realize that wouldn't be funny. Not for either of us. Instead, I remain silent, rubbing my hand up and down her side.

"You're really good at this," she says, changing the subject.

"Good at what?"

"Making me feel better."

"Misery loves company, right? My mother always taught me that comfort is the best kind of medicine."

"Your mother is wise."

"That, she is."

Snaking an arm around my waist, she snuggles even closer before she murmurs, "Michael?"

"Yes?"

"You'll make me fall asleep if you keep touching me like that."

I smirk down at her, even though she can't see me do it, and remind her, "You could use the rest."

She hums sleepily but offers up nothing else. She falls silent for so long, I think that she's sleeping. Then she surprises me when she asks, "Michael?"

"Hmm?"

"Why don't you have any children?"

My hand at her side slows to a stop as I gaze down at her. We've been getting to know each other for two months now. We've been intimate for more than half of that time. I don't know how it is that her desire for complete honesty between us still has the ability to catch me off guard, but it does. She's not afraid of the truth. Or, rather, she's not afraid to *face* the truth head on. In so many ways, she's shown me that I've underestimated her, and I shouldn't. In this relationship, all the doors are wide open—it's merely a matter of when we'll walk through them.

"Sorry, is that a sore subject?" she asks, giving my waist a weak squeeze. "I just think you'd be good at it. Being a dad, I mean."

I furrow my brow, regret tugging at my heart. It takes me a second to find my words, but when I do, I don't hesitate to offer her the answers she seeks.

"Veronica can't have children. Of course, I believe that with God anything is possible; but the doctors said we'd never conceive, and a decade later, we still haven't."

Tilting her head back, she looks up at me as she whispers, "You wanted kids?"

"Yes."

"And you never explored other options?"

Shaking my head, I confess, "It's a very delicate subject for Veronica. I won't claim to fully understand, because it's not something she ever wishes to discuss. Nonetheless, I know that after we first found out, we talked about adoption and she wasn't ready."

"Now?"

"Now, there's you. Even if she was open to exploring the idea, which she isn't, we're clearly not at a place in our relationship to be parents."

She nods her understanding and then dips her head, resuming her snuggling position. When she doesn't say anything else, neither do I. Instead, I continue rubbing my hand up and down her side. A few minutes later, when it's time for me to leave, she's fast asleep.

I carefully ease my way out of her bed, resting her on her pillows. After putting my shoes on, I kiss her forehead and quietly make my exit.

As I head back to the town car, I think about our conversation. It isn't until I'm reaching for the handle on the back passenger-side door that I realize I didn't ask her if she wanted children—neither did she offer up the information. I don't know if she neglected to mention it because she *doesn't* want them, or because she *does*. I pause, looking up the length of her building, taking stock of what I know about the woman I just left. Remembering that I should never underestimate her, I come to the conclusion that whatever her answer may be, she didn't tell me on purpose. Whatever her answer may be, she didn't want it juxtaposed against my history with Veronica.

Finally climbing into the backseat of the car, I sigh—in awe of the woman who is taking my heart, one piece at a time.

I'M GETTING READY to leave work when a text comes through. Hesitating at my office door, I slide my phone from my pocket and see that Blaine has sent me a photo message. When I open it, it's a picture of her smiling eyes—the rest of her face hidden behind the bouquet of flowers I left in her kitchen earlier.

Before I have a chance to black out the screen, another text comes through.

Thank you. You're the best medicine I've ever known. xoxo

I read the message twice, hiding my accomplished grin as I

slip the device back into my pocket and take my leave. Clay falls into step behind me as I pass through the reception area, and neither of us speaks a word as we head toward the car. All the way home, I think of Blaine. I play back our short time together, remembering the way she felt as she fell asleep in my arms, her warm body pressed against mine as she lay battling her illness. I think about our conversation, and my thoughts easily drift in an entirely different direction.

She asked me if Veronica and I had ever considered other ways to bring a child into our marriage. It seems like such an obvious solution to her diagnoses; and yet, *alternative options* have never been *obvious* for us. For *her*. Year after year, it's never felt like the right time. We've been waiting and waiting. We've been busy. I dropped the topic. It always felt easier that way—easier then getting into yet another argument about timing, and whether or not either of us was ready to let go of the seemingly *impossible* dream we had clung to in our younger years. We'd hoped for a family, conceived in our marriage bed; a pregnancy that she longed to experience.

"Sir?"

I'm pulled from my thoughts at the sound of Clay's voice, and I look around to see that we've arrived in the garage of the mansion. Still trudging through my thoughts, I nod a silent *thank you* and then climb out of the vehicle. I immediately make my way to the bedroom, with every intention of changing out of my suit. I'm surprised when I find Veronica busy folding laundry on the bed.

"Oh," she mutters, looking from me to the clock on the nightstand and then back at me. "I didn't realize it was so late. I haven't even started dinner. I wasn't sure when you'd be home."

"It's fine. Dinner can wait. Or we can eat leftovers. Doesn't matter," I reply, walking into the room. I take a seat on the bench at the foot of the bed and make quick work of my shoelaces.

"How was your day?"

I sit up straight, toeing the heels of my shoes from off of my feet, my back to my wife as I automatically reply, "It was fine."

"*Just* fine? Nothing else?" she asks casually.

Leaning forward slightly, I prop my elbows on my knees.

We talked about adoption, and she was never ready.

I replay my response to Blaine this afternoon one last time before I hear her soft voice asking—

Now?

I told her that *now* there was her; *now,* Veronica and I weren't in a place to consider bringing children into our home. However, the longer I think about it, the more I question whether or not that's true. *Now*, I find myself questioning if we were ready before I met Blaine? Were we ready last year? Or the year before that? Or has each day led us farther and farther away from being in a healthy place where fostering the hope of a family is a good idea?

"Mike?"

Twisting my head, I speak over my shoulder without looking at her as I inquire, "We're never having children, are we?"

She gasps softly, causing me to turn and look at her directly. Her lips are parted open in what appears to be surprise, and she seems to be at a loss for words.

"We never talk about it," I go on to say, wishing to do just that—*talk about it.* "I'll be thirty-eight in a few months. You're not far behind me, and we never discuss it."

She opens and closes her mouth a couple of times before sealing her lips. She shakes her head, as if to clear her muddled thoughts, and then her brown eyes sharpen as she stares at me purposefully. "This isn't a matter of a biological clock, Mike."

"I didn't say that it was."

"Then what does our age have to do with it?" she asks, reaching for one of my undershirts.

I watch her as she folds it, her hands showcasing her agitation at my chosen topic of conversation.

"All I'm saying is that we've never seriously discussed it."

"That's not true," she snaps, reaching for another shirt. "We have talked about it. I told you, I *told* you that when I was ready, we would explore our other options."

Stifling a sigh, I gently remind her, "It's been years, Veronica. We're not getting any younger."

"Well, you're not getting any less ambitious, are you? I might not be capable of bringing a child into this world, but any child we welcome into this family will be a responsibility that falls heavily on my shoulders. You might be our breadwinner, but my life is still full. And you? First the D.A. office and then governor? You're gone so often now, I can hardly tell when you're coming or going, and—"

"Don't," I grind out, unable to keep the scowl from pulling at my brow. "Don't put this on me."

"Why not? Why do I have to carry all the blame?"

"Veronica, I didn't say that. I'm not *blaming* you for anything—I just want to talk."

She draws in a deep breath, closing her eyes for a moment as she composes herself. I watch as her shoulders relax on her slow exhale. When she looks at me again, she offers me a small, apologetic smile, and I can see it in her eyes. I see that the door on this subject has been closed. *Again.*

"You're right. I'm sorry. Look, it's been a long day for me. I really need to finish this laundry and then start on dinner. I don't want to fight. Can we—can we table this for now? Just for now?"

I don't bother answering her. Instead, I stand and pick up my shoes before heading toward the closet.

The truth of the matter is, it doesn't have to be a fight. I didn't bring it up to fight. Yet, here we are—her grasping hold of the key, refusing to unlock that door; refusing to walk through it with me. Here we are *again, not* communicating. As I toss my shoes into the bottom of the closet, I think about all the years that have been *lost* in this *limbo.* Unbuttoning my shirt, I question how it is that we got here? How it is that neither of us noticed? Or when it was that we got complacent?

Fifteen years, we've been married. Fifteen years, she has been the only woman in my heart. And yet, somewhere along the way, all that we don't discuss, all that we don't say to one another, all that we sweep under the rug, it created room. Now, there is a gap; there is an opening; there is a *hole* in our marriage—a hole I didn't notice until one gorgeous woman with the smile of an angel sought entrance.

Discarding my shirt into the laundry, I reach into my pant's pocket for my phone. I check over my shoulder to ensure I'm alone and then open up my most recent thread of messages. Tapping on Blaine's picture to enlarge it, I admire her hazel eyes—still puffy from sleep—and the war in my inner most being rages on.

How can I possibly stay?

How can I possibly go?

Twenty

Michael

My phone vibrated at least twenty times during dinner. With every new alert, I wanted to pull it out and check to see if it was Blaine. I don't like being this far away from her. It's nonsensical, I know. Two days in our nation's Capital is nothing compared to the four days that came before it—the four days that we were in the same city but still unable to see each other. Perhaps it's Veronica's constant presence that has me feeling anxious. I haven't had a single moment alone since we landed in D.C. to return any of Blaine's messages.

This weekend, duty calls.

"Politics and opinions on their character set aside, you can't deny that the First Lady knows how to host a Governor's Dinner," Veronica says, pulling me from my thoughts.

Her hand is resting on my thigh, but even as she speaks, her gaze is trained out the window. She doesn't always get the chance to accompany me on my trips to Washington. After last year's event, she insisted she didn't want to miss this one. While I know that a part of her is here because she wants my peers to see that she and I are a united front, there's another part of her that enjoys the lavishness of gatherings such as these. Not because she's materialistic in any way, but because she's always looking for inspiration for her own galas and charity events.

"Yes," I agree, admiring her profile, lit by the moonlight pouring in through the window. "It was nice."

Humming a laugh, she turns to look at me as she mutters, "You're such a man."

I wink at her in reply and she squeezes my leg before shifting her attention back out onto the city. We ride in a comfortable silence for the duration of our trip back to the hotel. It's been a long day, and an even longer evening, and I know she's as tired as I am.

Upon reaching our destination, I help her out of the backseat, holding her hand all the way to our room. We say goodnight to Noah and Clay, and then we're alone in our suite.

"Oh, my goodness, stop," she begs, planting a hand on my shoulder.

I look back at her, the both of us just a couple steps into the room, and watch as she slips one high heel and then the other from her feet.

"Much better. Thanks, sweetie."

She reaches up and kisses my cheek before continuing into the room. I shed my tuxedo jacket as she pulls her phone from her little purse to check for notifications. When she presses the phone to her ear and I know she's distracted, I turn my back to do some checking of my own. I find three missed calls, fifteen emails, a text from my mother and a missed call with a voicemail from Blaine. I navigate my way to Blaine's message, guiltily taking an extra step away from my wife as I bring my device to my ear.

"Hey, Michael. I know you're busy being all governory, but I haven't heard your voice in a few days. I don't expect you to call me back. I know you're not alone. Anyway, listening to your voicemail greeting was nice. That's pathetic, right? Which means calling back to hear it again would also make me a pretty sad individual, right? Yeah, maybe I won't do that…"

I stifle a laugh, my chest swelling with my own contentment from simply hearing the sound of her voice. I find her absolutely adorable—her candidness and vulnerability alluring and sexy. As I continue to listen to her message, all I can think about is how anxious I am to return home.

"I miss you. Do you realize that I haven't been able to kiss you in almost two weeks? I'm all better now…so whenever you feel like being rude, I'm ready. Okay. You probably have to go. I miss you. Dammit, I said that. Oh, well, I mean it enough to say it twice. Anyway—bye, baby."

I save the message, certain that I'll listen to it again later, and ignore my other notifications. I then black out my screen, discard my phone on the dresser, and proceed to loosen my tie.

"My mom called," says Veronica. I look up and find her walking toward me. She stops when she's closed the distance between us, gathering her hair to one shoulder as she turns her back to me. Without instruction, I unzip her dress as she goes on to inform me, "Dad has pneumonia. She promised me it was nothing serious, but it's just one more reason why I wish they hadn't decided to retire in San Diego." Holding the front of her dress in place, she turns back to look at me and states, "He's seventy years old. I know he's not in the grave, but how am I supposed to help them during times like this if they're so far away?"

"Hey," I murmur, sliding a hand over her bare shoulder. I graze my thumb back and forth across her skin, wishing only to calm her down. "First, don't stress. You know your mother. She doesn't sugar coat things. If she thinks your dad's going to be okay, then I'm sure he'll recover."

"I know. I just want to be able to help."

As I replay her words in my head, an idea comes to me. The second after I think it, my guilt from a moment ago returns. However, along with it comes an anticipation that overrules my moral compass. I justify my thoughts, arguing with myself, claiming that this is the perfect opportunity for us both to get what we want.

"Why don't you go see them?" I suggest. "When we get home tomorrow, you can look into some flights. Maybe spend the weekend with them. What does your schedule look like for the rest of the week?"

"Um," she hesitates, knitting her eyebrows together in concentration before shaking her head. "I don't think I have anything that can't be moved around." Meeting my eyes again, she inquires, "You wouldn't mind?"

"Babe, why would I mind? You haven't seen your parents in a few months. If you want to go, then go."

"I do want to go," she insists with a nod, taking a step closer to me. "I know we talked about us going out there together in the fall—"

"We'll play it by ear," I tell her, sliding my hand down her back before wrapping my arm around her waist. "I think now's a good time. I can't go, but—"

"No, I understand. That's okay. Like you said, we'll figure it out." Letting go of her dress, she presses her chest to mine as she circles her arms around my neck.

The top of the garment slips a little, and I can see the generous swell of her breasts as I look down at her. It's been a while since we've had sex. At least four weeks. For obvious reasons, I haven't been in the mood, and she hasn't pushed. Even still, my body has been responding to hers for more than half my life—so it comes as no surprise when it begins to respond to her now.

"Thank you for suggesting this, sweetie. It means a lot to me."

"You're welcome."

I lean down to kiss her out of habit. It's almost like a period to the sentence that marks the end of our discussion. Except, we both linger a little longer than usual, and then I feel her tongue brush against my lips. I follow her lead, deepening our kiss, and it's not long before we're both naked, falling onto the bed.

It isn't until I'm inside of her that I sense that this is wrong. I'm on my back, watching as my wife rides me slow and gentle, and I'm desperate for more. Only, it's not a *more* that she's capable of giving me. As she takes from me, as I *let* her *take* from me, I can't stop my thoughts from wrapping around the reality that hers is not the taste that I crave. Her passion, her *fire*, it does not stoke mine. I now know another. More than that, I now *thirst* for another. Nevertheless, Veronica's warm, soft, wet heat works my dick until I come. And when I do, I'm not satisfied. Not even close.

Blaine

I PICK UP MY phone and the screen lights up, showing me what I already know—I haven't missed any new notifications. I set the device back on the table and push the remains of my dinner around my plate. I haven't heard from Michael since Thursday evening. He called right as I was getting ready to leave for my shift at the Lounge. Over the last several weeks, he's made it a point to call me as often as he can. Even if we can only talk for two minutes, it's always nice to hear his voice.

Now, I miss it more than ever.

Thinking about his trip to Washington, I wonder if I miss him more because I know how far away he is. There's also the fact that he's with Veronica. No, it's not different than any other day—except it *is*. As his wife, she gets to go to things like *the Governor's Dinner,* and I don't. That's not to say that I have any great desire to attend such a function, but that's not the point. It simply begs the question—will I *ever* get to be on his arm in public? Or will we always be a secret?

"You seem awfully anxious about that phone," dad grunts, yanking me from my thoughts.

"What?" I gasp, my head shooting up to look at him. He cocks an eyebrow at me, and I shrink a little in my chair. "Sorry, dad."

"Is something going on that I need to know about?"

I shake my head and stand to my feet, sure that I'm not ready to tell my dad about Michael. "Are you done? Do you want anymore?" I ask, pointing at his empty plate.

"No, Lulu, I'm done. Thank you."

"There's plenty more," I assure him. Taking his dish along with mine, I make my way to the kitchen sink as I instruct, "You can pack it for your lunches this week."

"All right."

As I rinse our plates and load them in the dishwasher, my thoughts wander back to Michael. He flies into town tomorrow morning, but he warned me that he might not be able to get away to join me for lunch.

"Baby girl, your phone just went off."

"It did?" I abandon my task of wrapping up leftovers and race back to the table. The second I see *Mateo* lit up across my screen, my heart sinks. I hesitate to even open it, my disappointment so distracting, but then decide I should read it and get it over with. I'm a little taken aback by what I find.

I miss you.

I haven't heard from him since he moved out. Not once. Now, I don't know how to respond to that. I'm sure that whatever honest response I can give him will not be what he wants to hear. The truth is, I *don't* miss him. Furthermore, being with Michael—even in the limited capacity that I can have him—I've learned that there's so much more to *love* than what Mateo was willing to give.

I set my phone back down with a sigh and start for the kitchen again before dad calls out, "Lulu, sit your ass down."

Startled, I glance at him with a confused frown. "Dad, I'm putting away—"

"Something's going on with you, baby girl, and I intend to find out what."

Now, I can't help but fight a smile as I obediently return to my seat. Propping the heel of my left foot against the edge of the chair, I wrap my arms around my leg and wait patiently for him to speak again. Not that I need reminding, but it's during moments like this one when I *am* reminded that my dad does more than all right. We're all each other has left. He watches me just as closely as I watch him. We might not be able to offer one another exactly what mom did, but we do our best.

"You seein' someone you neglected to mention?"

I bite the inside of my cheek as I stall, not sure how I'd like to answer his question.

He sees right through me and asks, "This that guy you told me about a while back? Right before you broke up with Mateo? You two an item, now?"

My cheeks warm in a blush, and I do the only thing I *can* do—I tell the truth. "Yeah. Well, kind of. I mean—it's not official, I guess. I don't know."

"Jesus," he sighs, scratching at his jaw. "Make it plain, Lulu."

I cough out a laugh, slightly amused and slightly terrified as I admit, "That's the thing. It's not plain. It's complicated. Really, really complicated."

"Is that what's got you all twisted up? Checkin' your phone every two minutes?"

"Kind of," I murmur.

"Who is this guy? Is he stringin' you along, or what?"

"No, dad. It's…" My voice trails off, my vocabulary suddenly insufficient for the topic at hand. Still sure that I'm not ready to see the look in dad's eyes when he finds out I'm dating a married man, I drop my foot to the floor and scoot to the edge of my chair. Reaching over to pat his hand, I tell him, "I like him." As soon as the words pass my lips, my heart tells me that's a gross understatement. "A *lot*," I tack on. "Anyway, we just—I don't know—we met under unusual circumstances and so it's taking longer than normal for us to, I guess, figure out what we are. Just know that when I'm ready, I'll tell you all about him. Okay? Can you trust me?"

He studies me for a second before offering me a decisive nod, and I smile at him.

"Let me finish putting away the food. You'll make me miss kickoff to the first Sunday night pre-season game," I tease, raising an eyebrow.

"Shit, that starts in a minute, doesn't it?" he grunts as he pushes himself out of his chair. "Bring some popcorn when you come, will ya?"

"Yeah, dad," I mutter, rolling my eyes. I suppose popcorn isn't the worst dessert he could ask for. "I'm right behind you."

I FINALLY HEAR from Michael just before noon on Monday. Having kept my phone annoyingly close all weekend, I don't have to go hunting for it when the text alert sounds. I pull it out of my pocket and open the message right away.

I didn't know I was capable of missing someone this much.

A grin lights up my face as I read his words over and over again. I'm just beginning to type a response when another text comes through.

I have a surprise for you. Can you get Friday off?

My smile slips as I pull the nub on my cheek between my teeth. Last week, I was out of commission for three days. I only ended up missing two scheduled shifts, but pulling favors to get Friday off won't be easy.

I can try…
Try hard. I'm ready to see you in that little black dress.

A squeal of excitement fills my apartment at the possibility of us going out—*out* on a real date. I make up my mind that I'll find someone to cover my shift if it's the last thing I do.

I'll make it happen. I'll proposition myself if I have to.
Blaine...

Giggling, I start to construct my reply when there's a knock at the door. My head still lost in my exchange with Michael, my feet move slowly across the loft to answer. I hit send and then don't bother looking through the peephole before twisting the knob to see who's in the hallway. When I find Michael standing before me, dressed in a light gray suit, my stomach clenches at the same time that my heartrate speeds up a few notches.

"Hi," I greet him breathlessly.

He takes a step toward me, then another, causing me to retreat a bit. He slams the door shut at the same time that he hooks an arm around my waist. Bringing his lips a hair's breadth away from mine, he grumbles, "You'll proposition yourself to *no one*."

I smile up at him, grabbing hold of the lapels of his jacket and pulling him even closer. My mouth grazing his, I whisper, "Yes, sir."

He growls before taking me in a hard, deep, burning hot kiss. As our tongues dance, my entire body tingles with a desire that makes me want to come out of my skin. I moan, circling my arms around his shoulders, and he crushes me against him with both of his arms. I'm not sure how I could possibly forget how fucking fantastic his kisses are, but I get lost in his affection like it's the first time I've ever experienced it.

"I want you," I mumble, hiking my leg up around his thigh.

"I want you, too—but I can't stay."

"I know you said—*god*," I groan as he kisses down the column of my neck. "I know you said you'd never fuck me and leave me, but can we? Just this once?"

"*Dios, no sabes lo difícil que es para mi decirte que no? Y aún así me pides hacer lo imposible?*"

"Baby, I don't know what you're saying. Is that a yes?" I pant.

He spins me around, grabbing hold of the back of my thighs as he lifts me off of my feet. I wrap my legs around his hips as he presses my back against the door, groaning when I feel the bulge of his erection align perfectly at my center.

"No, angel. I can't. I'm sorry. I literally only have five minutes. I went home to shower and change, and now I'm headed into the office."

"Dammit," I whine before kissing him desperately.

"Friday," he mutters into my mouth.

I nod, not separating my lips from his, and he indulges me for a moment longer. When at last his self-discipline bests my attempts to kiss him until I can no longer feel my lips, I try not to pout. I know I don't do very well when he sets me back on my feet and smirks at me while running his thumb across my lips.

"Friday. I'll be here no later than six to pick you up."

My eyes grow wide in surprise, and my slight frown disappears completely as I smile up at him. "We get to ride together, too?"

Chuckling, he slips his hand around the back of my neck, gently drawing me close. After kissing the tip of my nose, he tells me, "There'll be plenty of riding on our agenda—and we'll do *all* of it *together*."

"*God*, get out of here," I say on a laugh, pushing him away from me. "I won't be held accountable for my actions if you don't."

His sexy grin firmly in place, he travels the short distance to the door before opening it and stepping across the threshold. Winking back at me, he murmurs, "Goodbye, Blaine."

"See you soon."

He closes me inside of my apartment, leaving me all alone, and my mind immediately replays the last few minutes. I'm standing in the spot he left me, my fingertips barely grazing my lips in awe, when my phone chimes from within my pocket. After opening my latest message from Michael, I remember that we were in the middle of a conversation when he arrived. His response to my last text makes my heart swell, and I promise myself—one more time—I'm getting Friday off if it's the last thing I do.

Kidding! Though...I could proposition you, if you'd like...

That won't be necessary. I'll simply tie you up and take what I wish until you've come so many times you're begging me to stop.

Twenty-One

Blaine

Turns out, it wasn't that hard to get someone to cover my Friday night shift. Apparently, Dodger had the night off, and he was looking to pick up a few extra hours. He not only agreed to take my place, but he also told me that any time I needed to give up hours that he wasn't already working, he should be my first call. He was so nonchalant about it, and I was so relieved and thrilled that I'd managed to clear up my Friday night, that I didn't put too much thought into it. Now, as I'm finishing up my hair and makeup, I can't help but wonder what it is he's saving for.

I'm distracted from my thoughts when my phone vibrates across my small bathroom counter. I grin when I see it's Michael trying to reach me, and I don't hesitate to answer.

"Hey, baby."

"Hey, angel. Slight change of plans."

"Oh..." I mutter, feeling instantly deflated. I know how it is with us. It's the nature of our relationship—our plans always get dropped first. "Are you canceling?"

"No. Absolutely not. I'm leaving now. I'll be there in ten minutes. Traffic looks to be a nightmare, and I don't want to delay our departure anymore than we have to. Can you be ready when I arrive?"

Glancing up at my reflection, my grin returns as I assure him, "Yes. I'll be ready."

"Good. I'll see you in a few."

Setting my phone aside, I take one last look at myself in the mirror. While Michael has never said it out loud, I get the impression that he likes it better when my hair is down—so I curled it and left it loose, making my wavy locks look fuller. Given the color of my dress, I kept my makeup fairly neutral, applying the full works. Eye shadow, a hint of blush, and pale pink lip gloss. However, keeping in mind that it's my first Friday night out with my man, I made sure to add a generous amount of dark eyeliner, along with a double coat of mascara to give my eyes that extra pop.

Satisfied with my handiwork, I hurry to my closet to finish getting dressed. I know that I promised Michael a little black dress tonight, but when I unearthed my choice—buried in the back of my dress stash—I changed my mind. After discarding my bra onto the floor, I reach for the strapless, dusty-rose, bodycon dress I'm hoping Michael will appreciate. The bustier cut on top is accented with a subtle scalloped edge around the neckline, which matches the cut of the hem, falling halfway down my thigh. I manage to get the zipper up with little trouble, and then I smooth my hands over my stomach, feeling suddenly nervous.

Ignoring my anxious butterflies, I grab the shoes set aside for tonight. I hope, wherever we're going, I don't have to do a lot of walking, because these things were meant to be *admired* and not much else. My gold cage stilettos have a closed back and a peep toe. Across the top of the shoe, the straps make it look exactly like the name implies—*a cage*, which goes all the way up to my ankles. I bring in a little more gold with my dangling earrings, leaving my neck and shoulders bare, and my outfit is complete.

Once I'm dressed, I snatch my teal clutch from off of my top shelf before returning to the bathroom to get my phone. I drop it inside and then search for my bag. It takes me a second to dig out my keys, ID and debit card, but I manage to find them by the time a knock sounds at the door. The butterflies in my stomach remind me that they are there as I twist my head to look at the barrier that stands between me and my *date*. It's in this moment that I understand *why* I'm nervous.

It's true that I didn't know who the governor of our state was until Michael introduced himself as such, but Dodger knew him—*Dodger!* I'm sure there are plenty of people who pay attention to what's happening in our government, on every level, *including* Michael's, which means he's not exactly an *unknown* around here. While I trust that Michael wouldn't put his reputation in jeopardy, I still worry about the possibility of us getting caught tonight.

Maybe I shouldn't have worn a pink dress, after all.

Michael knocks again, and I shake my head clear before crossing the room. As soon as I see him standing in the hallway, all my nerves and worry vanish. He doesn't look a whole lot different than he usually does, but that doesn't stop me from drinking him in hungrily. He's dressed in a pair of charcoal gray suit pants with a matching vest over his lavender button-up. He's not wearing a tie, his collar is undone, and he's got his sleeves cuffed up to his elbows. The beginning stages of his five o'clock shadow is evident along his jaw, and just *looking* at him makes me feel like the luckiest girl I know.

Except, when I take in the frustrated expression tugging at his brow, I wonder if I've done something wrong. I look down at myself and then up at him before I softly acknowledge, "I know I said I'd wear black, but then I remembered the first time we made plans to go out. I was wearing a little black dress. I didn't want to jinx tonight, so I—I changed my mind. Is this okay?" I ask, peering down at myself one more time.

He chokes out a strangled laugh before he grunts, "Do you want to know what I'm thinking about right now?"

Peeking at him from beneath my lashes, I whisper, "What?"

"I'm thinking about the criminal who was sentenced with twenty years that I've been asked to pardon this week. I'm thinking about the new bill that I vetoed yesterday morning. I'm thinking of my intern, Larry, who needs to seriously reconsider his personal hygiene practices—angel, I'm thinking of *anything* that'll prevent my dick from making me extremely uncomfortable in these tailored pants. Blaine, your dress is a lot better than *okay*."

I try really hard to stifle my giggle, but it bubbles out of me anyway. As I take a step toward him, I ask softly, "Does that mean I *shouldn't* kiss you hello?"

Chuckling, he leans down and presses his lips against my temple before he mumbles, "Kiss me now and we might not make it out of this apartment."

"No kisses then. Got it."

Taking a step back, he clears his throat and offers me his elbow. "Lock up. Let's get out of here."

Smiling in utter excitement, I do as he says, dropping my keys in my clutch before slipping my hand into the crook of his arm. As he escorts me down the stairs for the first time, I know already that this is going to be the best date ever.

How could it not be? I'm learning that Michael—he's all I've ever wanted, and all I didn't know I wanted, too.

Michael

It takes us over an hour and a half to reach our destination; but if it weren't for my watch, I wouldn't know it. Blaine sat in the middle seat, her fingers laced with mine and her shoulder pressed against my shoulder the entire way. She spoke in a hushed voice, obviously wishing to prevent Clay from picking up most of our conversation. While I found it unnecessary, as Clay is far from ignorant about our relationship, my hushed responses made for an intimate exchange that I rather enjoyed. With our heads close and our eyes focused on one another, talking about the ordinary seemed to become extraordinary. It also made it easy for me to deliver more than a few chaste kisses, all of which made her smile at me sweetly.

I'm in love with her smile.

When we finally come to a stop in front of the Motif Jazz Café, Blaine squeezes my hand and whispers, "What if someone recognizes you?"

With my free hand, I trace the back of my knuckles over the apple of her cheek and remind her, "We're outside of my usual, every day territory."

"I think you underestimate yourself. You're not just the *youngest* governor in the country, you're also the *hottest.* And that's not me being biased—I looked them all up. It's definitely a fact."

I smirk at her before tipping her chin and touching my lips to hers. I tease us both when I sneak my tongue out for a taste, and she moans so softly I'm not sure I was meant to hear it. As I pull away, I assure her, "I picked this place for a reason. It has an intimate setting that would make it hard for anyone to spot me in the crowd, even if they *thought* they recognized me. To be on the safe side, we won't touch."

"Okay." She nods and then reaches for one more kiss—hanging on a moment longer than before. When she pulls away, she unlaces our fingers and frees herself from the confines of her seatbelt. I do the same, and then we exit the car and make our way inside, careful not to touch one another.

In spite of being a few minutes late for the reservation I made earlier in the week, we're seated right away. Our table for two is located on the periphery of the room, to the left of the stage. Just as I had seen in the pictures online, the lighting of the room is dim, the focal point and spotlight cast on the stage. There's nobody playing right now, but the piano, the upright bass, the drum set and the abandoned saxophone imply that the band is here. When our waitress arrives to take our drink order, she informs us that the music will begin in fifteen minutes.

By the time my order of bourbon and Blaine's Cosmo has been delivered, we've decided on the tapas that we'd like to share. With our decisions made, our orders taken, and a true moment alone, I prop myself against my forearms on the table, gazing at the gorgeous woman across from me. It feels good, being out with her. In this setting, what we have feels like less of a secret, and I pride myself on giving her an evening that she deserves.

"I didn't know you liked jazz," she says before sipping at her drink.

"I do. Or, I should say, I appreciate it for what it is. I don't normally go out of my way to listen to it, but it seemed like a romantic idea."

Setting her drink down, she sucks in a breath through her teeth before mumbling, "This is awkward. I mean, you'd be right…if I liked jazz."

My stomach drops as I tug my eyebrows together, instantly regretting having not asked her if she'd be interested in a place like this.

Before I can apologize, she laughs, leaning against the table as she says, "Baby, I'm *kidding!*" I let out a sigh of relief, and she sobers up a bit before she admits, "Michael, you could have brought me anywhere tonight and I would have loved it."

Quirking an eyebrow at her, I challenge, "McDonald's?"

"As long as you bought me French fries and ice cream, I wouldn't care. I'd just be happy to be out with *you*."

I fight the urge to reach for her hand or her face. Knowing that we'll have plenty of time to appreciate each other's bodies later, I simply reply, "For the record, I care for you and your digestive system far too much to ever take you to McDonald's."

"I appreciate that," she says with a giggle.

We're finished with our first round of drinks by the time our tapas have arrived, and we order more as the band takes the stage. Everything is great—the music, the food, the drinks, and especially my company. Her chair is situated so that she has to turn in order to see the band. She's twisted around so often, captivated by the musicians, that I suggest we switch places. She agrees only after I insist, and then it is I who is captivated, admiring her in this setting.

After her third Cosmo, she slips her phone out of her small

purse and types out a message. When my phone vibrates in my pocket, I smile at her before taking it out to see what she's up to.

I'm drunk. You're really, really sexy. If you don't take me home soon, you won't have time to fuck me before you have to go to the mansion—and I'll die.

Laughing under my breath, I'm quick to reply.

I'm not going home tonight, angel. It's just you and me all night.

I know when she reads my text when she gasps, looks at me with wide eyes, and then taps her thumbs on the screen excitedly.

Holy shit!!!!! You just made my nipples hard. Can we go?!?!?

The thought of her hard nipples makes my cock stir. I clear my throat, trying to distract myself as I slip my phone into my pocket and stand. Leaning down to whisper in her ear, I mutter, "Sit tight. I'll be back in a minute."

Anxious to close our tab, I flag our waitress down as she fills drink orders at the bar. I hand her my card with instructions to return it with the check to our table. She nods her understanding, and I step outside to make a phone call. It's a little after nine o'clock here, which makes it eight o'clock in California. I know that Veronica is likely to call at some point before she goes to bed, as she always does when she's out of town, so I decide to take the initiative. I'm certain that as soon as I leave with Blaine, she'll be the only woman I'll be able to think about.

When I get dropped into Veronica's voicemail, I don't know

whether to feel relieved or disappointed. As I listen to her recording, I try and think of something convincing to say.

"Hey, babe. I thought maybe I could catch you, but I guess not. Um, I'm turning in early tonight, so if I miss your call, I'll give you a buzz tomorrow. Hope you get some sleep. Talk to you soon."

I hang up and then stare down at my phone, taking a moment to contemplate how easy it was to lie to her—how easy it's been for weeks. Each lie I tell is like chipping away at who I thought I was. *Honest Abe* is full of lies; and yet, thinking about the woman I've left inside, the woman who yearns for me as I yearn for her, I know that I've never felt more *alive.* Perhaps I am not *Honest Abe.* Or maybe I am, professionally speaking, at least. Maybe the *Michael* I've come to know over the last decade is just a cover.

Covering up the pain of regret.

Covering up the ache of disappointment.

Covering up the numbness of routine.

With Blaine, there's so much *more.* I've told her before that Veronica is not her competition; that there isn't a lack I'm trying to account for with her body or her mind. Rather, I simply understand that they are different—unique to the time in which they exist. Lately, Veronica feels like nothing more than my past; a piece of my present identity that is slipping out of my grasp. But Blaine…

The spark that I felt between us in the beginning, it's grown into a blazing inferno. I thought that I couldn't deny myself this angel before—and *now,* just the thought of losing what we have seems like a tragedy; like without her, my future would be cold and barren. This evening, there is no room for guilt, shame, or condemnation. There is the truth, the truth that what we have was birthed in immorality. Yet, what we share, it's genuine. It's real. Furthermore, it comes with a passion that is all consuming.

I reenter the club and search the bar for Clay. He's sitting at the end, closest to the door, and notices me as I approach. These last several weeks, he's earned more than his keep. As always, his sense of duty to maintain his professionalism is paramount, and he has respected my privacy probably more than I deserve. I haven't been able to get a read on him to understand how he feels about my actions—if he has any feelings at all on the matter—but that is, of course, beside the point. Nevertheless, I will be forever grateful for his discretion, for his courtesy, and for his respect.

"We'll be leaving in a moment," I tell him. Keeping my voice low, I instruct, "You'll drop me off and return to the house. I insist. I won't have you sleeping in the car. Show up at her building at the crack of dawn for all I care, but I won't accept you waiting on me. I'll call you should something arise, which is not likely."

He studies me a moment, as if he's going to argue against my wishes, but then jerks his chin in an affirmative nod. Pulling the car keys from his pocket, he holds them up as a silent signal, then leaves the establishment to pull the vehicle around front. I don't waste any more time getting back to Blaine. When she sees me approach, her eyes light up and my chest swells. I spot my credit card on the table, and I'm quick to sign the receipt before returning the card to my wallet. I don't bother sitting, and with a wink and a head nod, Blaine knows it's time for us to leave.

The moment we step outside, she reaches for my hand, lacing her fingers with mine. It feels good. *No*—it feels *right*. Without even thinking, I hold on tighter and then lift our conjoined hands, leaning a little to kiss the back of her palm. She props her shoulder against my arm just as Clay pulls up, and I glance down at her as I say, "Let's get you home."

Smirking at me, she coyly replies, "Yes, sir."

Blaine

I'VE HAD ENOUGH to drink that when Clay starts to drive, I don't hesitate to cup my hand around Michael's opposite cheek. I'm beyond the point of caring that we aren't alone. If I don't get a taste of him soon, I'll go crazy.

Turning his face toward mine, I brazenly admit, "I've been fantasizing about your tongue in my mouth all night."

His eyes flick away from me, and I know he's looking into the driver's seat. I'm afraid he's going to deny me, until I hear a soft hissing noise. My head jerks, and I watch as the partition panel between the rear and front of the car slides up. I gasp, wishing I had known that was there before, and turn back to Michael to tell him as much. Except, I don't get out a single word.

An unabashed moan vibrates my chest as he fills my mouth with is tongue, and the desire that makes my belly clench is overwhelming. He cradles my neck as he leans into the kiss, and I shift as much as my seatbelt will allow, hooking one of my legs over his. When he reaches down and grabs the back of my thigh, pulling my knee further up between his legs, I whimper at the feel of his erection, trying the seam of his pants. My arousal pools in my panties, my heart pounding at the fact that I could get him hard so quickly—

Or perhaps he's been aching for me as long as I've been aching for him.

I have no idea how long it takes to get back to the loft. All I'm sure of is that Michael's lips don't leave my body for even a second of the duration of our ride. As much as I want to do more than kiss, lick, and touch over each other's clothing, Michael stays in control—keeping *me* under control. When Clay knocks on the partition, announcing our arrival, I don't know whether or not I'm still drunk, or if it's Michael that has me feeling so twisted up and buzzing with a heady high.

"Come on, angel. You've been a very handsy girl," Michael mumbles against my lips. "I think it's time we tied you up."

"Oh, my god," I whine on a shiver. I try untangling myself from him in order to get to my seatbelt, but I'm so excited, I'm trembling and my hands feel useless. "Shit, get me out of this thing!"

Chuckling, his voice deep and unbelievably sexy, he frees me from the belt and then unfastens his. When he doesn't reach for the door handle right away, I bite my bottom lip and peer at him through the darkness, wondering *what the hell?*

He takes hold of my chin with his forefinger and his thumb and then begins delivering his instructions. "I want you to go upstairs. I want you to take off this dress. Leave your heels on, Blaine, do you understand?"

"Yeah," I breathe.

For a second, I don't know if I'm more turned on by his demands, or the fact that he noticed and appreciates my shoes.

"I want you on your back, spread wide open for me. I'll be right behind you."

I nod my head, incapable of speech, and he delivers one last hard, wet kiss before opening the door. He steps out first, then helps me to my feet before making his way toward the trunk. I don't linger and stare, knowing that I've been given a very important task. Rather, I walk as fast as my heels and my wobbly legs will let me. As soon as I step foot into my apartment, I flip on the lights and start tossing things. My keys end up on the kitchen counter. My clutch ends up on the dining room table. By the time I'm halfway up the stairs to my loft, my dress is unzipped. I shimmy out of it when I make it to the landing, and then I hear Michael open and close the front door.

I freeze, as does he, and our gazes lock. In this precious moment in time, I'm wholly and completely aware of one single truth—I want him. *For always.*

I've never felt more *alive* in all of my life. Earlier, when I told him I'd die if he didn't fuck me, I was only half kidding. Now, I don't care how dramatic or immature or naïve it sounds, I simply confess to myself that I'm so in this with him—there's no doubt in my mind or in my heart that without him, a part of me really will die. In such a short span of time, he's come to mean that much to me.

Then again, what is time when you've found a soul that connects with yours in such a way that you never imagined possible? It's more than physical. It's the way he looks *at me. The things he* says *to me. The way he* treats *me, as if I really am his angel.*

With my eyes still trained on him, I hook both of my thumbs into the waistband of my thong. Slowly, I remove it from my body, careful to keep my balance when I step out of the material. I dangle the scrap of fabric from my finger as I straighten and then extend my arm over the banister before letting the thong drop.

His small duffle bag makes a *thud* noise as it hits the hardwood floor, and I can see it as his nostrils flare before he turns to flip the deadbolt on the door. I'm still standing in my spot—naked in my heels—when he looks back up at me.

"Bed," he grunts, loosening the buttons on his vest. "*Now.*"

My clit pulses at the sound of his tone, and I follow his command immediately.

His shoes click across the floor at a steady, even pace as I toss the comforter onto the rug—certain that we won't need it, and too impatient to fold it at the foot of the mattress. As I spread myself across my sheets, my legs opened wide, and my fingers hooked around a couple of links on opposite sides of the headboard, I hear it as he approaches the stairs. I'm breathless with anticipation as he draws closer, and I'm panting when he reaches the loft's landing.

He's shirtless, the belt at his pants is undone, and his top button is loose. From this vantage point, the bulge at his groin is painfully obvious, and it makes me want to jump him. I don't, somehow knowing it would displease him. The last thing I want is to do anything to prolong the moment where his dick is inside of me.

I need him.

He doesn't ask me where the ropes are, too familiar with their storage space. Instead, he toes off his shoes and drops his pants before heading straight for the nightstand to my right. He pulls out both cords, dropping one on the bed as he begins to secure my right wrist to the headboard. Just like the last couple of times that we've been able to play, the soft texture of the rope against my skin makes my whole body breakout into goosebumps. My ache for him grows, and the slightest brush of his fingertips at my wrists makes me quiver.

"*Hurry*, Michael. I can't wait."

A smirk tugs at his lips as his eyes lift to meet mine. My hand jerks as he tightens the knot on my left wrist, and I test his handiwork, fighting against the restraints. When I find that I'm not going anywhere any time soon, excitement trickles down my spine, and I arch my back with a moan.

"*Michael…*"

"What is it? Hmm?" he hums, teasingly tracing his fingertips along the inside of my arm.

"Baby—I need you," I confess, not the least bit embarrassed.

I admire him as his gaze precedes his touch, hinting at where he'll set me on fire next. My jaw falls open and I can feel my desire leaking from between my legs as he grazes his fingers over one of my peaked nipples.

"*Fuck*," I whine when he pinches and rolls my sensitive bud.

"Where do you need me?" he asks softly, his voice rumbly and seductive.

My god, the sweet agony of his foreplay.

I love it and hate it.

I hunger for it and despise it.

I'm *greedy* for it and tired of it.

I'm impatient with his teasing, and yet, enjoying every second of it.

I am in awe of the power he wields, the strength of his self-control, and his ability to take his time with me. I adore the way he savors every inch of my body, the way he *worships* me, making me feel like the most beautiful woman in the world. I'm *lost* in him, in *us*, knowing that what we do here, how he touches and tastes me, how he plays and pleasures me, it's *ours*; knowing that he's only ever experienced this kind of tantalizing, erotic ecstasy with *me.*

Only me.

"Blaine?" he grunts, dragging two fingers down my stomach. "Where do you need me?" he repeats.

I bend my knees, planting my heels flat on the bed as I open up for him. In this bed, completely at his mercy, I am not bashful. I am not shy. I am *desperate.*

"I need you in my pussy. Please, baby—I—"

I suck in a loud gasp when he grazes his fingers over my clit and then down to my soaking wet entrance. He groans, slipping inside of me with ease before shoving his other hand into his boxer briefs. I buck my hips at the sight of him stroking himself, clenching my jaw closed as I tug on the ropes.

"Is this what you need, angel? Is that what you want?"

"More," I pant.

He pumps in and out of me, my slick center coating his fingers in my abundant desire. He reaches into me as far as he can go, curling his knuckles and stroking me just right. My eyes roll into the back of my head when the welcome pressure of my building orgasm starts to overwhelm my senses. I'm on the brink of coming when he pulls out of me, and I whine at the loss of him.

My eyes shoot open just in time to see him drop his briefs before climbing into bed with me. I'm still mourning with the frustration that he's caused, after leaving me hanging, when he straddles my chest. He aims his dick right toward my mouth, and the *smell* of him makes my clit pulse and my hands itch, aching to touch him.

"Take me," he groans, touching the tip of his head against my parted lips.

My stare locked with his, I slowly lick his seam, and the muscles in his jaw jump as he clenches his teeth together and draws in a deep breath through his nose. Wanting to make him feel as out of control as I do, I open my mouth wide and lift my head, taking as much of him as I can swallow. Swirling my tongue around his shaft, I bob my head, all the while watching him watch me. His eyes are dark and dangerously sexy. The way he's looking at me, it's as if the tables have turned. Even in my vulnerable state, *I* feel powerful.

When he tenderly rakes his fingers through my hair, I moan in delight. Then he clenches his fingers into a fist around my wavy strands, causing me to cease my movements. His eyes grow even darker as he begins to move my head for me. I whimper, my sense of power being ripped away from me at the exact same time that I get my wish—to see him out of control. With his left hand, he takes hold of the top of my headboard. I see the muscles in that arm flex with his grip as he continues to guide my head up and down while he thrusts his hips back and forth.

"Blaine—you look so perfect just like this. *Mierda.* Mí ángel hermoso."

As I fight against my restraints yet again, I'm startled by the tears that spring to my eyes—and yet, I can't stop them. I was wrong to think that watching him lose control would bring me any sort of relief. It doesn't. Not even a little bit. It makes me more desperate than before. I want more—I want *him.*

When my first tear spills down the side of my face, he pulls out of me instantly, his expression melting from one of passion to one of worry. "Angel, are you okay? Am I hurting you?" he asks, cupping a hand around my cheek.

"No," I insist, shaking my head. "Fuck me. *Please*, Michael—fuck me, fuck me, *fuck me!*"

Still straddling my chest, he reaches over to the nightstand on my left and yanks out a condom. I can hardly breathe as I watch him sheath himself. Then, when he finally positions his body between my legs, I tuck my bottom lip between my teeth in heightened, anxious anticipation. Except—he doesn't enter me right away.

Propping himself up on his forearms, he traces his nose along mine as he whispers, "I like to hear you beg." He pauses, kissing me tenderly before he tells me, "But I hate to see you cry."

"Oh, *shit—yes!*" I mewl as he slams his big cock inside of me.

I circle my legs around him, digging my heels into his ass as he pushes up onto his hands and pounds into me over and over.

The sound of our slapping skin mixed with that of my wetness drenching us both is so damn hot, I can hardly stand it.

"Harder, baby!"

With a growl, he rams into me, and I arch my back and tighten my legs as my climax barrels through me like a mighty storm. While my core pulses around his cock, constricting him, he slows down a notch, rolling his hips. Every thrust is precise, hard and yet gentle—or rather gentle, as he grazes his pelvis over my swollen clit, and hard, when he thrusts all the way home. Before I start to come down from my first orgasm, I feel it turning into a second.

"No way. No way, no way—oh, god, baby—I'm coming!"

My entire body trembles, and I throw my head back as I pull at the ropes. I can't think. *That's* how intense my pleasure is, how all consuming, how *perfect.*

Michael grunts as his hips slow down even further, his strokes deep and staccato. It's obvious he's having difficulty holding on, the muscles in his neck straining as he tries to keep it together.

"Let go, baby. Come for me, Michael," I pant.

He roars, throwing his own head back as he drives into me twice more before I feel him twitch inside of me. His arms are shaking, and I know he must be as spent as I am. He doesn't sever our intimate connection right away, and neither does he relax. He drops his chin to his chest, taking a few deep breaths before he lifts his head once more. With one hand, he reaches to unfasten my left wrist. That accomplished, he repeats the act with his opposite hand on the other side. Not until I'm free does he collapse on top of me.

I close my eyes, clinging to him with all of my limbs. He's heavy, and I can hardly catch my breath with him pressing against my chest, but I don't care. To touch him is *heaven*, and I'm not ready for him to move. Silently, I say as much as I tenderly run my fingers through his hair.

A squeak spills from between my lips when he rolls us over together. My arms stay firmly locked around his shoulders, and my legs straddle his hips as he settles on his back. We lose our connection, and I feel it as he reaches around me to slide off the condom. Burying my face in his neck, I hide my smile when he simply tosses it onto the floor before securing one of his arms around my back. With his free hand, he grazes his fingers over my ass, feeling all the way down to my tender entrance. His touch is light as he strokes me, and I shudder, tightening my grip around him.

"Rest, angel," he mumbles. "I'm nowhere near done with you tonight."

His reminder that I get to keep him, just like this, all night long—it does something to me. Something unexplainable. I'm not sure that I've ever been as happy as I am in this very moment; this moment where, no matter what might be happening outside of my front door, what *reality* exists outside of our little bubble, we have each other—we have *right now*—and we have *us.*

I touch the tip of my tongue to his neck, tasting his skin as I kiss him before I whisper, "Yes, sir."

Twenty-Two

Michael

I WAKE UP, AND ALL I'M COGNIZANT of are my five senses.

I *smell* her. I smell the evidence of her arousal and the five orgasms she had before we fell asleep. I smell her sweat on my skin. I smell *her*—my angel, and the scent of flowers in springtime that is all *Blaine.*

I *taste* her. I taste her on my lips—reminding me of how I savored every inch of her body last night.

I *feel* her. I feel her warm, small body pressed up against mine—her back to my front, and our legs tangled together. Her arm rests over the one I have draped across her stomach, and our fingers are laced together as if, even in our sleep, we knew that the night was precious. We couldn't afford to let go of each other for even a moment.

I *hear* her. I hear the soft murmur of her slow, even breaths. I marvel at the sound, having never had it upon waking before.

Finally, as I open my eyes, I *see* her. I see her mess of brown hair fanned around her head like a crown on the pillow that we share. I see the three condom wrappers discarded on the nightstand in my line of sight. I see that the sun has already made its entrance as it shines through the window above us, casting its light across the loft—and I know that I am not where I belong.

Yet, I am home.

Right here, in this bed, with this woman—*I am home.*

There is a comfort here that I don't feel in my own bed. In the silence of morning, without a word spoken, without a touch given, in this stillness that only exists as one shakes off sleep, there is a sense of security that insists that I stay. That *here* I am safe. *Here* I am free. *Here* I am *home.*

I hold Blaine closer, burying my nose in her neck as I breathe her in. My heart swells and my chest aches as I realize that while last night was the best night of my life, it does not compare to the serenity of *this* quiet moment; this awareness of who Blaine is to me—of who *I am* when I am with her. She allows me to be all that I am, and she does so with more grace and mercy than I can remember experiencing with another human being.

I am a man—a man that she cares for.

I am a believer—a Christian that she neither judges nor condemns.

I am a husband—a husband that does not belong to her, and yet, with every passing day she gives me grace and *time* to figure out what the hell I'm to do with the pieces of my marriage that hold me captive.

I am a *savage*—a wild thing that she coaxes into her bed; a man unhinged in the throes of passion that she *begs* for.

I am *hers.*

The bed in which I lay may not be the place where I belong, but the woman in my arms belongs to *me.*

She gasps, her body going rigid before she twists her neck to peek at me from over her shoulder. I lift my head to meet her beautiful hazel eyes, and she frees a soft whimper as she lets go of my hand in order to shift. Her front now flush against mine, she peppers my face and my neck with kisses. When my dick grows stiff, she reaches between us and wraps me in her small hand. My hips jerk when she tightens her grip and runs her thumb over the head.

We had more sex last night than I've had in one night for *years.* That said, it doesn't stop me from wanting her right now. With my arm locked around her waist, I hold her to me as I flip onto my back. She buries her fingers in my hair as she licks and nibbles across my scruffy jaw, and I take hold of her ass, using both hands. She sighs as I groan when I drag her pussy across my dick, finding her already wet for me. Her fingers close in a tight fist in my hair as I continue to move her back and forth. She feels so good—warm, silky, and soft—and I can't stop myself from easing my way inside of her bare.

"*Michael,*" she whispers on a shudder.

I moan in response, my hands sliding up her smooth back and into her hair. Gently, I tug her head up, just enough to align our lips. "Kiss me, Blaine."

She doesn't deny me, but plunges her tongue into my mouth, kissing me slowly—sensually. It's a kiss lazy mornings are made of, and it makes me want to take my time. As she continues to work my mouth, I slide my hands back down her body. I graze the side of her breasts, and she rocks her hips, silently telling me what she needs. Taking hold of her ass once more, I guide her movements, syncing them with mine.

When I can no longer stand the restrictions of our current position, I roll her onto her back, never breaking our connection. She looks up at me, her gaze sweet and affectionate, and I roll my hips, thrusting as deep as I can go. I hold myself still for a second and then gently ease my way out before repeating the sequence. She shudders beneath me, her hands feeling their way along my neck, over my shoulders, and down my chest. When her fingertips graze over my nipples, I groan, plunging inside of her.

"*Michael,*" she whimpers, hitching her knees up against my sides. I fall into her deeper, pressing in until my balls rub up against her, taking on her wet arousal. Wishing to keep her exactly where she is, I reach beside me and guide her ankle around my back. Without a word, she crosses her feet behind me, and we breathe together as I continue to roll my hips.

"God—you feel so good."

She mewls into my mouth when I close my lips around hers and then circles her arms around my shoulders. We love on each other, savoring the moment with all that we are, and it's incredible. I'm so lost in her that nothing else exists—nothing else matters. Not here. Not now. She's my only focus.

When the feel of her tight, wet center is too much for me, and I know I can't hold back much longer, I sever our kiss and stare down at her face. Keeping my steady pace, I slip my hand between us, finding her clit with my thumb. She gasps, arching her back, and I smear her arousal slowly, yet firmly, until she's trembling all around me. I know she's close. I'm now well versed with her body, and I'm sure I've brought her to the edge.

"Come with me, angel," I murmur, my balls tightening as they gear up for my release. My thrusts become jerky as I try to keep myself together, and I quicken my thumb on her clit. Touching the tip of my nose to the tip of hers, I groan, "Let go, baby."

Her nails dig into my shoulders as she wails with her orgasm, the walls of her core strangling my dick so hard, I lose my grip on my control. I grunt incoherently as I drive into her once, and then once more before I spill my seed inside of her.

Blaine

I'M IN LOVE with him.

As my body continues to tremble with the aftershock of what we just shared, as he gathers me in his arms and rolls us onto our sides—as he *holds me*, I know that there's no other way for me to describe how I feel. He's it for me. Going to sleep with him and waking up with him, I've never felt more safe and protected. It's not simply that he's *larger* than Mateo was. It's not that he's more dominate in bed than any guy I've ever been with. It's more than that. It's *deeper* than that. It's the realization that he's been taking care of me since the moment we met. In one way or another, my well-being has always mattered to him. We still have so much to learn about each other, and I want that—more than anything, I want that—but even now, I'm sure. My heart is sure.

I learned, while mom was dying, that there are some things that you can never speak aloud; things that can't be expressed with mere *words*. There's an understanding between two people who love each other that is conveyed through a touch or a look or just their presence. When mom died, I was in the room. That *connection* that I had with her, I felt it leave. All that was left was my love for her and my broken heart. I didn't think that I'd feel anything as strong as the *bond* I had with my mother ever again. Then I met Michael.

What we just did wasn't sex. We've had sex. Last night, we had lots of sex—but just now, that was something more. That was a forging of a bond that made my heart feel so full. Full of *love.* Love…and terror.

I know that so long as he wears that wedding band, he'll never be wholly mine. The thought of losing him makes me question if my love is actually the same thing as my terror.

"Hey," he hums, running a hand over my hair. "I'm right here, angel. Don't cry."

I suck in a breath and lift my head, surprised that the *aftershock* of my orgasm is actually my body shaking with my sob. When my gaze crashes into his, his gorgeous, blue eyes dancing around my face, I know that I'm not ready to tell him all that's in my heart. Not yet. Not like this. But I also know that we made a deal. We don't keep secrets from each other. So I do the next best thing and address my fear head on.

"I want you to be mine."

A small smile curls one corner of his mouth as he gently runs the back of his knuckles down my cheek, drying my tears. "I already am."

Pressing my body closer to his, I whisper, "I want you—I want you to stop having sex with Veronica." His body freezes around me, but I'm not finished. "I know you probably have sex with her. She's your wife. It would be weird and suspicious if you stopped, but I—I just—"

"It's done," he declares, circling both arms around me and crushing me against him. "I'll spare you the details, but I'm already yours, Blaine. It's done. I won't have sex with her anymore."

I sag with relief in his hold, tucking my face in his neck as I breathe, "Thank you."

"You deserve so much more. It's the least I can do."

Michael

I HOLD HER UNTIL I think she's fallen back to sleep, and then I move to see about breakfast.

When she makes an incomprehensible noise and holds onto me, I can't silence my chuckle as I ask, "What was that?"

"Where are you going?"

"I thought you might like some breakfast."

Her head pops up, and her wide eyes meet mine as she murmurs, "Breakfast?"

"If you have all I need, yes. I make some damn fine pancakes, if I do say so myself."

She brings her hands up and holds both sides of my face as she stares at me silently. I don't move or speak, waiting for her to say whatever it is that's on her mind. Finally, she tells me, "I love pancakes." She presses her lips against mine and then playfully shoves at my shoulder. "Chop, chop, Governor. I could definitely use the carbs."

Grinning, I reach around and pinch her ass, making her squeal and wiggle out of my grasp. I roll out of bed to the sound of her melodic giggle, and then head for my duffel, which I brought up last night. After donning a fresh pair of boxer briefs, I run my fingers through my hair and look back at the bed. Blaine has the sheet pulled up over her chest, and she's smiling at me—as if she's proud for having been caught staring.

"You're so hot. Did you know that?"

I wink at her before starting for the stairs. A few steps down, while she's still in view, I instruct, "Come keep me company."

"'Kay."

I hear her rustling around, but I don't wait for her. She's not the only one who could use the carbs. My grumbling stomach makes that fact quite clear. I'm washing my hands at her kitchen sink when I see her round the bottom of the staircase. Her petite frame is swallowed up in the button-up shirt I wore last night. Even with the sleeves rolled to her elbows, she's practically swimming in the material. It's cute as hell. Then, as she draws closer, I see that the first three buttons have been left undone, cluing me into the fact that her breasts are still bare. My dick twitches as I watch her finger-comb her messy locks into a small bun on top of her head, and I'm left wondering which I want more—*pancakes* or *Blaine.*

Knowing that I can have both, I set about pulling out the necessary ingredients for a batch of pancakes. I've had the recipe memorized since I was fourteen, when my mother told me I could have pancakes every weekend, so long as *I* was the one who made them and I made enough to share. My memory served me well when I was an undergrad, too. Saved me from having to resort to Ramen Noodles on a regular basis.

Blaine perches herself up on one of her stools on the opposite side of the kitchen counter, telling me where to find what I need. Fortunately, she's fully stocked up on eggs, milk, flour, brown sugar, and honey. She's a little dubious as to how they'll turn out, having never had anything other than homemade buttermilk pancakes, but I tell her to trust me. The smile I get when she agrees makes me wish I could make her pancakes every damn Saturday.

It's not long before we've got a healthy stack of flap-jacks piled on each of our plates. Blaine pours us each a small mason jar full of orange juice, and we settle at the dining room table. She moans her delight after taking the first bite, and I don't hesitate to mutter, "What'd I tell you? You've got to trust me."

"Never again will I doubt you," she promises around her mouthful, fighting a grin as she chews.

"Good," I say before stealing a forkful from her plate.

"Hey!" I shrug at her, feigning innocence, and she narrows her eyes at me. I fight my own smile when she doesn't put up anymore fight. Instead, her carefree expression fades as she dips her next bite in a pool of syrup. Then she murmurs, "This is nice. *Really* nice. I like waking up with you here."

"The feeling is mutual."

She nods, looking down at her plate before she quietly inquires, "When do you have to leave?"

I don't answer her right away. The truth is, I had only planned on staying one night. Seemed like the prudent thing to do, given the sensitive nature of our circumstances. I don't want to get sloppy. Then I got up this morning. I won't pretend that I don't want another morning just like this one. Confident that I can think of some excuse as to why I won't make it to church tomorrow, I reach over and tuck a loose strand of hair behind Blaine's ear as I inform her, "Veronica doesn't get back into town until tomorrow evening."

Peeking over at me from beneath her lashes, she doesn't repeat the question I see in her eyes; and I don't force her to.

"I'd like to stay," I assure her. "That is, if you're free."

She drops her fork and takes my hand, drawing it away from her ear and pressing it to her chest. "Please stay."

"It's settled then."

Beaming at me, she drops my hand and picks up her fork. Before I have the chance to do the same, she steals a bite of pancake from my plate, giggling as I shake my head.

God, I adore her.

"What do you normally do when you're by yourself at *the mansion?*" she asks, mockingly dropping her voice at the end.

Smirking her way, I reply, "Enjoy the quiet. I take my time with the paper, catch up on the news, things of that sort."

She quirks an eyebrow at me and mutters, "That's it? That's how you unwind on your weekend? You immerse yourself in all that's wrong with the world?"

"It's so rare that I have a weekend to relax. If I'm not working, Veronica is dragging me to one event or another. You know that." She nods, having been on the disappointed end of my obligations more than once. "Weekends are also the best times for the family to get together. Even when I do have an evening to kick back, Veronica has a hard time being *idle*. Closing myself in my office is the best escape—so the news is what I indulge in. If I can, I try and catch a ball game every once in a while. Sometimes I can get away with turning it on in the den, or I'll go out with some buddies of mine, or my brother, to a bar. Sometimes we'll snag tickets, too. Being the governor has its perks."

"All right, well," she pauses, pushing around her last bite of breakfast. "I don't have cable. Or a television—so sports are out. I'm also of the generation that doesn't get the newspaper, but you can use my laptop if you want to scour the Net for stuff. I can read or something while you—"

"Angel, look at me," I insist, shoving aside my plate.

She does as I've requested, and I hold out my hand. When she slips her palm against mine, I grip her fingers and gently tug her toward me. Taking the hint, she stands from her chair as I push my seat away from the table, making room for her. She straddles my lap, and the warmth of her body over my groin immediately makes my cock twitch. Forcing myself to concentrate on our conversation, I close my left hand around the side of her waist and slide my right one around the back of her neck.

"I don't want to do what I normally do on any given weekend when I find myself alone. I'm not alone." I lean in and peck her lips before reminding her, "I'm here with you. We can do whatever you want."

She leans into me a little closer, her fingertips absentmindedly grazing back and forth over my pecs and through my chest hair as she asks, "Even if that means cuddling with me and binge watching Netflix all day?"

"*Especially* if that means cuddling with you and binge watching Netflix all day—so long as you don't make me watch something utterly ridiculous. No teen drama. No politics. Oh, and no singing."

"Who do you think I am?" she asks on a laugh with a confused scowl.

Circling my arms around her, I pull her flush against me. Her breath hitches in her throat as she lifts her hands to hold my face, and I look straight into her hazel eyes as I answer, "Mine."

"Wow. Good answer," she breathes.

Unable to ignore the feel of her body on mine a second longer, I reach for a kiss. When I trace my tongue across the seam of her lips, she opens up for me and gives me what I want. She tastes like syrup, sweet pancakes, and *home*. My hunger for her returns; and as our exchange becomes more heated, I'm absolutely certain of what is quickly becoming a proven fact.

When it comes to Blaine, I'll never have my fill.

Blaine

I CAN FEEL IT as his dick grows stiff beneath me, and the warmth in my belly stirs my desire. I hold onto his jaw as he works my mouth, loving the feel of his scruffy skin rubbing against the palms of my hands. When he reaches underneath the hem of his shirt and grabs one of my ass cheeks, I moan and rock my hips. I know the thong I threw on is doing little to *nothing* to prevent my wetness from smearing against the cloth of his underwear, but I don't care. I want him to feel how wet I am—how wet he makes me—how turned on I get just knowing that he wants me as much as I want him.

"You want to ride me, angel? Hmm?" he mumbles against my lips.

I grind down on him harder, whimpering as I rub my clit against his bulge.

"Up," he commands, tapping my ass.

Biting my lower lip, I do as he says and stand to my feet before waiting further instructions. When he lifts his hips and simply slides his underwear to his ankles, I'm quick to follow suit. Without a word, I straddle his lap again, this time reaching for his dick. I position him at my entrance, hesitating for a second as I look into his stormy, dark blue eyes.

"Before—before, we didn't—"

"It's just you and me, Blaine," he assures me, taking hold of my hips and gently sitting me on top of him. "No more rubbers."

I nod, my jaw falling open as I get used to this position. He's never surrendered complete control to me before, and it's both unnerving and thrilling all at once. Grabbing hold of his shoulders, I take what I want—what I *need*. Setting a steady pace, I rock my hips, captivated by the way Michael is looking at me.

Like maybe he loves me, too.

I shake the thought away, not wishing to get ahead of myself, and just allow myself to get lost in this moment; in our connection; in the promise of this day and all the hours we get to spend together.

It's not long before I begin to sweat. When I start to peel his shirt off of my body, he's quick to assist me. Before the fabric even hits the floor, his mouth is wrapped around one of my nipples.

His facial hair scrapes against my soft flesh, and I hold his head to me, enjoying the sensation. While he sucks and licks me, I buck my hips, my movements growing wilder as he helps bring me closer to the brink of my climax. When he shifts his mouth from one nipple to the other, I let my head fall back. I close my eyes and whisper his name, enamored by the way he owns me even when he's offered me control.

Then I feel his hand graze over my ass before he dips a single finger between my cheeks. I gasp, fisting my fingers in his hair as I thrust my hips forward with as much force as I can muster. All the while, he massages my back entrance with slow, sure circles, and I can barely breathe.

"*Michael!*" I mewl.

"You like that, hmm? Do you want more?"

"*More*," I insist.

I come the moment he teases my hole with the tip of his finger, shuddering even as my body locks up around his. Then, my center still pulsing around his dick, he grabs hold of my thighs and stands to his feet. Planting my ass on the table, he angles his body over mine and begins to pound into me relentlessly. I'm so sensitive that it nearly hurts, but it doesn't last long. He comes almost right away, filling me with his release as his groan invades the entire loft.

Neither one of us moves a muscle for a minute as we work to catch our breath. The ecstatic high of my orgasm begins to fade, and my brain registers that Michael just fucked me on my dining room table. I bite down on the inside of my cheek, fighting a giggle as I cling to his shoulders.

It's not the kitchen—but it's one step closer.

He kisses my lips, and my smile breaks free before he suggests, "How about we get cleaned up?"

"That's probably a good idea. I could use a shower."

"Me too," he chuckles.

"Does that mean this is about to go?" I ask, dragging my knuckles along the side of his cheek.

He studies me a moment, as if trying to decipher my meaning before he asks, "Do you want it to go?"

I shake my head, silently hoping that my answer will make him keep it. I'll love him with or without a little scruff—but I swear, he was made to sport a little hair *everywhere*.

"All right then. It stays."

"Yes!" I cheer, feeling positively giddy with the news.

He kisses me before finally breaking our intimate connection. Then he says, "I'll clean up out here. You hit the shower first."

Hooking my legs around his ass, I stop him from pulling away from me completely and suggest, "Or we could shower *together*."

"We do that, angel, and it might be a while before we get to that cuddling you asked for."

"Netflix can wait, can't it?"

"*Mierda.*" He makes a noise that's something between a laugh and a grunt before he moves my legs from around him and quickly scoops me up into his arms. "Yeah. Netflix can wait."

Twenty-Three

Blaine

On Tuesday night, I'm still floating on a cloud *every place* I go. I've seen Michael for the last *four* days in a row, and two of those days I went to sleep wrapped in his arms. I won't get to see him today, but he called me before my shift started. While it's admittedly a bit disappointing to be in bed without him now, I still have the memory of our fabulous weekend to hang on to. Aside from the twenty minutes he stepped out to talk to his wife on Saturday night, he was *all mine*. Getting a glimpse of what that's like was heaven and hell mixed into one.

When I allow my thoughts to go there, *there* being the realm otherwise known as reality, where Michael is a married man and a high profile politician, the uncertainty I feel about our future makes me anxious. Though, in order to keep my happy cloud afloat, I decide not to think about all that we're up against.

I trust Michael. Even though we haven't had a serious

conversation about whether or not he plans on leaving his wife any time soon, I trust his heart. I trust his intentions. I know that he cares for me deeply. I can sense it all through my body when he makes love to me, or when he ties me up to fuck me, or even when he simply *looks* at me from across the room. Besides, he's rightfully claimed me to be his, promising me that he is mine.

"All right, I'm back," says Irene as she enters the galley behind the bar, clocking back in from her dinner break. "What'd I miss?"

"Not much. People drinking. You know, the usual," I reply with a grin.

"That, and the guy who keeps staring at B from the far end of the bar," Dodger mumbles as he passes by behind us.

Rolling my eyes, I insist, "He is *not*."

"Don't listen to her, Irene. She's in denial."

"Oh, wow, he's *cute*," she observes, pretending to straighten the liquor bottles on the shelves. Turning her neck to address me, she asks, "Are you serving him?"

"Nope," I proclaim triumphantly. "Dodger's got that end right now."

"Hey, Dodge, is it time for your break yet?"

My jaw falls open as she speaks over my head. I turn to face Dodger, knowing good and well that he hasn't had his dinner yet. He smirks at me before shifting his gaze to Irene.

"You know what? I'm *starving*."

"Dodger," I hiss.

I chance a glance over my shoulder, to the guy sitting in the same exact spot Michael sat the first night he came to the Lounge. By the looks of him, I wouldn't put him at any older than twenty-nine. He's not wearing a suit jacket, but he's got on a button-up and a tie. Judging by the loosened knot and the opened collar, I'm guessing he's had a long day, and he's simply here to enjoy a drink or two. Then again, if I'm to go by the way he's looking at me *right now*, I'd also have to admit that maybe he wishes *I* was on the menu, too.

Unfortunately for him, not only does Michael fill his dress shirts a hell of a lot better, but he's made me a taken woman.

Unfortunately for me, *my friends don't know that—and I can't tell them.*

Facing Dodger once more, I open my mouth to fabricate some excuse as to why him leaving me with his guests is a bad idea, but he beats me to it.

"Come on, B. Just go talk to him. You never know. You could like him."

"Or not," I counter.

"At the very least, he could be the perfect rebound. Seriously—he's cute, and I know cute when I see it," says Irene before abandoning our conversation to help a new customer.

"Good luck, B." Dodger grins at me, and I glare at him before he winks and takes his leave.

Knowing that there's nothing to be done at this point, I get back to work. I help my few patrons first, but there's no avoiding the far end of the bar. Eventually, when the staring stranger runs low on the scotch I'm pretty sure he's drinking, I head his way.

"Hi, there. Would you like another?" I ask, nodding down at his glass.

"That depends," he replies, swirling around the ice in his tumbler, a small, mischievous smile on his lips.

"Okay. Depends on what?"

"Depends on if the woman who is offering will tell me her name."

Tilting my head slightly, I ask, "Not that I mind telling you my name, but how could that possibly have anything to do with your scotch?"

His smile stretches into a grin before he replies, "Because a woman who knows her liquor deserves to be addressed by her name. How did you know it was scotch?"

I can't help but laugh as I confess, "Because I saw the bottle out after Dodger poured your first glass. Besides, I certainly *hope* I know my liquor—for your sake, for their sakes," I continue, nodding back at my other guests. "And especially for mine. It would be kind of hard to keep my job otherwise."

"I like you," he tells me, his grin still firmly in place. "What's your name?"

"You don't know me well enough to like me. And I'm Blaine."

"Well, let's change that, shall we? I'm Lewis."

"And would Lewis like another glass of scotch?"

"Please."

"Coming right up."

Instead of reaching for the glass in his hand, I go about filling up a fresh one. I pour a couple shots over the rocks, and return in no time. I don't plan on lingering, but then he asks, "What's your favorite book?"

"My favorite book?"

"Yes. I'm convinced you can learn a lot about someone if you know their favorite book."

"I see," I reply, stepping closer to the edge of the bar as I grab my hips. "Well, I don't have a favorite book. What's yours?"

"Hmm," he hums, tugging his eyebrows together disconcertingly. "Curious. You don't like to read?"

Smirking, I remind him, "You didn't answer my question."

"*The Catcher and the Rye.*"

"Wow. Your favorite book is about an adolescent who gets expelled, gets his ass kicked more than once, can't get laid to save his life, and whose greatest confidant is his ten-year-old sister. What does that say about you?" I tease.

Laughing, he props himself on his forearms against the bar as he says, "So she *does* read."

"I never said I didn't. Furthermore, I think that a person who is capable of picking just *one* book out of the *millions* that exist in the world to mark as their favorite lacks imagination. Or, perhaps, they don't read that often. So in a way, I suppose you were right after all. You can tell a lot about a person if you know their favorite book. Now, if you'll excuse me, I should get back to work."

I leave him with a shit-eating grin on his face, which only makes me laugh. I thought for sure that my quip would turn him off somehow, but over the course of the next hour, I find out that it had the opposite effect. Dodger comes back, much to my relief, but that doesn't stop *Lewis* from catching my attention. When he calls me over, Irene chuckles and nudges me with her elbow, encouraging me to respond. I roll my eyes at her but walk the distance toward Lewis anyway.

"If I stay much longer, I won't be able to drive home—but you know I can't leave without your number."

Deciding that I've let this go on long enough, I shrug and reply, "Sorry. I don't give my number to customers. It's kind of against my own personal code."

I say this knowing that while I'm not lying, I have made an exception. Just once. Even though I can't admit that to anyone, I have no intention of ever going out with Lewis. *Ever.*

"Fair enough," he says with a nod. "Do you have a pen?"

"I do," answers Dodger, offering him the writing tool from over my shoulder.

I cut my eyes up at him, but he only smiles before *conveniently* disappearing.

When I turn my attention back on Lewis, I see him scribbling something on his cocktail napkin. Once finished, he folds it in quarters and then tucks it between his forefinger and middle finger. Propping his elbow on the bar, he extends his hand, offering it to me.

"If I can't have your number, you can have mine."

"Lewis, I—"

"Just take it. What harm will it do?"

I stare at the folded napkin long enough to come to the conclusion that if I *do* take it, not only will Lewis leave, but Dodger and Irene will leave me alone for the rest of the night. My mind made up, I snatch the napkin from his grasp and shove it into the back pocket of my slacks.

"Have a good evening, Lewis," I say from over my shoulder, walking away from him. "Get home safe."

"I *totally* saw that," Irene practically sings as I pass her on the way to the register.

"It was nothing," I insist with a shrug.

"Yup. Nothing at all. Just a cute guy who is *totally* into you."

My mind races toward another guy—my unbelievably hot guy—and I suddenly get the urge to remind him that even when other guys are hitting on me, I'm still his.

Pulling out my phone, I construct a quick text and send it before either Dodger or Irene can catch me.

Missing you – always, your angel. xoxo

Michael

"So, you're really going to keep that? This is really going to be a thing? Little hairs in the sink every morning?"

Looking away from my reflection, I cast my eyes on my wife. She's sitting on her vanity stool, her back to her own mirror and her gaze aimed at me. She's still in her negligee and matching robe. For a split second, I try to remember the last time she walked around in one of my discarded dress shirts. When I can't remember, my memory fills with images of Blaine, who lounged in my shirt all day Saturday. There was something about it that I loved. Not in the sense that it stroked my ego or played into my vanity, it merely spoke of her idea of comfort, which is vastly different juxtaposed with Veronica's.

Forcing my thoughts to remain in the here and now, I reply, "I don't leave *little hairs* in the sink."

"Oh, yes, you do. You just don't notice because I've been going behind you after you leave for the office."

Resisting the urge to scowl at her, I return my focus to my task as I remind her, "We don't share a sink. Feel free to *not* go behind me."

"I just don't understand why—"

"Are we really going to have this argument? We're really going to argue about my beard?"

"Is that what it's called? You keep it so short, it looks like you simply *forgot* to shave over the weekend. It's not professional, Mike."

"All right," I mutter as I continue to shape my new *beard*. "I guess we really *are* going to argue about it."

"I leave for three days, and I come back to this. It's a *surprise*."

"Perhaps it was a surprise on Sunday. It's Wednesday now."

"Right. You're right. Now it's just annoying."

I draw in a deep breath, taking a moment to collect myself. The last couple of days have been more difficult than I could have foreseen. I was under no false impression that being back in *the mansion* and sleeping next to Veronica would be as it had been before. Nothing with Veronica is the same. Her touch. Her kiss. Her presence in bed—even the sound of her voice reminds me that what we have is broken. It's *been* broken. I just didn't notice it until I noticed Blaine. Now, every crack and crevice that has eroded over the last two decades is hard to ignore.

The last thing I want is to be the reason why this argument escalates and turns into something it's not. I don't want to say something that I'll regret. I knew that the facial hair would be an adjustment for her—but it's not *her* I'm aiming to please. Not anymore. Since I was eighteen years old, she's made it perfectly clear that she prefers my face clean shaven. She's never asked me what I prefer when, in fact, I *like* the beard. I always have. However, it wasn't until Blaine that I realized its worth.

Turning to address her directly, I keep my voice low and even as I explain, "It stays. I'm sorry you don't like it. Now, if you wouldn't mind leaving me in peace to finish? I'll be late otherwise."

We stare at each other, both of us silently standing our ground until she rises to her feet and takes her leave. I watch her go, knowing that she's angry, but not giving a damn. After all—it's *my* face.

My morning doesn't get any better. It's as if the conclusion of one argument makes way for the beginning of another. A cabinet meeting ends up being a disaster, with nothing but bad reports, and a bill that I did not wish to pass was passed anyway. My foul mood runs so deep, when Heidi reminds me of Everly's class field trip, of which I promised to make a special appearance, I almost decide to back out of it. Except, thinking about the disappointed look on my niece's face the next time I see her if I skip, I change my mind.

Schools bring kids to the Capitol Building all throughout the year. Some travel far, and reservations are made months in advance. Everly's fourth grade class is the first of the fall session, school having started only a few days ago.

"Do you know where they are?" I ask Heidi on a sigh.

"Yes, Governor. Except, you're going to have to look a touch more pleasant than that before I let you stand in front of five classes full of nine and ten-year-olds."

I force a smile, knowing that she's right, and then drag my hand down my face. "Tough day."

"I know. But you love your niece, and she'll be happy to see you, so perk up. It'll do you some good."

"All right," I mutter, smirking down at her. "Enough with the pep-talk. Let's go."

We run into the students as they are exiting the House of Representatives. Their hushed tones as they whisper to one another makes me smile, certain that the teachers and volunteer parents are responsible for striking the fear of God in them, no doubt insisting that this is a building that mandates respect and *inside voices*.

This is why, when I hear Everly yell, "Uncle Mike!" I can't help but laugh.

"Everly Cavanaugh!" I hear Gabriel before I see him. After spotting my niece—shrinking at her father's tone, her cheeks red in a blush, and her eyes peeking his way—I follow her gaze and spot him. "You know better," he mumbles quietly.

"Sorry, daddy."

Wishing to play the roll of doting uncle, I shift my attention back toward my niece and call out, "Miss Cavanaugh?"

"Sorry, Uncle Mi—I mean, Governor Cavanaugh."

I stifle my grin and hold out my hand. "Come here, please."

She makes her way through her classmates quickly, most of them offering her compassionate glances as she passes. The snots of the group are easily detected, their smirks a clear giveaway as to what they think is about to happen.

When she's standing right in front of me, I crouch down so that I'm the one that must look up at her. Turning my head, I tap my cheek, silently requesting a kiss. She giggles before pressing her cool lips to my face, and I nod my approval before nipping at her nose with my thumb and forefinger.

"You have a beard," she observes.

I run my hand over my jaw and declare, "I do. Do you like it?" She nods her head enthusiastically. Grinning at her, I instruct, "Be sure to tell your Aunt Veronica that the next time you see her, all right?"

"Okay!" she agrees innocently.

"Would you like to introduce me to your classmates?" She nods once more, and I stand to full height, reaching for her hand as I go.

Shifting her little body until she's standing directly beside me, she clears her throat and sweeps a few stray strands of hair from out of her face. I smirk down at her when she rolls her shoulders and begins her introduction.

"Everyone, this is Governor Michael Cavanaugh. He's been governor since I was seven. So…two and a half years. Right?" she asks, whipping her head up to glance at me.

"Yes, very good."

"All right, Everly—time to join the rest of your class," Gabe commands.

I wink down at my niece before letting go of her hand. She smiles up at me and then obeys her father, returning to her previously occupied spot. For the next ten minutes, the teachers of the group facilitate a small question and answer session. When Heidi interrupts, reminding me of my next appointment, in approximately twenty minutes, the teachers are quick to thank me for my time before they all bid me farewell.

I say goodbye to the little guests, and they continue on their tour as I start back for my office. I've barely made it two steps before I hear Gabriel call out to me. I turn to address him and see him jogging the short distance between us.

"Got a minute to spare for your older brother?"

"Of course."

His eyes flick behind me, where I know Heidi still stands, and then return to meet mine. "In private. I'll catch up with the kids when we're through. It'll only take a minute," he murmurs.

"Okay. Let's go to my office." We walk in silence a few paces before I ask, "Where's Tamara today?"

"I handle field trips, you know that."

"Right. My mistake."

Sensing his demeanor is not particularly *warm* and *friendly* this afternoon, I don't try and engage in any further small talk. When I close us into my office and he refuses to sit down, I remember that I was in a foul mood not too long ago, and it seems to be returning rather quickly.

"What's going on, Gabe?"

"Where were you last weekend?"

Surprised by the question, I furrow my brow and ask, "What do you mean?"

"Don't do that. Don't lie to me now. Veronica went out of town, and you suddenly forgot to set your alarm clock? Honestly, Mikey, of all the excuses you could possibly use—you *overslept* Sunday morning?"

Folding my arms across my chest, I feel my hackles rise as I ask, "What do you want me to say?"

He doesn't answer me right away, but stares at me—*studies* me. "*Dios, estás colado por ella ya, cierto?*[12]" When I don't respond, he reaches up to rake his fingers through his hair and mutters, "So, you're definitely having sex with her, then. I'm guessing you stayed at her place all weekend?"

I drop my arms to my sides, no longer feeling defensive. More than anything, I wish only for my brother to understand.

"Gabe—"

"I can't. I'm sorry. I've got a group of nine-year-olds I've got to help chaperone for the next couple of hours, and I don't have it in me to hear you right now." Shaking his head, he gives me a look that, up until this moment, he's never given me before. At least, not as far as Blaine is concerned.

He looks *angry*.

"I don't know what's going on with you, Mike. It's like you're turning into a different man right before my eyes. I love you, you know I love the hell out of you; and I understand that perhaps your relationship with Veronica has run its course. I want you to be happy. I don't wish for you to stay in a marriage that makes you

---

12 God, you're falling for her already, aren't you?

more miserable than not—but what you're doing? It's gone beyond *risky*. You're getting reckless. People are going to get *hurt* because of your actions. This isn't fair to Veronica and we both know it."

"I realize that. But, Gabe—"

"*Arregla tu lío, hermano,*[13]" he interrupts. "I mean it. You were taught better. You weren't raised to be this selfish. None of us were. You can't have them both."

"Gabe!" I call out as he turns his back on me.

One hand on the door handle, he looks over his shoulder and says, "When you're ready, whichever woman you choose, I'm here for you. I'll never turn on you, Mike. I swear it—but you *have* to choose. Hell, give them both up for all I care. Just know that right now, you're being a dick."

He leaves without another word, and for the first time since this affair began, my sense of *shame* overwhelms me.

I LEAVE THE office at five o'clock on the dot. I need to get out of here. I need to see Blaine—to be reminded of the reason behind all of these lies; to be reminded that while the path we traverse is dishonorable, it is paved with a connection that's *real* and unlike any either of us has ever experienced. I need to be reminded that in the end, *this* will all have been worth it, because *she's* worth it.

Always my angel.

"Take me to Blaine," I grumble as soon as I slip into the backseat of the town car.

Clay catches my eye in the rearview mirror and offers me a nod before starting the engine.

13 Get your shit together, brother.

Blaine

I'M IN MY closet, tucking my black, button-up shirt into my black pants, when I hear a loud knock at the front door. Frowning, I peek my head out of the closet, as if that'll somehow give me some clue as to who is in the hallway. I have to leave for work in twenty minutes, so I'm certainly not expecting anyone.

At the sound of another round of knocking, I decide to answer. I'm halfway to the door when I hear Michael's muffled voice as he announces, "Angel, baby, it's me."

My stomach tingles instantly, and my feet move in double time as I hurry the rest of the way to the barrier that stands between us. I'm quick to switch the locks before swinging open the door. I smile up at Michael, excited about his surprise visit, but then notice the expression he wears. He doesn't exactly look happy to see me.

"Hi," I murmur cautiously.

It isn't until he takes a step toward me, hooking an arm around my waist, that I start to feel somewhat at ease again. When he leans down and kisses me hello, I relax even further into his hold.

"Hi," he breathes.

"Hi, baby," I semi repeat. Gripping the sides of his neck, I ask, "Is everything okay? You seem upset."

"Yeah." As he speaks the word, he pulls away from me, walking further into the apartment.

I watch him, not certain what his one-word reply means. *Yeah,* he's all right, or *yeah*, he's upset. After closing the door behind us, I follow him into the kitchen. He's now standing with his back to me, his hands propped on the edge of the counter as he hangs his head.

"Michael?" I run my hand down the length of his back, waiting for him to respond. When I feel him stiffen, I wonder what's going through his mind.

"What the hell is this?"

My stomach bottoms out, and I knit my eyebrows together, confused and afraid of what he means by *this*.

Is he talking about us?

I'm still trying to figure out what he's questioning, so I can decide what to say, when he turns around, holding the napkin with Lewis's number scribbled across the front. I immediately deflate in relief. I forgot that I tossed it there after I got home this morning.

"That? That's nothing. Some guy at the bar gave me his number last night."

Michael's brow dips in a deep scowl, and I suddenly don't feel relieved anymore.

"He flirted with you?"

"Yes, but—"

"Did you give him your number?"

My eyes grow wide in disbelief. I take a step closer to him, resting my hands on his waist as I insist, "No. Of course not."

"And you kept this because why? Because you intend on using it?"

My disbelief gives way to frustration as I return his scowl with one of my own, declaring, "Why would you even think that?"

"Why would you *keep it?*"

I scoff as I take a step away from him, irritated that he's questioning me so irrationally. "I don't know—because when I emptied my pockets after my shift it was after two in the morning. I was tired and dumped all my shit on the counter, like I always do."

"It's not two in the morning now."

"Oh, my god," I mutter, snatching the napkin from his grasp. I rip the soft paper in two and then crumble it into a fist before tossing it in the trash can. "It was nothing, Michael. He flirted. I took his number so that he'd leave me alone. Seriously, what is wrong with you?"

Folding his arms across his chest, he argues, "For him to have felt confident enough to give his number, you had to have given him some glimmer of hope. You flirted with him."

Resisting the urge to stomp my foot in anger, I counter, "I'm a *bartender*. All I have to do is *smile* and people think I'm flirting. I don't understand why we're even talking about this."

"I don't like coming over here and seeing other men's *things* laying around. You could have thrown away his number as soon as he left the bar."

"No, actually, I couldn't have. If I *did*, I'd have Irene and Dodger all up my *ass* about not giving the *cute guy* a chance. It's not like I can tell them that I already have a boyfriend, now can I?"

"Why can't you?" he asks with a shrug.

My jaw falls open at the same time that my eyes widen once more in shock. "You're kidding, right? These are my friends we're talking about. I can't just tell them I have some *secret* boyfriend. They'll never let me get away with that. They'll want to meet you. I'd have to come up with excuses for you all the time. I can only keep up with so many lies, Michael."

He gives me a *fraudulent* smile, the expression so disingenuous it hurts my heart. He then drops his arms to his sides and leans toward me as he grumbles, "So I'm just supposed to accept this? You flirting with guys, night after night, accepting their numbers for the sake of your ignorant friends?"

His question is like a blow to my chest, and I force out a harsh sigh, ignoring the burning sensation behind my eyes. He's being completely unfair right now, and I don't understand how he doesn't see it.

"Let me get this straight." I force the words out, speaking around the knot in my throat. "You're mad at *me* for flirting with *one* guy while you go home to your *wife* every night?"

"This has *nothing* to do with her," he grunts.

I gasp softly, taking another step away from him. The mere fact that he's so quick to take his wife out of the conversation brings me back to *reality*—where Michael is a married man and a high profile politician. Only, right now, I find no comfort in his presence. I see no *promise* in it. He's holding me to a double standard, and it's like he doesn't even care.

Now, wholly aware that we're in the middle of our first fight, I can't stop my tears from falling. He stares at me, unmoving, and neither of us speaks a word for what feels like *hours*, even though I'm sure it's no longer than a minute. The muscles of his jaw jump across his cheek as he clenches his teeth together in frustration, and I don't know what to say.

How could he not know that I'm completely in love with him? How could he think that I would go behind his back to be with anyone else?

"I would never cheat on you, Michael," I whisper.

He stares at me for a minute longer. Then, to my utter disbelief, he storms out.

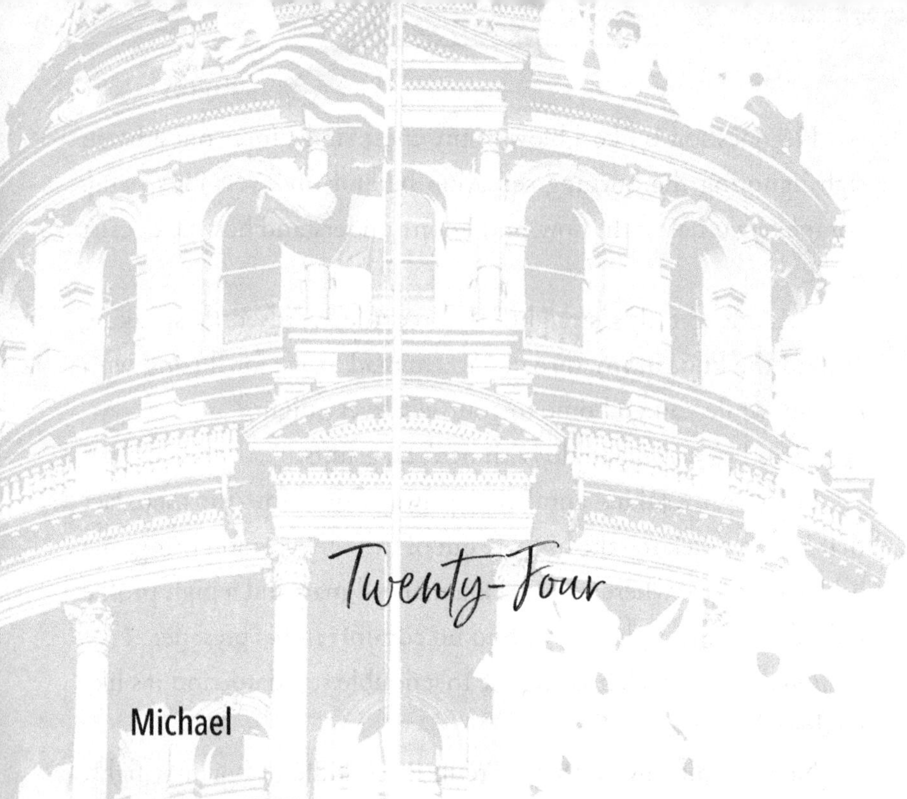

Twenty-Four

Michael

I REGRET LEAVING AS SOON AS I SHUT the door behind me. I pause before slowly turning back around. I place my hand on the doorknob, but I can't make myself twist it open. Softly resting my head against the solid barrier, I let it all sink in.

The argument I had this morning with Veronica.

The demands given to me by my brother.

The fight I just had with Blaine.

I would never cheat on you, Michael

My angel—she's not responsible for the guilt and the shame that weighs heavily on me in this moment. She's not responsible for the horrendous day this has turned out to be. Her promise of fidelity wasn't meant as a blow to my conscience, which is wholly aware of my complete lack of self control and my apparent inability to remain faithful in my marriage. Even more than that, she's not to blame for the overpowering sensation of *jealousy* that burns hotter inside of me than I've ever experienced before. Just the *thought* of another man *thinking* he could have what is mine—

Only, she's not mine. Not so long as I am bound by covenant to another.

I feel like a bastard when I finally make my way down the stairs. I should go back. I should apologize for taking my frustrations out on her, but I can't. I'm too consumed by them to get around them.

When I close myself into the backseat of the town car, I open my mouth to tell Clay to take me home, but then I stop. Looking up at the building in front of us, I remember that I already *am* home. At least I was before I walked away. Now, the last place I want to be is at the mansion. I'll never be able to explain my mood to Veronica. She no longer holds the place of my confidant. In fact, it's been some time since that has been the case.

For a moment, I get lost in my thoughts, wondering when my deepest secrets and insecurities went from something I felt comfortable sharing with her, to dark truths that I decided to harbor on my own. I'm not sure I could even pinpoint a moment in time, or if one closed door simply led to a plethora of *open* doors we stopped bothering to even darken.

"Sir?"

I snap my gaze toward the front seat and find Clay watching me through the rearview mirror.

"You look like you could use a drink."

I cough out a humorless laugh, surprised both by his suggestion and his willingness to even say such a thing.

"You're right."

"Where to?"

Peering out the window, I know that I can't be seen at the Lounge. Not tonight. Blaine was dressed for work, which means she'll likely be headed there any moment now. When my stomach growls, it's as if it makes up my mind for me.

Meeting Clay's gaze once more, I inquire, "Care for some pizza?"

He nods his response and then shifts the car in reverse, needing no more of an answer.

WHILE WE WAIT for our order to arrive, we don't say much to one another. Clay sips at his water as I nurse my beer, my thoughts occupied. I know I should be polite and make conversation, but I can't get the look on Blaine's face out of my head. I left her crying, like a jackass. The more I think about it, the more troubled I become.

She was right to call me out for holding her to a double standard. Even still, the reality of our situation is so *maddening.* I've made it impossible for both of us. We're doing the best we can, and yet, it's not good enough. It's not what either of us wants. I know that I'm not being fair. I've known that since the beginning. However, my actions moving forward could alter the course of my entire life in ways I can't even begin to comprehend. It's not as simple as getting a divorce. Not in my position. Not with the eyes of so many pointing in my direction. I need time to figure out how to do this as gracefully as possible, all the while knowing that the difficulty of the situation is my fault entirely.

Furthermore, I must also consider Veronica. I've yet to figure out the best way to tell her, the best way to go about ending what she might not even realize is our broken marriage. I do not wish to be callous with her. I do not wish to inflict anymore pain than the truth itself will cause. I cannot simply cast her onto the street, leaving her with nothing—I still care for her, regardless of the fact that my feelings are not the same as they once were.

"You're a smart man," says Clay, pulling me from my thoughts.

"Excuse me?" I ask, shaking my head clear.

"You're a smart man, Governor. You're tactful, you're generous, and you're far from cruel."

Frowning at him slightly, I inquire, "Why are you saying these things?"

"You'll figure it out. You're not one to be bested by a challenge, sir. It's how you got to where you are today."

I try to grab hold of his words—of his undue *confidence* in my ability to get through this like I get through my work day. I can't. I don't know what I'm doing *now* anymore than I did when it all began. I know what I feel. I know what I want. I know *who* I want—but I'm not entirely sure how I got here or where to go from here. I don't know how to explain this to my wife, to my family. It just *happened*, and yet, I know that's not true.

"I have a sister. Older. She's thirty-nine, now. She got married when she was twenty-five. Real nice guy. Successful. White collar career. In it for the long haul."

On the tip of my tongue is my question *why?* I don't know why he's telling me this, but I don't ask. He's never been particularly forthright with personal information, and I get the impression that I'll understand his reasons if I'm patient enough to hear him out—so I do.

"Five years in, my sister started acting different. At first, it was her wardrobe. Then it was her personality. She'd put on airs one day, and the next she'd barely be able to get out of bed. It didn't take long for me to figure out that she was having an affair. Her husband either pretended not to notice or pretended not to care. He loved her.

"The other guy, he was wild. He was rich. He was powerful. But more than all of that, he was manipulative. He didn't make her happy, he made her unstable and insecure. I'm not sure how she couldn't tell the difference. Blinded by love or some shit. Six months in, he convinced her to leave her husband. Six months after that, she was at my doorstep with nothing."

He pauses, props his forearms against the table, and leans toward me before continuing in a hushed voice.

"The state of your marriage is none of my business. That said, *you* are my business. I'm your shadow. I go where you go. I see what you see. I see *more* than you see."

Mimicking his stance, I lean toward him as I ask, "What is it that you see?"

"I see that *this* is not *that.* Pardon me saying so, but it seems *better.* She makes you happy. She lightens your burdens. She relaxes you. To her, you are not the governor. You are not the former D.A. You're not even a Harvard Law graduate—you're merely a man; a man for which she cares a great deal."

"So what are you saying?" I furrow my brow in curiosity as I go on to question, "Do you mean to imply that I am *not* merely a man to Veronica?"

"In my opinion? No. You're not. I surmise it's no one's fault—but she appears to have misunderstood your ambition and your drive, mistaking it for your identity and your highest purpose. Or perhaps it is *her* ambition and *her* drive that has shielded her eyes to the *man* she sleeps next to night after night. I suppose I wouldn't know. I'm not her shadow."

Our pizza arrives, interrupting our conversation, and we both lean back as the hot dish is placed in between us. Once the waitress has delivered our plates and napkins, she takes her leave, and I stare down and the deep-dish in front of me.

I sensed that Clay had an opinion about what's been going on between Blaine and me. Though, I never guessed that he'd admit to it. Furthermore, I never imagined that his observations would be so telling. The truth is, I do not know how either woman views me. I do not feel at liberty to make such assumptions. All I can do is base my opinions on my experiences. I must admit, Clay's theory holds some weight.

Since the day I was sworn in, I've said that Veronica was made to be the First Lady of our state. She's always done her best to fill the role of my biggest supporter as the woman at my side. In many ways, I think her *role* as my wife has helped her to bury her *desire* to be a mother. While I can't hold it against her, it doesn't change the fact that as we've grown, as we've matured and settled into one career advancement after another, we haven't exactly changed *together*. In retrospect, it's almost as though we've changed to *accommodate* one another.

It's not that complicated with Blaine. As messy as the circumstances of our affair may be, what we share is quite simple—quite *pure*. It is honest and open. It is transparent and *liberating*. Even more, it is passionate and real—it is *extraordinary*.

It is all that I want.

She is all that I want.

Thinking back on his story, I furrow my brow at the thought of his sister. Curious as to how she's currently fairing, I boldly inquire, "How is she now? Your sister?"

Sliding a slice of pizza onto his plate, he informs me, "Remarried her ex a year after she showed up at my place. They've got two kids."

Taken aback by his answer, I hesitate to reach for my own slice. "Are they happy?"

"Very. Love covers a multitude of sins, or so I'm told."

Love.

Over the last thirty-seven years, I've come to learn that there are various shades of *love*. I knew I had fallen in love with Veronica when I couldn't imagine my life without her. However, I was seventeen, and I didn't understand that I knew nothing of love. I've been so often told that *love* is a choice—one that is to be made every single day. To an extent, I can appreciate that as a wise proverb not to be forgotten; yet, the unadulterated fear I felt when I saw that napkin on Blaine's kitchen counter, that was not a choice. My inability to comprehend her lack of interest while I was busy combatting my panic at the thought of another taking my place in her life—*that* was not a choice.

It's not that I can't imagine my future without Blaine. Rather, it's the fear of who I'll be without her that breathes life into my hope.

"I need to see her," I mutter under my breath, trying to think of way to get her alone as soon as possible.

"There's a twenty-four-hour fitness center a couple of blocks away from where she lives."

I look across from me, speechless at Clay's suggestion. It only takes me a second to recognize the genius of his plan. Tonight, he is full of surprises.

"I'll need a membership," I state obviously.

"I can swing you by after dinner."

"Excellent."

Blaine

When I used to get into a fight with Mateo before a shift, working through the evening was like pretending to ignore a papercut on my dominate hand. Working a shift after my fight with Michael feels like pretending to ignore a gaping wound across my entire chest. What's worse is that the Lounge has had a pretty slow evening, giving me plenty of time to replay our exchange over and over again. Each time, it hits me anew that after I mentioned his wife, he had nothing else to say. I don't know what that means, and it scares the shit out of me.

It's not unusual for neither of us to know the next time we'll be able to arrange to see each other. Sometimes it's spur of the moment. When Michael has a spare hour and I'm home, he'll sneak by. Other times, we could go more than a week without getting the chance to be together. I wasn't expecting his visit earlier in the night. After that fight, I have no idea when I'll see him again. The thought of going *days* without talking to him, without figuring out what the hell happened, it makes me anxious and sick to my stomach.

I don't *want* to think that he was somehow defending his marital status. I don't *want* to think that he got mad when I brought up his wife because he expects me to put up with her presence for *forever*. I don't *want* to think that the fact that we've yet to have a conversation about what *our* future will look like is a telling sign that I *should* be reading into. I don't want to feel this lost, wandering around in *reality*. I want to trust my heart. I want to trust *his*. I want to find my happy cloud again and go back to last weekend, when it was just him and me—but that's not possible. Not with my *gaping wound*.

With my phone nestled in my back pocket, I know I'd feel a text notification or a call come through. Even still, I pull it out to check for any possible missed communication from Michael at least a hundred times between the beginning and the end of my shift. When two o'clock finally arrives, I'm mentally and emotionally exhausted. Yet, something tells me I won't be getting much sleep tonight.

"Yo, B—hold up a sec, will you?" calls out Dodger as I push open the front door.

"Yeah. I'll be right outside," I assure him. I force a smile before making my way out into the cool, late summer, morning air. While I'm gazing up at the moon, I feel him come to stand beside me, and I shift my focus in his direction.

"It's just you and me, now. Tell me what's going on. I can tell you've been upset all night."

I can feel the urge to cry coming on fast at his invitation, and I'm at a loss as to what to do. I hear Michael in my head, flippantly suggesting that I tell my friends I have a boyfriend, and *reality* hits me in my sore spot, yet again. I wonder if anything between Michael and me will ever be normal. If I'll ever get to introduce him to my friends, or if we'll crack under the weight of our secret and never make it that far. Or worse, if we *do* make it that far and he doesn't *like* my friends, all of whom are still in their early twenties—except Simone.

"Yeah, okay, now you *really* need to tell me—what the fuck, Blaine?"

I'm startled out of my fearful thoughts when Dodger swipes a tear from my cheek. I hadn't realized I started crying.

"I'll be okay," I murmur, brushing my fingertips under my eyes.

"Bullshit."

"You wouldn't understand anyway."

Folding his arms across his chest, he shrugs and challenges, "Try me."

I hesitate for a moment. Then, my exhaustion getting the better of me, I blurt, "Remember that guy from last night? The one who gave me his number?"

"Yeah," he mutters with a scowl. "Did you call him or something?"

"No. God, no—but my…boyfriend found his number on accident and got really pissed."

"Whoa, your *what?* Did you get back with Mateo? Fuck, B, why didn't—"

"It's not Mateo. It's someone else. I didn't tell you because it's complicated. Anyway, we got into a fight about it, and I don't know what it all means."

"Shit. Now I feel like a dick for egging you on last night."

"No, don't," I insist, shaking my head at him. "It's not your fault. I should have thrown it away. I wasn't thinking. I didn't know it would be that big of a deal. I wasn't planning on calling the guy."

"You told your—*mystery* boyfriend this?"

"Yes. Of course."

He shrugs again and says, "Well, I don't know, B. Maybe he just needed a minute to cool off. You're still pretty new, right? This could be a mild case of jealousy. Trust me, it happens to the best of us." He smirks, dropping his arms before he lightly taps my arm. "When you catch a good one, the thought of losing her while you're not around is terrifying."

My muddled mind tries wrapping itself around his theory, but I can't let go of the fact that Michael is *married* and I am not. If anyone should be afraid of losing to another, it's *me.*

"Maybe," I sigh.

"Come on," he insists, throwing an arm around my shoulders. "I'll walk you to your car. You both probably need to sleep it off. If he's still being a douche tomorrow, maybe he's got a small dick and you should ditch him."

In spite of how I feel, I cough out a laugh, imagining Michael's dick—which is anything but *small.*

"Hmm. I'm guessing that means you've seen the goods?" he teases, giving me a small shake.

"You could say that." I bite the inside of my cheek, sweeping my hair behind my ears before I softly admit, "The goods are good...*really* good."

"In that case, I hope things are a little brighter in the morning."

"Thanks, Dodge."

When we reach my car, he waits for me to sink into the driver's seat and then closes me in. He taps the top of the vehicle before he yells, "Get some sleep, B."

I nod in reply, knowing good and well that my mind is far too anxious to make any such promises.

I SIT STRAIGHT up in bed, waking from a restless sleep. Trying to get my bearings, I peer through the darkness, the dim light from the setting moon shining through my tall windows across the bed. When I realize that it was my phone that startled me, I pat around for the device. I know I didn't plug it in and leave it on my nightstand like usual. I may or may not have spent an hour scrolling through images of Michael on Google while trying to fall asleep. By the time I find the device, tucked underneath my pillow, it's no longer ringing.

Just as I see that *My Lover* was trying to reach me, there's a knock at my front door. I snap my gaze through my banister, my heart rate speeding up as I stare down at my entryway. My phone starts ringing again, and when I see Michael's calling, a ridiculous amount of hope fills my chest. There's another knock, and I'm quick to scramble out of bed. My thoughts and emotions are so jumbled, I almost forget that it's four in the morning, and I should probably answer my phone before whipping open the door.

"Hello?" I answer, my feet carrying me swiftly down the stairs.

"Angel, open the door. It's me."

My hope intensifies at the sound of his term of endearment, and I can't even bother to answer him. I drop my phone on the dining room table as I pass and race toward the door. My hands are shaking as I fumble with the locks, but I manage to get them turned. Opening the barrier between us, I see Michael standing in the hallway, dressed in a pair of tennis shoes, gym shorts, and a muscle shirt. All the fear and insecurities I've been battling since he stormed out come rising to the surface, and I don't even hesitate to throw myself at him.

I jump up and circle my arms around his shoulders, and he's quick to crush me against his chest. His strong embrace is my undoing, and I bury my face in his neck as I let my tears fall. I barely even notice as he carries me over the threshold before shutting the door behind us with his foot. He soothes me, rubbing one of his hands across my back. Neither of us speaks right away, but I don't mind. We've been in a fight for less than twelve hours, but it feels like much longer.

With Michael, everything is greater—brighter, more vibrant, and more passionate. With him, I feel deeper, I love harder—but I also hurt harder, too.

I stole one of his undershirts from his duffel over the weekend, when he wasn't looking. It's what I changed into before I climbed into bed a couple of hours ago. So when I hitch my legs up, wrapping them around his hips, and he drops a hand to graze my thigh, my skin is bare. His touch makes me hold him tighter.

"I shouldn't have left. I'm sorry," he mumbles, his lips grazing my ear. "I had a bad day. I took it out on you, and I shouldn't have. There's no excuse. I'm sorry, Blaine."

"I'm sorry, too. I'm sorry I took his number. I didn't mean—"

"I was jealous," he admits, holding me closer. "I didn't have the right to be, but I was—*am*. I hate that you feel like you can't tell people about us. I hate that you can't introduce me to your friends; that I can't be the one flirting with you in public."

He spins us around, pressing my back against the door as he grabs my sides and holds me—his thumbs right below the small swell of my breasts.

"It's my fault. I know that I've put us in this situation, and I'm sorry. I'm going to figure this out, angel," he promises, peering through the darkness into my eyes. He touches his forehead to mine, and my heart aches with the crushing weight of my love for this man. "I'm going to leave Veronica. I need you to know that. I—"

Having heard enough, I lean forward and cut him off with a kiss. "I know you will, baby. You'll figure it out. *We'll* figure it out," I mutter before delivering another kiss. "This isn't all your fault."

He plunges his tongue into my mouth, momentarily silencing us both before he grumbles, "I started this."

"*We* started this," I mumble against his lips, burying my fingers in his hair. "I'm in this with you, Michael. I always have been."

I'm about to confess that I love him, but he interrupts me. He kisses me fervently, and I don't stop him. Instead, I try and convey the depths of all that I feel—my love, my fear, my frustration, my relief, and my hope—using my mouth and my greedy hands. I kiss him hard, clinging to him fiercely, unable to get him close enough. When he reaches down between us and shoves my panties aside, sliding his fingers along my slick center, I moan unabashedly.

"Yes—*please*, baby," I beg.

It's all I have to say. The next thing I know, he's inside of me—and it's *perfect.*

Michael

I SWALLOW BLAINE'S moan as I coat my dick in her arousal. She feels incredible, her body wrapped tightly around mine, and I regret having ever upset her—I regret having hurt her. My angel. My love. I hardly slept last night, anxious for the excuse to get out of bed; aching for the woman who now occupies my thoughts more than any other. Sleeping beside Veronica has become *less* than a routine. It's as if I wake up every morning in a place that has somehow become *foreign* to me. Gabriel wasn't wrong—I am changing. My heart is changing. *Has changed.*

I knew, the moment she opened the door, that I'm not falling anymore. I'm there, and I'm not going anywhere.

I buck my hips up harder, feeling my way underneath the shirt on her back. *My* shirt. She whimpers when I palm her breast, and I sense myself losing control like I so often do with this woman. *My* woman. I massage her tit while I hold tight to her opposite hip, all the while fucking her tight, wet pussy. *My* pussy.

She hums the sound of her pleasure, her warm breath fanning across my lips, and I can no longer keep my silence.

"*Te amo,* Blaine. *Te amo más de lo que me sabía capaz de amar. Siempre,* angel—*siempre serás mi* angel."

A strangled cry spills from her throat, her hands holding my face close to hers as she begs, "Again. Tell me again, baby."

"*Te amo, Blaine.* I love you. I love you more than I knew I was capable of loving. Always, angel—you'll always be my angel."

Her lips close around mine in a desperate kiss, and I can taste the salt of her tears even as she giggles into my mouth. "*Michael,*" she whispers on a sigh. "I love you, too. I love you so much."

Her declaration unhinges me, and I need her to come—I need her to come *right now.*

I drive into her unyieldingly and rapidly. With every thrust of my hips, I press her harder against the door, causing it to make a rattling sound. She moans loudly, and I grunt in response, loving every single noise she makes while I'm inside of her. This is the soundtrack of our passion—our love—or *need.* It is *ours,* and I wouldn't trade it for anything.

"*God—just like that,*" she groans, her head falling back against the door. "You feel *so* good, baby."

Sliding my hand down her chest and slipping it between us, I press my thumb against her clit and demand, "Come, Blaine. Strangle my cock."

She grips the collar of my shirt, arching her back away from the door as her legs begin to shake. "*Shit,*" she murmurs when her core clenches all around me.

My own pleasure hits me instantly, a zing racing up my spine, and I bury myself balls deep—going still as she milks me dry.

"Hell, yes," I grunt, pressing my forehead to the side of her neck.

Her body continues to tremble as we both work to catch our breath, and it's not until she speaks that I realize that she's crying.

"Tell me it'll be enough," she pleads, her arms locking around the back of my neck. "Tell me again that you love me and that it'll be enough."

Not understanding what has her so upset, I pepper kisses along the side of her neck until I've reached her ear. Her hair tickles my lips as I whisper, "I love you."

"I love you, too," she stammers.

"I'm going to put you down. I need to see you."

She nods and loosens her legs, causing me to slip out of her heat. Once she's on her feet, she sniffles, wiping away her tears before we both right our clothing. Not wanting to blind her with the overhead light, I gently take her hand and lead the way up to her loft. We sit on the edge of the bed together, and I switch on her nearest bedside lamp. Groaning, she closes her eyes and presses her forehead against my shoulder. I touch my lips to the top of her head, cupping my hand around the back of her neck.

"Talk to me. Tell me what's wrong."

Rather than answer me right away, she burrows her way into my side, hooking both of her legs over my thigh as she wraps her arms around my waist. I rest one arm around her hips, tucking her hair behind her ear with my other hand, waiting as patiently as possible for her to respond.

"I don't want to lose you," she finally confesses.

"Blaine, look at me," I command, a small smile playing at my lips. I quirk my eyebrows at her when her hazel gaze collides with mine. I then go on to say, "Were you with me just now? I could have sworn you were there. I could have sworn you said you loved me, too."

"What if you don't like my friends? And your family—what if they hate me? What if you leave Veronica and *reality* tears us apart?"

I tug my eyebrows together, momentarily reminded that I'm the reason these insecurities exist. Deciding that I can only deal with this one mountain at a time, I shove aside my blame and do my best to assure her of my commitment. "There's no *if*." I shake my head, remembering what it felt like to climb out of bed a little while ago. Touching my forehead to Blaine's, I explain, "I don't belong to her any longer. Do you have any idea how hard it is for me to even be in that house? Or how hard it is for me to share a bed with her, knowing that the woman I'd prefer to hold in my arms is sleeping here, *alone?*"

"Why are you still with her, then?"

"You know why," I insist tenderly.

"Yes, but how long are we supposed to hang onto that excuse? Until you're reelected for a second term? Until you're no longer governor at all? Will we even be able to exist as something *more* than a secret? Will we know how?"

Her questions strike a cord deep within me. *Waiting* for the right time—it's an issue I've been up against before. It's a challenge that drove an invisible wedge between Veronica and me long ago. If there's one thing I adore about Blaine more than any other, it's her vulnerability and her desire to be open and honest about her insecurities in regards to our relationship. She may be more than a decade younger than me, and we will always have our differences, but they're not enough to best who we're capable of being *together.* She's not afraid to *feel.* She's not afraid to let me see her—*all* of her. Even more, she's made it abundantly clear that she craves the same in return. All of me. That is what she wants, and that is what she shall have.

She gasps when I fall back onto the bed, taking her with me before rolling until I'm on my side, hovering over her. I rest my hand on her hip, giving her a squeeze as I press a soft kiss against her lips.

"Labor Day weekend is in a couple of weeks. My family uses it as an opportunity to travel together. Graham's grandparents own a beach house in Oregon. I'll think of an excuse to get out of it. I'll take you away—just you and me. Can you get the time off?"

Frowning at me curiously, she mumbles, "I can try. But, Michael, that doesn't—"

"Blaine, things will be a little tough once word is out. I've never been up against something like this before. I need to gather my wits about me. I need a little calm before the storm."

"Okay," she whispers, reaching up to run her fingers along my jaw. "You'll tell her when we get back?"

"Let me get some advice. I'll set up a few meetings with people I trust, people who helped me get into office—people who I'm sure will keep their lips sealed. I need to know how to handle this with as little scandal as possible thrown at all of us."

She nods her understanding and then presses, "*Then* you'll tell her?"

"Yes," I promise, brushing my lips over hers. "Then I'll tell her."

"'Kay," she murmurs. Her eyes staring up into mine, she bites the inside of her cheek, stalling before she asks, "When do you have to leave?"

"My suit is out in the car. I should be in the shower at six, out the door no later than twenty 'til."

"Will you hold me until you have to get up?"

"I'd love to."

Blaine

I'M SO TIRED, I feel my eyes drooping almost as soon as he shuts out the light. When he joins me underneath the covers, he pulls me into his arms—my back against his chest. *Relief* pales in comparison to how I feel having him here. I didn't expect for my morning to go as it has, but here I am, drifting to sleep in the arms of the man I love. I know he'll be gone by the time I wake up, but I don't let that trouble me. Not anymore.

He loves me.

"Michael?" I mumble, fighting against sleep for just a second longer.

"What is it, angel?"

"There's a key. In the drawer by the dishwasher, there's a key."

Holding me tighter, he buries his nose in my hair and mutters, "If you're offering me a key, I won't be able to stay away. I'll be here every morning before I get ready for work, even if all I get to do is *this*."

A weak smile pulls at the corner of my mouth as I breathe, "Promise?"

"I love you," he murmurs in reply.

"Love you," I barely manage, finally succumbing to the pull of sleep.

Twenty-Five

Michael

"I STILL CAN'T BELIEVE YOU'RE NOT GOING," Veronica states, emerging from the closet with another handful of clothing.

I watch her from where I sit, on the cushioned bench at the foot of the bed. She stacks her outfits in her suitcase, laying open beside me.

"Don't even get me started on your mother. Every day this week, she's been calling me, trying to get me to convince you that you can just bring your work with you."

I shake my head, mentally pulling on the truth that I wouldn't be able to get any work done with everyone around. We're not exactly a quiet bunch, a fact that everyone can admit. Regardless of the fact that I won't actually be working this weekend, I still defend myself as I say, "You know I wouldn't be able to concentrate."

"Yes, I know," she says with a sigh. She stops what she's doing, frowning at me before she reaches over and runs her fingers through the front of my hair. "You've never missed a weekend before. We've been doing this since Abigail got engaged. Eight years, Mike."

"I realize that, Vee, but I've also never had a quarter like the one I'm currently having. We've been over this. I didn't make this decision lightly."

"You've been working too hard, lately. I know your job is important, but you need down time just like the rest of us."

I don't say anything in reply, not in the mood to rehash the argument we had when I first told her that I wouldn't be joining the family over the holiday weekend. I knew that everyone would be disappointed, most of all Veronica and my mother, but I need the space. I need the chance to take a breath before I rip apart one of the longest and most meaningful relationships that I've had in my whole life. More than that, I need another weekend with Blaine. The days are getting longer and the nights are getting harder without her. I'm not so prideful that I can't admit that a weekend with my woman is what I need before I face the turmoil I know lies in front of us.

As I admire the woman that's been my wife for more than fifteen years, I'm certain that while I will always care for her, she no longer has my heart. It's the most difficult truth I've ever had to face, and I'd be lying if I said that I was anxious to be done with her. It is not my intent to be cruel. I'm not a heartless man, and I'm aware of the pain my secret will cause. Yet, at the end of it all, I know that the truth will set us both free. She deserves to be loved the way I'm no longer capable of loving her.

"I'm sorry," she says, giving my shoulder a squeeze and pulling me from my thoughts. "I know this isn't your ideal choice, either. Maybe I should stay."

"What? No—why would you do that?" I ask, furrowing my eyebrows to disguise my rising sense of panic.

"It was only a couple of weeks ago that I left to visit my parents. Now this? We haven't really had a lot of time to spend together recently. Maybe it would be better if I stuck around for when you could take a break."

"Veronica, I'll be fine. You're going," I insist, reaching up with one hand to grip her waist. It isn't until after I say the words that I realize that this will be the last Labor Day weekend she'll be spending with the family. She doesn't know it yet, but she needs this time away just as much as I do. Taking hold of the opposite side of her waist, I position her in front of me, so that she's standing between my legs. Looking up at her with honest sincerity, I tell her, "I want you to go. They'll want you there. Besides, I know how much you enjoy the beach house this time of year."

"I do," she says on a sigh, running her fingers through my hair again.

"Then it's settled."

She stares at me for a second and then sits herself in my lap, resting her arms around my shoulders. When she presses a kiss to my lips, I kiss her back, pulling away before she does.

"I'll miss you."

"You'll have a good time," I reply.

I deliver another short kiss, intending only to bring this conversation to an end, but she leans into me. When she flicks out her tongue, I indulge her, wishing not to appear cold. It's not long before I can tell where she wants this to go. I feel guilty denying her. I know, without me, she won't find the relief she's after, while I was fully satisfied this morning—but I made Blaine a promise, and I won't go back on my word.

"I can't, babe. Not tonight," I mutter, slowing down our kiss. "Besides, you have to finish packing. Your flight leaves early tomorrow."

"Yeah. You're right," she concedes, touching her forehead to mine.

"I should go give Lawrence a call."

Raking her fingers through her hair, she murmurs, "Oh, that's right."

I offer her a small smile. It's the best I can give. To cover my tracks, I've decided to tell her *half* of the truth. While she thinks that I'll be locked away working all weekend, I told her I wouldn't be doing it here at the mansion. Lawrence has a cabin up in Vail. I told her he intended to lend me his space for peace and quiet. Seeing as it *is* a holiday, the excuse of getting out of the city felt like a good one to fall back on. All that she doesn't know is that I won't be alone.

"Don't stay down there too long," she insists, checking the time on the alarm clock as she stands from my lap.

I see that it's a few minutes past eight, and my first thought is to wonder when Blaine will be taking her break tonight.

"I'll be back up in a bit," I assure her, pulling my phone from my pocket as I take my leave.

Blaine

My phone vibrates from my back pocket, and I smile as I pour the cocktail from the shaker into the martini glass in front of me. Something tells me that it's Michael, and just the thought of him makes me stupidly happy.

We've had the most amazing week and a half. After he took the key, he kept his promise. Every morning, outside of Sunday when he goes to church with his family, he lets himself into my loft not long after four a.m. Occasionally, he'll hold me for an hour before he gets up and goes for a short run. When he's finished, he then comes back to get ready for his day, always kissing me goodbye before he leaves. Those mornings, it seems I can't really fall asleep until after he's left, too anxious for any and all time with him. Mostly, though, I'm more than happy to be coaxed out of sleep for a *different* kind of exercise. On those mornings, we'll play for as long as we can, after which I fall into a deep, restful sleep while he gets dressed for work.

It's not perfect, but it's a routine that belongs to us. For now, I won't take it for granted.

I've been looking forward to our weekend plans since the moment I ensured my time off. Dodger was able to cover my shifts on Friday and Sunday, regardless of the fact that that meant he wouldn't get a day off for two weeks straight, and I worked it out for my boss to schedule me off on Monday. Even though I'll only be gone for three nights, I've been slowly packing all week. I also may have made a trip to Victoria's Secret to up my underwear game for the holiday. This is the first time I've ever had plans to go away with my boyfriend before. Of course, Mateo and I went out of town a couple of times, but it was never a romantic getaway so much as it was a weekend meant to be spent with friends.

I deliver the drink I was making before refilling another patron's beer. Finally having a moment to spare, I make my way toward the register, turning my back before pulling out my phone. When I see a message waiting for me from *My Forever*, my smile from before returns.

That's what he is to me. I'm sure of it. I'll never love another as much as I love him. Never.

Unlocking my screen, I pull up his text, reading it quickly.

Don't forget the rope, angel. We'll be needing it.

I bite down hard on the inside of my cheek, willing my body to remain calm. I can't manage to stop the shiver that races up my spine as my stomach clenches, and I can only hope to keep a blush from blossoming across my cheeks as I type out my reply.

Tossed them in my bag after you got in the shower this morning. One step ahead of you, baby.

I wait a second to see if he's able to respond right away, and a grin breaks out across my face when my phone vibrates with his reply seconds later.

My angel is kinky.
Only at the hands of her governor…
I love you.

My heart melts, and I'm quick to respond. Only Michael would talk dirty to me one second, and be completely sweet to me the next.

I love you so, so, so much!!!! I can't wait for tomorrow.
I'll pick you up at two.
I'll be ready.
Night, angel.
Night, baby. xoxo

"So, when am I going to get to meet this guy?"

My head snaps up in surprise, and my heart leaps when I realize Dodger is leaning against the back counter not even a foot away from me.

"Shit, Dodge—you scared me," I whisper, sliding my phone back into my pocket.

He grins at me, folding his arms across his chest before he asks, "Well? *Mystery* boyfriend can't stay a mystery forever—especially not if he makes you smile like that. I've never seen you this happy, B."

I shrug, not denying his observation as I admit, "Me neither."

"So? Date and time. Hope and I will be there."

"Soon. I'll tell you more about him soon. I just—things are still a little complicated," I state, my understatement so grand that it feels like a lie. "Anyway, we're not entirely official. I want to wait. I want to wait until we are."

"All right, I get it."

"What about you?" I ask, nudging his leg with my knee. Wanting to shift the conversation off of me and onto him, I question, "What's with you working all of these hours? You're saving for something. What is it?"

His grin stretches even wider, his dark eyes dancing with excitement as he vaguely answers. "It's time."

"Time for what?"

"Time to get my shit together and pop the question."

I gasp so loudly it sounds like a shriek. I clap both hands over my mouth, chancing a quick glance behind me to see if I've disturbed anyone with my outburst. I don't get a good look, too distracted by Dodger's laughter.

Joining in with my own amusement, I playfully smack his chest before I mutter, "I can't believe you've been holding out on me."

Lifting a single eyebrow, he counters, "You really want to go there? Miss *Mystery* Boyfriend."

"This is so not the same thing. This is *Hope!* Oh, my god—she's going to say yes."

"She better," he chuckles.

Sobering up a bit, I think about the two of them. They've been together for a while now, having met only a couple months before Mateo and I first got together. It's pretty obvious that they're an almost perfect match, and I know they've loved each other through good times and not so great ones, too.

"In all seriousness, I'm truly happy for you. I think that's great news."

"Thanks, B."

Someone catches his attention and he pats me on the shoulder before getting back to work. I watch him go and then check on my guests, as well. For the rest of the night, my thoughts are all over the place. Between my weekend with Michael and Dodger's news of wishing to get married, I can't keep my ideas from bouncing all over the place. In the back of my mind, I know that my trip to Vail isn't *just* an excuse to get out of town. I know that it's for *us*—for Michael and myself—but it's also for *Governor Cavanaugh.* He promised me that as soon as we got back, he was going to start the delicate processes of making it so that we could be together. For *real.*

At the end of my shift, I'm completely drained. Even still, all the way home, I can't shove aside my thoughts of the future. For a while now, I've felt as though my future was this illusive place with undiscovered dreams. Since graduating college, it's felt too daunting to think too hard about it. Facing one day at a time has been my tactic for the last couple of years; but with Michael, it's different. With Michael, I'm not afraid to dream.

Logically speaking, that doesn't make much sense. There's so much about our future that is unknown. As Simone told me, there are variables that we're up against, variables that we're not in control of—variables that could play a part in where we go and how we get there. We're having an affair, for Christ's sake. Except, none of that matters to me. None of that scares me. Michael *is* my future. The woman I want to be, the life that I wish to have, they don't exist without him. My love. My *forever*.

Since I know it'll take us a couple of hours to drive to Vail, and I imagine we'll be laying low for the evening, I decide to keep my travel attire casual. After towel drying my hair and slathering my body in lotion, I make my way to the closet to dress in the clothes I set out the day before. I giggle to myself when I realize just about all of it is new—my black, holey, skinny jeans, my ankle bracelet, and black gladiator sandals being the exceptions.

I slip into my dark pink, lacey, cheeky panties and matching sheer bra, hoping that Michael will appreciate them. When my jeans are on and cuffed at the bottom, I toss my newest t-shirt over my head. It's gray, the red letters on the front reading: *Harvard Law*. Right below that, in smaller font, it says: *Just Kidding*. The moment I saw it, I knew I had to have it. It arrived the day before yesterday—just in time. It's got a deep V-neck, showing off a generous amount of my chest, and it hangs loosely around my frame. I opt to add a last minute accessary and throw on a simple necklace to complete the outfit.

I then set my shoes outside the closet, beside my small carry-on bag, and head for the coffee table, where I abandoned my phone.

Making myself comfortable on the couch, I reach for the device and pull up dad's number, hitting *call* without a second thought. He took today off, so that he could enjoy a four-day weekend. He's probably out shopping for food and supplies for his fishing trip tomorrow with some of the guys, which is why he doesn't answer until after the fourth ring.

"Hello?"

"Hey, dad. What are you doing?"

"Shoppin'," he grunts.

I smirk, amused at how well I know my old man. "Don't go crazy, all right?"

"It's a holiday, Lulu. I don't want to hear it."

Rolling my eyes, I mumble, "Yeah, okay."

"You didn't call me to give me grief about my snacks, did you?"

"No. I just wanted to remind you that I'll be out of town this weekend. I won't be back until Monday night, but I'll try to stop by and see you Tuesday before I head into work."

"Oh. Right. This that guy that's stringin' my baby girl along?"

"He's not stringing me along, dad," I laugh. "But *yes*. It's him. Mike," I murmur, offering his name for the first time, much like I did with Simone.

"Mike, huh? When do I get to meet this *Mike?*"

For a second, I get nervous even *thinking* about introducing them. I still haven't forgotten the look on my dad's face when I first alluded to Michael. I know that he doesn't condone cheating. In many ways, *I* don't either, so I can't blame him. That said, I still want him to approve of my choice. Not my choice to lie and covet and steal—but my choice to love and adore and commit to the man I never saw coming.

In the end, it's my feelings for Michael that give me the courage to answer, "Soon. I promise."

"You'll let me know when you get to where you're goin'?"

"Yeah."

"And when you get back?"

"I promise."

"All right, baby girl. Hope you have a good time."

"Thanks, dad. You, too. I'll talk to you later."

"Love you, Lulu."

"Love you, too."

I end the call and check the time, feeling instantly impatient when I see that it's barely past one-thirty. Trying to kill time, I triple check my bag to make sure I have everything, and then I go mess with my hair. I end up braiding the front in a short French braid, then piling the rest on the crown of my head in a little messy bun. I pull a few tendrils loose to dangle from above my ears, and then I check the time again. When I see that I've killed all of *eleven* minutes, I decide to pace while I scroll through my social media platforms. Not two minutes later, and I'm struck with a realization I hadn't thought of before.

Michael and I have not one *picture together.*

While it's quite obvious that I couldn't share photo proof of our time together and our happy memories, that doesn't mean we can't have them or that I shouldn't capture them from time to time. I've never been someone who feels like it's necessary to take a picture of everything, but I'd be a hell of a lot less *stalker-like* if I had my own images of Michael to scroll through, instead of whatever I can find on Google.

When a knock sounds at the door, I gasp excitedly, noting that it's ten minutes to two. Slipping my phone into my back pocket, I hurry to answer, grinning wildly at the sight of Michael standing just beyond the threshold. He looks delicious in a blue and white checkered button-up, undone enough for me to get a peek at his chest hairs, and his sleeves are rolled up to his elbows. He's in a pair of navy khaki shorts, and he's got flip-flops on, a sight I've never seen before—a sight that speaks of his intentions to enjoy a relaxing weekend with *me*.

"You're early," I say in greeting, playfully pretending I wasn't ready for him to be here an hour ago.

"I didn't get my cuddles this morning," he teases, stepping toward me and caging me in his arms. I reach up to hold the sides of his face, covered in his light beard, the why I like it best. Leaning toward me, he murmurs, "I couldn't wait any longer."

"Good. I was *dying*," I whisper. Pressing up on my tiptoes, I bring my lips to his.

He keeps our kiss short, and a little better than sweet, before he pulls away. "I like your shirt," he tells me, speaking through a smirk.

"I thought you might," I giggle.

He smiles, kisses the tip of my nose, and then asks, "You ready to go?"

"*So* ready."

"Let's get out of here, then."

"Yes, sir."

Twenty-Six

Michael

I DON'T REMEMBER MUCH OF OUR RIDE into the mountains. As soon as Clay merged onto the interstate, Blaine and I somehow got lost in one another. We made-out like a couple of teenagers almost the whole trip.

Before Blaine, I'm not sure that I even remember the last time I enjoyed the simple act of *kissing* so much. I'm certain there was a point in my adolescence where all I could think about was kissing Veronica, but that era has long since passed. I'm not naïve. I'm sure that as the *newness* of my relationship with Blaine begins to shift into something else, something *more*, that we won't always be this love struck. However, the mere fact that just her kiss could leave me with such a heady feeling even now, being the grown man that I am, it takes me back. Back to that ball field, when my lips first met hers. I knew then that her kiss would change me forever. Now I'm without a doubt that I'll never be the same.

Hers is a kiss I can't live without. Hers is a kiss I *won't* live without. And this afternoon, hers is a kiss I won't deny. This weekend is *ours*, and I plan on savoring every moment of it.

When I feel the car come to a stop, I caress the side of Blaine's neck and pull my lips away from hers. She tugs her bottom one between her teeth, her gaze lowered and glued to my mouth. I smile at her, the sight of her swollen pink lips and her greedy stare reminding me that I've found in her something I thought I'd never have. Sexually speaking, I've not known better. Granted, before her, I'd only ever been with my wife—and I won't claim to never have enjoyed her, as that would be a cruel lie. Nevertheless, I didn't know how strong a pull you could have toward someone who not only understands your sexual desires but *appreciates* them. It only intensifies my craving.

"Don't worry, angel. There's more where that came from," I assure her, my voice soft and low so as not to shatter the charged atmosphere in which we're still wrapped.

The hand she's got resting at my side grips my shirt as she leans into me a bit more. Slowly lifting her eyes to meet mine, she murmurs, "You make me so happy."

"As do you."

She closes her eyes and shakes her head, giggling quietly as she hides her face in my neck. "Are we there yet?"

I draw in a deep breath, finally taking a look out of the window as we continue to move. Noticing that we've made it to town, I reach for the button to roll down the partition between us and Clay.

Before I get the chance to ask, Clay informs us, "We should arrive in less than five minutes."

"Thank you," I reply with a nod.

"Five minutes?" Blaine questions, looking over her shoulder through the window on the opposite side of the car. "I thought you said this guy lived in a secluded area. We can't really be five minutes away, can we?"

"No. Not quite. We have to make a stop first."

"Oh. Where?" she asks, returning her attention toward me.

Smirking, I answer, "The grocery store. I thought maybe I'd buy us some food before we locked ourselves in."

"Mmm, sustenance. Good idea," she hums.

Just as Clay predicted, we arrive at the local grocery store five minutes later. We all exit the car together, and I grab my ball cap out of the trunk. While I don't anticipate running into anyone I may know, I'm smart enough to take the precaution and slide the hat down low in disguise. I then take Blaine's hand and escort her inside, winking down at her when she laces her fingers between mine.

"I'll push, you load?" I ask as I reach for a cart. She answers with a nod and a sweet smile, dropping my hand before resting hers in the crook of my arm. "I thought I'd teach you how to make empanadas tonight."

"Really?"

If her tone wasn't enough to give away her excitement, the way she tightens her grip around my arm certainly tells me she likes my idea.

"Yeah. Outside of that and pancakes, I hadn't really planned much of a menu. If you see something you want, toss it in the basket."

"*Anything?*" she inquires teasingly, quirking an eyebrow up at me.

"It's your weekend, baby. Anything you want."

She grins at me and then pulls her phone from her purse before she announces, "This requires a quick look at my Pinterest. Oh, and we should probably make a stop at the liquor store. There's this recipe I've been wanting to try, and it calls for wine. Wait, do you want to do chicken or beef?" she asks, her focus still directed at her phone as she scrolls through what looks like dozens of recipes.

Her feet slowing us down as her mind works, I admire her for a second, acknowledging how much I like her like this. We've never done something as simple as go to the grocery store together, or plan our meals for the next few days. To most people, this might be a trivial moment, but it's not. It's something I've *robbed* us of, something that obviously makes her happy, and something that she deserves. She deserves all the small things. She's *worth* all the big things.

"Baby?" she asks, looking up at me when I don't answer her.

No longer remembering her question, I lean down and press a kiss to her temple as I mumble, "Repeat the question?"

"Chicken or beef?"

This time, I don't hesitate to reply, "Why choose? We've got all weekend."

"We do, don't we?" Squeezing my arm once more, she hides her smile as she returns her attention to her phone before she says, "Chicken and beef it is."

Blaine

WE'RE IN THE grocery store for nearly an hour, and I love every minute of it. It's a mundane task, shopping for food, but getting to wander up and down every aisle on Michael's arm feels more like a *date* than a *chore*. To top things off, when we pass the floral section, he won't let us leave before I pick out an arrangement I want—*just because*.

My love—so sweet.

I almost forget that Clay came into the store with us, until I spot him checking out at the same time as we are. Michael told me a couple of days ago that Clay will be staying down the road from us, in a rented condo. I think about all the time that Michael has spent with me over the last couple of months, and I suddenly feel kind of bad for Clay. I know it's his job to watch over Michael, but I'm sure it must get boring sometimes—especially when Michael's at the loft with me. I decide to buy him a bottle of wine and a six pack of beer when we stop at the liquor store, hoping he'll appreciate the gesture. It's not enough, but it's the least I can do.

Luckily, the liquor store is only right next door. Unlike in the grocery store, Michael doesn't want me to go inside with him. I don't understand, until I remember that he'll have to show his ID at the register, so I don't protest. Instead, I give him my list, whispering to him that I want Clay to have what he wants, and he nods and winks at me before they leave me in the car.

Fifteen minutes later, our errands complete, we're back on the road. It takes us another twenty minutes to reach our destination. When we pull into the driveway, I can't keep my jaw from falling open. The house is *gorgeous*. It's also at least three times the size of dad's house.

"When you said *house in the mountains*..." My voice trails off as I gape at Michael.

"Wait until you see the inside."

"You've stayed here before?" I ask, wondering if he's ever brought Veronica, and wishing the thought never crossed my mind.

"No," he insists, resting a hand on my leg. "I've *been* here before. Day trip. Lawrence likes to play golf. He invited me up back when I first decided I wanted to run for governor."

"Oh." I nod, feeling relieved. As selfish as it might be, I want everything about this weekend to be ours—just mine and Michael's.

"Come on, angel. Let's get inside and put these groceries away. If we don't start the dough for the empanadas soon, we'll never eat."

While his words imply that *I'll* be carrying something inside, all I end up taking are my flowers and my purse. Clay and Michael bring in everything else, leaving me to stand in awe of this place. The main level is basically one *huge* space. With the light of the evening sun shining through the wall-to-wall windows that make up the back of the house, I can see why the architect didn't want to divide the room with any type of barrier. The only thing breaking up the space is a stone faced fire place between the living room and the dining room, as well as the kitchen cabinetry, which actually sits right up against the stairwell that leads to the second level.

The view is *outrageous*, making the deck just outside the dining room and living room space incredibly inviting. Even with so much exposure, there's no need for fear of privacy. The backyard, if you could even call it that, looks to be acres of wood and trees—some of which are already starting to turn with the colors of autumn.

All of the furniture—from the living space, to the dining room, and into the kitchen—is very *modern mountain lodge chic*, with lots of muted, neutral colors and warm, dark accents; yet, there's a touch of comfort in the details, causing me to assume that a man didn't decorate this place on his own.

"There's a hot tub out back," Michael mumbles into my ear as he comes up behind me, surprising me when he slips his arms around my waist.

"I didn't know. I didn't bring a suit."

He chuckles softly, his grip tightening as he replies, "Neither did I."

Smiling, I tilt my head so that I can see him. He waggles his eyebrows at me, making me laugh before he kisses me.

"It's just us now. What do you say to cracking open a couple beers and getting started on that cooking lesson?"

"I say: *yes, please!*"

After I set my bag down, we search the kitchen for something in which to store my flowers. While I arrange them in a glass pitcher, Michael finds everything we'll need to fix dinner. After we make the dough and set it aside to let it rest, we prepare the filling. I must admit, as much as I love watching Michael cook *for* me, cooking *with* him is probably equally as awesome. Even though the kitchen is industrial size in comparison to mine, we do everything side by side, flirting and laughing the entire time.

We're both on our second beer when we've got all the empanadas filled and ready to fry. I let Michael handle that part while I follow his directions with the avocado sauce. After the sauce is ready, I go about cleaning up a little, so we won't have much to do when we're done with dinner. Once that's finished, I hop up onto the counter top to watch him fry the last batch.

"Oh!" I cry, immediately hopping down and hurrying to my bag.

"Everything okay?" he calls out after me.

"Mmmhmm," I hum excitedly as I retrieve my phone. Returning to the kitchen, I resume my perch on the counter and open up my camera app. Pointing the lens at him, I explain, "I'm documenting our weekend. I don't have any pictures of you, and that's not allowed."

"Not *allowed*?" he asks with a smirk, glancing over at me.

I snap a quick shot, but it comes out blurry and I have to delete it. "Yeah. Since I love you and all, it's like a requirement that I have pictures of you on my phone, at the very least. Smile!"

He makes a goofy face, causing me to laugh, and I capture the image.

"Now I need a real one."

"How about…" He abandons his station at the stove and comes to stand in front of me. After pecking my lips with his own, he says, "How about we do this right?" He then spreads my knees apart, making room for himself. Turning around, he leans back a little, and I don't even try to contain my grin as I prop my chin on his shoulder. With my arms extended around him, I hold up my phone and take our very first picture together. Before he can move, I press my lips to his scruffy cheek and snap one more.

"Thanks, baby," I whisper into his ear, setting aside the device.

He kisses me in response and then goes back to attending to our dinner. It's not long before I'm searching cabinets and drawers for plates and silverware so that I can set the table. When Michael brings the food, asking me if I want another beer while we eat, I grin, knowing I'm already halfway drunk, but not caring in the slightest. We both open another, polishing off our six-pack as we sit down to enjoy our meal.

"So—is it me, is it the beer, or is it just *fact* that this is *so freaking* good? Like, way better with the homemade dough?" I mutter around my mouthful.

"Fact," he states with a wink. He takes a bite of his own, chewing before he repeats, "Definitely fact."

I reach over and rest my hand on his wrist, giving him the most serious face I can muster in my intoxicated state as I tell him, "If we ever get into a really big fight, like—*really* big, and it sucks, and we're both super upset—when we're ready to make-up, promise we'll do it with empanadas and lots of sex."

He stares at me for a moment, amusement dancing in his eyes before he turns his wrist and takes my hand in his. "First—" He pauses and kisses the back of my hand before he goes on to say, "Let's try and *avoid* as many *really* big fights as we can manage. I don't like fighting with you. Not even a little bit."

"Me neither," I whisper, appreciating that he would say such a thing, setting a precedent here and now.

"Second," he continues, "We don't have to fight to have empanadas and lots of sex." Speaking through a crooked smile, he lowers his voice and mumbles, "We're not fighting now."

"Governor Cavanaugh," I murmur coyly. "Are you *implying* something?"

"Not implying. Promising."

My breath hitches in my throat, and I give my hand a tug before I ask, "In that case, can I have my hand back?"

He grins at me and then kisses my knuckles before letting me go.

I finish my dinner in record time.

Michael

When I hear Blaine's fork hit her plate as she lets out a contented sigh, I pull my focus away from the beautiful view in front of us and shift my attention to the gorgeous vision beside me. She's now leaning back in her chair, her glass of wine in her hand, and her eyes closed. We decided to dine out on the deck tonight, the patio furniture making it pretty impossible for us to stay inside another night, and the weather just warm enough as the sun began its slow descent.

We've been here for a little more than twenty-four hours, and already I wish I could slow down time and make it stop. Just for a little while. I feel at peace right here and right now, sure that I'm in the right place with the right woman. I know that it is a peace that will not last—not with what lies ahead of us—and I want to hang onto it for as long as possible.

Today was spectacular. We slept in so late that we didn't even bother with breakfast. We took our time in the shower before getting dressed for the day, and then snacked on leftover empanadas before heading outside for the afternoon. There's a trail behind the house, leading to a clearing about a half a mile away. The view of the mountains from there was so amazing, I can understand why Lawrence likes it so much up here. I wasn't sure I was going to be able to get Blaine to leave. Ultimately, it was her hunger that led us back to the house.

After we got cleaned up, we started on an early dinner. Now, it's a few minutes past six, and my angel looks as content as her sigh would imply.

"You know what would be awesome?" she asks, her voice soft and almost reverent, her eyes still closed.

"What's that?"

"If we had our own place, tucked away in one of these mountain towns. Someplace for us to runaway to when we felt like shutting out the world. It wouldn't have to be this big, of course, not so long as it had the essentials."

"And what would those be?"

She smiles, cradling her glass against her chest, and I imagine she's envisioning this dream escape as she tells me, "It'd have to have a pretty great kitchen. We'd spend a lot of time in there. A living room with really comfortable furniture—oh, and a fireplace, in case we came during the winter, so we could snuggle by the fire. Obviously, we'd need a master bedroom—maybe even a playroom…"

Her voice trails off, and I watch as she bites the inside of her cheek, like she's contemplating what that sort of room would entail. My dick twitches as I get a few ideas myself.

"Yeah," she murmurs contemplatively. "Definitely a playroom. And a big bathroom with a tub large enough for the both of us. Oh, and a deck. Can't forget that—with an epic view."

Leaning back in my own chair, I smile at her as I tack on, "I'm picturing a rancher, with a basement. We could put in a home theater down there."

"Oh, yeah," she agrees, her eyebrows shooting up in excitement. "It could be baseball themed." Speaking through a little laugh, she adds, "I get the impression we'd end up watching more baseball than movies anyway."

Smirking at her, I ask, "Would you watch the games with me?"

Finally opening her eyes, her smile soft and her gaze affectionate, she replies, "Every one."

We stare at each other in silence for a moment. When I can stand the distance that separates us no longer, I push out my chair and command, "Come here."

She sets her wine glass aside as she stands. After pushing her chair back, her gaze flicks across the deck before it settles on me again. She takes one step in my direction, but then she stops. I lose her eyes once more, and then she retreats a step before a mischievous grin spreads across her face. The next thing I know, she's taking her shirt off and dropping it into her vacated chair.

"What are you doing?" I ask curiously.

"Getting naked," she tells me as she slides her shorts to her ankles.

I'm distracted for a moment at the sight of the body I've come to know more intimately than I've known any other. Her small, perky breasts are covered in a black bra; and as my eyes travel down beyond her flat belly and narrow hips, I see the matching, lacey boy shorts she put on this morning.

Clearing my throat, I gather my wits about me and inquire, "I see that you're getting naked, Blaine, but *why?*"

Seductively, she eases her way out of her bra as she informs me, "Because I'm hoping you'll get naked, too."

Unable to contain my grin, I resist the urge to adjust myself in my shorts as I question, "No doubt, I will—but *why,* angel?"

"Because I think we should continue this conversation naked—in the hot tub."

Now rid of all of her clothing, she smiles at me suggestively before walking around the table toward the water.

The Jacuzzi is built into the deck on the other side of the fire pit, beyond the patio dining area. I opened the automatic cover before dinner, curious to see if I could get it going. Now, I'm glad that I did. I'm naked before she immerses herself in the water, and I join her just as she turns to beckon me. I don't miss the happy look in her eyes when she sees that she doesn't have to.

Once inside the warm water, I walk straight toward her, my hands immediately reaching for her waist as I pull her against me. As if we're of one mind, she lifts up on her tiptoes, pressing into me for a kiss just as I lean down to capture her lips. We stay this way only long enough to get a proper taste, and then I pull away, guiding us both toward the edge so we can sit. The bench seat is wide enough that she settles herself between my legs, leaning back against me as I rest my arms around her middle.

She frees another contented sigh as she rests her head on my shoulder, and I stare down at her body, wrapped in mine. I think about how breathtaking she is. Not simply because she's naked, but because she's everything I didn't know I could have. The more I think on it, the more in awe I am of what we've managed to find in one another.

"I don't know why life turned out this way," I mutter contemplatively.

"What do you mean?" Her voice is so soft as she traces her fingers back and forth across my forearm.

"I don't know why I found you when I did. If I believed in something other than God, I would think it was the universe playing a cruel joke. But I do believe in God. In some ways, that belief makes all of this pretty black and white. Yet, at the same time, His grace makes it gray."

She turns her head, as if to signal that she's listening closely before she repeats, "What do you mean?"

"Nowhere in the Bible does it even suggest that what I'm doing with you—what we're doing together—is right. It's not moral. The fact that I found you at this stage in my life, it was like a test that I failed. I couldn't stay away from you when I should have, and now I'm incapable of letting you go. While it's wrong for us to be together now, I'm going to make it right; and when I do, you know what I believe?"

"Hmmm?"

"I believe that God's promise will stand true. It already has."

"What promise?"

"All things work together for the good of those who love Him—Blaine…" I pause and she shifts, turning her body so that her legs are hooked over my thigh. She rests a hand on my side, her attention focused on me intently. "You're already a manifestation of that promise. I know that what we have right now is not ideal. It's not fair. It's not right—and yet, in the same breath, I can't deny that I've never wanted anything more than I want you. Having you, being with you, it's right even when it's wrong."

"Michael," she breathes, reaching up to cover my cheek with one of her hands.

"I've been married for fifteen years, but I've never been more *myself* than I am when I'm with you. I've never felt more comfortable in my own skin. I'm almost thirty-eight years old, angel—do you even understand how liberating that is? To have found you—Blaine, it's so good. I don't just mean that it feels good, it *is* good. What we have is *good.* No matter what anyone says, no matter what we face in the coming future, I will not let anyone tell me otherwise.

"I choose you. I love you, and I need you to know—"

She cuts me off, her grip around my cheek causing me to follow her lead when she presses her mouth to mine in a hard kiss. I don't stop her. I part my lips instead, offering her an open invitation. She takes it, plunging her tongue inside of me. Reaching up to circle her arms around my shoulders, she pulls herself closer as she kisses me long and hard. I let her, *listening* to all the words she's not saying as she moans into my mouth.

Stopping our kiss momentarily, she mumbles against my lips, "You mean everything to me. *Everything.*" Then, before I can say a word, our tongues are tangled together once more.

I tighten my arms around her waist, causing her breasts to

crush against my chest. Soon, our sweet, sensual exchange shifts into something else—something hotter, more desperate and more urgent.

"Michael," Blaine pants, her hands sinking into my hair before her fingers clench into fists around the strands. Speaking into my mouth, she begs, "I need you to fuck me."

"Where?"

"*Now,*" she whines.

A low growl sounds from deep within me, and I cradle her against my chest as I stand to my feet. I climb out of the tub with ease, carrying her in my arms toward the nearest surface. When nothing within sight seems comfortable enough for me to set her on, I plant her feet in front of one of the stone faced pillars holding up the awning over the outdoor dining set. Taking hold of her wrists, I position her hands above her head, signaling for her to hold on.

I grip my fingers around her hips, pressing my erection against her ass as I bring my lips to her ear and command, "You're not bound, but you're not to move your hands, understand?"

"Yes, sir," she moans, arching her lower back and pushing against my cock.

I mutter a curse under my breath as I reach down and position myself at her entrance, then I drive into her—*hard.*

"Yes!" she cries, bending over a little further, her hands still obediently braced above her head.

I'm not the least bit gentle as I pound into her over and over, her pussy growing wetter with our friction. The little sounds she makes as I take her from behind turn me on even more, and the warm breeze that blows against our drying skin reminds me that we're still outside.

Freedom.

My gaze is locked in on our connection, and I'm transfixed by the way I fit inside of her as perfectly as I do. With every thrust, I know I'm home, and I groan in pleasure.

"Oh, *god*, you fuck so good, baby."

I barely register her words, distracted by her movement. When I look up and see that she's dropped one of her hands to palm her breast, I act before I can even process my movements. She gasps, rearing back against me when I slap my hand down on the side of her ass.

"Michael!" she moans.

"Hands," I bark.

Quickly lifting her hand to join her other, she whimpers, "*Fuck*."

"Next time, I'll do more than slap your ass, angel."

Her head falls, hanging in what appears to be despair as she whines, "Don't tease me, baby—please, don't tease me."

My eyes flash in surprise as a new hunger burns from within. I spread her ass cheeks, studying her back entrance. Memories of the orgasm that wracked her body the last time I played with her asshole cause my shaft to grow more rigid. I understand what it is she wants, because I want it just as much—I want to take her there, my kinky angel.

My left hand still holding her hip, I continue to ram in and out of her as I slide my right hand up her side. I mold my palm around her tit, giving her a light squeeze before I continue to feel my way up. When I get to her neck, I ease her head back, tracing my thumb across her lips. I don't even have to say a word, and she sucks it into her mouth. I grunt, my length twitching in excitement, her tongue greedily swirling around and tasting my skin.

Impatient to put my thumb to use, I tug it out of her hold and bring it to its intended destination. She mutters something incoherently, bending over even further as I tease her entrance.

"*More,* baby—*more*, please," she begs, meeting me thrust for thrust as she tries to impale herself with my cock.

I slow down my hips. As I pound into her with my firm, steady strokes, I press my thumb into her entrance. She throws her head back, a shudder causing her whole body to quake, and I know I've got her exactly where I want her. I own her pussy while I gently fuck her ass until her legs are so wobbly I'm certain I've brought her to the edge. Longing to push her over, I slide my freehand down between her legs.

"Shit!" she mewls, her entire body locking up as I rub two fingers against her clit.

I pull my thumb free, plastering my arm across her chest as she loses her grip on the pillar, her pussy clamping tightly around my cock as she rides the wave of her orgasm. Her frame trembles against me as I continue to circle her clit, smearing around the evidence of her release. I only stop when her legs give out. Catching her around the waist, I slip from out of her core. I then hold her for a moment before setting her down on her knees.

She's panting on all fours, trying to gather herself as her body quakes with the aftershock of her ecstasy. I stroke myself, aching to find my own release.

"Turn around, angel. Give me that mouth."

"Help me," she sighs, holding up a hand.

I offer her my assistance as she braces herself against my forearm, turning around on her knees to face me. With my erection now pointed at her face, she hums as she grips the back of my legs and takes as much of me as she can manage into her mouth.

A deep, long groan spills from my throat as I bury my fingers in her hair, watching her head bob back and forth across my dick. Her eyes are closed as she sucks me, and there's something about the expression on her face that makes me certain that I'm not the only one enjoying the hell out of this. The longer she goes, the more into it she gets. When she grabs my shaft with one of her hands, pumping me with her fist as she sucks on my balls, my grip in her hair tightens.

She opens her eyes when she takes my dick back into her mouth. Her hazel gaze locked with mine, she slowly presses forward until I feel my head hit the back of her throat. It's then that my balls start to lift, tightening as I draw closer to my climax. She pulls away, her saliva coating my length as she takes a breath, and then she's back at it—easing forward until she's gagging on my tip.

I lose grip of my control at the same time that I lose my patience. Burying both hands in her hair, I take over—my eyes never leaving hers—fucking her mouth until I'm coming down her throat. When I've spilled my release completely, I ease my way out of her before gently wiping her mouth clean. The look of adoration I see expressed on her face as she gazes at me from her knees is enough to almost bring me to my own. Instead, I reach down and help her to her feet before scooping her up into my arms.

She doesn't say a word of protest as I take her back to the hot tub. When I sit in the water, I don't let her go. Though, it wouldn't matter anyway—because she doesn't let me go, either.

Blaine

I BREATHE IN deeply, smiling when I inhale my favorite scent—the delicious, manly smell that I've come to know as Michael's. I burrow deeper into my pillow, giggling groggily when I realize that said pillow is his chest. With my eyes still closed, I uncurl my fingers, flattening my palm against what must be his side. I then feel my way over his hard, raised pec, grazing his nipple on my way to my desired destination. My leg is hitched up over his, and I feel his cock jerk against my thigh in response to my touch. I snuggle against him closer, sleep falling away from me with each new intake of air I breathe. I can hear his heart beating beneath my ear as I play with his fine, dark chest hairs, and I've never felt so relaxed in all my life.

Without having to look, I know that he's already awake. The hand attached to the arm draped across my back is absentmindedly tracing circles on my hip, just above where the sheet rests over us. It feels nice, and I don't want to move, so I don't. By now, I'm certain he knows I'm awake, too—but he doesn't move or speak. It's almost as if we're both under the false impression that the longer we stay here, pretending that our Sunday has yet to begin, then it'll last as long as we want it to.

So far, this weekend has exceeded all of my expectations—which is saying a hell of a lot, because I had some pretty high expectations. I knew all along that I'd enjoy my time with Michael, but I didn't imagine that I would enjoy it this much. I didn't think that a few days locked away in a secluded house in the mountains would make me fall in love with him even more, but that's exactly what's happened.

I try not to think about what it'll be like to return to reality; but in trying *not* to think about it, my thoughts rush me there faster than I can help it. After tonight, I'll be back in my own bed. While I certainly don't mind my place, it's the thought that I'll be climbing into my sheets alone that disappoints me. I know that it won't be like this forever. He's promised me that he'll make things right, and I believe him. With all my heart, I believe him—but I know things won't change over night.

Then, of course, I can't forget who he is. Even after he's parted ways with Veronica, he'll still be the governor of Colorado. He'll still have the mansion. Knowing how he feels about that place, on top of the fact that it's the house he shares with his *wife*, I'm not exactly keen on moving in with him.

Moving in with him.

Is that what we'll do? Move in together? Is the governor allowed to shack up with his girlfriend without it being some sort of scandal? Or will we live apart until…

Even just the thought of marriage frightens me. Not because I don't want it, but because I'm afraid *he* won't.

I've never been in any hurry to get married. With Mateo, I didn't really even think about it. Of course, it's something that I want. Growing up in my house, watching the way dad loved mom—especially in the end—I want that. I couldn't really see a future with that much love with Mateo. I thought maybe we could get there, but then I met Michael. I realized that it wasn't *time* that was holding back the potential between Mateo and me, it was *us*. Now that I have the sort of love I never truly understood—the kind of love *no one* can understand until they have it—I want those promises of forever. Except, it's not exactly that simple. Not for Michael and me.

Will he want to make that kind of commitment after getting out of a fifteen-year marriage?

My mind drifts toward thoughts of Dodger and Hope. I remember the look in his eyes when he told me he was ready to ask her to marry him. He's a couple years older than me, but not so many years older than Michael was when he married Veronica. Michael's not old, but he's not young—not mentally. He's experienced life that I haven't. Not to mention, he's obviously not the same guy that he was back then, and I'm not Veronica.

"Something's bothering you." Michael's deep, gravely, morning voice rumbles in his chest beneath my cheek.

My eyes fly open, and I feel a blush rush to my face as I try to avoid broaching the topic of my most recent thoughts. "What makes you say that?"

He presses a kiss on top of my head before he replies, "Your fingers. They stopped tickling my chest. What's wrong?"

I don't want to lie to him, but I'm embarrassed to confess the truth, so I say nothing.

"Blaine?" he mumbles into my hair.

I sigh deeply, sealing my eyes closed tight as I whisper, "I…I'm embarrassed to tell you," I admit. "And scared."

Why it's easier to tell him *that* and not the truth is beyond me, but there it is.

"*Quiero todos tus secretos, angel.*" He kisses the top of my head again and then says, "I want all of your secrets, angel. All of your insecurities. All of your doubts. All of your fears. I don't want you to hide from me. I don't want you to feel as though you have to hide from me. I don't want to lose you while you're trying to fight some mental battle that you don't have to face alone."

Why I'm surprised by his response, I have no idea, but here I am.

His words giving me courage, I open my eyes and stare across the landscape of his chest before I ask, "Will you ever want to get married again?"

When he doesn't answer right away, I pull the nub on my cheek between my teeth and roll it around anxiously. He doesn't speak for so long, I wonder if he even really meant all that he just said—and then he takes me by surprise *again.*

He rolls us over, forcing me onto my back. My legs open for him naturally, and he fits his hips between them, propping himself up on his forearms. I stare up at him, wide-eyed, wondering what's going through his head as his eyes dance around my face. Still, he says nothing—and then he takes me by surprise a-freaking-gain.

His pretty blue eyes stare straight into mine as he lifts his hips and slowly fills me with his hard length. What's *not* surprising is that I'm already wet enough for him to slip right in. Then again, with the man on top of me between my legs, no one could blame me.

Once he's fully seated, he doesn't move and he doesn't speak. I wonder which will make me go insane first, and then he rolls his hips. A soft moan forces its way between my lips as my knees fall open, my body answering my question for me.

Then, *finally,* he speaks.

"Right here," he whispers, tenderly thrusting inside of me. "This is home. *Right here.*"

My breath catches in my throat, but he's not finished.

"Just you. You hear me? Only you. *Only ever you.*"

I nod, my center now so drenched, I can *hear* it as I soak his cock.

"The answer to your question is no, baby. I won't one day *want* to get married again. I've already made up my mind. I *will* get married—to *you.*"

He fills me yet again, and I gasp when his pelvis rubs against my swollen clit. I can't take my eyes away from his—the blue of his irises dark and yet so calm, so certain, so confident. I stare into the depths of his soul—bottomless, like the ocean—and I see nothing but his love. It breaks my heart wide open. My own eyes fill with tears as I wrap my fingers around the back of his neck, holding on tight, trying to cling to his promise with all that I am.

"You feel this?" he grunts, plunging into me deep and hard.

He glides out slowly, then pounds into me forcefully, causing me to lose my breath.

"Do you feel me? Hmm?"

"Yeah—yes," I stammer with a nod.

"This is *all* of me. It's yours. I'm *yours*. All of me."

When he drives into me again, jarring my whole body, I cry out. My back arches as tears spill from my eyes, and I know what he's telling me. I know, without him having to explain it, that I don't have to hang onto his promises. He's given me *more* than his promises—he's given me more than he's given anyone. *Anyone*. Including his wife.

"All of you," I mewl as he rams his hips against mine.

"Only ever you," he repeats.

We don't say anything else to each other after that. At least, not with our words. As he makes love to me, gently and fervently, I take all that he gives and I give all that I am in return. When we come, we come together, and it's earth-shatteringly beautiful.

I cling to him as he collapses on top of me, our bodies coated in a thin layer of sweat. I don't let go when he tries to move off of me to give me space to breathe. Catching on to the fact that I don't plan on going anywhere any time soon, he kisses my neck before shoving a hand beneath me. He then rolls onto his back, taking me with him so that I'm plastered to his front—and this is how we stay.

Until he bribes me out of bed with pancakes, of course.

Twenty-Seven

Blaine

"I WISH YOU COULD STAY," I MUTTER into Michael's chest.

"I know."

It's all he says as he holds me in front of my apartment door. It's nearly eight o'clock, and I know he should be going, but I don't want to let him go.

"Listen, it might be a couple of days before I'm back. I have to catch up on a few things, which means earlier mornings in the office. I also have plans to meet with my attorney this week, along with a few advisors and my campaign manager."

He buries his fingers in my hair, gently pulling on the strands until I'm looking up at him. He kisses me, and I tighten my arms around his waist, opening my mouth to express what I want. What I *need.* He doesn't disappoint me, but tangles his tongue with mine—tasting me in that way only he ever has.

He pulls away abruptly, touching his forehead to mine as he

breathes, "I love you. I'm tired of loving you in secret. It's time I made this right."

"I love you, too," I whisper in reply.

"We have to be ready for anything."

"I know." And I do.

While Michael is *my* Michael right here in my arms, I know that as soon as he walks out that door, he's Governor Cavanaugh. I know that he has regular conversations with the press, and that he's no stranger to television. I know that his name is in the news when he pisses people off or accomplishes something great—and I know that *divorce* and *affair* are words that could make headlines.

"Are you scared?" I ask, fisting his t-shirt at his back into my hands.

"No." He furrows his brow, as if he's trying to make sense of his own answer. He goes on to explain, "I probably should be, but I'm not going to carry around fear on top of everything else. I'm about to have a fight on my hands. I won't lose everything I've worked so hard for simply because I fell in love. Besides, I have my family to consider. There's only so much a man can shoulder."

Thinking about his family fills me with anxiety. Just because Michael loves me doesn't mean they will, and I know how very important they are to him. Eventually, I'll meet them, and I wonder what they'll see when they look at me—a home wrecker? Or the woman that he loves? Honestly, it's not fair for me to blame them if they only see the former. They don't know me like I've already come to know them.

"Hey," Michael mumbles, his lips pressed against my forehead. "I don't want you to be scared, either."

"It *is* scary, Michael. As much as I don't want to hide anymore, it feels safe here in our little bubble where no one can touch us."

"Angel," he pauses, taking hold of either side of my face. His gaze locked with mine, his eyes filled with enough confidence to empower my own, he says, "We're going to weather this storm. It's not going to be easy, but every storm ends. When this one does, you'll be right by my side—right where you belong. Understand?"

"Yes."

"Good." He kisses me softly, pulling away slightly as he whispers, "I have to go."

"I know," I reply, nodding as much as his hold will allow.

"I love you."

"I love you, too."

He touches his lips to mine once more and then pulls away from me entirely. This goodbye feels heavier than normal, but I try to fight the foreboding feeling that's attempting to fill my chest. Instead, I think back over our weekend—the most romantic weekend I've ever had—and I cling to those memories with the hope that they are only the beginning of our forever.

"I'll talk to you soon."

Offering him a small wave and as much of a smile as I can muster, I murmur, "Bye, baby."

When I climb into bed, I feel lonelier than I've felt in a long time. I miss Michael, and it hurts me in a way that it hasn't before—the truth that he's in bed with another woman. As I lay alone, staring up at the ceiling, I come to the conclusion that I would endure *anything* to have Michael as mine. Whatever comes our way in the coming weeks, no matter how scary it might be, I won't let him go. I can't.

Wishing to see his face, I reach for my phone, like I so often do when the urge strikes. Only this time, I smile, remembering that I have pictures of my own I can look at—photos that remind me that what we have might be hidden in the shadows now, but it doesn't make it any less real. As I scroll through the pictures, my belly fills with a comforting warmth, and I can't stop myself from smiling. For the first time, I realize that I wasn't the only one taking pictures. Michael obviously got a hold of my phone while I was sleeping. Most of the ones he took are of me—*naked.* They aren't exactly indecent, the sheet covering my most intimate parts, and I decide to keep them so I can send them to him later.

Then I come across one that makes me stop.

It was taken this morning. I'm on my side, my arms curled up against my chest and my cheek resting on my hands. Michael is behind me, his body curled around mine. In the picture, he's kissing the back of my head, and all I can see of his face are his eyes as he looks directly into the lens. My heart swells, and I will myself not to cry—remembering that we'll be together again soon. Sooner than ever before.

Michael

"Governor?"

I draw in a deep breath, lifting my head from where it was propped on top of my fist, and shift my attention toward my office door.

"Heidi," I speak with a furrowed brow. "What are you still doing here?" Flipping my wrist to verify the time, I note that it's almost seven o'clock. I thought she had left with the others a couple of hours ago. People don't tend to stick around on Friday afternoons.

"I'm getting ready to leave. I wanted to check in on you first. Do you need anything?"

"No," I reply, forcing a smile. "Thank you."

"You should get out of here, too. You've had a busy week."

"I'm right behind you," I lie.

"All right. Have a good weekend. I'll see you Monday."

I dip my chin in a nod, and she takes her leave, shutting the door behind her. Freeing a sigh, I lean back in my chair, trying and failing to mentally prepare myself for what's ahead. It's time for me to tell Veronica the truth. I can't keep lying to her. I can't keep pretending. Furthermore, I can't begin to deal with the fall out if I don't first come clean.

Privacy. I was reminded this week that I have very little of it. The best advice that I was given by my advisors was to *not* go through with this; to break things off with Blaine, and pay her off, if need be, to keep her quiet. Upon hearing what they had to say, I felt like I had entered into some terrible plotline on primetime television. When I informed them that their suggestions weren't an option, they were forced to help me brainstorm my other choices.

Plan B is to keep Blaine hidden for a while longer while I deal with the end of my marriage. It's impossible for me to get a divorce without notice, this much I knew. I also planned on a press release, explaining the situation as delicately as I can manage—pleading with the public for privacy as I continue to serve them in the midst of a trying time for my family. I was instructed to keep *the other woman* out of it as much as possible. However, this can only be accomplished under best case scenario—best case being Veronica doesn't go to the press herself. While I don't think that it's in her character to do that, as she's not a vindictive woman, I can't be sure. I've never cheated on her before.

I'm well aware that what I intend to tell her this very evening will turn her world upside down. The pang of regret in my heart reminds me that it'll flip my world, too. There is, of course, a contingency plan that has been thought of should the best case scenario fail, but I can hardly worry about that now. Before I face the public, before I concern myself with my career, I have to admit the truth to my family.

When my affair began, I didn't know how to address the issue of my divided heart. I was confused. I felt conflicted. On the one hand, there was a woman who wanted me; a woman who excited me and connected with me in the most effortless way. I needed her for reasons I couldn't explain. I felt drawn to her to the point that it couldn't be denied. Yet, on the other hand, there was my wife; a woman I had loved for most of my life; a woman I had somehow managed to fall away from in ways I wasn't even aware of until it was too late. I didn't know how to break her heart without breaking mine. I didn't know how to let her go anymore than I knew how to deny myself the satisfaction of being *seen* for the first time in *years*. I didn't know how to chase after the future I was desperate for with my past grafted into my very being.

Now, all these months later, I still don't know what I'm doing—only that it must be done.

My cell phone rings from inside of my pocket, and I know without even looking that it's my call to head home. Sliding the device from out of my pants, I see Veronica's name lit up on my screen. I swipe my thumb across the answer key before bringing it to my ear.

"Hello?"

"Hey, sweetie. Where are you?"

"I'm still at the office."

"Oh. I wish you had told me you were going to be staying late. I made dinner. It's getting cold."

Running my hand down my face, I combat the guilt warring inside of me as I tell her, "I'm sorry. I'm leaving now."

"Okay. I'll pop it back in the oven for a minute."

"Sure. I'll see you in a few."

I stand to my feet as we exchange our farewells, grabbing my jacket from the back of my chair before heading for the door. No sooner do I cross the threshold, and another call rings through. Thinking it's Veronica calling me back for one reason or another, I don't bother paying attention to who's calling before I answer.

"Hello?"

"Michael—I need you!"

I stop dead in my tracks, my back rigid as a chill races down my spine. The dread I was feeling a moment ago at the thought of going home is now replaced with a rising sense of panic. It's seven o'clock on a Friday night. Blaine should be at work, not on the other other end of the phone sounding hysterical.

"Angel, what's the matter?"

"It's my dad. Shit, shit, *shit,*" she cries.

I hear what sounds like keys falling, then I'm sure it's her phone that clatters to the ground next.

"Blaine—Blaine!" I call out, my eyes locked with Clay's as I begin to hurry toward the exit. "Blaine!" I repeat a third time, my voice echoing through the quiet hallway.

"I'm sorry, I'm sorry. I can't stop shaking. I keep dropping my shit."

"Where are you?" I demand to know, my feet moving faster now.

"I'm at the bar—I'm leaving. Uh, the, uh—um—"

"Don't get behind the wheel. Do you hear me?"

"I have to go! The hospital—"

"Angel, *do not* move. I'm coming."

I hang up on her, hoping that by cutting her off, she'll know I'm not to be argued with right now. I've never heard her voice like that before. It does something to me, and I feel as though I'm on autopilot. All that matters is that I get to her. *Now.*

"The Lounge," I bark over my shoulder as I rush down the stairs out of the building. "It's an emergency." Clay catches up with me easily. When we reach the vehicle, I pause only long enough to deliver one last instruction. "Haul ass."

He's quick to mutter his own in reply. "Call your wife."

Blaine

I SAW HIM Tuesday. I made him dinner before he got home, and then we hung out until I had to go to work. He was *fine* on Tuesday.

I close my eyes and more tears race down my cheeks. Gripping the steering wheel with my trembling hands, I try to get control of my breathing, but I can't. The sob I'm trying to keep at bay is clogging my airway.

He was *fine* on Tuesday!

Fuck.

It's been five minutes since Michael hung up on me. The only thing keeping me from speeding down the street right now is the fact that I've already tried to insert my key into the ignition three times, but my hands are shaking too much and I keep dropping them. My frustration only ruins my ability to concentrate even more, and my inability to breathe is starting to make me lightheaded. I can't fall apart. Not yet. I have to get to him—I have to get to my dad.

It's been eight minutes since the hospital called, informing me that he had been brought in a little while ago—by *ambulance*. He collapsed.

I gasp loudly when my car door opens. Whipping my head around, I find Michael already reaching for me. He pries my fingers away from the steering wheel and helps me out of the car. His hand clasped firmly around mine, he leans across the driver's seat and snatches up my purse, grabbing my keys while he's at it, before shutting and locking my door.

"Let's go."

I follow his lead, comforted by his obvious ability to be cool during a crisis. I, on the other hand, remain a complete mess.

"Where to?" Clay asks from the front seat as Michael closes us inside of his town car.

"Um—St. Luke's. South Denver."

His response comes by way of stepping on the gas. I'm so relieved to finally be moving, I sag against Michael's side. When he wraps me in both of his arms, I lose a little bit of my grip on my emotions. A whimper sounds from my throat, my fear almost all consuming.

"Talk to me, Blaine. Tell me what's happening," Michael commands, his voice soft but adamant.

"He was at the store. He collapsed. The nurse—the nurse—she said—"

"Hey, take a breath, angel. Just breathe. Talk slow."

I nod, drawing in a shaky breath as I grab a fistful of his shirt. "He had another heart attack. She said—when she called, she said that they were admitting him for surgery. They have to open him up. His chest, Michael—they're going to cut inside of his chest and—"

Thinking about my dad in open-heart surgery is my breaking point. Saying it out loud makes it more real, and I start to fall apart. I sob into Michael's chest, feeling helpless and scared.

"I'm right here, baby. I'm right here. You're not alone, all right? I'm right here."

He holds me so tight, it's like he's the one keeping me in one piece, and I let him. I cry for the entire trip. I'm not even sure how long it takes us to reach our destination, only that Michael doesn't let me go. When we finally come to a stop and Clay kills the engine, I'm quick to jump out of the car, but Michael stops me.

"What are you—?"

"Look at me, angel," he insists. I do as he says, and he dries my tears before pressing a kiss to my forehead. Without pulling away, he mumbles, "Remember to breathe, no matter what. He'll need you to be the strong one."

I jerk away from him, frightened that he's telling me this now because he won't be with me later. I don't hesitate before I blurt, "You're coming with me, right? You're not leaving, are you?"

Sliding his hand around the side of my neck, he gives me a gentle squeeze before he declares, "You need me, I'm here."

"I do. I do—I need you," I insist.

"Okay. It's settled, then. Let's go."

All three of us make our way into the hospital through the emergency room. It's Michael who takes the lead, asking where we're to go in order to get an update on a patient in cardiac surgery. We're instructed to find our way to the seventh floor, where upon arrival, we head straight for the nurse's station. When we inquire about my dad, we aren't given very much information—only that he's been in surgery for thirty minutes now. Apparently, the procedure is four hours long, but a doctor should be out to inform us of their progress and my dad's status after being notified that I've arrived.

As I turn to take a seat in the waiting area, I stop short when Michael continues talking to the attending nurse.

"I understand this may be a request that you might not be able to grant; however, as we're to be here for a few hours, I would appreciate any accommodations you could make for some privacy."

I watch the woman on the other side of the desk raise her eyebrows in surprise as she asks, "Excuse me?"

Clay steps in before Michael can speak another word and explains, "The Governor would like a private room. Can this be arranged?"

"Oh—um, gosh," she stammers, a blush rising to her cheeks. "I'm sorry, I didn't—"

"It's quite all right," Michael interrupts, stopping her before she draws more attention. "Is there any available space?"

"Yes. Yes, I'm sure I can find something."

"I appreciate that very much."

"Sure, Governor."

"Nurse…" He leaves the word hanging, obviously trying to catch her name.

Her blush returns as she fills in the blank. "Connie. My name is Connie."

"Nurse Connie, I would also appreciate as much discretion as you can manage. If you can imagine, I don't want anyone *tweeting* about my whereabouts."

"Certainly! I understand completely."

Michael merely nods in response. Five minutes later, we're

escorted to a private, empty room. Connie promises that a doctor will be along shortly, and then we're left alone. Clay closes the door behind her and then keeps post in the hallway. I stare at Michael, a little taken aback by all that just happened.

"Are you all right?" he asks, closing the distance between us.

I shake my head, in awe of the man before me. "The last time—the last time dad had a heart attack, it was a nightmare getting to the hospital and finding someone to get me information. You got me here and got us a private room without even batting an eyelash."

"Oh, I don't know," he starts to say, his tone leaning toward playful as he tucks my hair behind my ears. "I'd like to think it was my charming personality that won over that nurse."

I cough out a laugh, turning my cheek to rest it against his chest as I tease, "Yours, or maybe Clay's. You're not the only one with pretty eyes around here."

"Are you telling me I need to keep tabs on my security detail or he might steal my woman?" he murmurs, folding me in his arms.

Snuggling against him, I whisper, "I'm telling you that I love you; that we've been here for all of five minutes, and already I don't know what I'd do without you; and that nurse Connie better steer clear—because you're mine."

"There's my girl."

"Tell me he'll be okay," I beg softly. "Just tell me he'll be okay."

"I'm praying that he will be, baby. We'll know more, soon."

Soon feels more like an eternity. When Michael gets tired of standing, he sits in one of the chairs against the wall, inviting me to join him in the empty one at his side. I refuse, unable to sit still as my patience wanes. I pace back and forth while we wait, wondering if *no* news in this case is *good* or *bad.* It's a half an hour before there's a knock at the door, a doctor on the other side to tell me what I'm so anxious to hear.

I learn—from a surprisingly pretty doctor in peach hued scrubs and a matching scrub cap—that my dad is in the middle of CABG surgery. She explains to both Michael and me that the procedure will help widen the arteries of his heart to allow for better blood flow. When she informs me that he's currently on a bypass machine, I start to lose my balance—but Michael is at my side in a second. I grab hold of his hand, squeezing it for dear life as I try and concentrate on what the doctor is saying. Something about taking a vein from his leg to graft into his heart.

It isn't until after she describes the procedure that she tells me it's a very common surgery, one that they perform at this hospital often enough—*whatever that means*. She then assures me that someone will be back to update us further as the surgery progresses, but that she doesn't anticipate any complications.

"If you wouldn't mind, could it be *you* who delivers all of the updates moving forward? Until we can speak with the head surgeon on John's case?" asks Michael. Before I can figure out why he's made such a request, he goes on to clarify, "I prefer the consistency. It's easier to trust the information coming from the same source."

"Absolutely, Governor. As I said, Mr. Foster is doing great so far. I see no reason to worry at this juncture. I'll let you know as soon as he's off bypass."

"Thank you."

"Yes, thank you," I echo, watching her leave.

"That was favorable news," says Michael. He leans down and presses a kiss against my temple, and I nod, letting out a sigh.

"I'll feel better when I can see him."

"Well, we've got a few hours. Sit with me."

This time, when he takes a seat, he doesn't invite me into the chair at his side. His hand still wrapped around mine, he guides me into his lap. I go willingly, curling up against him as I close my eyes and try to relax. Michael grazes his hand back and forth across my thigh, and I concentrate on his touch, willing the hours to pass by faster. Then it dawns on me that while I'm here, instead of at work, Michael's here, instead of *at home*.

"Oh, shit," I mutter, sitting up straight so that I can see his face. "Veronica."

"I told her I had an emergency, that I didn't know how long I'd be, and that I'd text her when I knew."

"But—tonight, you were going to..."

My voice trails off as he shakes his head at me. "One crisis at a time, angel. I'm where I need to be right now."

I stare at him for a minute. My mind a little less muddled than before, I realize how quickly he dropped everything to be here with me. Not *just* to sit with me, but to take care of me—take care of everything.

Reaching up to hold either side of his neck, I run my thumbs across his scruffy jaw and lean in to kiss him. I kiss him lovingly, tasting his lips a little before touching the tip of my nose to the tip of his.

"Thank you," I whisper.

"You don't have to thank me, Blaine."

"Maybe not," I say, snuggling against him once more. "But I mean it anyway."

Michael

It's nearly midnight by the time we're taken back to the ICU to see John. Blaine grips my hand tightly the entire way to his room, inhaling a shuddered breath when she finally lays eyes on him. As she goes to stand by his bedside, I stay back and allow her to have a moment. I watch as she slips her small hand into his large one, her tears returning as she dips down to kiss his cheek. Sniffling, she murmurs something in his ear that I can't make out, and it hits me for the first time that I'm seeing a side of her I've never seen before.

Blaine as daughter.

Admiring her now, I regret having not met this part of her before. Even more so, I'm sorry that it had to be under these circumstances. We've been told that it'll take John some time to come out of the anesthesia. While I plan on staying for as long as Blaine asks me to, it's only a matter of time before I have to answer about my whereabouts to my wife. Any chance I have at meeting Blaine's father properly before that time is slim to none.

As if she can hear my thoughts, Blaine looks over her shoulder at me. "Come 'ere," she murmurs.

Accepting her invitation, I stop right behind her, resting my hands on her shoulders.

"This is my dad," she states. "John Foster."

"Looks like he's going to be all right."

"Yeah," she sighs, giving me her slight weight as she relaxes against me. "I'm never going to let him eat fried chicken again, but he'll be all right."

I smirk down at her, both amused and attracted to her protective side. I then lower my lips to her ear as I ask, "What about bacon?"

She hums a giggle, shaking her head as she tells me, "I'm no match against the bacon. I don't want him to disown me. I love him too much."

We're interrupted by a knock on the door. I straighten behind Blaine as we both look at the man who enters the room. He introduces himself as the head surgeon before shaking both of our hands. He then gives us a thorough run-down of the successful surgery and what can be expected throughout the duration of John's recovery. Blaine has a couple of questions, which he's patient enough to answer, and then we're left alone again.

"Do you mind if we stay? Just a little while longer? I want to see him when he wakes up. I know you need to go home, and if you can't—"

"Whenever you're ready. We'll take you to your car, and I'll see you home."

She turns around to face me and circles her arms around my waist. Tilting her chin up, her gaze aligns with mine as she frees a heavy sigh. "I know you said I didn't have to thank you—but how about an I love you?"

"Those are always welcome."

"In that case—I love you, Michael Cavanaugh. I love you so much."

"I love you, too, angel. Don't forget it."

"I won't," she promises, giving me a squeeze. "Not ever."

Twenty-Eight

Michael

It's after four when I arrive back at the mansion. I'm exhausted, and yet I'm without a doubt that sleep isn't in my near future. I ignored half a dozen texts from Veronica last night, only informing her that I'd be home as soon as I could and that I would explain it to her upon my arrival. That's why I'm not at all surprised when I quietly make my way into the bedroom and find her asleep, but with the bedside lamp still lit.

I don't bother waking her. Rather, I take a seat on the bench at the foot of the bed and wait. At this point, there's no reason to rehearse what it is I'll say. There are no right words. There's only the truth. The truth that last night—I wasn't Blaine's husband. I wasn't her boyfriend—I was *the governor*, pulling favors for her. To the woman I love, it didn't matter. Her concern was her father, as it should have been. However, to me, it mattered a great deal.

I'm not stupid. There's no explanation as to why *the governor* came into the hospital with a woman who is not his wife and sat with her all night. There's only room for speculation. I'd be an idiot to assume that such speculations weren't made. I'm not worried about them. I'm not concerned with word getting out. It was one hospital, one ghost staff, one night. I'm merely tired of it all. Tired of the lies, of the secrets, of the hiding. I can't do it anymore.

Propping my elbows on my knees, I close my eyes and rest my face in my hands. I can feel it as sleep starts to wash over me at the same time that there's a rustling in the sheets behind me.

"Mike?" Veronica mutters groggily.

"I'm here."

"My God," she sighs. I hear it as she pushes herself up to sitting before she asks, "Where have you been? I've been worried and you've been vague. What's going on?"

"I was at the hospital," I admit.

"What?" she asks, sounding more awake. There's more rustling as she goes on to question, "Why? Are you okay? Did something happen?"

I don't answer her right away. For a moment, I embrace the silence—I embrace the last moment of her ignorance. I embrace what it feels like to be *us* for just a second longer. With my eyes still closed, it's like I see our whole lives flash before my eyes. It amazes me how, in one instant, it can all shatter.

"Sweetie, you're scaring me," she tells me, her voice now closer than it was before.

When I feel her occupy the space next to me, I lift my head from out of my hands and I look at my wife. I notice that even in her worried state, she went to bed last night in a red negligee. It's ironic to me—how perfectly her nightgown depicts her character. From the outside looking in, you can't tell anything is wrong; you can't see her broken spirit—*I* can't see the pieces of herself that she's hidden from me.

"Why were you at the hospital? Mike! Talk to me!" she demands, grabbing hold of my arm.

"I was with Blaine. Her father had a heart attack. I stayed with her and waited with her while he was in surgery and then in recovery. She didn't want to leave until he woke up."

A confused expression pulls at the features of her face as she shakes her head at me slowly. "What are you talking about? Who is Blaine?"

I want to touch her. I want to hold her hand. I want to comfort her. I want to make this easier for the woman I still care for, but I know that's impossible. Not only that, but it's no longer my place.

"*Michael!*"

She says my name like a demand, and all I can hear in response is Blaine's voice.

I love you, Michael Cavanaugh. I love you so much.

"Blaine…Blaine is the woman with whom I've been having an affair."

Veronica's spine straightens as her hand falls away from my arm. The shock she wears on her face is unmasked as she studies me. Her dark eyes are calculating, like she's trying to make sense of what I've just told her. Finally, she replies, "I—I can't have heard you correctly. Right? I—"

She cuts herself off, as if she thinks that it's my cue to speak. When I say nothing, I see it as the truth begins to sink in and take root. I see it when her eyes grow glassy with tears, and her breathing becomes shallow and uneven. I see it when the beginning stages of *pain* strikes her heart.

"You're—you're sleeping with someone," she states, her voice thick. She doesn't phrase it as a question, but like a truth she's trying to taste.

"No." I straighten, shifting my body so that I'm facing her fully. Resisting the urge to take her hands in mine, I explain, "I'm not just sleeping with her."

"*Just*," she mutters, fidgeting with her fingers. "So you *are* having sex with her? Is that what you're telling me?"

"We're intimate, yes," I answer with a slow nod.

Tears spill over and down her face, but she's quick to wipe them away—as if they're not meant for me to see. Regardless, I can *see* them. For the first time in a *long* time, I can *see* her—and I can't look away. She's crumbling right before my eyes, and I can't look away.

"How long?" she asks, sweeping her fingers across her cheeks once more.

"I met her in June."

"Three months," she murmurs, her voice so soft I'm not sure she meant to speak aloud. "Three months. So—you barely know her."

I hear the glimmer of hope in her voice, and I know that she does not understand. It's as if she thinks I'm confessing an indiscretion—a mistake for which I seek absolution. Except, Blaine is not a mistake.

"Veronica, listen to me—"

"You have to end it," she states, standing to her feet. Her tone is calm, in spite of the fact that I know *calm* is not how she's feeling. "We'll go to counseling. We'll sit down with your dad and he'll suggest someone."

"Veronica—"

"We've been together for a long time. This happens. In every marriage, it's a risk, right? There's always a chance of infidelity. Nobody is perfect. I know I'm not, so I can't expect you to be, either."

My back stiffens when her meaning becomes clear to me.

Nobody is perfect.

She thinks I find her *imperfect* because she can't have children. She's justifying my affair because of her *lack* when that has *nothing* to do with it.

"Veronica," I say softly, joining her as I stand to my own feet. I take a step toward her, but she retreats. I raise my hands in surrender, understanding her desire for distance, but still determined to get through to her.

"Obviously, we've got issues, but we can fix them. We'll get through this, and—"

"Veronica," I try again, wishing she would take a breath and *listen* to me.

"I can learn to forgive you. I can. I will. You're my husband, and I'm your wife. Marriage is—"

Eliminating the space between us, I gently grab hold of her shoulders and confess, "I'm in love with her. I'm in love with Blaine."

"I'm your *wife!*" she shouts, suddenly fighting against my hold.

My eyes widen in surprise, but I let her go. She then proceeds to beat her fists against my chest, her pain unleashed. I don't stop her. Nevertheless, it only lasts for a moment. Then she's not beating me, she's clinging to me as she dissolves into a fit of tears.

"I'm your wife," she sobs. "Your *wife!*"

I hold her, my heart aching as she leans into me, surrendering to her feelings. I don't speak, certain that there are no words to make this better. There's nothing I can say to ease her shock or her pain. As she reveals herself to me, as she gives me the pieces of herself that she's been holding back, all I can think is that it's too late. We're broken beyond repair.

With a gasp, she pulls away from me abruptly. Her legs are unsteady, so she almost loses her balance, but then she catches herself. Shoving a finger in my chest, she weakly demands, "Take a shower. Wash her off. I can *smell* her."

"Vee, I'm not taking a shower. We need to talk."

"Obviously," she bites, burying her fingers in her hair. "But I can't *think* knowing that you've been with her all night. I can't look at you. I can't even begin to fathom what we're supposed to do next *until you take a shower.*"

"Veronica, please. I need you to *listen* to me. I need you to understand that I'm in love with Blaine."

"Stop saying that!"

"It's the truth."

Dropping her arms to her sides, she narrows her eyes at me and asks, "How could you *possibly* love her? You don't even know her."

"I do, Vee. I know it might be hard for you to believe that, but—"

"We've been together for *decades* and you've been sleeping with her for three months."

I take a deep breath, scrubbing my hands over my face before I try and explain, "It's not like that."

"Isn't it? You admitted that you two were having sex." Her breath hitches in her throat as more tears spill down her cheeks. She folds her arms across her chest before she chokes out, "Which explains why you haven't wanted to touch me in *weeks*."

"It's not that simple, Veronica. I told you, it's not just about the sex."

"I know I'm not very adventurous in bed, but you never complained. We've both always been satisfied."

I clench my teeth together, biting my tongue. The last thing I want to do right now is compare sex with Veronica to sex with Blaine. It doesn't matter, as I've been trying to explain.

"Do you not find me sexually appealing anymore? Is that it?"

"Babe—you're not listening to me," I mutter, begging with her to hear me.

"I *am* listening to you," she cries. "You cheated on me. You *cheated!* But nobody cheats for no reason, and we can fix this."

"Vee—"

"You made a vow to me!" she states, speaking over me. "You're my husband. My *husband.* You made a vow to me, and I made a vow to you. That matters. That matters more than some other woman who gets you off."

"Veronica—don't talk about her like that."

She flinches at my request and then narrows her eyes at me. "I'll talk about the woman who thinks she can have my husband the way I *want* to."

Raking my fingers through my hair, I try to think of what to say—how to be more clear without being cruel. Then I realize that even with the best of intentions, in her eyes, no matter what I say or how I say it, I'll always be the bad guy at this point in our marriage. Looking at her now, reading her stance and hearing her adamancy, I concede to the fact that there is no way to be kind *and* defend my love for Blaine. I have to make a choice.

No—I've already made my choice, weeks ago. Now, I can't live *without* that choice.

"This is my decision, Veronica. I'm sorry. I'm sorry for lying to you; I'm sorry for being untrue to you; I'm sorry for being *unfair* to you. I won't claim to be in the right, but I can't go back. I can't undo what I've done. I can't change the way I feel."

She stares at me, unmoving, for an entire minute. Then, without a word, she turns on her heel, headed for the closet.

"Veronica, wait—"

"If you won't take a shower, I will," she says. "You want to go out in the clothes you wore yesterday, *be my guest!*"

"Go out?" I mutter, furrowing my brow in confusion. "It's four-thirty in the morning. Where do you think you're going?"

"We!" she shouts, turning around and taking a couple steps back in my direction. "*We* are going to your parents' house. We need help. *I* need help. I can't fight for this marriage all on my own."

Feeling defeated, I ask, "Veronica, do you hear yourself? You shouldn't *have* to fight by yourself. I'm sorry, but they can't help us. We have to talk about divorce. I can't keep doing this—I can't keep pretending. I'm in love with another woman, Veronica, and you deserve better than that. You deserve to be with someone who can love you as a husband should. I'm not proud to admit it, but I…I'm not him."

"Bullshit," she cries, her face crumbling as her tears return. "I *deserve* to be with the man *I chose* to be my husband. And that's *you*. So, like I said—wear that, or change, I don't care, we're going to your parents."

I watch her disappear into the closet, and I find myself at a loss. I hadn't anticipated that she would fight. I didn't imagine that she would fight for *us* after I admitted that I'd stepped out of our marriage. Seeing her do so breaks something inside of me—something I didn't even know was still there. All at once, I'm overwhelmed with disappointment. I'm disappointed in myself for giving up—for claiming defeat when faced with a challenge that felt impossible to rise above.

I don't know when it happened, when I gave up. I don't know when my marriage became nothing more than the status quo; when *I* became a husband by routine. It breaks my heart to know that I didn't even notice. It breaks my heart to see it only now, now when it's too late. It breaks my heart to see Veronica shove aside her anger, her pain, all because she refuses to give up a fight that I stopped fighting even before I met Blaine.

Is that the man I am?

"Mike..."

I don't realize that my eyes have filled with tears until I look across the room at her soft call. As she stares at me, more broken than I've ever seen her, I'm reminded of how selfish I've been. Seeing my reflection in her gaze, I know that this is not the man that I wish to be. I want to be better. Stronger.

"It's going to be okay," she whispers through her trembling lips. "We're going to be okay."

My first tear falls as she turns toward the bathroom.

She starts the shower, and I say a prayer—that she isn't wrong. That we'll both be okay. That we'll both get through this. But most of all, that God would forgive me for being less of a man than He designed me to be.

THE DRIVE TO my parents' house is completely silent. I managed to stall our departure, opting to take a shower at the last minute, but it's still barely past six in the morning when we arrive. The second the car comes to a stop, before Clay can even shift the gear into park, Veronica is out the door. I watch her go, pulling in a deep breath before exhaling it slowly. I glance into the rearview mirror, catching Clay's reflection, and he offers me a small nod. Sure that I can't postpone the inevitable any longer, I follow after my wife.

The front door opens before either of us even reaches the porch. Dad steps out in his house shoes and night clothes, his robe hanging open, and greets us with a concerned scowl.

"This isn't exactly how I anticipated starting my Saturday morning."

"It couldn't wait," murmurs Veronica, her voice tight and strained.

"Sorry, dad."

He looks between the two of us suspiciously before instructing, "We'll take this to my study. The girls are still sleeping."

"The girls?" I ask.

"Your mother hosted girl's night yesterday evening. Your nieces are scattered and sprawled across the living room floor."

"Is mom up?" Veronica inquires, fidgeting with her fingers.

"She's making coffee," he answers with a nod.

"It couldn't wait," Veronica repeats.

Instinctively, I reach up to press my hand on the small of her back—the act nothing more than a habitual sign of comfort—but she's quick to jerk away from my touch. It's a reaction that doesn't go unnoticed. Dad's scowl returns before he leads us inside. Speaking in a hushed whisper, he tells us to go to his study while he gets mom. Both Veronica and I decline when he offers coffee, and then we part ways.

Dad's study is more like a sitting room with a desk on the far wall, right below a large picture window. There's a couch, a coffee table, and two sitting chairs in the middle of the space. Veronica takes a chair, but I remain standing, my attention focused out the window. The sun is on its way up, and I find it incredibly ironic, given the circumstances in which I currently find myself.

"I wish you hadn't brought them into this," I state softly.

"I wish you hadn't brought *another woman* into *our marriage*," she argues.

"I'm sorry, Veronica," I tell her, turning to face her. "I can imagine those words don't mean much right now, but I mean them. I'm sorry for hurting you. That wasn't my intention."

"You've been having an affair for three months. *Three* months, you've been having sex with another woman, and you honestly have the gall to tell me it wasn't your intention to hurt me?"

Running my hand over my face in frustration, I shake my head before I explain, "It wasn't about you, Veronica. This wasn't about vengeance. I needed—"

"Stop talking. Please. Nothing you say—*nothing* will justify what you've done."

"If you believe that," I start to say, staring straight into her angry gaze. "If you *truly* believe that, then why are we here? What is there to save? What are you fighting for, Vee?"

"Us! My marriage, my husband—my *life!*"

I don't get a chance to respond before my parents darken the doorway. The cautious look on my mother's face makes me pause. My chest tightens, knowing that in a few minutes, Veronica's won't be the only heart I've broken with my news. I'm reminded that fifteen years of marriage isn't merely a promise made on paper, or a vow said before God. My relationship with Veronica is twenty-one years of my life. Twenty-one years of my *family's* life. She's a Cavanaugh. *I* made her a Cavanaugh. Now, I can't just *undo* that anymore than I can *undo* the affair that has brought us here.

"What's going on?" asks mom as she and dad make their way into the room.

They sit together on the couch, and neither Veronica nor I saying a word.

"We can't help if we don't know what's going on," dad offers.

When Veronica starts crying, I look down at my feet, needing a second to gather my courage. Telling my father—my pastor—that I've been unfaithful to my wife is only going to make this harder. Convincing my mother that I choose another, it will be as if I'm tearing away one of her children from the fold. Closing my eyes, I think of Blaine, and my heart fills with both grief and love.

Now, more than ever, I despise myself for the mess I've created. I hate that *this* is how my family will come to know the woman who owns my heart. I hate that I was the coward who didn't face this moment when I should have. I hate that I let my fear of the unknown, of the seemingly indecipherable, of *this moment* cloud my judgement. I regret that *Blaine* will always be at the center of the end of my marriage, as if she's to blame, when that is not the truth at all.

Shoving aside my shame, I lift my eyes as I tell my parents, "I'm in love with another woman."

"An affair!" Veronica grinds out. "You're having an *affair*. It's not the same thing as *love*. Fifteen years of commitment to your marriage is love. Three months with a woman you barely know—that's not love. That's *lust*."

"I know you want to believe that, but you're wrong. I know how I feel. I know what I want."

"What? What is it that you want, Michael?" dad interjects.

"A divorce."

"You can't mean that," says mom, her hand clutching at the

robe over her chest. "You made a vow before God. You are in covenant with Veronica. You can't just *throw* that away."

"I'm not throwing anything or *anyone* away. I'm doing what's best for us. For the first time in *months* I'm doing what's fair—what's *right*."

Standing abruptly, Veronica argues, "How is this either of those things? How is *lying* and *cheating* and *abandonment* fair and right? In what *world*, Michael? In *whose* world?"

"You're not listening to me," I reply, taking a step toward her. I beseech her to hear me as I say, "I am here, taking full responsibility for what I've done. I'm not proud of myself! I know what I've done is wrong. I know that I've hurt you—I've been unfair to you—"

"You've made me into a fool!" she yells, shortening the distance between us. "Everything I do, it's for you—it's for us! And here you are, off screwing some other woman."

"Everything you do is *not* for me," I mutter, suddenly feeling angry. "You take care of me, yes. But you take care of yourself more. You're so *busy* being *busy* that you don't see that I never asked for that."

She scoffs, rearing her head back in surprise before she asks, "So now this is *my* fault? What—I was so busy that you had to seek another woman's company?"

"I didn't go looking for her. But I met her, and you know what? From the *moment* I laid eyes on her, she didn't hide from me. I knew her for all of five minutes, and I could see her pain—she *let* me chase it away. And it felt good—*God*—it felt good."

"A hero? Is that it? You needed to be someone's hero? It wasn't enough for you to be my husband? To be my partner?"

"We're not partners," I mutter, reaching up to bury my fingers in my hair. "Partners don't hide from each other. You've been hiding from me for years."

"How could you say that? I tell you everything. You're my best friend!"

"I was. I *was* your best friend. Then you stopped letting me in. We found out we couldn't have children, and you stopped letting me in."

"That's not true," she whispers, her tears resurfacing.

"It is true. Our dreams died together. It was hard, and it was devastating, and it was painful—and on the road of *coping*, I went left, and you veered right. So I went right, and you turned left. I chased after you until I couldn't chase after you anymore, and we changed. We grew up. We're not the same people we were ten years ago. We're not the same couple."

"Of course, we're not! That's not grounds for divorce. Tell him," she insists, looking to my parents for help.

"Emotions are high right now," dad says, glancing between the two of us. "I think you both need to sit down, take a minute, and then *listen* to one another. If you're going to get through this, you have to get to the root of the issue. Trust has been broken. We're starting from the ground up here."

"Dad—" I shake my head with a sigh, wishing it was that easy. "I appreciate what you're saying, but I've made up my mind."

"Son, you have a wife to consider. She's right here, in this room, fighting for you—don't disrespect that."

I cough out a humorless laugh, my exhaustion overwhelming, and my fight just about gone. Dropping my chin to my chest, I claim defeat.

"It's too late," I remind them. "I already gave my heart away, and I can't get it back. I don't want it back. I can't live without it—without her—and I don't want to."

I look up only when I hear the study door open and slam shut.

I watch as mom rushes after Veronica, leaving me alone with my father.

"What have you done, Michael?" he asks, staring at me dumfounded. "What have you done?"

Blaine

DAD'S STILL IN the ICU when I return to the hospital at nine in the morning. I was home long enough to shower, nap, eat, and then come back. I didn't want to stay away as long as I did, but I knew that I'd be useless if I didn't get at least a couple hours of sleep. Now, as I enter the room, I find that he's still asleep. I'm grateful for this, knowing that his body could use all the rest it can get.

I pull the chair against the wall close to his bedside and then sit with my legs curled against my chest as I hold his hand. He was pretty groggy when he first came out of the anesthesia, around three a.m. He didn't even say anything, really, but I was relieved to see those baby blues of his. The look he gave me was enough for me to know that he really is going to be okay.

"Knock, knock."

I smile even before I see Simone come into the room. It wasn't until this morning that I remembered to call her. She forgave me, of course, knowing how I get when I'm panicked. She then promised that she'd drop by to pay dad a visit with me. I stand when she rounds the end of the bed, and she gives me a hug.

"How is he holding up?"

"His heart is beating," I answer, holding her a little tighter as I say the words. Even thinking how things could have turned out differently—it makes me so thankful to be able to deliver that simple report.

"This is good news. Has he woken up?"

"I'm awake now," he grumbles, his voice deep and raspy.

I gasp, letting go of Simone as I turn toward dad. Taking his hand once more, I hold his fingers tight and breathe, "Hi, daddy."

"Baby girl," he grunts, squeezing my fingers lightly. He then nods slightly, his focus now beyond me as he greets Simone. "Good to see you."

I don't look away from my old man, but I don't have to in order to know Simone is smiling. I hear it in her voice when she says, "You stole my line."

"How are you feeling, dad?"

He grunts again before he mutters, "Like someone sawed my damn chest in half."

I frown as I ask, "Do you need me to call a nurse or a doctor? Do you need more pain meds? I can—"

"Relax, Lulu. Nothin' I can't handle."

"Are you sure? I—"

"Nurse told me I should expect to feel sore. Don't fret."

Chuckling softly, Simone replies, "John, you know she'll be on you like white on rice for the foreseeable future. Might as well get used to it."

He grumbles, but I don't miss the smirk he throws her way. Though, it disappears when his eyes settle on me again.

"Nurse also said I should consider myself someone special. Said I must be, seeing as I had an important guest who made sure I was getting the best care."

My eyes widen at his statement, and I think back over last night and the earliest hours of the morning. Michael was incredible. He was attentive and, just like dad said, he made sure that dad was getting looked after to the best of the staff's ability.

"You were with a man last night," he says, interrupting my thoughts. "Can't say I remember his face, but you weren't alone when I opened my eyes. Who was he?"

I bite the inside of my cheek, somehow knowing that dad already knows who he was. Michael asked that the nurses be discreet, but they can't have known that meant not telling their patient about his visitor, either. One would assume, given the fact that he stayed through the night, that John Foster and Michael Cavanaugh were well acquainted.

"Mike. That's the name of your boyfriend, or whatever he is, isn't it?"

"Yes," I whisper, my heartbeat accelerating as he continues to stare at me pointedly.

"Mike happen to be short for *Michael?*"

"Dad…"

"Am I missing something?" pipes in Simone. "You told me Mike was a professor."

His eyes shift to Simone. I look over my shoulder, feeling slightly short of breath as I find her standing at the foot of the bed, watching my father and me.

"You know about Mike?" he asks gruffly.

Her gaze flicks from me to dad before she answers, "Only what Blaine has told me."

"Did you know he was married?"

I gasp, whipping my head around to look at dad. I knew. I knew that when I told him, that he would be disappointed. I know his thoughts on marriage and cheating. I know. And yet, the disappointment I see in his eyes isn't what I was expecting. It's *worse.*

When Simone doesn't answer him, he focuses his gaze on her. Narrowing his eyes, he purses his lips, as if he's trying to keep himself from saying something unfiltered. A second later, he relaxes a bit and mutters, "You knew more than me—but she still lied to us both."

"Daddy," I whisper, squeezing his hand.

He ignores me, his focus still on Simone as he tells her, "Mike is short for Michael. Seems my daughter, here, has been havin' an affair with our governor."

All the air in my lungs rushes out as I sink down onto the edge of my chair.

"Dear God," Simone whispers.

"I was going to tell you. I was going to tell you when—"

"I don't want to hear it right now, Blaine."

My vision grows blurry with my unshed tears as my gaze collides with his. "Daddy, let me explain," I beg.

"We made a deal," he grunts, squeezing my fingers in his.

"I know. I didn't break it. I swear to you, I didn't—"

"We'll talk about it later."

"But dad—"

"Blaine Luella, I mean it. I don't want to hear it right now."

I nod, deciding it's better if I don't speak at all. Bowing my head, I try to get control of myself, willing my tears to stop. It takes me a minute; but when I remember that we're in a hospital, that my dad just had major heart surgery, and that it's completely fair that he doesn't want to discuss something so heavy as my affair with a married politician, I put my selfishness aside and get myself together.

I draw in a deep breath, wiping away the last of my tears before I ask him, "Do you need anything, dad?"

"Bucket of KFC would be nice."

My breath hitches in my throat as my eyes snap up to meet his. "That's not funny."

Smirking, he mumbles, "It was a little funny."

A small smile breaks across my face, *not* because it's funny but because I know his attempt at a bad joke is his way of telling me that even if he's disappointed, he still loves me enough to bug me.

My smile starts to slip when I get teary again. Only this time, it's for completely *different* selfish reasons.

"I'm really glad you're okay. You scared the shit out of me."

"Can't get rid of me that easily. We made a deal," he grunts.

How's your dad, angel?

He's doing okay. They moved him from the ICU and took out his chest tubes. Doctor says he's recovering well and should be able to go home in three or four days.

Good.

Veronica knows. I'll call you when I can.

Okay. Are you all right? I love you…

And I you.

I REACH FOR MY phone as I head for the door, stopping before I exit to check my messages. I find nothing new, which isn't surprising. I've been glued to my phone pretty much every moment of every day—except when I'm in the shower—and it's nearly impossible that I've missed anything. Still, I check to make sure anyway. Reading over my short exchange with Michael from Saturday, it takes a great deal of self restraint not to call him or text him right now. I haven't heard from him in three days. Not a word. I've been sleeping like shit, bouncing from work, to home, and to the hospital. Between worrying over my dad and wondering about Michael, I'm exhausted.

Reluctantly sliding my phone back into my pocket, I reach for the duffle bag I sat by the door a few minutes ago and strap it over my shoulder. With dad coming home from the hospital today, I plan on spending my nights in my old room. I know that he'll hate having me all over his ass every minute I can spare, but he'll have to get over it. At least for a couple of weeks. Besides, he needs me. He can't drive anywhere for the next month, and he needs to make sure he's eating the right foods. I'll be sticking close whether he likes it or not.

Glancing back into my apartment, I look up to the loft and think of Michael. He hasn't come for any early morning visits since before our weekend in Vail. Obviously, he won't be able to sneak into my bed while I'm at dad's, but with the silence that stretches between us, I have no idea what to expect moving forward. If his wife knows, then I imagine he can come and go as he pleases—except, he hasn't come at all.

Not wishing to read into what that means, I remind myself that we love each other and that I shouldn't worry. Right now, I've got enough on my plate with dad—which is exactly why I finally open the door and step into the hallway, locking up behind me.

"ARE YOU ALL right? Do you need anything?" I ask dad as I grab his empty plate. "The leftovers are in the fridge if you get hungry later. I didn't have much to work with, so what you've got will only last one more meal. If you're feeling all right, I was going to run to the grocery store before I had to leave for work. I can buy a few things and do some meal prepping for you on Friday. I have the day off. And I—"

"Lulu, sit down."

"Dad, if I'm going to—"

"Sit your ass down, dammit," he grumbles.

I stifle a sigh as I set his plate down on the coffee table and sit on the couch. When he doesn't say anything right away, I stare at him impatiently and remind him, "Dad, I only have an hour and a half before I have to go to work. If you're going to eat, I need—"

"You're going to run yourself ragged if you don't stop. You been gettin' any sleep at all? You're startin' to look pale, Lulu, and I don't like it."

His observation makes me feel self-conscious. I look down to my lap as I rake my fingers through my hair, tossing it to one side. "I'm fine, dad. Honest."

"Well, the store can wait, I won't starve, and that dish won't rot if you leave it be for a minute."

A small smile tugs at the corner of my mouth as I lift my gaze to meet his once more. "It's fine. Really. I don't mind looking after you."

"Know you don't," he grunts. "I mind seein' you work yourself into the ground. I appreciate what you're doin' here, baby girl, but I can see you're tired."

"It'll pass. I've got a lot on my mind, is all."

"Can see that, too. Know it's not me making those eyes sad."

"Dad…" I don't know what else to say, so I don't say anything.

"You told me it was complicated. That was a fuckin' understatement."

I shrink back into the couch, cognizant of the fact that dad's apparently ready to talk to me about Michael. Though, I feel more like I'm about to get *scolded* like a child.

"You broke your promise."

"I didn't," I insist lamely.

"No less than you deserve, Blaine—*no less than you deserve*. You are worth far more than what that man can give you."

"No, dad, you don't understand—"

"I understand he's a married man. I understand that whatever you two might have, you can't be more than his dirty little secret."

"Dad!" I cry, my spine straightening as my eyes begin to burn with tears.

"He's a goddamn politician, Blaine. He's a public figure with a ring on his finger, which means he keeps you in the dark. Tell me I'm wrong."

"You're wrong," I mutter without hesitation.

"Yeah? He take you out on dates? He hold your hand in public? Huh? Answer me, baby girl."

I swallow hard, trying to stay in control of my emotions. It doesn't stop the tears in my eyes from spilling over my cheeks.

"I love him," I whisper.

"That doesn't make it right, Lulu. I see you. I see you checking your phone every five minutes. Know what that says to me? You aren't his number one priority."

"Stop it," I beg, my tears coming faster now. "It's not that simple."

"Don't you get it? That's what I'm sayin', Lulu. It *should* be that simple. It's complicated because he's married—because you don't have a claim over him. He's got you hangin' on, waitin' for his scraps, and I've got to sit here listenin' to you tell me you aren't breaking your promise? No, baby girl, I won't stand for it. You deserve a hell of a lot better than what I'm seein'."

"He's leaving her. For me—he's leaving her *for me.*"

I see it as the fight leaves my dad's face, pity taking its place. My heart aches as he shakes his head at me. His *pity* hurts so much more than his disappointment.

"He loves me, daddy," I declare, my voice thick and shaky with my rising sob. "He *loves* me."

"Then where is he, baby girl?"

I close my eyes and shake my head. I won't allow my dad's doubt to take root. He doesn't know Michael. He doesn't understand what we have. *I* do. I know that Michael is my forever. I know that won't change.

He loves me.

He loves me.

He loves me.

Needing to be finished with this conversation, I stand abruptly, sweeping my fingertips across my face to dry my tears. I then grab dad's plate and start for the kitchen.

"Lulu!"

I stop suddenly, turning to face my father. Before he can say another word, I tell him, "I'm going to spend the rest of my life with him. You'll see. You'll see, daddy—you'll see that you were wrong; that I'm *not* going back on our deal; that he loves me and I love him and it doesn't matter how it happened, only that it *did.* I found him. I found the man I'll love as much as mom loved you. You'll see." Turning away from him once more, I call back over my shoulder, "I'm going to the store. I'll be back before I have to leave for work."

I hurry into the kitchen, discarding his dish in the sink. Needing just one more second to gather myself, I pause and take a few deep breaths. When I'm sure I can leave the house without bursting into tears, I find my purse and my keys, and I walk out the door.

Twenty-Nine

Michael

I STARE UNSEEINGLY INTO THE DARKNESS, sleep evading me. I've been staying in one of the guest rooms since the night I told Veronica about Blaine—but it's not the unfamiliar bed that has me feeling so restless. As exhausted as I am, I can't stop my mind from reeling. Over the last several days, when I'm not fighting with Veronica, I'm listening to angry voicemails from my sister, fielding texts from my brother, or avoiding calls from my mother. Work has become more than an escape. It's an oasis—my responsibilities my greatest distractions. Though, try as I might, I can't hide there forever. Even in the darkness, when I'm all alone, I can't ignore the mess I've made—the heartbreak I've caused—the *chaos* I've unleashed.

Even in the darkness, God is here.

He sees me.

He knows me.

He forgives me.

But He also convicts me.

He's never been so far away that I didn't question the morality of what I was doing with Blaine. Except here, in the aftermath, it's not about *morality.* It's about love. It's about the meaning behind the word. It's about *His* love for me. Knowing that God loves me anyway, it crushes me—it breaks me to know that I, a man so undeserving, am a recipient of such grace.

In the quiet, in the stillness of night—I *see.* I see not just the hurt that I've caused the woman who is my wife, but also the way in which I've broken my family. I see the ways in which I've compromised my own character and my beliefs. I see that I got lost in the lies and forgot that there is grace and honor in *truth.* Had I been honest from the beginning, maybe none of this would hurt so much. Maybe I wouldn't be *that guy* who lied to his wife and hid the other woman—the woman who deserves so much more than I've ever given her.

I don't deserve Blaine. Not like this.

Not like this.

I'm unaware that I'm not alone until I feel the bed sink beside me. When I see the dim outline of Veronica's form at my side, I push myself up onto my elbows. I don't speak. It's a lesson I've learned in the last couple of days. It's better to let her lead the conversation.

"Blaine," she says, her voice so low I can hardly hear it. "That's her name, right?"

"Yes."

"Do you have a picture of her?"

I frown, even though she can't see me do it, and reply, "Veronica, I don't—"

As if she can sense that I'm about to deny her, she interrupts and asks, "How old is she?"

Drawing in a deep breath, I stall. To be honest, I'm surprised these questions didn't come a lot sooner. Nevertheless, I still don't feel comfortable answering them. It's not that I'm ashamed of who Blaine is. Rather, I don't believe her *details* should be exploited in a conversation like this.

"How old is she?" she repeats, her voice a little louder.

"She'll be twenty-five in a few months."

I hear it as she draws in a shaky breath, blowing it out slowly. She does this twice more, causing me to sit up completely.

"Veronica..."

"When did I become—too old? When did I become not good enough?"

"It was never a competition, Vee. It was never as meaningless as all of that. It just happened—it just...happened."

"I still love you," she cries.

"Hey," I murmur, cautiously reaching for her. When my hand finds hers, resting next to my leg, I wrap my fingers around it. She doesn't pull away, so I don't hesitate to tell her, "I know my words don't carry much weight anymore, but a part of me will always care for you. Always. I want you to be happy. I do. I mean that. I just—I can't be that guy for you. Too much has happened. Too much has changed. I'm sorry. I truly am."

"You broke my heart," she chokes out, slipping her hand out of mine.

I curl my fingers into a fist, a wave of guilt and remorse crashing over me. One would think I'd be used to it by now, but I'm not. Not by a long shot.

She stands and makes her way across the room. I barely see

the silhouette of her body in the doorway as she informs me, "I'm going to California. Abbie and Tamara—they'll be by to help pack my things." She hiccups, and I know she's restraining a sob as she says, "I won't go to the papers. I've been humiliated enough. I don't need to be dragged through the mud anymore."

Without another word, she leaves me alone again.

I should be relieved by her decision to stay away from the press. That was the plan. That was the best case scenario—to save my career from being cast in the shadow of a scandal that's a distraction from the job that I was elected to do. Yet, there's something dishonest in keeping it all in the dark.

Here, in the darkness, I can't help but feel as though I long to be in the light.

Only secrets are kept in the dark.

I'm so tired of secrets.

Blaine

It's a few minutes after five on Friday night when my phone alerts me to a new message. I jump, like I do every time it sounds, and search the kitchen for a towel. I just finished meal prepping for dad, and I'm elbow deep in a sink full of soapy water. Remembering that I threw the towel over my shoulder, I'm quick to reach for it and dry my hands before pulling my phone from out of my pocket.

My heart leaps at the sight of *My Forever* lit up across the screen.

I need to see you.

When? Where?

My stomach is in knots. I'm so anxious to see him. It's been a week since dad's heart attack, and I haven't seen Michael since he saw me home Saturday morning.

Tonight. Wherever you are.

I smile as I type my reply, the urgency in his need matching my own.

I'm at dad's. But I can meet you at my place, if you want. Just tell me when.

No, I'll come to you. Send the address. I'm on my way.

I do as he asks right away, and then hurry to finish up the dishes, sure that it'll take him at least thirty minutes to get here from the Capitol. Twenty minutes later, I'm racing up the stairs to take a quick look at myself. I flip on the light in the bathroom and glance at my reflection with a grimace. My hair is a mess, having been thrown up without the assistance of a mirror before I started cooking, and I look like I haven't slept in a week.

Coming to the conclusion that there's only so much I can do in the next few minutes, I take out my hair-tie and re-do my messy ponytail. I tug out a few strands around my face and then reach for my tiny makeup bag on the sink. I pull out my lip gloss and apply a thin coat, rubbing my lips together as I replace the cap and then smooth down my t-shirt. This one says: *Classy. But I cuss a little.* I'm wearing it over a pair of black sweatpants—sweatpants I have a mind to change out of right as the doorbell rings.

My eyes widen, and I rush out of the bathroom, racing down the hallway as I shout down to dad, "I'll get it!"

"It's my door, Lulu. I can answer it."

"No, dad, really!" I insist, my bare feet slapping against the steps as I take them as fast as I can.

"I'm up."

"Sit back down!"

I'm slightly breathless when I reach the bottom of the stairs at the same time he does. He scowls at me and grunts, "I'm not an invalid, Lulu. I can answer the door."

"I know, it's just—"

I don't get a chance to finish my sentence before he's turning away from me and walking the short distance to the front door. I hold my breath, trailing behind him, all the while wondering why Michael insisted that we meet *here*.

When the door swings open and reveals Michael standing on the porch—his suit jacket nowhere in sight, his shirt sleeves hugging his huge, beautiful biceps and cuffed at his elbows, and his hands buried in his pockets—I forget to breathe for a second.

I've missed him so much.

I snap out of my thoughts when dad looks at me from over his shoulder, quirking an eyebrow at me. I try to hide my *I told you so* smile, but it slips a little as I murmur, "Well—are you going to let him in?"

Feeling far too impatient, I don't even wait for his reply before I squeeze between him and the door, unlatching the screen and opening it wide. "Come in."

Michael offers me no more than a small smile as he holds open the screen and extends his opposite hand toward dad. I try not to read into his subdued demeanor as I watch him properly introduce himself to my father.

"I'm glad to see you're recovering well."

"Thanks," dad huffs, accepting Michael's hand.

"I'm Michael. It's nice to finally meet you."

"John." Dad shifts his eyes toward me, then back to Michael, and then drops his hand to his side. "Well, come in, if you want to."

"I appreciate the offer," Michael starts to say with a nod, "but I can't stay for long."

My heart sinks, knowing instantly that something must be wrong. As if Michael can hear the descent of my heart in my chest, his eyes meet mine before he extends his hand toward me.

"May I speak with you for a moment?"

I nod, afraid to say a word as I slip my palm into his. He closes his fingers around mine, leading me out onto the porch, and I let the screen shut behind us. We both look toward the house when the latch of the front door clicks softly, signaling that dad has left us in private. Sure that we're now alone, I can't help myself. I launch myself at Michael, pressing up on my tiptoes and circling my arms around his broad shoulders.

"I've missed you so much!"

When he pulls me close, his arms locking around my waist, I relax in his hold. With my face buried in his neck, I pepper kisses across his skin.

"Angel—"

"Whatever it is you're going to say, I don't want to hear it yet," I whimper, squeezing him tighter. "Please? Will you please just hold me for a minute?"

I feel his chest expand as he takes in a deep breath, his arms crushing me against him as he exhales. Still, the foreboding I sense in my gut, it won't go away. I hate it that he hasn't told me that he missed me too, or that he loves me, or *anything* that makes this feel like the hopeful reunion I was yearning for.

"Blaine, we need to talk."

"That sounds bad," I whisper, still refusing to let him go.

"Come on," he encourages, gently pinching the back of my neck. "Sit with me a minute."

Reluctantly, I let him go. He takes my hand and laces our fingers together before we sit side my side on the top step, leading down to the walkway.

"Baby, what's happening?"

"I've made a mess. A mess I don't even know how to begin to clean up."

He looks at me with sad eyes, and mine start to burn as we stare at one another.

"Veronica left this morning. She'll be staying with her parents for a while. The paperwork for our divorce should be drawn up soon."

"Isn't this—isn't this what you wanted?" I ask, my voice soft and timid.

"Angel…" he sighs, furrowing his brow at me in what appears to be regret.

I let go of him, my heart breaking as I interpret all that he's *not* saying.

"Are you—are you—oh, my god," I cry, covering my mouth with my hands.

He's quick to comfort me, cradling the back of my neck as he presses his lips against my forehead. "I need some time. That's all. I need for us to push the pause button."

"No. No!" Dropping my hands, I argue, "We're supposed to be *together*. You promised me—you—"

Lifting his head away from mine, our gazes collide. The sight of his troubled, deep blue irises swimming in his own tears causes a sob to erupt from within me.

"Shhh, baby," he hushes gently, touching a whisper of a kiss against my lips. "It's going to be okay."

"You're leaving me! You said you loved me—you said—"

"I do. I *do* love you," he states, his voice adamant and strong. "I want to be with you. If you think that I want to be apart from you, then you're wrong."

"Then don't," I plead, resting my hands against his chest as I lean into him. "I'm right here. We can be together right now."

"I can't." He closes his eyes, and as tears trickle into his beard, the pain inside of me intensifies. "I have devastated my family. I've shattered a woman's heart—I barely recognize myself. This is not who I am, Blaine."

Closing my fingers around his shirt, I cling to him as I admit, "I don't understand what you're saying."

"I want to be better." He opens his eyes to look into mine and repeats, "I want to be better—for you. I want to be a man that you can be proud to call yours. I want to be a man who's worthy of you."

"You are—"

"I'm not," he mutters, shaking his head at me. "The fact that you think so is only a testament to how I've mistreated you."

"That's not fair," I argue.

"I know." Using the pads of his thumbs, he wipes away my tears. It's no use, as more continue to fall, but he catches those, too. "I'll be back," he assures me.

"When?"

"I don't know. I can't tell you that. I just need a little space—a little time to piece together what I've broken."

"I don't want to lose you. I love you. I *love* you, Michael."

"You won't lose me," he mumbles, bringing his mouth to mine.

"I love you, too."

I take advantage of his parted lips, slipping my tongue between them. Still holding tight to his shirt, I bring myself even closer as I steal his kiss. He opens up for me, and I hum in response, needing more of him—needing *all* of him.

When he buries his fingers in the back of my hair, holding my head still as he tilts his and deepens the kiss, I think maybe I can convince him to change his mind. But then, before I'm ready, he starts to pull away from me. He's stronger, so he wins, and I know there will be no changing his mind.

"I should go."

A deep frown tugs at my brow as I confess, "I don't want you to."

"I know," he whispers.

We stare at each other, neither of us making a move to get up, and I hold onto every second. When at long last he leans toward me and kisses my forehead, I know our time is up. He stands, helping me to my feet, and wipes away more of my tears. My entire chest hurts with an ache I've never felt before, realizing that I don't know the next time I'll see him.

"Come back to me," I beg, not the least bit ashamed. I love him too much to give a shit about how pathetic I sound.

"I will."

"Promise?"

"I do."

He takes one step away from me, then another. The farther he retreats, the hollower my chest feels.

"I love you," I call out as his foot hits the bottom stair.

"I love you too, angel. More than you know."

I watch him get into his town car and ride away, a shock of

numbness circulating through my veins. I don't bother hiding my tears as I head back inside. I don't say a word to dad as I make my way up the stairs and straight to my room. It isn't until I close the door behind me that reality shocks my system, chasing away the numbness. When I sink to the floor and lean against the wall, letting loose my cry, I surrender to my greatest fear. I surrender to *reality,* which has seen fit to remind me that Michael's a married politician, and this has always been our fate.

We were robbing time with every stolen moment we thought was ours, and now time has come to rob us.

Michael

I've been in the house for all of ten minutes before I'm notified that this evening's guests have arrived. Abigail and Tamara have been by a couple of times this week, helping Veronica pack the things that I'll ship to California in a few days. I've been informed that they know what's left, and they'll be taking over the task of finishing up, now that Veronica is gone.

Truth be told, I wouldn't mind if all Veronica left were my clothes and the contents of my study. I'm not attached to any of our things. Not anymore. I'll be starting over. It's what I need. After all of these years, a blank slate seems like the necessary canvas by which I can begin again.

As I make my way into the foyer, which serves as the entryway for the private front entrance, I spot Tamara with a couple of collapsed boxes underneath her arm. Abigail holds a plastic sack in her hand, no doubt filled with the supplies to seal and label the boxes they fill this evening.

"Hi. Can I help you with that? Where are you headed?" I inquire, walking toward my sister-in-law.

"I've got it. Thanks," Tamara replies coolly, offering me a tight, false smile. "There are a few things left in the bedroom, and then we have the kitchen to do before we're done."

"Wait!" Abigail calls out, catching Tamara around her bicep before she can walk around me. Narrowing her eyes on me, she asks, "Your side piece isn't upstairs, is she?"

My brow dips in a scowl, my chest tightening with an ache that's becoming quite familiar. "Of course not. Please don't call her that."

Abigail folds her arms across her chest, making her growing belly more visible. Tamara clears her throat, taking advantage of her freedom, and scoots around me—but my sister stays rooted to her spot.

"I sure as hell have no intention of calling her by her name. She doesn't deserve that much of my respect. Quite frankly, *you* don't either."

I sigh, reaching up to run my fingers through my hair as I look down at my feet. Over the last week, I've had my share of wrath thrown my way. I won't for one second stand here and argue that I'm not deserving of it. Yet, at the same time, there's only so much that I can apologize for. What's done is done, and I can't change any of it. Now, it's the grace that my father preaches about—the grace that we *all* believe in—that I seek. Grace and forgiveness.

Lifting my eyes to meet Abbie's, I murmur, "I understand that you're angry, disappointed, and hurt. I know that as your older brother, I've let you down—I've let our whole family down."

"You have no idea," she scoffs, shaking her head at me.

"It's my marriage that has been destroyed—I think I *do* have an idea."

"What, so, I'm supposed to feel *sorry* for you? Your marriage was destroyed by *your* hands. God—I don't even want to *think* about who your hands have touched. I don't want to know what that home-wrecker even looks like."

"Abigail, stop it. Just *stop it,*" I demand, taking a step toward her.

With our gazes locked, she glares at me in disapproval, but all I can see in my mind's eye is Blaine. I remember the look on her face when I told her that I needed some space to deal with moments just like this one. It breaks my heart that my sister has predetermined what kind of woman Blaine is without even giving her so much as a chance. Cognizant of the fact that it's my fault, I can't even begin to figure out how to fix this—how to fix *any* of it. All I have to hang onto is my assurance that Blaine is the woman that I love.

"You don't have to like it," I inform her. "You don't have to like *me*. I won't hold it against you. But Blaine is innocent."

"Oh, do not give her that!" Abbie yells. "She is not—"

"She's innocent because I say that she is," I mutter, raising my voice to cover hers. "She's innocent because *I* chose *her*. *I* pursued *her*. I *fell in love* with *her*. She didn't do this—I did. So take your anger out on me, but leave her out of this."

"You are *unbelievable,*" she spits as she begins to walk by me. "You're the governor of Colorado. You're powerful, you're rich, you're *married,* and she spread her legs. I will not leave her out of *anything*. She's a woman capable of making her own decisions, just like the rest of us—and she chose *wrong*."

As she stomps up the stairs, following after Tamara, I don't say a word. Rather, I let her go, certain that this is a battle I'm incapable of winning today. Hanging my head, I lift my hand to squeeze the back of my neck, sealing my eyes closed with a frown. I wonder if this is a battle I'll ever be capable of winning—or if Blaine and I are simply doomed, our love too tarnished to survive this war.

Blaine

I DON'T BOTHER waiting for Dodger after we finish our closing tasks, like I normally do. I've got to get out of here. My shift was long, and at least nine people ordered the steak tonight—each request a reminder of Michael that sliced through my chest like a fucking machete to the heart. It's been four days since I've heard from him, and I'm barely keeping it together. While it's true that we've gone longer without speaking, it's never been like this. The *indefinite* nature of this silence makes it incredibly hard to bear. Tonight, I've reached my limit.

As soon as I close myself into my car, I press my forehead against my steering wheel and let my tears fall. The absence of him has never felt this consuming. What's worse is that Veronica is gone. Now, more than ever before, we have the freedom to be together, and he has chosen to press the *pause* button on our entire relationship—as if my heart was made to sustain suspended animation.

The sob that erupts from within me is proof that my heart can do no such thing.

While a part of me feels like I'm being overly dramatic, a bigger part of me simply cannot help it. I'm hurting, I'm having difficulty sleeping, I'm overwhelmed with the state of my dad's health—it's just all so much at once, and I feel myself cracking under the pressure.

I gasp loudly when I'm startled out of my thoughts at the

sound of knuckles rapping against my driver's-side window. When I jolt upright and look outside, I smack my hand against my chest in minor relief at the sight of Dodger standing on the opposite side of my door. He signals for me to roll down my window, so I power up my car and press the button to lower the barrier between us.

"What gives, B?"

I sigh, offering him a shrug, not even bothering to use my words.

"That boyfriend of yours being a douche, or what?"

My breath catches in my throat as I try to hold back another sob from breaking free, and Dodger nods.

Tapping the top of my vehicle, he demands, "You need a drink. Come over."

"Oh, god. No, Dodge. It's late—I don't want to—"

"You've been quiet and standoffish for the past couple of days. I'm worried. Bars are closed. We've got two options. You make me stand here in the middle of the street while you tell me what's up, or you come to my place and I get you a drink. Either way, you're unloading some shit—so what'll it be, B?"

I don't respond right away. Instead, I gape at him. For a long time, I stare and I think. Dodger has always been a good friend to me. No, a *great* friend. Even now, his insistence is nothing but kind and generous. Except, if he knew the truth, would he still look at me with the same compassion in his eyes that he has now? Or would he judge me? Or worse?

It's the pity that I can't stand. The pity is what hurts the most.

"Yeah, okay. You know the address. I'll see you in a minute," he demands, clapping his hand on my roof once more before he takes off toward his own car.

I peek my head out the window, opening my mouth to

call out to him, but no words are spoken. Truth is, I'm tired of keeping secrets. Hiding my pain, hiding the identity of the man I love, hiding the reason behind the complicated nature of our relationship—or the current lack-there-of—it's *exhausting.* So instead of declining his insistent invitation, I roll up my window, and I drive to Dodger's apartment.

It only takes fifteen minutes to get there. He pulls into the parking lot as I'm turning off my car. I step out at the same time that he does. He lifts his chin at me, and we climb the stairs to the third floor silently. Unlike my building, his door opens up to the outdoors, and the quiet of the early hour follows after us. Just like almost everything else these days, it reminds me of Michael—of the wee hours of the morning when he would come and sneak into my bed.

My heart aches.

"Hope's probably knocked out, so we can't get too rowdy," Dodger warns as he unlocks the door and steps inside.

A small smirk tugs at the side of my mouth, my amusement nudging my sadness as he flips on the lights in the main room. "Yeah. Okay. 'Cause I'm a real party animal these days."

"Make yourself at home, B," he insists, giving my shoulder a friendly squeeze. "I've got to take a leak. Beer's in the fridge. Hope might have some wine open, too. Whatever you want, it's yours. I'll be back."

I watch him disappear down the hallway and then head into the kitchen. When I open the fridge and spot a bottle of white wine, I decide to give it a try. I take it out and place it on the counter before I start hunting for something to drink it from. Remarkably, I open four different cabinets, finding nothing but food, before I give up.

"Fuck, Dodge—what kind of storage system is this?" I mumble to myself.

"We keep the dishes in the pantry."

I squeak my surprise, spinning around at the sound of Hope's voice. She's standing at the entrance of the small kitchen, her eyes squinting against the light. She's not wearing much more than what appears to be one of Dodger's t-shirts; her wild, blonde curls piled on top of her head in a messy bun that seems to be coming loose.

"I woke you. Shit. I'm sorry."

"Mm-mm," she mutters, dragging her feet as she walks by me. "My baby pees as loud as a horse. Besides, I only went to bed about an hour ago." I watch her as she disappears into the pantry before coming out with two wine glasses. She flashes me a tired smile, handing me both. "Pour me one, too, will you?"

"Yeah," I agree, reaching for the stems as I take them from her.

"Babe, you're up," Dodger observes as he joins us.

"I heard you come in, saw the light on, came to investigate."

With my back turned, I don't see him greet her with a kiss—but I hear it.

Another machete to the heart.

God, I miss Michael.

"B's got man problems," murmurs Dodge. "Thought she could use a drink."

"Oh?" Hope replies, suddenly sounding more awake.

I turn toward her just as Dodger leaves her side to grab himself a beer from the fridge. I hand her a glass of wine and take a sip of mine as she lifts her eyebrows at me in curiosity.

"Well, are these *man problems* something you're going to spill, or what?"

My stomach knots up with nerves as I bite the inside of my

cheek. Dodger pops the cap of his beer and then props himself against the counter across from me, nonchalantly pulling Hope under his arm. She never once takes her eyes off of me as she leans into his side and takes a sip of her drink.

"Lay it on us, B," Dodger grunts before taking a swig from his bottle.

I draw in deep breath, pushing aside all of my doubt and my fear as I confess, "My boyfriend's name is Michael. Michael Cavanaugh."

Dodger chokes as he swallows, coughing into his elbow before he stares at me with wide eyes. "What? Run that by me again?" he stammers.

Pulling my lower lip between my teeth, I don't say a word, sure that I don't need to. Reading into my silence, Dodger's eyes grow wider still.

"Holy fuck."

"Wait," Hope mumbles, frowning as she looks back and forth between Dodger and me. "What'd I miss?"

"For the last three months, I've been having an affair with our state's governor. We met at the Lounge—and it just…*happened.* It's hard to explain, but—"

"Hold on, he's *married?*" Hope asks, trying to catch up.

"Shit, Hope, what high ranked government official do you know who isn't married? B—this is serious shit."

I cling to my glass, pleading with them as I beg, "Please don't judge him. Don't judge me. I know it's complicated. *Messy.* It's *messy*, but I love him."

"Wow," Hope breathes, turning to set her wine down behind her. She then takes a step toward me and removes my glass from my hand. Setting it on the counter at my back with one hand, she reaches to open the freezer with her other. "Forget wine—we need something better." She pulls out a container of ice cream and lifts her brow at me. "You're going to have to start from the beginning. I need all the hairy details. I'm also going to need to see what this guy looks like. Is he old? Aren't most *high ranked government officials* old? Oh, and, honey?" She pauses, cupping a hand around my cheek. "No judgment. We love you. This is a safe place."

"Yeah, B. No judgment here—but—*fuck*."

I nod, peering down at my shoes as I whisper, "I know."

Hope's hand falls from my cheek to my shoulder. She gives me a gentle squeeze and then leaves my side, headed for the pantry. When she returns with two spoons, I can't help but to stare at her in utter confusion.

"How have I never noticed that you keep your dishes in the pantry? And why do you?"

Dodge chuckles, shaking his head with a shrug, and Hope grins as she hands me a spoon.

"That's another story for another time. Right now, you've got some dirt to unload. Come on," she insists, exiting the kitchen. "I have a feeling we need to be sitting down for this."

"No shit," mutters Dodge, throwing his arm around my shoulders.

As he escorts me out to join Hope, I take another deep, fortifying breath. There's something cathartic about speaking the truth. While dad and Simone know about Michael and me, it's not enough. It's never been enough. What I feel for Michael, it wouldn't be enough if the whole world knew.

For now, I'll take what I can get.

Tonight—I'll start with two.

Thirty

Three Months Later

Blaine

I'M STARVING. I KNOW THAT I SHOULD EAT, but even with my food smelling delicious in front of me, my mind is slow on the uptake. Right now, my thoughts are consumed. On a good day, it's hard for me to feel optimistic and hopeful about my future—a future that I've filled with dreams and purpose over the last several months, for the first time in a long time. On a good day, it takes all the extra energy I have to hang onto Michael's promises and to the memories of our time together. But today is not a good day.

Today, I miss my mom. Today, I miss *My Forever*. Today is Christmas Eve, and instead of feeling festive and happy, I feel lonely and sad. It doesn't help with Simone looking at me the way she is. I know she's worried. Her and dad both. I haven't exactly been a ball of sunshine lately. They've been more supportive than they realize I need them to be, for which I am grateful; but they don't understand what I'm going through. Not exactly. Not completely.

"What if he doesn't?"

I look up from my *Wisconsin Brat*, catching her gaze from across the table. Absentmindedly tracing my finger along the edge of the red, plastic basket, I ask, "What if he doesn't *what?*"

Her pretty brown eyes grow sad, and my heart aches at the pity I see in her expression. I've seen a lot of that lately. From my dad, from Simone, even from Irene and Dodger—the former I confided in when word got out that our governor was going through a divorce. It's as if none of them believe he's going to come back to me.

"Blaine—darling, what if he doesn't actually leave her? What if he doesn't come back?"

I shift my gaze down into my lap and stare at my hand. With my thumb, I spin the ring around my middle finger over and over, all the while reminding myself that her *what ifs* are just words. I convince myself that what he and I have, it's bigger than our circumstances. I shield my heart against the lies that lie in *what if*—in the silence—in the *waiting*. I know in my heart that there's no chance of reconciliation between Michael and Veronica. Just because he hasn't been seeing *me* doesn't mean he's seeing *her*—at least not for reasons other than to discuss the end of their marriage, I'm sure.

"Blaine…" Simone murmurs, leaning against the table to shorten the distance between us.

I curl my fingers into a fist and lift my eyes to meet hers once more. I ignore the way her worry tugs at her brow and the regret I know she harbors in her thoughts. I'm certain that she finds herself partly to blame for my current state, having not discouraged me from the beginning. But I ignore it. I ignore it all. I have to. For Michael, for *us*, I have to.

"He will," I state resolutely. "He'll come back to me."

"But—"

"He *will!*" I insist, pounding my fist against my thigh. "He has to. He *has* to."

"Okay, all right. I hear you," Simone comforts, reaching across the table to hold my opposite hand. "Why don't we just finish eating? Tell me what you're making your dad for Christmas dinner."

It takes me a second to blink away the excess moisture in my eyes, and I swallow back my desperation as I offer her a nod. When I take a bite of my lunch, my mouth rejoices, and my stomach is soon to follow. Grabbing hold of joy wherever I can, I don't take this lunch date for granted. I relax, willing myself to simply enjoy Simone's company.

Michael

Isabella grows heavy in my arms, her dead weight resting against my shoulder as she naps. It's not even noon yet; though, judging by the tired look I noticed in my sister's eyes upon their arrival, I'd wager a guess that their three-year-old had the whole house up before the sun, too excited to wait for presents. I wonder, if I hold her long enough, if some of her Christmas spirit will rub off on me.

I've been surrounded by all things Christmas for weeks now. The mansion was decorated by the staff the day after Thanksgiving, and the city of Denver has been decked out for the holiday. I feel as though there are Christmas trees in every building I enter, and yet I can't seem to get in the mood to celebrate. It's been a long three and a half months. Now, I'm anxious for a new year. I need a fresh start—to put the mistakes, the regret, and the pain of this year behind me and start anew.

Except, as I stare out the window, at the snow covered view of the mountains seen beyond my parents' backyard, I can't help but question whether or not it's time. Time to move on. Time to chase after the future that I intend to claim as mine. Time to chase after the woman that I love—the way she *deserves* to be chased. I wonder if I'm that man—or if I'm still the fool capable of creating more hurt and division than I ever thought possible.

"There are beds, you know," says Abigail. I feel her hand glide down my back before she comes into view at my side. As she reaches up and runs her fingers through Isabella's hair, she tells me, "She's been up since three a.m. I'm sure if you laid her down, she wouldn't wake up for a while."

Gazing down at my beautiful niece, I shake my head and murmur, "I'm all right."

Abbie sighs, dropping her hands to rest them upon her protruding belly. She then shifts her focus out the window. We stare together, neither of us attempting to exchange a word. I'm sure that today, of all days, my little sister has been instructed to play nice. Of everyone in my family, she's been the most outspoken about what I did to Veronica. Even now, with the divorce mere days away from being final, she's still standing up for my wife.

My ex-wife.

"She should be here," she murmurs, as if she can't help herself.

"Abigail, don't," I warn.

"We're all thinking it. I'm sorry, but someone has to actually *say* it."

"Say what?" asks Gabriel as he casually joins our conversation. He stands on the other side of Abbie, a steaming mug of dad's signature hot cocoa in his hand and a knowing expression on his face.

"Veronica should be here. We're her family."

"I think you mean *Blaine* should be here," he replies before sipping at his drink.

Folding her arms across her chest, Abbie asks, "Did you really just say that out loud? You've got to be kidding me. That woman is *not* family."

"*That woman* is about to be family. You're going to have to get on board with that eventually."

Abbie snorts, and I stare at my older brother in shock, taken aback by what he's just said.

"Honestly, Abbie, I don't know how you don't see it. Or maybe you just *won't* see it—and I get that. I do. These last few months, something's been missing every time we get together. Part of that is Ronnie, yes—but the other part of it is *our brother*."

"Yeah, well, that makes sense, doesn't it? Proof that he should have stuck it out and stayed married."

"No. You're wrong. Veronica doesn't have a piece of him anymore. Look at him. It's Blaine he's pining over. It's Blaine who should be here. He loves her, Abbie. There's nothing any of us can do about it."

"I'm telling you now, if that woman showed her face here, I'd leave."

"Enough," I mutter, finally finding my voice.

I snuggle Isabella a little closer, hoping her warm, heavy weight will ease the pain my sister's wrath has caused. It's during moments like this one that I'm reminded of what I have with Blaine—what I *hope* I still have with Blaine—and how it will forever be tainted. It's my fault, and I hate that. I hate that I can't change it.

"She's not here," I point out. "Neither of them are here. You're stuck with me. I'm sorry if that disappoints you. Now, can you stop? Just—for one day, can we not?"

Abbie huffs out a sigh, immediately turning on her heel and leaving me with Gabriel. We look at one another and he shrugs before he says, "She'll get over it."

"You keep saying that."

"She will. We all will. Life goes on. *Your* life must go on."

I nod, wanting his words to be true, all the while afraid that they aren't.

"I mean it, Mike. You can't keep doing this."

"Doing what?"

"Punishing yourself. We're all going to forgive you. A couple of us already have. For some of us, it might take longer—the point is, you can't be the last one to forgive yourself. You're miserable. You don't even hide it that well," he jokes, clapping me on the shoulder.

"You heard her," I mutter, ignoring his last comment as I nod back in the direction Abbie fled. "Blaine isn't welcome here. It seems selfish, inviting her into my life—into the vacancy at my side. She's not Veronica. She can't fill Veronica's shoes, and I don't want her to feel like she has to. I screwed this all up. I took away her chance to simply be the woman that I want."

"Listen to me," he insists, now gripping my shoulder to hold my attention. "Taking some time to adjust, it was smart. One of your smarter moves, actually. But don't get stuck. Don't let other people's opinions dictate your next step. You have to do what's right for you—for *your* relationship. If it's serious, and I know that it is, two things are going to happen if you don't go get your girl.

"First, everything you sacrificed for her, everything you *risked* for her—your marriage, your career, your family, *all* of it—it'll have been for nothing. Second, we'll never understand why you did it. It's easy to judge someone when you don't know them. If she is as amazing as you believe she is, how could we not learn to love her?"

I shift my attention back out the window as I let his words take root. He's not wrong. Every day I spend away from her is another day lost. I was willing to go down fighting for her, and here I am, doing the exact opposite.

"What if…what if I hurt her? What if I'm not the man that I thought I was?"

He coughs out a quiet laugh, earning my attention once more. Shaking his head at me, he mutters, "You're scared."

"Sometimes, I swear, what I feel for her is more than love. With Veronica, we had our seasons—but none of them felt like this."

"Then my advice to you is don't be the man you thought you were. Be better. Be better for her. That's all you can do. *Choose* to be the man that loves her. Every day."

I draw in a deep breath, absentmindedly reaching up to run a hand down Isabella's back. I think of Blaine, of the man I wish to be for her, and I know I have some ground to cover. Three and a half months, I've made her wait. Three and a half months, I've been coming to terms with my new reality—only, I don't like this reality. It's missing *her*, and it's time I fixed that.

"She is, you know," I murmur, looking down at Isabella as she squirms restlessly in her sleep.

"She is what?" asks Gabe.

"Amazing."

"I don't doubt that she is, brother. I look forward to finally meeting her." He clears his throat, glancing over his shoulder before he adds in a mock whisper, "Just don't tell Abbie I said that."

"You kept my secrets," I reply with a smirk. "I'll keep yours."

Blaine

I WAS GLAD to see my name on the schedule for New Years Eve. Being scheduled to work meant that I didn't have to come up with excuses as to why I didn't feel like going out and drinking with my friends as we all rang in the new year. It also meant that if someone wanted to find me to deliver a kiss at midnight, he'd only have to come looking for me at the place we first met—except, I knew better than to have even hoped for such a thing.

A girl can't help but dream, though.

Now, as I lay awake in bed, the first day of the year more than half gone, I rub my hungry belly and try not to cry. More than anything, I could really go for some pancakes right now. Not just *any* pancakes, but Michael's pancakes. When I think about the last time he made them for me, the dam breaks, and all the tears I've been holding back come rushing out of me. It's been a few days since I've had a good cry, so I let it all out before I force myself to get out of bed.

I drag myself to the shower, taking my time underneath the hot spray of water. With my mind made up to head over to dad's and whip up some pancakes, I make quick work of an outfit. Since I worked last night, I get tonight off, which means I can hang out and watch college bowl games for the rest of the day. That said, I keep it comfortable, tugging on my favorite pair of navy, printed, fleece-lined leggings and my oversized gray sweatshirt. It reads: *Kinda Care. Kinda Don't,* which is exactly how I feel right now.

Next, I take the time to blow-dry my hair. The last thing I

want is to catch a cold, which is exactly what wet hair in freezing temperatures would get me. With the sound of the blow-drier in my ear, I don't hear the front door open and close. Neither do I hear his footfalls as he enters the apartment. So when I walk out of my bathroom and see Michael standing outside of the kitchen, staring at me from across the distance that separates us, I scream.

And then I cry.

I cry so hard, it's almost as if I hadn't cried less than an hour ago already.

I cry so hard, I can't move my feet to get to him.

Then he's all around me, holding me, comforting me, loving me—so, naturally, I cry harder.

I wrap my arms around his waist and hold on tight, soaking his sweater with my tears. He doesn't say anything, but lets me cry until I start to calm down. When I can catch my breath, I pull away only enough to look up at him. He looks as gorgeous as ever—with just the right amount of dark scruff covering his jaw, and those beautiful, dark blue eyes that I love so much, and his thick, curly hair, which is longer than it was the last time I saw him. He smiles at me softly, and I swear my heart skips a beat. He then cradles my head at my nape with one hand before carefully wiping my cheeks dry. When he uses the end of his sleeve to wipe away my snot, I can feel a blush creeping into my face at the same time that I giggle. His smile turns into a grin, but I don't get to enjoy it for long. I can't complain, though; the next thing I know, he's kissing me.

Instantly—*I'm lost.*

Michael

I BRUSH MY lips against hers tenderly, silently whispering my apology.

I press my lips against hers gently, seeking her forgiveness.

I sweep my tongue across her lips slowly, needing to taste her.

Then she opens up for me, pushing herself up onto her tiptoes, her fingers curling into fists around my sweater at my back, and I no longer know the meaning of restraint.

I kiss her desperately, declaring how much I've missed her.

I kiss her greedily, informing her that I am here to stay.

I kiss her ardently, reminding her that she is *mine.*

Siempre mía. Por siempre mi angel.[14]

She whimpers, kissing me fervently in return, and I am *lost.*

Blaine

I CAN'T GET close enough. I claw at his sweater, longing to *feel* him, and he reaches down to grab hold of my ass. A moan spills from my mouth into his as I circle my arms around his shoulders, holding on as he lifts me from my feet and carries me. I don't know where we're going, but I don't care—not so long as he doesn't take his lips away from mine.

He sets me back down on my feet only to grab hold of my hips and lift me up again, setting me down on the counter, and I know we're in the kitchen. He kisses me deeper, burying his fingers in my hair and moving my head where he wants it. I go where he leads

---

14 Always mine. Forever my angel.

me, twisting my tongue with his, my panties so soaked that I'm uncomfortable.

Aching to feel his bare skin, I seek out the hem of his sweater and slip my hands beneath his undershirt. Smoothing my fingers over his abs and up his chest only makes me want him *more*, and my clit pulses with my need. I didn't know that I could crave him anymore than I have been over the last three-and-a-half months, but I was wrong. Here and now, I feel *crazed* with my desire for him.

He lets me go, severing our kiss before yanking both his sweater and his undershirt over his head. He drops the garments onto the floor, and I immediately busy my mouth with licking and kissing my way across his chest. For a moment, he lets me have my way, and then his hands are in my hair again. Pulling at the strands, he forces me to arch my neck before he leaves a trail of hot, wet kisses up my neck and over my chin. He then plunges his tongue inside of my mouth, and my stomach clenches in excitement. I hook my legs around his hips and he grunts, nibbling on my bottom lip.

Then he releases my hair and drops his hands to reach for the hem of my sweatshirt. In an instant, I'm yanked out of the high of our passionate exchange. I gasp, batting his hands away from me impulsively, my eyes growing wide when I realize where I am—*when* I am. I choke on a sob as I shake away my lust filled haze, my heart so incredibly full when it dawns on me that I'm suddenly in a moment I've been waiting for for *months*. A moment I don't wish to *rush*.

I lift my gaze to find his, and when I see his eyes dance around my face, a warm sense of *calm* settles over me. For the first time since he spoke the words, calling me his *home,* I understand what he meant in the most profound way. Tears spill from the corners of my eyes, my joy and relief uncontainable. With a sigh, I lean forward and prop my forehead in the middle of his chest.

There's a slight tremble in my fingers as I rest them against his bare sides, and I wonder if he can feel it. When he soothingly rubs his strong, steady hands down my back, pressing a kiss on the crown of my head, something tells me that he can.

"I got carried away. I'm sorry, angel," he mumbles into my hair.

A shiver races down my spine hearing him call me *angel*—hearing him speak *at all.* Though, his apology is unnecessary. He's misunderstood my reasons for stopping.

"I don't want to stop," I whisper. My hands still at his sides, I brace myself against him as I slip off of the counter and down onto my feet. Peeking up at him from beneath my lashes, I murmur, "I just want to slow down."

I draw in a deep breath, both anxious and nervous to reveal myself to him. I feel as though I've been covering myself up for so long, hiding from anyone who isn't *Michael.* I can hardly believe that finally—*finally*—I don't have to hide anymore.

I lift my arms up in the air, inviting him to continue where he left off. With his focus trained on my face, he blindly reaches for the bottom of my sweatshirt and begins peeling it off of me. When he stops moving, the soft fabric of my top bunched around my wrists, I can't breathe. I watch as he takes me in, studying me in awe and confusion.

"Blaine…" he mutters, his voice thick and his gaze still locked on my belly.

I'm not showing very much, but to someone who knows my body as intimately as Michael does, I know my progress is hard to miss. Aside from my pudgy looking middle, my boobs are starting to outgrow my current collection of bras—a problem I'll have to remedy really soon.

Trying to keep my own emotions in check, I barely manage to reply, "Welcome home, daddy."

A strangled noise falls from his lips as he drops my sweatshirt to the floor. A second later, he's on one knee, *his* hands now the ones trembling as he holds me around my waist. He touches his lips to my small baby bump, a single tear trickling down his cheek as he mumbles, "You're pregnant?"

"Yeah, baby," I choke out, no longer holding back my cry. Running my fingers through his hair, I giggle through my tears as he rains down kisses all over my belly.

"When?" he asks between his showers of affection.

"I'm—I mean, *we're* eighteen weeks along. Our due date is in June."

He stops kissing me, tilting his head back as his gaze collides with mine. "Eighteen weeks…"

I read the disappointment and the questions on his face as it dawns on him that we've been apart for almost four months, and I never once tried to get in touch to tell him. I cup his jaw in my hands, hoping that he'll understand what I have to say. Even thinking about how hard it's been to keep my distance and grant him the space that he asked for makes my chest ache; and yet, I can't deny that this baby—*our* baby has given me the strength to hold onto the hope that Michael would return. On my hardest days, I was reminded that our child—*his* child was conceived in a love that would stand the test of time. I just had to be patient.

"I wanted you to come back when you were ready," I explain. "I wanted you to come back because you wanted me—not because you thought I'd trapped you." I shrug my shoulders feebly before I add, "I haven't told anyone. I wanted you to be the first."

"Angel, I'm sorry. I'm sorry it took me so long to find my way back," he breathes, touching his forehead just below my breasts.

"It's okay," I cry softly as he hugs my hips.

I mean the words I say. I know he wouldn't have left me if he didn't need to. I trust him. I've always trusted him. It's been difficult, but I'd endure anything for the man who now kneels before me. I also know, simply by the way he holds me, that this hasn't been easy for him, either. *Nothing* about our journey has been ideal. But we're here. *He's* here. That's all that matters.

Holding his head, I resume running my fingers through his hair as I remind him, "You're here now. You came back to me. You came back to *us*—and we can be together now."

"*No me voy a ninguna parte.* I'm here to stay. I'll never leave you again."

Michael

I MEAN THE words I say. Even still, it's not enough to *speak* them. I know that I must show her—that I must fight for her, every day. Starting now.

When I stand to my feet and scoop her into my arms, cradling her against my chest, she squeaks and giggles in surprise, but she doesn't protest. Wrapping her arms around my shoulders, she presses a kiss to my cheek before she whispers, "Where are we going, baby?"

"I'm taking you to bed—*our* bed." I stop at the foot of the spiral staircase and smirk at her. Leaning in until my lips are a breath away from hers, I murmur, "You said you wanted us to slow down. I'll take you slow, Blaine. I'll take my time and love you the way a woman like you ought to be loved."

"A woman like me?" she breathes, her breaths coming faster now.

My smirk turns into a grin, my cock twitching in response to her growing excitement.

"Keeper of my heart. Mother of my child."

"Michael," she moans, hugging me tighter as she presses a kiss to my lips. "Say it again."

"You're the keeper of my heart, angel. You're the mother of my child—you're my world, and I'm going to show you just how much you mean to me."

"Oh, god, I need you so badly. I've missed you so much, baby. *Hurry.*"

My need matching hers, I don't waste another second before I carry her up to the loft. I set her on her feet at the foot of the bed, bringing my mouth to hers an instant later. I taste her lips as I unfasten her bra, and palm her breasts as soon as they are free. She whimpers, reaching for the belt at my jeans, and I pull away abruptly.

"Right now, this is about you. Not me," I tell her, hooking my thumbs into the waistband of her leggings and panties. She acknowledges me with a nod, and I push the soft fabric off of her legs. Holding onto my shoulders for balance, she steps out of the last of her clothing. I take advantage of my crouched position, skimming my hands up the back of her legs and over her ass. I place a soft kiss against her belly, my heart swelling with the act, and then return to full height.

Taking a step back, I admire the woman I've gone without for the last several months. If it's even possible, she's more gorgeous now than ever before. Aside from the slight growth around her middle and her fuller breasts, her hair is longer—her wavy, brown locks hanging past her shoulders now.

"Michael—if you don't fuck me soon, I'll die."

Stifling a chuckle, I jerk my chin at her and command, "On your back. Wrists held together."

I see it as her eyes widen in excited anticipation before she moves to do my bidding. While she gets settled, I make my way to the nightstand, where I know she houses our rope. When I pull open the drawer, my eyebrows shoot up in surprise at what I find.

"Angel?" I mumble, reaching inside of the drawer. I pull out a black leather paddle, gripping it tightly in my hand, and shift my eyes in her direction, seeking an explanation.

She lowers her hands, joined together as I had instructed, and blushes as her gaze locks with mine. "Um," she hums before she goes silent. I wait, somewhat impatiently, as she bites the side of her cheek. Finally offering me a shrug, she admits, "On nights when I couldn't sleep, I did some online shopping."

"You mean, on nights when you couldn't sleep, you bought us *sex* toys?"

"Among other things," she replies sheepishly.

I take a second look at the paddle in my hand. The thought of using it on her—the thought of her purchasing the item *for me* to use on her—it has my erection pressing uncomfortably against the zipper of my jeans. I set it aside, a smile tugging at the corner of my mouth as I reach for the stick of a riding crop. On the end is a piece of purple leather, cut out into the shape of a heart.

This time, when I look at my beloved, she giggles and shrugs before she says, "I thought it was cute."

"I'll show you cute, all right," I mutter teasingly, playfully swatting at the side of her leg.

She grins at me, and I toss her a wink as I return the crop to the drawer and continue my search. Along with the navy satin ropes we've been using, there's a new set of black ones. However, there's something else inside that intrigues me even more. My fingers trace along the inside of the purple leather, fur-lined cuff that I find. When I pull out one, and then another, I raise a quizzical eyebrow at Blaine in hopes that she'll tell me how they work.

"There should be a couple restraint clips inside," she explains. "You could clip my wrists together, or—um—separately, to the bed."

Without another word, I set to work. In no time, her wrists are cuffed, and the restraints are chained through a couple of links above her head. When I'm finished, I can smell her arousal, and I have to remind myself that we're taking things slow. I undress myself completely, stroking myself a few times to relieve my urgent need, and then position myself at the foot of the bed.

She gasps loudly when I grab her behind her knees, lifting the lower half of her body up in order to hook her legs over my shoulders. With her settled right where I want her, I take hold of her hips to keep her steady, and then drag my tongue through her wet slit.

"Oh, *shit*," she moans, digging her heels into my back. I grin, knowing that I'm just getting started, and then proceed to devour her like the starved man that I am. Every little noise she makes turns me on, and my dick aches to be inside of her. When she comes on my tongue, I groan as I lap up the evidence of her climax, her body trembling in my hold.

After I've had my fill, I ease her back down on the bed. She tries circling her legs around me in an attempt to get me closer, but I take hold of her ankles and spread her legs apart, pinning them to the mattress.

"Patience, angel."

"That's not fair," she argues, pulling at her restraints. "I've waited *months* for you. I need you. *Now*. Please, baby!"

I almost give in to her, but then I remember how much I love to make her desperate with want. It's a game we haven't played in too long, and I intend to play it now. I flash a mischievous smile, and she groans, as if in protest. The grin that accompanies the noise gives her away, and I chuckle as I slowly skim my fingertips up her legs. When I reach her knees, I trace my touch along the inside of her thighs, and she shudders. I then lower myself over her, planting a wet kiss against her lower abdomen, right at the bottom of her newly swollen belly.

I kiss, nibble, and lick my way up her torso, reacquainting myself with what is mine. I take my time when I reach her tits, sucking on her nipples until she's fighting against her restraints—just the way I like. Just the way I *crave.*

"Michael Isidro Cavanaugh!"

Smirking, I look up at her from where my head is lowered and blow across her wet nipple.

Her eyes roll into the back of her head and she arches her back as she grumbles, "I'm horny, I'm hormonal, and if you don't stop toying with me—"

Before she can finish her threat, I grab hold of her behind her knees and spread her legs wide, sliding into her drenched heat. I thrust inside of her until I'm seated to the hilt—until I'm *home*—and my heart is full.

Blaine

"Oh, my god—*I love you!*" I mumble on a moan.

I'm sure I sound half manic, but I don't even care. He feels so fucking good! As he takes me hard yet slow, his strokes even yet adamant, the volatile feelings that consumed me a moment ago give way to something else. Now, as he stares down at me while plunging inside of my center, I have to fight the urge to cry.

He's home.

My lover. My forever.

He's home.

When he starts pumping his hips faster, I know he's right on the edge. Then his thumb is pressed against my clit, rubbing firm, perfect circles around my bundle of nerves. I arch my back, pulling on my restraints, desperate for *touch* as my second orgasm rushes to the surface.

"Come for me, angel. Let go," he growls, driving into me harder.

I do as he says, my body giving me little choice. As my core pulses, clenching his shaft, he roars with his own release. Buried deep inside of me, he stills as he fills me with his seed, and I marvel at the beauty of my man.

He props himself up with a hand on either side of my torso, his arms trembling as he looks down at me. We're both breathless, our connection still intact as he asks, "Are you okay? Was that too rough? I lost con—"

"It was *perfect*. Now, get down here and kiss me."

He grins at me slightly before he crashes his mouth against mine. We moan together when our tongues begin to dance, and my stomach clenches. Without breaking our kiss, he blindly fumbles with my restraints, unhooking me from the bed. As soon as my hands are free, I'm all over him. Chest. Arms. Shoulders. Back. Ass. Anything within my reach, I touch, grab, *feel*—and it's amazing.

We kiss until he grows hard again. I mewl when I feel him pull out slightly and push back in slowly, alerting me to his readiness to go another round. Only this time, he loves me slow and tender. This time, I don't fight my tears. When I come for a third time, it's so hard, I swear I see stars.

After he fills me again with his release, he rolls us until I'm plastered against his side. The room is filled with the heady scent of our lovemaking, and our skin is sticky and coated in sweat. I don't even care. It makes me smile, and I snuggle against him even more.

Then it hits me—like a jolt to my system—and I pop my head up to seek out his eyes.

"Baby?" I murmur, running a finger along his jaw to get his attention. He looks down at me, and I smile at the sight of my favorite blue eyes before I ask, "Will you make me pancakes?"

"Sure, angel."

"Like…right now? My cravings are no joke."

At the mention of my cravings, his face breaks out into the most beautiful grin, making my heart flutter. He then rolls me onto my back and presses a quick kiss to my lips before he mutters, "My girls want daddy's famous pancakes, then how can I refuse?"

His words make me want to kiss him until my lips are raw and chapped—but its my hunger that lets him go.

As I watch him pull on his boxer briefs, I smooth my hand over my slight bump and remind him, "It could be a boy, you know?"

He chuckles, not bothering with his pants as he starts for the kitchen. "Blaine, I have four and three-quarter nieces and one nephew. That baby is not a boy."

Giggling to myself, I smile up at the ceiling, marveling at how happy I am. I can hardly believe that only a few hours ago, the tears I was shedding in this bed were those of heartache—not at all like the tears of complete ecstasy and joy that I cried with my love inside of me. It's uncanny, how quickly your whole life can change.

One second I'm craving pancakes so much it wrecks me; the next second, the man of my dreams is half naked, whipping up a batch to feed me after three amazing orgasms.

I linger in bed with a goofy smile on my face only for a moment, and then I climb out to follow after Michael. I look around the floor for his sweater, knowing it's exactly what I want to wear, and then remember that he took it off in the kitchen. I unashamedly leave the loft completely naked in search of it.

He's busy hunting for ingredients in my cupboards when I pick up his sweater and undershirt and hurry toward the bathroom. I clean up a little, stepping into my closet for a fresh pair of panties before I continue to make my way back into the kitchen. He spots me when I enter the room as he turns away from the fridge. He doesn't move or speak for a second, and I rake my fingers through my hair a bit self-consciously, wondering what he's thinking.

He answers my unasked question when he murmurs, "I missed you."

It feels so good to hear him say it that I almost forget to reply, "I missed you, too. So much."

With my half-gallon jug of milk in one hand and a carton of eggs in the other, he closes the distance between us and kisses my lips. Pulling away slightly, he mumbles, "Lets get you two fed." He then kisses me once more before he gets to work.

Michael

"So, um, do you *want* to know the sex of the baby?" she asks.

I look over at her as she hops up onto the counter, perching herself in the corner between the sink and the stove. She crosses her ankles, fidgeting with the sleeves of my sweater as she bites the side of her cheek. It takes me a second to really think about what she's asked. I've never had to give such a question a thought before. Even while I'm in the middle of satisfying her current pregnancy craving, I'm still wrapping my head around the fact that she is, indeed, *with child.*

"I don't know. I suppose it would be nice to know. Do *you* want to know?"

She nods, sweeping her hair behind her ears as she tells me, "I have a doctor's appointment tomorrow afternoon. It was too early to tell last visit, but I was told that there was a good chance I'd be able to find out this time."

"What time is your appointment? I'd like to be there."

"Really?" she sighs, the expression on her face hopeful.

I furrow my brow slightly, picking up the bowl full of batter and closing the distance between us. I rest my hand on her bare thigh and rub her soft skin gently as I inform her, "From this day forward, when it comes to my personal life—*you* are my top priority. Professionally, I have obligations that will sometimes interfere with our lives, you know this. That doesn't make you any less important to me. And this child," I pause, gently placing a hand on her stomach. "I will be there, every step of the way."

She nods, drawing in a deep breath as she places both of her hands over mine, keeping my hand against her belly. After a hard swallow, she murmurs, "Two o'clock. My appointment is at two o'clock."

"I'll check in with Paul sometime this afternoon to make sure I can get away for an hour. Then, moving forward, I'd like you to connect with him before scheduling your visits."

"Okay," she mutters, frowning at me slightly. "But who's Paul?"

Slipping my hand from underneath hers, I flip on the burner beneath the skillet on the stove as I explain, "Paul took Heidi's position after she resigned."

"Heidi resigned? Why?"

I think back on the day she delivered her letter of resignation. It was only a couple of days after Veronica had mailed back signed copies of the divorce papers. Not exactly my best day.

"She was quite fond of Veronica," I admit, scooping a measuring cup of batter onto the warm pan. "News of our affair is not widespread. Only those in my closest circle are aware, but she's one of the few who caught wind of it. She told me that she wasn't a gossip and I didn't have to worry about her going to the press, but that she couldn't work for a man she no longer respected."

I hear Blaine's quiet gasp before she whispers, "Michael—I'm so sorry. I know that she was important to your staff."

"It was a tough loss, but with every transition comes some growing pains. We're adjusting fine."

"Baby," she mumbles, sounding defeated. I look to her and find her fidgeting with my sweater sleeves again. Her gaze is trained down in her lap, and her shoulders are slumped as if she's carrying the weight of the world on them. "Why do I suddenly get the feeling that this isn't going to be any easier than it was before?"

"Hey," I grunt, reaching for her chin. I lift her head until her gaze aligns with mine. "I'm right here, Blaine. I'm *right here*. This won't be like before. You know why?"

She tries to fight her smile, but I see it light up her hazel eyes as she says, "Because you're right here."

"Exactly. Whatever comes our way, we'll face it together. Hear me?"

"I hear you," she assures me with a nod.

"Good."

I lean in to press a kiss against her lips, and she hums, returning my affection happily.

Taking hold of the sides of my face, she keeps me close, mumbling, "I love you so much. Thank you. Thank you for coming back to me."

"I was always coming back for you, angel," I mumble in return.

"I know," she whispers.

Thirty-One

Michael

I STARE DOWN AT THE SMALL, BLACK VELVET BOX in my hand as I twirl it around and around between my fingers. The sun has barely begun to make its late entrance as another day dawns, but I can't sleep any longer. Sitting on the edge of the bed, with my back to Blaine, I think over the last week and a half. It only took me about three days to come to the conclusion that our arrangement isn't working—but I suppose, in the back of my mind, I always knew that would be the case.

With our schedules the way that they are, it seems as though we've slipped into the same patterns we had before. The bed we share is no longer morally impure, but I still feel as if I'm *sneaking* into it when I come to hold her for a couple hours before work. I only spend the night on the evenings when she's not working, as that seems to make the most sense, but I've reached my limit. I've had enough. This is not the life that I imagined for us, so it's time I rebuilt what we have. For the last week, I've been laying the groundwork. Today, I intend for us to start our lives together—as *one.*

As we were meant to be.

I'm not sure how long I sit up, waiting for Blaine to wake, but I don't wish to disturb her. We had a late night, and I know that she needs her rest. Aside from what seems to be an attempt to make up for lost time, her sexual appetite is more ravenous than it's ever been before. Given that she's capable of satisfying me in ways I never imagined possible, I'm certainly happy to oblige—but I know her body is also working to grow and nurture a life, and I respect that more than anything.

When at long last I hear her start to stir behind me, I stop spinning the ring box and wait. As if right on cue, I feel the bed dip slightly as she rolls toward me. The tips of her fingers graze across my lower back as she mumbles, "What are you doing, baby?"

Looking at her from over my shoulder, I can't help but smirk at the sight of her. She's beautiful, even with her messy bed head—*especially* with her messy bed head—and the look in her eyes causes my chest to swell a bit with pride. I can't predict how my plans will affect the future of my political career. However, as I stare into her warm, hazel gaze, I'm assured that she's mine. No matter what happens, I won't go down without a fight, that much I'm sure of; but at the end of it all, as long as she's still looking at me the way she's looking at me now, I'll live to fight another day.

This is how I know that what we have is right. *This* is how I know that she truly is the great love of my life. I would risk anything for her—I *will* risk everything for her—and I'll harbor zero regrets.

Closing the box in my fist in order to hide it, I signal with a small nod as I command, "Come 'ere. We need to talk."

I see the apprehension in her eyes as she processes my words. It wasn't so long ago that I used those same words before delivering news that broke her heart. Nevertheless, I watch as she draws in a deep breath before sitting up and scooting toward me. When she doesn't sit beside me, but rather presses her naked chest against my back and circles her arms around my waist, I allow it. I want her to feel comfortable and safe, not anxious and afraid of what I'm about to say.

Resting her chin on my shoulder, she whispers, "Is everything okay?"

"It will be," I promise, touching my forehead to hers.

Her arms tighten around me as she insists, "Tell me."

"I have an interview tomorrow afternoon with the press corp. I set it up last week. I intend to make a public announcement, introducing them to my new wife."

I can feel it the instant her body goes rigid all around me. "Wh—what?" she breathes. "Michael, what are you talking about?"

Without looking away from her, I reveal the small box in my grasp, holding it up for her to see. She doesn't break our stare, but even still, I know she sees it when her breathing starts to quicken.

"Michael?"

"Our marriage license is in the backseat of the town car. This afternoon, after my parents return home from church, I'd like for you to meet them. If all goes well, I intend to marry you with my father acting as the officiant."

"Michael…"

"If he refuses, I have more than one judge who I could ask a favor from. Either way, by the end of this day, you will be Blaine Luella Cavanaugh."

She blows out a heavy breath, dropping her forehead to my shoulder. As she shakes her head, she pleads, "Wait. Slow down."

I reach around to grab hold of the back of her neck while I press a kiss into her hair. Holding her tenderly, I go on to explain, "That's just it, angel—we can't slow down. We've missed our chance to take things slow."

"Why?" she whimpers. Pulling away from me so that she can look at me directly. "Are you rushing this because of the baby?"

"Yes—*and* no." Immediately picking up on her disappointment, I instruct one more time, "Angel, come here."

This time, when I open my arms, she crawls out from around me and settles herself in my lap. She brings her hands to the center of my chest, absentmindedly grazing her fingers through my short hairs as she admits, "This isn't what I wanted. I told you that I didn't want you to feel trapped."

"That's not how I feel."

"But you just said—"

With one arm around her waist, the other draped over her thighs, I pull her even closer as I explain, "You are not *some woman* that I'm casually dating. You're not my rebound. You're not my *mistress*. You're the woman with whom I intend to spend the rest of my life. You're the mother of my child—a child that I do not wish to hide.

"Blaine, I'm done hiding. I'm done hiding *you*. Would things be different if you weren't pregnant? Maybe. I don't know, and it doesn't matter. What matters is that I want you by my side, where you belong—and that means telling the truth. I believe that it's my responsibility—as a governor, as a Christian, as a *father*, and as the man who loves you—it is my duty to be honest. It's who I am. It's who I want to be.

"And you, my beloved—I don't ever want you to feel as though I am ashamed of you or the precious gift that you're carrying. Our life together starts now, and I want to do it right."

Her eyes now brimming with tears, she sniffles as she asks, "What if they hate you? What if they lose respect for you? I mean, look what happened with Heidi. What if this messes up your entire career? What then? I don't want you to resent me—"

"What if I never met you? What if I never came into that bar? We can't live our lives wondering *what if?* We can only face *what is.* You know me. You know my history. You know that I didn't get to where I am today without putting up a fight. If I lose their respect, I'll earn it back. I won't let the best thing that has ever happened to me *ruin* anything. I have a family to provide for—and I won't let you down."

She erupts with a sob at the same time that she takes hold of my face and pulls me to her. With our lips smashed together, she tells me, "Yes. Yes, I'll marry you." Giggling, she rears her head back a little. Her tears still streaming down her cheeks, she says, "Wait—I don't think you asked."

I grin, bringing my mouth back to hers as I mutter, "I didn't. And I'm not going to. You know what I *am* going to do?"

"What?"

"I'm going to make love to my fiancée," I reply, scooping her up as I stand to lay her across the bed.

"Okay," she breathes.

I let go of the little box in my hand as I settle myself between her spread legs. Somehow, I lose track of the ring in the sheets—but as we get tangled up in each other, neither one of us has a thought to care.

Blaine

I STARE DOWN at my hand, resting on top of my knee, and admire my new ring. It's quite simple—the two carat, round-cut solitaire diamond perched on a rose-gold band, held in place by six prongs—but I love it. It's elegant and beautiful, and it makes me happy that Michael picked it out himself.

"Can I see the others, again?" I ask softly, speaking of our wedding bands.

Reaching into his wool coat, he pulls out the small box that houses both rings and hands it to me. I smile at him as I take it, then shift my attention to the contents inside. Each band is made of rose gold. While mine is fitted with diamonds, his flat, matte band has a more signature touch to it. Since I had no part in choosing either of our rings, he went out of his way to make sure I knew that he'd had me in mind when he chose his. My name—*Blaine Luella*—is engraved on the inside.

"There are a few other things we need to discuss, Blaine," he tells me, pulling me from my thoughts.

I close the ring box and give it back to him, hugging his arm as I give him my full attention. We're on our way to dad's place, so we can tell him our news. My guess is that we'll arrive in less than ten minutes. I'm both anxious and excited to be there, but not entirely sure what to expect. Given my history with Michael, I know that dad doesn't fully trust him. I'm hoping that today will be the day he changes his mind. I don't know any other way to express to him that Michael is all that I want; and if the ring on my finger isn't proof that Michael loves me as much as I'd always dreamed a man would, enough to keep my end of the promise with my father, then I don't know what is.

"What things?" I ask as he tucks away the box.

Placing a possessive hand on my knee, making my stomach tingle, he answers, "I know how much the loft means to you, but we can't live there. It's too small. It has no living quarters for our security detail, and there's certainly not enough room for a baby."

I tug on the nub inside of my cheek, thinking over what he's just said. Of course, as soon as I got confirmation that I was pregnant, I knew that the loft wasn't a suitable living space for us. Not only is it too small for a family, it's not exactly baby friendly. With my child's safety in mind, giving up the loft has been a sacrifice I've been willing to make for awhile now. That's not what makes me pause.

"*Our* security detail? Do you mean I'll have my own?"

"Yes," he replies matter-of-factly.

"Oh."

"We'll discuss those details later. Right now, I want us to be on the same page in terms of where we will live. It's something I want to assure your father we're agreed upon."

A small smile graces my lips, as I'm both proud and humbled that I love a man who respects my father and our relationship in the way that Michael does. Then I think about moving into the governor's mansion, and that same smile fades.

"Are you going to want me to—"

"No," he insists. I know he's accurately read my thoughts when he goes on to say, "I don't have to live in the mansion. It's not a requirement. Besides, I want us to start this family in a place that's *ours*—not *yours* or *mine*. I want us to make a home with new memories."

"Yes. I want that, too."

"Good," he says before pressing a soft kiss to my forehead. "I'll arrange for us to meet with a realtor this week."

I nod, holding his arm tighter, trying not to freak out about how fast everything is moving. I understand, given who he is, that these steps are necessary. I don't just mean Michael, the governor of Colorado, but Michael, my driven, ambitious, crazy smart, super hot, thirty-eight-year-old fiancé. I also know, after everything he told me this morning, while it seems fast now—this is seven months in the making. He wants our life together to be just that, a life we live *together*. As scary as change may be, I'm certain that all of these changes are for the better. I'm ready for us to be together, too.

When we arrive at dad's place, Michael is quick to step out of the vehicle. He offers me his hand, and for a second, I merely stare up at him from the backseat of the town car. He's dressed in a fitted, mock-neck, white, pull-over sweater and a pair of navy blue slacks, his brown leather shoes matched with his belt. The flaps of his charcoal, wool coat are open, and he closes them, expertly fastening the top button with one hand as he waits for me to take his other.

I know, without an ounce of doubt, that I'm blessed beyond measure to have this man as mine. *He is totally out of my league.*

Finally accepting his hand, I allow him to help me out of the car. I look down at my own outfit, a bit surprised and a little thrilled at the fact that I'll be getting married in something so casual. Given the short notice that Michael gave me, and the shrinking number of clothes that I can fit these days, I did the best that I could. I got lucky and managed to fit into one of my favorite fall dresses. The bohemian t-shirt dress hangs loosely on my frame, my bump peeking out just slightly. The large, pink and cream rose floral pattern is on a dusty rose background, the leaves on the stems a dark green. The sleeves are cut at my elbow, and the hem stops about mid thigh. I matched it with my hunter green tights and my chocolate brown, leather ankle booties. In an attempt to dress it up a bit, I twisted my hair into a low chignon at the nape of my neck, leaving a few strands to dangle around my face. I also put on a little makeup.

The cold wind blows, and I hug my jacket around me. Today is the first day I've worn anything that shows even a hint of the progress of my pregnancy around dad, so I cling to the only garment hiding me as we make our way to the door. I ring the bell, knowing that I could go right in, but wanting to alert dad to our arrival.

Looking up at Michael, who stands by my side, his arm curled around my waist, I ask, "Are you ready for this?"

Smirking at me confidently, he simply replies, "Absolutely."

Michael

"Wait!" Blaine cries, reaching for my hand. She pulls it away from the door handle and looks at me, her terror like a beacon shining in her eyes. "I'm scared," she admits.

I slip my hand around the back of her neck, drawing her close as I press a kiss against her forehead. To be honest, I'm not certain how this will go anymore than she is. Aside from the fact that my mind is already made up about the fact that I'll be a married man in a couple of hours, I can't guarantee we'll have all the support I'm hoping for. My parents have no idea what I'm up to, only that I intended to come over this afternoon. I don't want to fill Blaine with any sort of false hope; nevertheless, I need her to know that I am unwavering.

"Angel, I've made you a promise I plan on keeping. I'm not going anywhere, no matter what."

"What if they don't want me in their house? What if they look at me and all they see is a homewrecker? Oh, my god—I'm freaking out," she gasps, pulling away from me.

"Blaine, did we not just leave your father's house with his blessing? He's getting ready, right now, to join us."

"Baby, no offense, but my dad is basically the shit. *Of course* he's coming to see me get married. I'm his one and only daughter. He's also *met* you before, and he's had months to wrap his head around how much you mean to me."

Taking hold of her chin, I level my gaze with hers and remind her, "He may have met me prior to our most recent visit, but that didn't exactly work in my favor, now did it? I had to spend the last hour convincing him than I'm more than the unfaithful bastard who left you crying on his porch last September."

"Yeah, well, you're a politician—and a good one at that. You're fantastic under pressure. I'm *nauseous* under pressure. At least I am so far as your family is concerned. I know how much they mean to you."

"Have you forgotten how much *you* mean to me?"

She clamps her lips closed tight, biting the inside of her cheek as she goes silent. I know I've made my point, but it doesn't stop me from reaching for her left hand and lifting it between us.

"I realize that I've taken the vow of forever before—a vow that I broke *for you*—but I intend to make it again. This time, I *will not* go back on my word. If I wasn't sure when I ended my previous marriage that *you* mean more to me than anything or anyone ever has, than the three miserable months that I spent without you solidified that fact.

"Now, you are not merely the keeper of my heart, but also the mother of my namesake. You mean *everything* to me. My parents will learn to respect that truth; and in time, they will not only forgive you as they have forgiven me, they will undoubtedly love you as their own. But they must meet my blushing bride in order to know how loveable you truly are."

"God—see what I mean?" she asks before pressing a quick kiss against my lips. "Fantastic under pressure." She squeezes the hand that still holds hers before she urges, "I'm ready. Let's go before you have to work your magic again."

Chuckling, I exit the vehicle, helping her out after me. With our fingers laced together, we make our way to my parent's front door. I ring the bell, and wait for them to answer, thinking it best to allow them the opportunity to invite Blaine into their home.

"Michael?" Blaine whispers as we hear approaching footsteps.

"What is it, angel?" I ask, gazing down at her.

"I love you."

A small smile tugs at the corner of my mouth as the lock of the door slides free. "I love you, too," I assure her as the barrier before us swings open.

"Oh," my dad utters in surprise, his eyes flicking back and forth between Blaine and me. "Hello."

"Hi, dad. Can we come in?"

"Yes. Yes, of course. Let me get your mother."

Blaine

My stomach is in knots. I can't imagine that my nerves are good for the baby, but I can't help it. As I pace back and forth across the length of Michael's office, I recollect the last twenty-four hours. Yesterday was emotionally exhausting. While telling dad about our engagement and the news of my pregnancy had gone over as well as we could have expected, telling Pastor and Mrs. Cavanaugh wasn't as easy.

The last thing I wanted was to cause a rift between Michael and his family. While he still maintains that time will heal, I can't forget all the arguing that happened between them yesterday. His dad was adamant that we were moving too quickly; that he didn't want to marry us without guiding us through pre-marital counseling; and that he didn't know me well enough to offer his blessing. Michael had been just as adamant. He held his ground, telling his parents that we were going to be married, whether Pastor Cavanaugh performed the ceremony or not. He fought with them, standing up for me, standing up for *us*—our little family of three—and providing counter argument after counter argument as to why our union was necessary.

In the end, Michael won. Or, rather, his parents' love for him and their bond as a family who supports each other, even when they can't *agree* with each other, led to a compromise of sorts. I was welcomed into their family an hour after everyone calmed down. Dad was there, as was Simone. I met Michael's brother and his wife, Tamara, along with their three children; but his sister and her family opted not to be there. I don't blame them, of course. The atmosphere in the room wasn't exactly warm and fuzzy.

A small ounce of calm settles in my chest as hope and happiness fills my heart at the memory of Michael reciting his vows to me. With my hands held in his, and his deep blue eyes—as calm and confident as the vast blue ocean itself—staring straight into mine, I'd never felt so cherished as I did in that moment. No, it wasn't ideal and it wasn't a wedding every girl dreams of, but it was *ours.*

Our wedding.

Our promises.

Our vows.

It was all *ours*—out in the open, with some of the most important people in our lives standing with us as witnesses. Now, all we can do is move forward. Then again, with Michael at the helm, moving forward is currently *not* our problem.

I gasp softly when the door opens. Halting my steps, I look over to see Michael making his entrance, Paul right on his heels.

"Lawrence called again," says Paul, not paying me any mind. "He still maintains that he needs to meet with you as soon as possible."

Michael smirks, heading straight for me as he replies, "Funny how I have to chase the man down when I'm walking a straight line—but the second I do something he disagrees with, he's leaving me messages every fifteen minutes." Hooking an arm around my waist and drawing me to him, he shifts his conversation toward me as he murmurs, "How are you feeling, angel?"

"Seconds away from hyperventilating," I half tease.

"That's not allowed," he tells me, dipping his head closer to mine. "You're breathing for two, now. Deep, *calm* breaths."

"Governor, I just want to warn you—"

"Paul," Michael starts to interrupt, twisting around to address his personal assistant. His arms still holding me close, he goes on to say, "In five minutes, I'm addressing the public, whether my advisors stand behind me or not. I know you're only the messenger, but I don't want to hear another word about it. If I were you, I'd make sure the press is ready—and I'd make sure *you* are ready. The backlash that's coming will keep the both of us busy for a while. Now, if you'll excuse me, I need a moment with my wife."

"Yes, Governor Cavanaugh." Paul nods before he takes his leave, the click of the latch on the door signaling that Michael and I are alone.

When he turns back to look at me, I can't seem to wipe the goofy smile off of my face.

"What's this look for?" he asks tenderly, tracing the tip of his nose along the length of mine.

"You called me *your wife*. It felt nice."

"Felt good saying it," he hums before pressing his lips to mine.

He kisses me until there's a knock on the door, and then we pull away from one another, looking as Clay peeks his head inside.

"It's time, sir."

Michael nods, letting me go in order to smooth out the front of his suit. He looks just as crisp and handsome as he did the first time I laid eyes on him—dressed in a black suit with a white shirt. The pale blue tie he wears matches my shirt. As he straightens it, I go about checking my own appearance.

Almost as soon as Michael and I exchanged *I dos* yesterday, Simone whisked us away to shop for the outfit I'm wearing now. My wardrobe isn't exactly *First Lady of Colorado* appropriate. While I have a long way to go before I feel comfortable wearing that title, at least I look the part today. My light blue, collared shirt is tucked into my high-waisted, horizontal black and white striped skirt. The hem sits right above my knee, and the cut makes the skirt poof out a little, giving me room to breathe without people speculating about my pregnancy. Simone insisted on buying my accent necklace as a wedding gift. I run my fingers over the silver pendant now, pulling strength and confidence from all the love and support she bestowed upon me yesterday. With my black tights along with my black and white Mary-Jane heels finishing off the outfit, I feel both *professional* and like *me*.

Brushing my hair over my shoulders, I stand up tall and will myself to take *deep, calm* breaths, as my husband instructed.

"Blaine?" he calls softly, holding out his hand.

"My palms are sweating," I confess, rubbing them against one another.

"I don't care."

I purse my lips, stifling my smile as I slip my hand into his. He weaves our fingers together and pulls me close to his side.

"No matter what happens, I'm *right here*."

"I know," I whisper. "Me, too."

Epilogue

Two Years Later

Michael

"Have you heard the rumors?" Gabriel asks as soon as Tamara gets up from the couch.

I don't take my eyes away from MJ as he plays with his cousin Aria. We're halfway through the day, and he's managed to not only keep all of his clothes on, but also keep them *clean.* His mother *insisted* he needed the baseball t-shirt with the green sleeves and a *white* front, in spite of his tendency to be incapable of eating without getting food on him someway, somehow—but the front reads: *Who needs mistletoe when you're this cute?,* and my angel wouldn't be denied.

Now, both cousins are tickled by the train that works its way around the tracks beneath my parents' gigantic Christmas Tree. At one and a half, my son is already completely captivated by any and all things with an engine.

"What rumors?" I mutter, only half curious as to what my brother is referring to.

"Talk radio is saying Pattington might be throwing his name in the hat for the republican party in the next presidential election."

I furrow my brow in annoyance, now giving him my full attention as I reply, "That's a horrible idea. He can barely hold his own in his senate seat as it is."

"I agree," he replies casually.

I squint at him, suddenly wondering why he's brought this up now. "Gabe?" I mumble cautiously.

"I'm just saying," he begins with a grin, even though he's said absolutely nothing. "If anyone can give him a run for his money—hell, if anyone can fight his way to the White House and win against all odds—it's *you*. The way you won your reelection the same year you came clean about you and Blaine? I mean, think about it, Mikey."

I stare at him, wondering if I'm finally ready to admit to myself that the thought *has* crossed my mind. More than once. While he's not the first person to suggest such a thing, I've always fought against the idea, even as it began to take root in the back of my mind. I enjoy my current role as governor. I have, for quite some time—but it's in my nature to always strive for the next best thing.

In two years, my term will be up, and I won't be eligible to run again. Since the moment my reelection was confirmed, I couldn't help but think about the change I wanted to help facilitate while in office, as well as the future that lay beyond. I'm far too ambitious to take a step backwards. I also have the future of my family to think about.

"All right, change of subject," mutters Abigail, plopping down on the cushion beside me.

Leaning to look at her from around me, Gabe replies, "You don't even know what we're talking about."

"I know it's got something to do with politics. Mike's got *that face*."

"What *face?*" I question.

"Please. Don't act like we can't tell when you slip into *Governor Cavanaugh* mode. Like I said, new subject—or I'll tell Tamara you two are talking shop on Christmas."

Gabe looks at me with a knowing smirk before conceding with a shrug. Chuckling softly, I turn to our sister and ask, "And what is it you wish to discuss?"

Her eyes meet mine, and I can sense her caution before she murmurs, "I talked to Veronica a couple of days ago."

I raise an eyebrow at her, not at all surprised by her chosen topic of conversation. Not only has she kept in touch with my ex-wife since she and I split, but this isn't the first time she's seen fit to tell me about it. I have no problem with their friendship—they've known each other more than half of Abbie's life—but it's taken a while for her to start delivering these updates *cordially*.

"She's doing well, in case you were wondering," she goes on to tell me when I remain silent.

Shaking my head slightly, I admit, "I wasn't, but I'm glad to hear that."

"She's finally seeing someone. I guess it's pretty serious."

"Good for her," I reply genuinely. "She deserves to be happy."

"All right—*change* of subject," Gabe interjects, clapping his hands on his knees. Leaning forward once more, he looks at Abbie and adds, "Or I'll tell Tamara *you* brought up Ronnie."

This time, it's Abbie who concedes.

"Mama!" cries MJ as he pushes himself up onto his feet.

I follow the direction of his gaze and see Blaine and my mother enter the room together. My wife is beautiful every day, but I love the way she looks the most on the days when we're laying low and she doesn't feel the need to get dressed up. It reminds me of the Blaine I fell in love with—before she was my wife; before she was a mother; before she was the First Lady of Colorado—all roles in which she's fallen into with such grace, strength, and love.

Her wavy locks, draped well beyond her shoulders these days, are loose; and her face is completely free of makeup, which I've always preferred. The oversized, black t-shirt she's got on reads: *OMG Chill,* the font written above a snowman. Her printed green leggings cling to her slim legs, and her feet are covered in thick, candy cane striped socks that she wears pulled up over her calves.

She smiles in response to MJ's greeting, stopping in her tracks as she leans over and holds out her hands in encouragement. "Hi, baby. Come here, handsome."

Abandoning his toys, as well as Aria, he toddles his way across the room, his arms lifted in the air as if to express exactly what he's after. As soon as he's in reaching distance, Blaine scoops him up and smothers his face in kisses. He giggles—one of my absolute favorite sounds in the whole world—happily accepting his mother's affection.

"My turn. Give mama kisses," Blaine says before puckering her lips.

MJ holds her face and delivers a smooch, making my wife light up with a gorgeous grin.

"Thank you! Now, kisses for *abuela*?"

She leans him over so he can reach my mother, and he plants a sweet kiss on her cheek.

Mom gasps excitedly, her eyes glimmering at my son as she murmurs, "*Gracias*, Mikey!"

He claps his hands, looking back to his mother for further approval, and she giggles—one of my absolute favorite sounds in the whole world—and touches her forehead to his as she tells him, "You're my sweet boy. Ornery when the mood strikes," she mumbles, shaking her head a little. "But so, so sweet. I love you."

As he jabbers his response, I feel Abigail nudge me with her elbow before she tells me, "This face I sort of love."

"What face?" I ask, my focus still trained across the room.

Blaine catches my eye and smiles at me as she runs her fingers through MJ's dark, curly hair.

"You're in *Michael* mode," says Gabe, clapping a hand on my shoulder.

Freeing a sigh, Abbie leans up against me, resting her head on my shoulder as she admits, "*Estás tan feliz que haces que el resto de nosotros se vea patético.*[15]"

Finally looking away from my angel, I grin down at my sister and reply, "*Yo tampoco lo siento.*[16]"

Blaine

I PAUSE FOR A moment, standing at the foot of the stairs as I watch my husband of almost two years carry our sleeping baby boy up to his room. It's during stolen moments like this one, where I can stop and admire the love of a father with his son, that my heart is so full I feel as though it could burst. Michael is incredible with our little Michael John; and every time I see them together, I feel blessed to have had the opportunity to give my great love the responsibility of fatherhood.

When they disappear around the corner, I finally make my way up the stairs, too. It's been a long day. After having spent our morning with my dad, and all afternoon with the Cavanaugh clan, I'm happy to be home. Once I'm in our room, I head straight for the bed. I kick off my boots and abandon my purse on the floor before laying out across the middle of the mattress. I'm far from tired, and as I lay staring up at the ceiling, I wait in anticipation for some alone time with my husband.

We got really lucky with MJ. He's been sleeping through the night since he was about four months old. Michael tries his best to make it home every night before MJ goes down, and then it's just us. Sometimes our moments still feel stolen, like when we first met—especially when work gets particularly hectic—but at his core, my man is a family man. He's always going out of his way to make up for the times when he can't be with us.

My thoughts of Michael are chased away by the man himself as he crawls on top of me, dipping his head to kiss and nibble on my neck. The whiskers of his beard tickle my skin, and I giggle, automatically wrapping myself around him. He's grown out his facial hair even more than usual during this holiday season, and I think it's sexy as hell. It feels really good, too. I can't possibly explain how it is that after all this time, I'm just as enamored with him as I was when we first started seeing each other, but *I totally am.*

"He's knocked out," Michael mumbles, kissing his way toward my lips.

"Does that mean we can go play?" I ask breathily, just the thought causing a shiver of excitement to race down my spine.

"It's been a day or two. I think we should. Besides, I got you something I think you'll like—something I couldn't give you until we were alone. Another little something for our playroom."

He doesn't give me a chance to respond as he closes his mouth around mine. I hum when he sweeps his tongue between my lips, tasting me and turning me on all at once. Reaching up, I sink my fingers into his hair, closing my fists around the strands and keeping him close.

The house he bought us a few weeks after we were married has four bedrooms and a loft space upstairs, with all of our living accommodations downstairs. The basement has an additional two rooms, where Clay and Joseph stay. There had only been one previous owner before us, and the house had been an ideal find when we moved in.

Then Michael suggested we make one of the spare rooms our playroom.

Moving in and having the chance to decorate a nursery *and* furnish a playroom was pretty hilariously spectacular. We didn't really get much use out of the playroom right away, with my progressing pregnancy, but as soon as I got the okay from the doctor after MJ was born, it quickly became one of my favorite rooms in the house. It's nothing too crazy, as Michael and I aren't what I would consider *hardcore*—but it's sexy and it's *ours*. It's furnished with my old bed, always conducive for bondage, a bench with a matching dresser full of lingerie and toys, and a St. Andrew's Cross. We keep it locked at all times—whether we're in it or not—and there's a video baby monitor mounted on the wall that we make sure to check between orgasms.

"Kiss me for much longer, and we won't make it to the playroom, baby," I mutter, my lips still pressed to his.

He chuckles and I feel his mouth stretch into a grin against mine before he kisses me once more and pulls away. He doesn't lift himself off of me, but rather stares down into my eyes before he says, "I want to talk to you about something first."

"Okay," I reply, tracing my fingers down his cheeks and into his beard. "What is it?"

His smile fades and he takes a deep breath, his eyes dancing around my face before he speaks. He's silent for so long, I furrow my brow a little in concern before I lift my head and kiss him softly.

"Tell me, baby."

"I'm thinking about running for president."

My eyes grow wide, and my lips part with a gasp before I ask, "Like—*United States* President?"

A smirk tugs at the corner of his mouth as he clarifies, "Yeah, angel. That one."

"Holy shit," I breathe, taking a moment to process his confession.

Gazing up at the man on top of me, it doesn't take me long before I'm not so much *surprised* as I am *afraid*. Michael is, without a doubt, the smartest man that I know. He still gets totally geeky and passionate at anything and everything related to politics, and I know how much he loves being governor. If I didn't know *before* the campaign for his reelection commenced, I certainly knew it after. He fought so hard to earn another four years in office, and the sex we had after he won—it was the best of my life.

"Angel," he murmurs, tracing the tip of his nose along the length of mine, pulling me from my thoughts. "What are you thinking?"

"I think—I think you would make a marvelous president. It's just—I don't know; it also scares me a little."

"That's fair. Tell me why," he insists, his dark blue eyes searching mine for understanding.

My mind fills with memories of the backlash he received after coming clean about our affair. He lost a lot of support, and he had to battle through hell to earn the trust of many. I remember the protestors and the reporters who wouldn't stop following us everywhere for *months.* Michael was incredible—as a governor, taking responsibility and working ten times harder than before—but even more so, he was incredible as *my husband.* Through it all, he kept his promise to stay at my side. He protected me, he fought for me, he fought for *us*. In the end, he didn't simply win, he conquered.

Except, running for president, being elected as president, that's taking it to a whole new level. I've never really been one to throw myself into the spotlight. Fortunately for me, Michael shines so bright, I can go almost entirely unnoticed when I want to. I do my best to hold my own as his wife—as his *partner* in all things—but I'm not filled with the same political prowess as him.

"It's a huge responsibility," I finally answer. "Like—*huge.*"

"This is true; but you know me and a challenge."

"Yes, but it's not just you. It's a huge responsibility for *all* of us. I barely know what I'm doing standing as your First Lady *now*. If you became President, you'd be so far out of my league, it's not even funny. I'm afraid of holding you back."

"Hey, don't talk like that. I don't want to hear that," he states adamantly. "You don't hold me back. You've *never* held me back. If anything, having you at my side has encouraged me to work harder—fight harder—every single day."

He delivers a slow, wet kiss, reminding my body of what we were doing just a moment ago. He then pulls away and informs me, "I love you. I can't live without you, and I certainly would never think to run for president if I didn't know that I could do it—if I didn't know that *we* could get through the battle of the campaign trail and win, *together*.

"You have to know that I wouldn't even mention the idea if I didn't think you were capable of holding your own at my side. My career is important to me, but my promise to you still stands. In my personal life, *you* come first. I don't want to put you through hell for my own personal gain—but you're better at being my First Lady than you think. Give yourself more credit. You've earned it."

I bite the inside of my cheek, staring up at him as my nervous anticipation makes my stomach flutter.

"You really think that?"

"Have I ever lied to you?"

I shake my head, certain that he's never been less than honest with me.

He is my *Honest Abe.*

"Do you…do you really think that you could win?"

"It's hard to say, for sure—but I think we have a chance. We just have to put our name in the ring."

I nod, pulling in a deep breath as I try and imagine life being married to the President of the United States. The longer the idea swirls around in my head, the more thrilled I become. The possibility of him winning still scares me, but he wouldn't be my Michael if he wasn't so ambitious—and I have to admit, it sort of turns me on, thinking of being married to the most powerful man in the country.

"Would you have to shave this?" I ask teasingly, running my fingers through his beard.

"Not if you don't want me to."

Shrugging, I explain, "I don't remember the last time we had a President who wasn't clean shaven."

"Maybe it's time," he grins.

"And when do you think was the last time there were two babies running around the White House?"

He furrows his brow in confusion before he mutters, "I don't—I don't know. Why?"

"Because, by my calculations, if you won, MJ would be two and a half, and his little brother or sister would be less than a year. Do you think it would be hard to baby proof the White House?"

"Blaine…"

I bite my lower lip, trying hard to fight my grin.

"Angel?" he asks softly, his eyes clearly expressing his unasked question.

"I'm pregnant, baby."

"Right now?"

Giggling, I nod and reply, "I was waiting to tell you when we were alone. You kind of side tracked me with talk of the playroom and then the whole president thing."

Bringing his lips to mine, he kisses me hard, stealing my breath away.

"You're making me another baby?" he whispers.

"Yes," I hum into his mouth with a quiet laugh. "Merry Christmas, Michael."

He grins down at me before pushing himself up and standing to his feet. He then reaches for my hands, pulling me into a seated position and helping me to my feet. Hooking one arm around my waist, he slips another hand around the back of my neck, holding me close.

"It's time for your gift."

"Oh, yeah?" I lean into him further, already excited for the remainder of the night ahead of us.

The hand around my waist slips down over my ass, and he

squeezes me delightfully hard before he orders, "I want you in black, on the bed."

I mentally sort through my favorite black underwear, and then smile at him coyly when I think of the exact pair that I'll wear. I lift up onto my tiptoes and press a kiss on the underside of his jaw before slowly backing out of his arms.

I reach for the hem of my shirt, and then pull the fabric over my head. Turning away from my husband, I drop the garment on the floor before looking back at him from over my shoulder. I offer my love a wink and obediently start to take my leave, already slipping into character.

With my eyes trained on his stormy blue ones, I murmur, "Yes, sir."

Author's Note

If you made it this far, all I can say is thank you. Thank you for giving me the chance to tell this story to completion. By nature, forbidden love is complicated, messy, ugly, and sometimes wrong. Nevertheless, we all have our stories to tell, our crosses to bear, and the grace to try again, to grow, and to be better people with the dawning of each new day.

xoxo

R.C.

Also by R.C. Martin

Made for Love Series

The Promises We Keep

Reckless Surrender

The O'Conners

So Much More

The Holloways

Fool For You

Chasing After Me

Mountains & Men Series

Encore Worthy

Worthy of the Harmony

Worthy of the Dissonance

Worthy of the Melody

Tennessee Grace Duet

Background Noise: A Tennessee Grace Short

Backwoods Belle

The Savior Series

Guarded

Tethered (Coming Winter 2018)

About the Author

I'm a born and bred Coloradan. While I now reside in Virginia, the land of the Rocky Mountains is where I've left a piece of my heart and where my characters come to life. I started writing love stories when I was seventeen, and I haven't been able to stop! With me, you'll find that I dabble in a few different romance genres, but my voice is one that's all about the heart. Writing is my dream; and as a dreamer, you can rest assured that there are many more novels in my head that I can hardly wait to share.

Subscribe to R.C. Martin's newsletter here:
www.rcmartinbooks.com

Keep in Touch with R.C. Martin:
www.facebook.com/rcmartinbooks
www.instagram.com/author_r.c.martin
www.twitter.com/AuthorRCMartin
www.goodreads.com/AuthorRCMartin

Made in the USA
Monee, IL
30 September 2024

66860404R00292